ARTIFICIAL HORIZON

ARTIFICIAL HORIZON

To my good friend Seb
Hope you enjoy it!
Much love
Raynor Woods

Raynor Woods

Strategic Book Publishing and Rights Co.

Strategic Book Publishing & Rights Co., LLC
USA | Singapore
www.sbpra.net

For information about special discounts for bulk purchases, please contact Strategic Book Publishing and Rights Co. Special Sales, at bookorder@sbpra.net.

ISBN: 978-1-951530-47-1

For Sandra and Ferris who flew away too soon

CONTENTS

1. A Middle Eastern dream, Jenny and Greg   1

2. Illusions fade   22

3. Reality bites and Peggy's shame   44

4. Jenny's world widens   58

5. Candy seeks love again   74

6. The hijack, Monique's fateful trip   99

7. Chips begin to fall   133

8. The betrayal, Greg and Sherrifa   161

9. Worlds are changing   173

10. Jenny's heartbreak.
    Nikos and Sherrifa play the odds   202

11. Reconciliations, revenge and political turmoil   224

12. Brutality and blame,
    Monique, Hussein and Nikos   244

13. A step too far, Nikos makes his move   274

14. Recovery   302

15. Trials and tears   332

16. Endings and beginnings   368

CONTENTS

1. A Middle Eastern dream, Jenny and Greg   1
2. Illusions fade   22
3. Reality bites and Peggy's shame   44
4. Jenny's world widens   58
5. Candy seeks love again   74
6. The hijack, Monique's fateful trip   99
7. Chips begin to fall   133
8. The betrayal, Greg and Sherrifa   161
9. Worlds are changing   173
10. Jenny's heartbreak.
    Nikos and Sherrifa play the odds   202
11. Reconciliations, revenge and political turmoil   224
12. Brutality and blame,
    Monique, Hussein and Nikos   244
13. A step too far, Nikos makes his move   274
14. Recovery   302
15. Trials and tears   332
16. Endings and beginnings   368

CHAPTER ONE

A Middle Eastern dream, Jenny and Greg

Jenny crossed the terrazzo tiled floor of her elegant lounge to shut out the intrusive rays of the harsh Middle Eastern noonday sun. Closing the heavy wooden shutters of the balcony window, she was gripped by a sudden, overwhelming sense of fear that brought a feeling of choking and nausea to her throat. For the first time in her twenty-five years, she felt that the people and events in her life were spinning, independently, out of her control. Her legs, now trembling, began to buckle under her modest weight, causing her to shake uncontrollably. Falling in the nearest chair, she tried hard to regain her self-control, however, it was beyond her. Great heaving sobs broke through the last vestiges of her composure. Finally, she succumbed to the complete misery that was mounting within her, and wept unceasingly for what seemed like hours. In reality, only half an hour had passed.

The release of all of the pent-up emotion proved to be cathartic for her, and she gradually became aware of the extreme pressure she was under. As she began to recover and review the shocking situation she found herself in, the sound of an aircraft heading towards the airport for landing caught her attention. Almost ritualistically, she went to the balcony and looked to the skies. On occasion, Greg would give a slight tilt of the aircraft wing in salute to her as he flew over their apartment building. Today, she knew that was not going to happen. Now, everything had changed, the old days had gone, and only the unmitigated strain of waiting for news from the hospital filled her mind.

Crossing the room again, Jenny caught sight of her reflection in the mirrored-back of the ornate cocktail cabinet and noted the need to repair the damage done by her recent outburst of tears. Soon she would have to face people and look composed. Peering closer at her reflection, she wondered whether her external appearance was reflecting the intense inner-turmoil that was gripping her. The stark reflection witnessed that little of her *visible* composure had been lost, only a strained pallor and a slight puffiness was evident. Her looks were not the kind that immediately stood out in a crowd. She had natural good looks that tended gently towards sensuality. Not possessing the necessary skills with makeup, she rarely emphasized her beauty to the maximum. Indeed, it had only been when she came to the Middle-East that she had learned how to apply even the most basic of cosmetics.

Forgetting about her appearance, she began methodically to sift through her thoughts. *How could I have got myself in this impossible mess? How did I ruin my marriage to Greg when I was so much in love with him? Life was so wonderful and exciting in that first year we were together.* Closing her eyes, her thoughts returned to the start of their first idyllic year before all the doubts and suspicions had begun. Greg had been a first officer then, on the brink of achieving his command. After a whirlwind courtship, taking place over a two-month period on Greg's night-stops in London, he proposed to Jenny and persuaded her to come and live with him in the Middle East.

Greg flew for Kharja Airways, a wealthy Middle Eastern airline that was staffed mostly by Western ex-patriot crew members. He was one of the few pilots who had actually joined the airline from the Middle East. Greg's father, Sami Youssef, was an Arab from the nearby state of Koudara, while his mother, Victoria, was British. Greg was (in the culture and the law of Kharjan society) an Arab, and this gave him a positive advantage when career opportunities arose. He was always given the same consideration afforded to the few other Kharjan pilots, so whenever a promotion was available, Greg was a prime candidate. Thus, as soon as he had completed the necessary Airline Transport Pilots License requirements, he was put forward for his command training. As most of the captains in the fleet were married, it was at this juncture that Greg decided his career would be better served if he too was married, and so he began his search for a suitable wife. In selecting a prospective wife, Greg had used the same kind of calculating rationale that he applied to every major decision in his thirty years of life. He wanted someone who was eminently presentable without being ostentatious and who would fit in the Euro/Arab culture in which he lived.

When he met Jenny, a young, good-looking nurse in London, he determined she was an ideal candidate. She was undoubtedly attractive but, probably through a lack of confidence, he'd observed, tended to underplay her assets. She wore little makeup and dressed rather modestly, disguising the seductive curves that lay beneath the baggy clothes she tended to wear. The fact that she was a North Country girl only added to her suitability, as his own adored mother came from the Yorkshire Dales. Greg felt confident that he would be able to gently mould her to his requirements as she was, clearly, infatuated with him.

Jenny remembered her arrival into Kharja, as it was a hot, sticky night that made breathing difficult. She was relieved when the car pulled up outside Greg's modest apartment and she could step inside to the welcome coolness of the air-conditioner unit, whirring fiendishly beneath the window. The apartment was modern and adequately furnished, although somewhat spartanly bereft of decoration. Jenny observed, approvingly, that Greg's house was kept immaculately clean and relished the thoughts of making a cosy home here for them both.

"I hope you are going to like it here, darling," said Greg considerately. "I know that I'm not offering you the most comfortable life in the world, and it is going to take you a while to adapt to the Arab culture and customs. But soon I will have my command, and then we can afford a much bigger apartment, or perhaps a villa, and then we can really start to live."

Jenny thought that this was a rather strange statement from Greg since, as far as she was concerned, she had already started to live. Indeed, she had been captivated by Greg's Mediterranean good-looks from the moment she had first laid eyes on him. Although only of average height, around five feet nine inches, his appearance was stunning. His physique tended towards the athletic without any sign of stockiness. His dark hair curled roguishly round his ears and neck, complementing his lightly tanned skin. However, for Jenny, it was his eyes that most captivated her. They were of a piercing azure blue which seemed to look straight into her heart. All in all, he was one of the most handsome men she had ever met. His considerable charm equaled his good looks. Jenny was completely won over. "Greg, darling, please don't be concerned about me. This apartment is really very nice, you don't have to apologize about it, and I will love getting to know all about the Arab people. You know that being with you is the most important thing in my life. In fact," she risked the old cliché, "I would be happy to live in a tent with you." Greg seemed unimpressed by her answer and told her that a tent was the last place that he intended to live, with or without her.

Falling deeper into reverie, Jenny recalled the day that Greg was scheduled for his final check before his command training was complete. Waiting at home, with the morning dragging on endlessly, she prayed fervently that all would go well for him. When he arrived home that afternoon at around four o' clock, she did not have to ask him if he had made it, as his ear-to-ear grin told her that he would, from now on, be referred to as "*captain*" Greg Youssef in command of Boeing 707s. Jenny had never seen Greg so happy.

The evening of the following weekend, whilst celebrating Greg's gaining of Command on the 707s, was the beginning of their problems, Jenny reflected. Greg had invited John Gallagher, the training captain who had cleared him on his final check, and his wife, Peggy, to join them at the Kharja Hilton. Whilst back at base, Greg had gone to the office of the chief pilot, Hussein Al Fayez, and in a much more formal manner, requested whether he and his wife Sherrifa would honour the evening with their presence. Hussein had enquired who else would be attending, and after establishing it would be only senior crew members and their wives, happily agreed to join the party. Rank and protocol were always observed amongst the senior air crew at home base, and Greg congratulated himself on being able to get the elite senior crew to attend his celebration, as it boded well for his future prospects.

On the day of the celebration, Greg had been at the airport completing paperwork. Returning home, he joined Jenny for a light snack, followed by a short siesta to revive them from the heat and the strain of the day. Awakening, Greg turned lazily to Jenny, "Darling, tonight is going to be very important for me. I've been lucky in getting most of the senior air crew to come out with us this evening, and I want you to really impress them, especially Hussein and Sherrifa. It looks as if Hussein has taken a liking to me, and I want you to make a huge effort to charm Sherrifa. In the Middle East it is important that you give those in high office, and their families, due respect, and it will be deemed an insult if you put yourself before her in any way."

"Don't worry, darling," replied Jenny playfully, "I'm used to bowing and scraping to people. I had to contend with the hospital doctors and consultants when they did their ward rounds, and they thought they were nothing short of being gods."

Greg chuckled and added, "That's the spirit, sweetheart, but don't forget that Sherrifa comes from a very influential family and is used to getting everything she wants. You will have to be very diplomatic, my love." Within seconds he had fallen asleep again, seeming satisfied that Jenny would adequately defer to Sherrifa's status.

Checking the time, Jenny noted that they had slept for about two hours, leaving her only a couple of hours to prepare herself for the evening. Jumping into the shower, she gathered her thoughts. She wanted to make an impression on their important guests, so she needed to make one of her infrequent visits to the hairdressers. Phoning ahead to check that she could get an appointment right away, Jenny sped off into the congested Kharjan traffic.

"Hello, Madam Youssef," fawned Leila, her hairdresser, speaking in stilted English, "do you have an engagement zis evening zat you wish to look beautiful for?"

"Yes," replied Jenny, wondering if she would ever get used to being addressed as "madam." At twenty-two, she barely felt like a "Mrs." never mind a "madam." *Still*, she reasoned, *it is the custom here to have ones status as a married woman acknowledged, and I had better get used to it.* "As a matter of fact, Leila, Captain Youssef and I are holding a dinner party tonight to celebrate him getting his command, and he has invited some of his bosses, so I want to look really special tonight."

Leila clucked and fussed over Jenny. She unfastened her long, golden brown hair from the hastily twisted French pleat that Jenny had skrawked up earlier, telling her not to worry, that she would make her look like a princess. Leila was glad that tonight Jenny allowed her a free rein with her hair, as Jenny usually told her to put it up and out of the way. *Well, tonight,* Leila determined mentally, *Jenny will have her hair down in a much more becoming style.*

Leila was true to her word and Jenny did look stunning after her ministrations, as her hair, coiffed into swirling waves and curls, fell enticingly round her slender shoulders. "Now Madam Youssef, please come and look in the boutique downstairs. I have a new dress in from Paris that will look beautiful on you." Leila gushed encouragingly, "You must look really special for all those important guests!"

I suppose I could do with a new cocktail dress, thought Jenny. *All I have is my little black number and that is severely dated.* "All right then, show me what you have, and if I can afford it, I will consider taking it."

"Oh, Madam Youssef, it weel be a special price for you," Leila replied in an almost wounded voice. *Yes* thought Jenny wryly, *it will probably be twice the normal price for me because I'm a foreigner.*

Leila unlocked a cupboard downstairs and showed Jenny a very elegantly coutured white, cotton jersey dress. Trying it on, Jenny was amazed at how well it suited her. The softly clinging bodice enhanced her slim figure, the design was suitably modest for Middle Eastern requirements, covering her arms, décolletage and shoulders. However, the back was scooped mischievously low, down to the centre of her back, where it gathered in again to fall in soft pleats to mid-calf length echoing the '70s fashion of the moment. She twirled around and noted how the soft fabric danced seductively around her hips. "This is a really lovely dress, Leila, but do you think that it will be all right, I mean, that no one will find it offensive? I don't want to do anything that will jeopardize the evening."

Looking steadily at Jenny, Leila told her that if the dress were not acceptable for the Middle East, she would not have gone to the expense of ordering and buying it herself. "Anyway," she continued, "I theenk that you are worrying too much. You know that the airline people are very Western in their ways because they travel very much, so who are you going to offend?"

Jenny conceded, "Yes, I think that you are right, and besides I have seen Arab women wearing quite daring outfits for the evening. How much is it?"

Surprisingly, Leila asked a reasonable price for the dress and told her that it would be a pleasure for her to think of Jenny wearing it that evening. "Just one more thing," smiled Leila, "you will allow me to put on your maquillage."

Jenny laughingly agreed, "You have done everything else, you might as well do my makeup." Leila's deft fingers worked busily for about fifteen minutes. "Look at yourself now, Madam Youssef. What do you think?"

Jenny stared at her reflection with amazement. Without significantly altering her appearance, Leila had subtly enhanced Jenny's clear hazel eyes so that they looked wider and more appealing. Her usually unmade-up lips had now been emphasized with lip pencil and a glossy lip gel, making them appear softer and sensuously full. Her clear skin had simply been highlighted with a touch of foundation and blusher, and her pert, slightly upturned nose had been given a dusting of matt powder to stop the shine. "Oh," exclaimed Jenny modestly, "is that really me? You have worked wonders Leila."

Leila beamed, happy that she was the one who transformed Jenny. Beauty is very important for women in the Middle East, and Leila was constantly amazed at how little effort Western women put in to their everyday appearance. Leila liked Jenny, and was happy to show her how to make the most of herself. She thought Jenny was very naive and sweet and, more importantly, she treated her very well, like a friend, not like some of the stuck-up wives of executives who behaved as if she were their servant. She waved Jenny on her way and genuinely wished her a successful evening.

Getting into her car, Jenny glanced at her watch, and began calculating: *nearly quarter till eight and we need to be at the Hilton by eight thirty. It will take me only a minute to slip on my dress and some perfume and that will leave us just enough time to get to the hotel on time if the traffic is not too bad.*

"Hi, Greg, I'm home," shouted Jenny, running for the bedroom.

"I'm just finishing in the bathroom. I'll only be five minutes, are you nearly ready, Jen?" replied Greg hurriedly.

"Five minutes for me too, love," Jenny rejoined. Greg finished showering and walked into the bedroom where Jenny was putting the final touches to her appearance.

"Wow," said Greg in amazement, as he looked at Jenny, "You look terrific. Is that a new dress?"

"Yes, do you like it?" asked Jenny hesitantly.

"Like it? I love it. You have never looked so beautiful. I only hope that you won't outshine Sherrifa."

"If you think that this is inappropriate, I can put my black dress on instead," Jenny volunteered somewhat reluctantly.

"No," countered Greg, "I think your dress is fine." Greg imagined the envious looks of the other men when they saw Jenny looking so young and beautiful. Most of the crew had been married for many years, and their wives had taken on that resigned, somewhat bored look of women who have a comfortable life but who are left too long on their own. *As for*

Sherrifa, thought Greg, *her ego is so large that she will not even perceive Jenny to be any competition for her at all.*

They reached the hotel with only seconds to spare. John and Peggy Gallagher arrived almost behind them, accompanied by Geoff and Clare Lambert. Geoff was also a training captain who had been instrumental in Greg's command training. Greg greeted them warmly, drawing heavily on his mother's British influence. "Welcome, welcome, old chaps, do come and meet Jenny, my wife. She is one of your fellow countrymen or should I say women?"

"Perhaps you should say country 'people,'" quipped Jenny jokingly. "I am pleased to meet you all. Shall we sit down and have a drink?" Jenny noted that both Peggy and Clare were obviously firm friends and both were significantly older than her. Often she found herself in this position, since she was a newcomer to the community and by far the youngest captain's wife in the airline. However, her experience as a nurse leant her an air of maturity that belied her twenty-two years. Jenny initiated various interesting topics of conversation with the two women that were of mutual interest (generally concerning health) to help the evening along. Of course, the evening could not properly begin until the guests of honour and their entourage arrived. Everyone knew Captain Hussein Al Fayez and Sherrifa would not arrive until, at least, an hour after the designated time. This was more or less an unwritten rule for important personages in the Middle East.

True to form, Hussein and Sherrifa arrived slightly more than an hour later than the others, accompanied by the executive flying crew. The entourage included Hussein's deputy, Captain Chuck Bonner, who was an extremely experienced American pilot who had begun his career at the latter end of the Second World War. Chuck was now semi-retired from flying, but his easygoing manner made him a popular Second in Command, and Hussein relied heavily upon him in the day-to-day running of the airline. Following Chuck and his rather unsophisticated wife, Betty, was Captain Nikos Stianou, the 707 fleet captain, with his charming French wife Monique. Jumping smartly to his feet, Greg greeted Hussein and Sherrifa profusely in Arabic and ushered Hussein to the head of the table, seating Sherrifa at his right. When the formal greetings had been made in Arabic, the conversation resumed in English, and Jenny was duly introduced to the rest of the party as dinner was ordered.

Jenny was relieved Sherrifa was not at all reluctant to join in the conversation. In fact, Jenny was amazed and somewhat flattered that she had been singled out for most of her attention. Sherrifa gave Jenny quite an interrogation, wanting to know what her job was, where she was from and where she had met Greg. "Jenny, my chèree, how is eet that I have not had ze pleasure of meeting you before?" enquired Sherrifa, her accent reflecting the expensive French education that she had received at the Sorbonne. Jenny longed to say that it was because, until tonight, she had been the wife of a lowly first officer and they would not have moved in the same circles. However, she settled for politely saying that she had been married to Greg for only a few months and had not had the chance to meet many people in the airline.

"Well, chèree, zat must change. I will make sure that you meet everyone in the airline," rejoined Sherrifa in dulcet tones. "Eet is so nice to have someone so young and beautiful around. You will come with me to all ze coffee mornings, and you will come with your new husband to all ze parties."

Jenny was taken aback at all this attention. Greg had prepared her to expect Sherrifa to be some kind of egotistical, over-spoiled woman, when, in fact, Jenny found her to be youthful, beautiful and utterly charming. Indeed, Sherrifa was closer to Jenny's age than many of the other wives. She was fifteen years younger than Hussein and, at thirty-three, could easily pass for ten years younger. She was a striking beauty with long, thick, wavy, shoulder-length hair as black as jet. At five feet, four inches, she stood the same height as Jenny, but where Jenny's figure was slender, Sherrifa's was full and voluptuous. Her ample breasts were emphasized by her tiny waist, and her full hips completed her hourglass figure. Jenny could see Greg glancing approvingly in her direction during the evening, and she anticipated his pleasure when he learned that Sherrifa was going to take her under her wing.

The evening continued on a pleasant note, and after the dinner was finished, some of the party began to wander onto the dance floor to the strains of an Italian band whose lead singer was crooning romantically. As usual, it was the foreign crew who took the lead. John Gallagher escorted Clare Lambert onto the floor as his wife, Peggy, was deep in conversation with Nikos. Geoff leaned over to Jenny and asked if she would care to dance.

"I would be delighted," replied Jenny, and they moved onto the dance floor.

"How are you finding it over here, Jenny?" enquired Geoff.

"Well," Jenny replied cautiously, "it does have its drawbacks, such as the heat and the lack of freedom for women, but on the whole, I am very happy. Greg takes good care of me and makes sure that we get out a lot when he's off duty."

"That's good to hear. A lot of the ex-patriot wives find it too stifling and find it hard to mix with the locals. Still, I suppose it's different for you because you have the best of both worlds with old Greg being half English and half Arabic."

"That's true," said Jenny matter-of-factly, "but you know that over here, Greg is considered to be completely Arabic because his father is an Arab."

"Yes, I've heard that before. Not much hope for women's lib over here then," Geoff joked.

"Mmm," replied Jenny, glancing back to the table where the rest of the party was sitting.

Sherrifa, Nikos and Monique seemed to be deep in conversation while most of the others were on the dance floor. Hussein had asked Betty to dance as none of the other wives were including her in their conversation. He felt sorry for Betty because she was overweight and had none of the social graces that were common to the other wives. She was a misfit and the others did not spare her feelings in letting her know it.

"Are you enjoying the evening, Betty?" asked Hussein, whose clipped English accent reflected his public school education at Uppingham.

"Well, I wouldn't exactly say enjoyin' but I am findin' it interesting," replied Betty in her deep Southern drawl. "I predict that sparks will begin to fly when those two good-lookin' young-bloods start doing the rounds," she said, indicating Greg and Jenny.

"I'm afraid that you are right, Betty," sighed Hussein as he whisked her off into the midst of dancers who were crowding the dance floor.

Jenny had been kept on her feet dancing for quite a while and was ready for a long, cool drink when Nikos approached her. "Ah, Jenny, I can see that you are tired, but when you have finished your drink, I insist that you spare a dance for me."

"Oh, I'm not really tired, only rather warm. Let me swallow this drink, and I will be right with you." Jenny found Nikos to be an excellent dancer. He had natural rhythm, and Jenny soon began swaying effortlessly with him. He was a handsome man of Greek extraction, about ten years older than Greg and gifted with the same easy charm her husband possessed. During the second slow dance with Nikos, Jenny became aware of his arm drawing her body closer to him, and she began to feel uncomfortable. Feeling her stiffen under his arm, he whispered to her, "Jenny, you sweet thing, don't pull away from me. I don't often get the chance to dance with someone as beautiful as you."

Feeling compromised she told him, "Nikos, you have a lovely and charming wife. I don't know how you can say that."

"Lovely she may be," returned Nikos, "but charming she is not."

"I think you are being rather disloyal to say that about her," Jenny shot back. Nikos laughed and held her even closer.

Back at the table, Jenny could still feel where Nikos' hands had touched her, and he made little effort to hide the fact that he was giving her long, penetrating stares that both excited her and terrified her. She looked for Greg to give her reassurance, but he was escorting Sherrifa to the dance floor. Monique was also conveniently out of the way too, as she was dancing with Hussein. The only ones at the table were Chuck and Betty. Jenny launched in to conversation with Betty, who could see her predicament.

"Say, Jenny, do you know where the john is in this place?" drawled Betty unceremoniously.

"Oh yes, yes," replied Jenny thankfully, "I will take you there myself." She could feel Nikos' eyes on her back as she left the room and was glad to escape to the relative sanctuary of the ladies' powder room. Jenny sank gratefully into the plush chair that had been thoughtfully provided, exhaling loudly. Turning to Betty she said, "Thank you for bailing me out back there. I was feeling quite uncomfortable with Nikos looking at me like that. I suppose that he must have had a bit too much to drink."

Betty countered, "No, I don't think so, honey. He's got an early flight in the mornin', and I've never known him to drink within eight hours of a flight. When it comes to flyin', he goes by the book. But unfortunately for you, dear, that's the only time he does go by the book."

"What do you mean?" asked Jenny.

"What I mean, honey, is that Nikos has got his eye set on you, and he ain't gonna quit until he's got you into the sack."

"Oh, you can't be serious," said Jenny.

"I'm real serious. I have known that son of a gun for the best part of ten years, and I've never seen him fail to get who or what he wants. And he don't care what method he uses either. Although, I gotta say that most of the ladies don't need much persuasion, but something tells me that you are different."

"You bet I'm different," protested Jenny indignantly. "I have only been married a few months, and I'm really in love with Greg. I don't want that egotistical so-and-so laying his hands on me."

"Well if that's the case, hon', you are gonna need some help because Nikos will put every kind of pressure on you, including threatening to make things difficult for Greg in the airline," said Betty seriously.

"Surely, he wouldn't do anything to affect Greg's career. It's totally unethical," responded Jenny rather indignantly.

Like I said, his personal flying is the only thing he does by the book. Everything else is fair game to him. Listen, honey, I will do what I can to help y'all. I'll explain things to Chuck and see if he can arrange the roster so that Nikos is always flying when Greg is. At least that will cut down his opportunities for gettin' to ya."

"Thank you, Betty, I really appreciate that. But how does he get away with doing that kind of thing?"

Betty looked at Jenny and wondered how much she should tell her. She was so young and naïve, and she did not want to shatter her illusions about the kind of things that went on amongst a lot of the crew. "Look, honey," Betty replied gently, "Nikos is a first-class bastard, and he will use anything or anyone to get what he wants. What's more, he's got a lot of influence with Hussein and uses that to reinforce his position of power."

"I rather thought that Hussein was a very straight sort of chap who would not stand for any messing about," stated Jenny.

"He is, Jenny, but that wife of his, Sherrifa, ain't. And she's got him over a barrel. Sherrifa's family is very influential in this country, and if she don't get things the way she wants them, she goes home and hollers to daddy. Then daddy goes to see Hussein and threatens him with everything under the sun for making his little girl unhappy. I swear that woman gets everything she wants, and what's more, Nikos is her best friend and ally. Years back, when Sherrifa first met Nikos, they went for each other in a big way. You could feel the fire between them from yards away. That little affair went on for a couple of years, but then Sherrifa cooled. She dumped Nikos for a while and then befriended him again when she realized that he was quite happy to be a middle-man in her little affairs. That little partnership is still going strong."

"What about Hussein?" said Jenny, somewhat shocked. "Does he know?"

"I expect he does know, but what can he do? Sherrifa knows that her father would not hear a bad word said about her, and she'd deny anything that Hussein said about her."

"Yes, I can see how that would work, but what about Monique? Why does she put up with her husband behaving in such a way?" queried Jenny.

"She puts up with it, honey, because the very elegant and sophisticated Monique has got nowhere else to go. When she met Nikos, she was engaged to a very eligible suitor in Paris, and her snobby family was delighted with the match. Then Nikos came along and couldn't keep his hands out of the cookie jar. He was determined to have her and stopped at nothing to keep Monique from marrying her French Count. To cut a sordid story short, he got her pregnant, and her family never forgave her. The French Count married her sister, and poor Monique woke up one day to find that she was married to a bastard who was happy to keep her around as an adornment, and that she had no one to turn to since her family had cut her off without a word or a cent."

"That's appalling," cried Jenny. "Can't she just leave him and start out on her own somewhere?"

"Well, it would be real difficult for her since she ain't got no money of her own and Nikos won't give her any. What's more, she was not raised to be anything other than being a society wife, and she's got her son to think of, you know. In any case, she is so stubborn that she does not want her folks to know what a big mistake she made in marrying Nikos, and I guess she has not forgiven them for cutting her off like that. Still, she gets her own back with Nikos. She does her social duty for him but that's it. The rest of the time she treats him with contempt."

"Well, I'm glad that someone does," said Jenny looking at her watch. "You know, we have been in here for fifteen minutes, Betty. I think we had better go back inside before it looks impolite."

"I guess you're right honey. Let's head on back. Just remember to watch out for that Nikos. If you need any more help, you can give me a call."

Returning to the party, Jenny noted Greg was obviously relieved to see her. "There you are, darling. Everyone was wondering where you were."

"Oh, I just spilled some wine on my dress, and it took quite some time to remove it. Betty was kind enough to help me," lied Jenny convincingly. Betty nodded to all as if to confirm the story.

The evening gradually began to wind down. It was almost eleven thirty and most of the pilots had early starts and wanted to grab some sleep before it got too late. Recognizing this need, Hussein gestured to Sherrifa that it was about time for them to go, giving opportunity for the others to leave without breaking protocol by leaving before them. Greg and Jenny stood up to bid their guests farewell. Sherrifa told them both how much she had enjoyed the evening and looked forward to seeing them again very soon. Turning to Jenny she insisted, "Jenny, chère, I weel call you tomorrow to arrange to have coffee or go shopping, that weel be so nice, ne ce pas?"

"That will be very nice," replied Jenny. "I look forward to it."

Sherrifa said her goodbyes to the other wives before she and Hussein made their exit. Nikos and Monique were the next to leave. Nikos was very friendly towards Greg and congratulated him again on getting his command. "Listen, Greg," said Nikos encouragingly, "now that you have made captain, I'm sure we'll be seeing a lot more of each other, and I want you to know that if you have any problems, you must come to me and I will help all I can."

Greg thanked him, pleased that Nikos had apparently taken a liking to him. He had heard that Nikos could be very difficult with those he did not like.

Greg bade goodnight to Monique while Nikos took Jenny's hand and whispered in her ear, "See how nice it can be for you and your husband when I am kept happy, sweetie?"

Jenny cringed at the threatening tone of his words and at the derogatory way he called her "sweetie." Not wishing to disrupt the evening in any way, Jenny smiled and replied, "It was so good of you and Monique to come, and I look forward to seeing you both again."

"Count on it," whispered Nikos as he left.

Chuck, Betty and the others followed them out, bidding their farewells to Greg and Jenny. Chuck smiled warmly at Jenny, "It's been a very pleasant evening. Betty has really enjoyed herself. Now if you need anything, you just come on over and talk to Betty. She will be only too happy to help you."

"I enjoyed Betty's company, and I certainly will be contacting her," replied Jenny sincerely, hoping that Betty would not forget what she had promised her earlier in the powder room. It looked as if Nikos was going to use Greg against her to get his way, and she felt defenseless.

When the guests had all departed, Greg and Jenny made their way home, holding a postmortem of the evening as they went. "Jenny, you were wonderful this evening," praised Greg. "You got along marvelously with Sherrifa, and it was a master stroke to befriend Betty like that. I noticed the other wives didn't bother with her very much."

"Well, I actually liked her, Greg," said Jenny seriously. "I know she does not fit the usual mould of a captain's wife, being so outspoken and unsophisticated, but she was very pleasant with me."

Jenny wondered whether it would be a good idea to tell Greg what Betty had told her about Nikos. Some inner instinct told her that it would not, so she approached the subject in a different way. "What did you think of Nikos?" queried Jenny.

"Nikos?" repeated Greg. "He's an ace pilot, you know, but he can be a bit of a bastard with anyone he doesn't like. But he was really pleasant with me, told me to come to him if I had any problems, and that's quite an honour coming from him. I think I am going to get on well with him. I noticed he danced with you for a long time. How did you find him?"

Thinking of how to carefully phrase her words, Jenny replied, "As a matter of fact, darling, he was a tiny bit fresh with me. I think he must have had a bit too much to drink."

Greg knew, as Betty did, that Nikos would not be drinking before his early morning flight and was rather thrown by Jenny's criticism. "Darling," he countered, "I'm sure that was all that it was, but you know that Nikos is a bit of a ladies' man and likes to flirt with all the pretty women."

Jenny was surprised at Greg's slightly untruthful answer, but she gave him the benefit of the doubt — perhaps he really didn't know that Nikos had an early morning flight. Not feeling happy to leave the situation as it was, she tried to convey her misgivings to Greg again. "Greg, I felt it was a bit more than just flirtation. He was a bit intimidating," complained Jenny.

"Jenny, you are very naive about some things," shot back Greg angrily, "and you are going to have to grow up a bit. This sort of thing is going to happen, and you are going to have to learn to deal with it on your own. Besides, the last thing I want to do is to alienate Nikos."

Jenny felt as if she has been slapped across the face and was reeling from the implications of what Greg had just said to her. He had made it clear that she must not rock the boat for him and that Nikos should be kept happy. It hurt to think that Greg might realize what that would mean for her, so she chose to ignore it. Tears stung her eyes but she forced them back. She was unable to think of anything to say, so she sat in silence the rest of the way home. By the time they reached home, Greg had cooled off but Jenny was subdued.

"Jenny, please don't think that I am a monster," he said to try and placate her. "You know that I love you. I want the best for us, and the only way we will get it is if we play the game well. We have made a good start this evening, and I'm sure we will get invited to all the right parties and mix with the right people. Without that, I will not move much further up the ladder than I am now. I have every chance of joining the executive staff in a year or two if we play our cards right, so let's not blow it now over a small issue that might turn out to be nothing."

The way Greg put it made Jenny feel like she had rather jumped the gun and ended up conceding that he was probably right. However, she could not shake the lingering feeling that Greg's ambitions came well before his love for her. *Still*, she reasoned, *she would not want to be married to a man who had no drive or ambition, and if she loved Greg she would have to love that part of him too.*

CHAPTER TWO

Illusions fade

The next morning, Hussein rose early as usual to get to his office by eight o'clock. He showered and dressed without disturbing Sherrifa. She had long since taken to sleeping in a room of her own, complaining that Hussein's irregular hours disturbed her sleep patterns. He was happy enough to comply with her wishes since they had no real reason to share a bed as the sexual side of their relationship had broken down a long time ago. The years of kow-towing to Sherrifa's demands had rendered him impotent when it came to making love to her. Besides, all desire for her had long since eroded. There had been a time when she could not get enough of him, but that was before they were married.

Hussein had been the best friend of Ezert, Sherrifa's brother. They were together at school in Uppingham and had gone on together to university where Ezert studied for a degree in business while Hussein studied for a degree in mathematics. Their close friendship had irked Sherrifa, who, since childhood, had always wanted whatever her brother had and thusly she set about winning Hussein away from Ezert. Sherrifa was then of marriageable age, and she knew Hussein would be acceptable to the family as a suitor. He was good looking and very Westernized, having studied for both his degree and Commercial Pilot's license in England. She quickly decided that Hussein, who had recently been appointed as a junior executive in the airline, would make a splendid husband for her. She would have all the freedom she had enjoyed during her studies at the Sorbonne in Paris and be able to travel and lead a relatively unrestricted life. Her father, Nabil Nasrawi, who adored her, had enough influence in the country to ensure that Hussein would move swiftly to a position of power and authority. Sherrifa pursued Hussein relentlessly, much to Ezert's consternation. All his life, he had played second fiddle to her. He hated her and her greed. However, Hussein quickly fell for Sherrifa's considerable charms.

As an unmarried woman, Sherrifa had been unable to move around with the freedom that she had been accustomed to in Paris. Her wings were clipped, and she could not indulge her passions with men in the way she had done whilst abroad. When she and Hussein began courting, he became the willing recipient of all the pent-up passion that had mounted within her in the six months since she had left Paris. Hussein was totally infatuated with her and found her irresistible. The first time they made love had taken Hussein by surprise. Sherrifa had engineered a meeting with Hussein in the house of one of her married friends who had conveniently gone out for the evening. Hussein had imagined that the evening might not be formal, but he was unprepared for Sherrifa's unbridled sexuality. When he arrived at the house, he was surprised to find the lights dimmed, soft music playing. Sherrifa was dressed in an expensive negligee from one of the couture houses of Paris and carried a large brandy in her hand. "Hussein, chère ami, you look so surprised!" drawled Sherrifa seductively in a hybrid of French and Arabic.

"I am, I don't know what to say," replied Hussein, hardly believing his eyes. It was inconceivable that an unmarried girl should behave this way in the Middle East, even if they were likely to someday be married. Moreover, Hussein was very aware of Sherrifa's position in society and was hesitant to be frivolous with her.

"Come here," she whispered enticingly, "I don't want you to say anything; I want you to do something."

"Sherrifa, what will happen if this gets out? What will your family say?"

"Leave my family to me. I can always handle my father. He is the only one who has any control over me, and he is not going to find out anything unless you tell him, or I do," she said dismissively, abandoning her French accent and snapping somewhat impatiently into Arabic.

Not wishing to upset her, Hussein went over to her and explained that he was only concerned for her and that he did not want to seem as if he were taking advantage of her. "Sherrifa, habibti, we can be married tomorrow if you like and then you won't jeopardize your position," urged Hussein.

"We will be married, chère, but not tomorrow. You know that my family needs a lot of time to arrange a wedding as important as ours, but tonight we will be as married people. I can't wait to make love to you any longer."

Hussein felt the heat of desire for her rise through his body until it threatened to choke him. He gasped, "If you are sure, Sherrifa, my love, there is nothing I want more than to make love to you."

Sherrifa stood tantalizingly before him and dropped her expensive negligee to the ground and waited for Hussein to come to her. Through his silk shirt, he could feel the heat of her body. Their lips met in an explosion of passion, each one fighting to devour the other. Sherrifa opened his shirt deftly, exposing his broad shoulders and slim waist. She pulled off his trousers effortlessly, and within seconds they were twisting and writhing on the carpeted floor, eagerly exploring each other's body, consumed by the passion that overtook them. Sherrifa was completely uninhibited, grabbing Hussein's hips and directing them so he penetrated her the way she wanted, groaning in ecstasy as he touched the most sensitive areas inside her. Hussein eagerly responded to her, finding her intoxicating and stimulating. He wanted to make love to her all night, yet his climax threatened to overtake him before he was ready. As if sensing this, Sherrifa gasped, "It's all right, I am ready too. We can orgasm together." Unable to control himself any longer, Hussein groaned deeply as he reached orgasm, and feeling Sherrifa convulse in orgasm with him only added to his pleasure. They lay together for some time, unable to move from the exertion of their lovemaking.

Recovering, Hussein caressed Sherrifa's face and whispered, "You are incredible. I have never felt like this with anyone else."

"You are such a good lover," replied Sherrifa. "You made me feel very excited. We will be so good for each other."

Hussein had become aware that, contrary to Arab custom, Sherrifa was obviously no virgin. This was not of importance to him, but he felt the issue ought to be put out of the way here and now in case it should worry her. Some Arab men would instantly annul their marriage if they found out their wives were not virgins. "Sherrifa, my sweet, this cannot be the first time you have made love, and I want you to know that it does not matter to me. In fact, your knowledge of lovemaking has given me great pleasure," said Hussein both generously and truthfully.

"I am happy to have given you so much pleasure, my love," responded Sherrifa in dulcet tones. "My education in Paris was very thorough," she added mischievously. "However," she continued, "if I thought that you were the kind of man that would have minded, I doubt that we would be here tonight."

Hussein was slightly amused at the audacity of her reply but felt the subject was now adequately dealt with. Their marriage followed within months, and Sherrifa's passion for him remained strong for some eighteen months. By then, Sherrifa had presented Hussein with a son, Samer, a cause for much celebration for both their families. In the Middle East, the birth of a son is always greatly welcomed. As attention began to focus on her son rather than her, Sherrifa began to resent her role as mother and soon found a nanny to take on the mundane chores of motherhood. She spent little time with Samer, only seeing him briefly in the afternoon and sometimes before she went out in the evening.

She quickly found someone outside her family unit who would give her all the attention she craved, as Nikos Stianou had just joined the airline. They met at one of the airline's parties and were immediately drawn to each other. They began a passionate, obsessive affair which they hardly bothered to disguise from anyone who was around them. Sherrifa was completely infatuated with Nikos; he filled her every waking thought. She turned away from Hussein time and time again in bed saying that she was ill or that she was not in the mood for his advances. After a few months of rejection, he confronted Sherrifa with his suspicions that she was having an affair with Nikos.

"How very clever of you to find out," sneered Sherrifa. "What are you going to do about it?"

"I don't know," replied Hussein, shocked and confused. He had not really expected Sherrifa to respond in this way. "Do you want a divorce?"

"Not really," she said confidently, "I want things to go on just the way they are, but I don't want to hear you complaining about whom I see, or what I do. We will be married in name only. You can see whoever you want as long as it's not someone from this country. I think that's a fair deal."

Hussein was taken aback at her words. He was prepared to forgive her for her indiscretion as he did feel that the demands of

26

his job had kept him away from her too much and that he might be partly responsible. He still loved her and wanted things to be the same as they used to be. "I still love you, Sherrifa," he said, his voice shaking with emotion. "Can't we try again and make things work out?"

"No," said Sherrifa firmly, "I am sick and tired of having to be a good little wife and mother. I want some control over my own life." Hussein became enraged at this. He had not made any real demands of her and gave her unquestioning freedom, giving way to her every whim. He felt her complaints were unwarranted and unjustified.

"You ungrateful whore," he snarled. "I have given you everything you wanted, and you repay me like this. Well, I will divorce you, and you can take the consequences on your own."

"I don't think so, my sweet," she replied calmly. "It is only thanks to my father that you have moved up so far in the airline. If I tell him that you are the one that is having an affair, and believe me I can find women who will be only too happy to testify that they slept with you if I offer them the sufficient incentive, then you will be out of the airline and the country so fast you won't have time to pack your bags."

Hussein shook with fury at this injustice. He was totally compromised. He knew she was quite capable of carrying out her threat. He had seen her deal ruthlessly with others who got in her way. All she ever had to do was appeal to her doting father.

Sherrifa's father, Nabil Nasrawi, had enormous influence in the country with his network of contacts built up through his successful business empire. If he thought his daughter was being maltreated by her husband, Hussein knew it would only take a phone call from Sherrifa to destroy everything that he had been working for and be disgraced. He also knew his own family would not be excluded from his disgrace. This was the only reason that he held back from the satisfaction of walking out on Sherrifa. In that instant, any love he had felt for her died; cold resolve took its place. Until the day he was free of her, he would dedicate his life to the airline and their son. He would do everything he could to prevent Samer from being manipulated by his conniving mother if it was the last thing he did. He turned and walked out of the room without another word.

Sherrifa ensured that Nikos was given a promotion within the airline so their social lives would inevitably coincide, giving her the opportunity for frequent meetings. Their passion burned for two years before Sherrifa tired of him. Indeed, they both became aware at the same time that their passion had burned out and it was time to part. Although their affair was over, and despite an initial awkwardness, they both cared for each other enough to remain friends. In many ways they were kindred spirits, as they understood each other's needs and wants in a way that others could not.

Hussein was forced to swallow his pride and endured the indignity of knowing that he was working closely with her ex-lover. However, he tried to protect Samer from the knowledge that he and his mother were estranged. Hussein opened the door to Samer's bedroom and looked at all the paraphernalia strewn around the room, common to most boys of twelve, and felt a pang of loneliness shoot through him. Samer was in boarding school in England and would not be home until the summer recess. Hussein missed him sorely but was nonetheless glad that he was away from Sherrifa's clutches.

Samer, however, had no feelings other than hostility for his mother. She had been absent in his formative years and only showed up for functions at his schools when it was really necessary. Hussein had been both father and mother to his son, and Samer's affection for him reflected that. He adored him and wanted to be like his father, to go to the same schools that he did and become a pilot like him.

Surprisingly. Sherrifa interfered very little in decisions concerning Samer, as if sensing, in some fleeting moment of compassion, that perhaps the best she could do for her son was to keep out of his life as much as possible. She did not have any real maternal feelings for him, but some sense of conscience prevented her from ever doing him any harm. She could see that he was devoted to Hussein, and she did not interfere with their relationship. Although Hussein was grateful for Sherrifa's lack of interference in Samer's life, he could not trust her to stay that way, and he believed she would even use him, if it served her purposes. Closing Samer's room, Hussein went to the dining room where the cook had laid out a plentiful breakfast. Hussein felt a wave of despondency come over him and took only a cup of coffee before leaving for the airport for the day.

Sherrifa awoke three hours later, at ten o'clock, and called for the maid to bring her some coffee and a croissant. After consuming her light breakfast, she lay back on her pillows and let the thoughts of the previous night flow through her mind. She was pleased with the way the evening had gone. Befriending the little English milk-sop, Jenny, was a good move. If she established a relationship with her, it would ensure that she had access to her goal, the very handsome Greg Youssef. *It is such a bonus having someone like him join our social circle*, she thought. *Things have been dull and lifeless for some time, and if my guess is correct, Greg will be just the man to change that.* He reminded her a little of Nikos, ten years ago, but there was something more about him, a challenge perhaps. She could feel that he was amenable to her wishes, yet she felt that he was not yet ready to fall into her arms. *He had been more than polite and attentive,* she thought, *yet he kept a distance. Yes,* she reflected in a predatory manner, *I am going*

29

to enjoy hunting down this prey. She took her time dressing and spent the next hour calling some of her female friends. Friends, that is, only in whatever context they could be of use to her. Those "friends" were afraid of her and the power she wielded through her father and knew the pitfalls of falling out of grace with her, whilst also being aware of the status that she could confer upon them through her friendship.

Her maid came into the salon timidly, announcing that Captain Nikos was here and was she at home.

"Yes, yes," replied Sherrifa impatiently, "you know that he is always allowed to come straight in, you stupid girl. Show him in immediately!"

Sherrifa was pleased Nikos had stopped by, as she was eager to talk to him about the evening's events. She had noticed that he had designs on Jenny, and that would work out well with her own plans for Greg. They would plan their strategy together.

Nikos walked in, still in uniform having come straight from the airport. "Salute, Chichi, comment ca va?" he enquired as he kissed her on both cheeks. Nikos and Sherrifa had found early in their relationship that the best language for their communication was French because his Arabic was weak, her Greek was none existent and her English was somewhat strained.

"Bien, bien, chèrie," she said excitedly, "now let me send for some coffee for you and we can talk. Are you hungry?"

"Just a little," replied Nikos, "I had a takeoff at five thirty and did not have time for breakfast on the flight as I had a new first officer and needed to keep my eye on him. It was a really short flight with a quick turnaround."

Sherrifa ordered her maid to bring some manaouche from the local bakery for him. She knew he loved the popular Arabic breakfast delicacy, comprising hot pizza-like dough, spread with thyme, sesame seeds and spices and baked in a traditional wood-burning oven. After finishing his late breakfast, they began plotting their strategy. "Am I right in believing that you have plans for the sweet little Jenny?" enquired Sherrifa.

"You are more than right my chèrie, but I don't think she is ready to fall for my charms. In fact, I think I got off to a bad start with her last night," answered Nikos seriously, telling her of his unfortunate conversation with Jenny.

"Fool!" she shot back at him. "I don't want you to mess things up for me with Greg. We will have to make some cosmetic repairs. I will talk to her and convince her that you have been under a lot of strain or something and you can back off for a while."

"Yes," he acknowledged, "that is probably a good idea. There is something about her that really attracts me. I don't want to lose her before I even start."

"What attracts you to her, Nikos Stianou, is the fact that she is indifferent to you. She is not overwhelmed by your good looks and charm. Just look at her husband. She is hardly desperate for someone like you, unlike some of the other wives who fling themselves at your feet," said Sherrifa astutely.

"You're right, Chichi," he agreed. "We will have to do something to make her desperate for me then."

"Yes, and I have very good plan," said Sherrifa smiling. "I have just heard from my father that the airline is planning to buy some wide-bodied jets at the end of the year, which means that the crew selected to fly the new aircraft will have to go to the States for training courses. You, Nikos, will ensure that Greg is selected for the course, which should be no problem since I have heard he's a hot-shot pilot, always passing exams with marks in the high nineties. The course will run for six weeks, and the airline will not be actively encouraging wives to go along since they are hoping that the crew will double-up in the villas that have been provided and keep their minds on the course and the studies. It will, of course, be necessary for me to go," she said expansively, "and one or two of the other senior wives, as there will be a few official goodwill functions to attend where some wives will be expected to be present. It is there that Greg will be most vulnerable, and quite amenable to my wishes. Until that time, you will become the model of propriety as far as Jenny is concerned. You will apologize for your conduct last night and say that you have been under a lot of strain. You will do everything to win her confidence and Greg's friendship. When it comes time for Jenny to hear about her darling husband's indiscretion from some friend of mine, you will be the shoulder for her to cry on and the rest will no doubt follow."

Nikos absorbed the news about the new aircraft, amazed that Sherrifa knew this information before anyone at the airline, probably even before her husband. He also rationalized that unless he did some fence-mending with Jenny, he would be faced with an unwilling lover rather than a grateful, adoring one. Sherrifa's plan seemed as ingenious — and as devious as always — and he did not doubt that she would be able to pull it off. Greg seemed to him to be hungry for promotion and position and would be most likely to comply with Sherrifa's wishes. He would be smart enough to know what benefits it could bring to him if he played his cards right, and conversely, the perils associated with earning her displeasure. Besides, even though Sherrifa was now thirty-five, she had lost none of her beauty or sexuality. Any man would be a fool to refuse her. "Chichi, you are a genius. What would I do without you?" he said in a complimentary tone, "That's a brilliant plan, but how am I going to wait months for the delectable Jenny?"

"The same way that I will have to wait for my new plaything, by enjoying the chase, flirting discretely from a distance, taking pleasure in each innuendo, letting the anticipation build so slowly that when the conquest finally comes, it will be so much the sweeter," replied Sherrifa with satisfaction. "Besides, we still have some affairs of the heart to attend to in the meantime. I am still seeing that Air France representative who wants to sell the airline some airbuses, and you have that interesting Moroccan hostess and dear, besotted Peggy Gallagher, who can't let you go, the fool," she added, showing her contempt at Peggy's weakness.

He considered Sherrifa's words and could see that she was right. It would certainly be a change and a challenge to slowly capture little Jenny, and he would savour every moment of the chase as she would gradually begin to respond to him. After all, he had sensed some attraction from her last night. No doubt, it was only her immature sense of morality that made her step back from the adventure of infidelity. *Well time and events will, no doubt, erode her admirable sense of morality*, he thought pleasurably.

"Now, cher Nikos, you must leave because I am going to phone your dear little Jenny and take her out for the afternoon and do a PR job on her for you," said Sherrifa sweetly.

"Bien chère, a plus tard, call me soon," he said as he kissed her gently on both cheeks.

Sherrifa watched Nikos drive away in his Mercedes sports car, feeling happy that she had such a friend in him. No one in her life, other than he, was able to understand the devils that drove her. He knew how much she needed to be the centre of power and attraction and about her need for adventure and stimulation. She knew she was not a good wife or mother, and yet there was precious little else she was allowed to be in Kharjan society. She wished she could be single and live a life of her own choosing, but she knew she needed to be married if she was to have any sexual freedom at all. Ever since her first taste of liberty in Paris, it was as if she was reborn. The independence that she experienced, coupled with her wealth, bought her a sybaritic lifestyle that she found impossible to give up. Returning to Kharja had been a nightmare until she met Hussein, who proved to be her passport to freedom. Sometimes she felt guilt about her treatment of Hussein and Samer, but it did not last long. Her needs, in the end, always outweighed any feelings of pity she might have for her husband and son.

Anyway, she reasoned, *I have bought Hussein a good position in society by marrying him, so it is not as if I have done nothing for him.*

Yes, Nikos, her thoughts returning to the new adventure about to start, *you and I are truly two of a kind. We share the same devil, that's why you understand me so well.*

Picking up the phone, Sherrifa dialed operations, "Is that you, Abdullah?" she barked at the dispatcher in Arabic.

Recognizing Sherrifa's voice, he swiftly answered, "Yes, Madam Al Fayez, how can I help you?" "Get me Captain Youssef's home telephone number," she instructed him. "Right away, madam", he answered, anxious not to displease her.

Having secured the number, she memorized it and made a call to Jenny, who was in the middle of preparing an elaborate recipe for the evening meal when the phone rang. She was surprised to hear Sherrifa's velvety tones inviting her to come out for coffee with her later that afternoon.

"I would be delighted," said Jenny. "What time shall we meet?"

"I weel pick you up at five o'clock and we weel go to one of ze 'otels and 'ave some coffee or perhaps tea since you are British. Ze British always drink ze afternoon tea, ne cest pas?"

Sherrifa crooned, her English sounding worse than usual, largely because she had been thinking and speaking in French earlier that morning.

"Well it is less of a ritual than it used to be," answered Jenny, wishing that she was able to speak to Sherrifa in either Arabic or French. "I will look forward to seeing you at five then."

Jenny looked in the mirror and decided a complete overhaul was needed. She could not be seen out with Sherrifa looking anything but perfect. She phoned Leila and asked if she was free to do her hair again today. "With pleasure, Madam Youssef," answered Leila happily, "come right away."

"Well, I must have a shower first so it will take me about half an hour," said Jenny.

"Okay, madam, I weel see you then," replied Leila, looking forward to hear about the events of the night before.

Arriving at the salon, Jenny explained that she was invited for coffee with Sherrifa in the afternoon and needed to look presentable. "Don't worry, madam, I weel take care of all. Now tell me about your evening. How was the dress, and did your husband like your hair?"

Jenny told Leila how well the evening had gone and that her dress and hair had been a success, only omitting the part that involved Nikos. "I am so happy for you, madam, and now you are invited to coffee with Madam Al Fayez. That ees a great honour. She ees a very powerful woman," she gushed happily. "Just take care zat you do not offend her," she continued on a less positive note. "She can be very deeficult if things are not to her liking."

"Yes, I have been warned," replied Jenny, "but so far I have found her to be quite charming."

Leila decided a more sedate hairstyle was required for the coffee invitation and put Jenny's hair back into an elegant chignon and insisted that she do her makeup for her again. Happy to submit herself to Leila's ministrations, Jenny relaxed and enjoyed the feeling of being pampered.

Back at home, Jenny thought carefully about what to wear and decided her smart blue linen suit that had been made for her in Bangkok would be ideal. As she dressed, she fondly remembered the time that she and Greg had spent in Bangkok together. It had been in place of a honeymoon as Greg was not due for leave at the time they married, so she accompanied him on a long-haul flight to Bangkok. The weather had been appalling as it was the rainy season and the flood waters had come right down into the city, making it impossible to go anywhere except the hotel and the shopping arcade that adjoined it. Jenny recalled how they had spent the whole week hardly moving from their room, spending most of the time in bed, making love and getting to know the delights of each other's bodies. They did surface in the late afternoons to visit the shopping arcade and take advantage of the wonderful tailor-made clothing that was abundant in the country. Later they had joined the rest of the crew for dinner and endured the inevitable jokes about honeymooners and their unsociability.

Jenny had been unbelievably happy and enjoyed all the sights and sounds of the Far East — she had never before travelled any further than the Spanish Algarve. She also enjoyed the camaraderie of the crew who seemed so much more relaxed when they were away from base. All the formalities that were observed on the aircraft and at home base were dropped, and the cabin staff mixed freely with the cockpit crew on an equal basis, all happy to enjoy each other's company. The week had flown by, but the cherished memories of that special, intimate time they spent together in Bangkok always remained close to her heart.

Glancing at the clock, Jenny realized it was three o'clock and she had not eaten anything since Greg had left in the morning for the airport. She made herself a large salad sandwich to allay hunger pangs since she likely would not eat dinner before eight o'clock in the evening. After her modest repast, she turned on the radio and sat down lazily on the sofa and listened to the soothing strains of Julio Iglesias playing on the local FM stereo station and let her thoughts drift back to the time she and Greg spent in Bangkok.

Jenny was dressed and ready by quarter to five, not wanting to be late for this important appointment. She left a note for Greg to say where she had gone and to put the casserole in the oven if she was not back before seven. Greg always liked to know her movements, and she guessed he would be delighted at her invitation today.

Jenny was a little surprised when she saw the large, black, chauffeur-driven American car pull up outside their modest apartment building. Somehow, she imagined that Sherrifa would be coming in person to pick her up. Then she realized that someone of Sherrifa's stature would, of course, be chauffeur-driven and that she had better stop thinking in her small-town way.

A few seconds later, Ahmed, the concierge, phoned upstairs to inform her that Madam Al Fayez had arrived and would wait downstairs for her in her car. Jenny thanked him and said she would be down immediately. She flew out of the apartment and into the elevator, anxious not to keep Sherrifa waiting.

"Jenny, chère," exclaimed Sherrifa, "how are you today? Eet ees so nice to see you again."

"Oh, I'm very well indeed. Thank you, Sherrifa, it's a real pleasure to see you again too. I'm looking forward to our coffee," Jenny responded pleasantly. Sherrifa eyed Jenny and was forced to admit to herself that the girl had style and beauty. She was every bit as well groomed and poised as she herself.

Settling herself in the back of the large, air-conditioned car, Jenny felt nervous and ill at ease. She was very flattered to be

37

the object of Sherrifa's attentions but could not help wondering what it was that Sherrifa found so interesting about her.

Sherrifa instructed her chauffeur to drive them to the Marriott Hotel and began making pleasant conversation with Jenny. Arriving at the Marriott, Sherrifa was greeted profusely by all the hotel staff she came into contact with — the waiters in the coffee lounge almost bent over double in subservience to her.

"Madam Al-Fayez, where would you like to sit? I will prepare a table for you immediately," crooned the head waiter.

"We will sit over there, by the window overlooking the pool," she instructed him in Arabic.

Jenny was amazed at the amount of power Sherrifa wielded. She was treated like royalty, and what's more, it was obvious she enjoyed it. They were ushered to their seats and offered cool glasses of water with lemon and ice to refresh them. Jenny was about to take a sip when Sherrifa stopped her.

"Is this bottled water?" she demanded of the waiter in Arabic. "No, Madam Al Fayez, it is filtered water. It is very pure," he replied reassuringly.

"Take this away and bring us bottled water. I never drink the filtered water. It has a back taste that is unpalatable to me," Sherrifa instructed him, registering disgust on her face.

"I am very sorry, madam. I will change it right away for you," replied the waiter, bowing in abject apology knowing that one word against him to the manager would result in his immediate dismissal. The power of Sherrifa's family was undisputed. Jenny could only watch in wonderment at what was transpiring. She wished fervently that she could speak Arabic and understand all the nuances of what was taking place. She had asked Greg to teach her, but he was never around long enough to make much of a job of it. She admired the fact that, in the Middle East, nearly everyone, from the humblest worker upwards, was able to communicate in either English or French — and in many cases, both languages in addition to their own.

Sherrifa smiled at Jenny, telling her she should not drink the water as it was not bottled and that the waiter would bring her some more. Jenny did not really mind the filtered water and quite enjoyed its slightly salty aftertaste. But not wishing to argue with Sherrifa, she kept her feelings to herself. Besides, she remembered, Greg had told her that in the Middle East, it was almost expected that important personages would criticize the service they received. Whilst she could not understand the logic of this, she was resigned to accept it.

"Jenny, you may 'ave wondered why I 'ave asked to see you again so soon," cooed Sherrifa. "Well zere ees a reason, my dear. You see, I 'ad a call from Nikos thees morning and 'e was very, very upset. He theenks that 'e was a leetle forward with you last night and 'e wanted me to apologize on 'ees behalf. You see, chère, 'e 'as been under a lot of strain lately. You know zat ze airline ees expanding very quickly and the commercial people 'ave been taking on more bookings than we can actually manage until we get some more crew. The 707s 'ave been ze work 'orses. Zey are back in ze air after every mechanical check. Poor Nikos, as ze 707 fleet captain, 'e has 'ad so much pressure to keep ze flights on schedule. 'e 'ad to take on many extra flights 'imself, as well as all ze work in ze office. Ze poor darling ees sometimes so tired zat he doesn't know what he ees saying. Also, he ees 'aving problems een ze 'ome with his wife. Maybe I should not tell you thees, but she ees a very cold woman and does not look after him properly, eef you know what I mean," she said with a conspiratorial gesture. "Anyway, he 'as asked me to apologize on his behalf and to tell you zat zis weel never 'appen again."

Sherrifa studied Jenny and saw that her little speech had been effective. Jenny was shocked at the fact that Nikos had spoken

39

to Sherrifa about last night and was rather at a loss for words. Remembering Betty's words about the relationship between Nikos and Sherrifa, perhaps she should not be surprised at his actions, she reflected. *Yet, on the other hand, what did she know about Betty; was it possible that she had some kind of an axe to grind and was being malicious about them? In the cold light of day, Sherrifa's explanation seemed quite plausible. Perhaps last night she had overreacted to the situation. She decided to take Sherrifa's explanation and Nikos's apology at face value and proceed as if nothing had happened.* "It's very kind of you to do this on Nikos' behalf, Sherrifa," replied Jenny thoughtfully. "I know that there has been a lot of pressure for management to keep the flights on schedule, so I can imagine how much stress it could cause him. Please tell him that I have forgotten all about last night and that he should too."

"Zat ees so kind of you, chère. I know 'e will feel much better about it now," purred Sherrifa.

The rest of the afternoon passed by pleasantly enough. Some of Sherrifa's friends arrived for coffee and joined them at their table at Sherrifa's request. Jenny felt a little left out at times as the conversation often broke into Arabic or French, leaving her feeling distinctly uncomfortable, especially when it was accompanied by peals of laughter. Jenny determined, there and then, that she would enroll for either Arabic or French lessons as soon as possible. She did not like the feeling of being excluded, even if it was unintentional.

Jenny's discomfort was not unwarranted. Sherrifa's friends had enquired, in Arabic, who she was. Sherrifa had replied that she was the latest of Nikos' fancies, and she was just preparing the ground for him. Why else would she bother with such a useless foreign weed?

Sherrifa's friends were cognizant of how unorthodox her rude conduct was for an Arab woman but, nonetheless, happily indulged her because of her elevated position in Kharjan society. They eagerly listened to the gossip of the airline and all the adventures of the crew. It made a diversion from their mundane lives as spoiled wives of executives.

Returning home with Sherrifa rather later than expected, Jenny saw Greg waiting for her downstairs in the compound of the apartment. "It looks as if Greg is wondering where I have got to. I can see him prowling around the compound," said Jenny.

Turning with a bright smile, Sherrifa told Jenny, "You must let me tell him zat eet ees all my fault zat we are a leetle late. I forget ze time when I start to talk weeth my friends, you know."

Greg walked swiftly to the car and opened the door for Jenny. Bending over to greet Sherrifa, he asked her if she would care to come inside for a drink before she left. Declining graciously, she offered her apologies for their late return. Then she broke into Arabic again and held a short conversation with Greg before taking her leave of them. Jenny felt the prick of annoyance again at being excluded from the conversation and strengthened her resolve to learn the language as soon as possible.

Walking upstairs to the apartment, Jenny was greeted by the delicious smells of their dinner cooking. Greg had obediently put the casserole in the oven at the appropriate time and thoughtfully turned it down when she was late in returning. Sitting down to dinner, they discussed her afternoon. Greg was clearly happy at her success with Sherrifa and complimentary on the way she looked. "You know, Jenny," said Greg smiling, "I have been getting lots of compliments for choosing such a beautiful wife. Everyone who saw you last night all said how lovely you were. The new dress and hairstyle really worked, so you are really going to live up to it now. No more ponytails and going without makeup, you have got a reputation to maintain!" Greg had always appreciated her beauty, but had not realized what an impact she would make on others. He had particularly enjoyed the compliments that had been paid to him on her account and wanted them to continue.

Jenny did not quite know how to respond to Greg's cautionary compliment. She was pleased to know that she had made a good impression with the others, yet she was surprised that Greg should expect her to promote herself as some kind of beauty. But remembering what Leila had told her about the importance of feminine beauty in the Middle East, she agreed to work hard on maintaining her beautiful new image. "Darling, there is something that I would like to ask of you too. I intend to take Arabic lessons, and until I have mastered the language, would you please conduct conversations where I am present in English? A couple of times today I have felt really excluded when people talked around me in Arabic, including you."

What was it that Sherrifa was saying to you before she left?" enquired Jenny.

"Don't worry, love," returned Greg, "she was only saying how much she was looking forward to seeing us again and mentioned that John and Peggy Gallagher were celebrating their wedding anniversary next week and were throwing a party. She said that she knew we were invited, and I told her that I had got the invitation card today in my pigeon-hole at the airport. That's all there was to it," said Greg reassuringly.

"Fine," retorted Jenny, "but why couldn't she have said that in English?"

"Oh, you know how it is here. She was just being formal by asking me etcetera, etcetera," drawled Greg.

"Well Sherrifa does not seem the type to abide by customs and conventions to me," argued Jenny.

"What are you being so paranoid for all of a sudden Jenny? It just happened, forget it. It's no big deal," said Greg trying to placate her. Leaving the table, he strolled into the kitchen and reappeared carrying something in an exaggerated waiter-style in the air.

"Here, madam, I bought you some of your most loved ice cream that has the gum Arabic in it, which makes it go stretchy. Let's go and eat it on the sofa and forget about Kharja Airways for a while," he coaxed.

"I don't need any more persuasion," she conceded, laughing at his parodying. "You've bought my silence for a tub of ice cream."

CHAPTER THREE

Reality bites and Peggy's shame

The months that followed Greg and Jenny's initiation into the elite social circle of the airline crew were marked by frequent invitations to functions and parties. Soon Jenny became familiar with all the regular attendees of these occasions. These evenings usually followed a familiar pattern with the men gathering together to compare flights in the early part of the evening and later joining the women for small talk and dancing. Jenny noted, with pleasure, on these occasions that Sherrifa always made a point of spending some time with her before moving on to her longer-standing friends. She was also impressed with the way that Nikos conducted himself around her, always the gentleman, with no hint of malice about him. Jenny tried her best to socialize with everyone on these occasions, but having little in common with many of the older wives, she often ended up sitting and chatting with Betty. Although Betty was probably the oldest of all the wives, Jenny enjoyed her unaffected forthrightness and was entertained by her numerous amusing anecdotes of former and present crew members. The only occasion when she felt distinctly uncomfortable was on the evening of Peggy and John Gallagher's wedding anniversary.

The evening had begun pleasantly, she and Greg were warmly welcomed into Peggy and John's elegant villa and introduced to those they didn't yet know. After the men had finished their usual pow-wow, a toast was made to Peggy and John and the dancing began. Peggy was unusually high-spirited that evening and was slightly the worse for drink. Cutting in on a conversation between Nikos and Sherrifa, she requested that Nikos dance with her. Obligingly, he took her to the dancing area and began to dance with her. The music was particularly soft and romantic, and Jenny was horrified to see Peggy moving closer to Nikos and begin kissing him on the neck. Turning to Betty, Jenny exclaimed, "What on earth is Peggy doing? This is her wedding anniversary and she behaving like that with Nikos?"

"That poor woman has been messed about badly by that rat Nikos," drawled Betty, "A couple of years ago, he noticed that she was very amenable to his charms, and decided to move in on her. The poor woman became besotted with him. She thought she'd found the love of her life, but he was only passin' time with her. In the beginnin', Nikos made sure that John was always away on long-haul flights or doin' long training sessions so he could get to see her regular. But true to form, Nikos' attenion soon wandered and he moved on to pastures new. He didn't stop seeing Peggy, like any decent sorta guy would. He just saw her less often, tellin' her all sorts'a lies about where he was. Peggy didn't know that he was seein' other women, until she heard 'bout it while she was on board one of our flights and heard the cabin staff talkin' about him. His latest conquest had been a Moroccan hostess who had bragged about her relationship with him. When she caught on that she was being two-timed with a hostess, she went berserk. She confronted Nikos with what she had heard. The bastard admitted his relationship with the hostess and told her that if she did not like it, she knew what she could do. That was the beginnin' of her instability. The poor thing had thought that Nikos was going to leave his wife for her and they would go away and start a new life together somewhere. The shock of knowing that she was just another notch on his gun was too much for her. That night, her friend Clare received a disturbing phone call from Peggy, sayin' that she wanted her to know that she had always been a good friend to her and just wanted to say goodbye. Clare, who knew about Nikos and all his philanderin', guessed that somethin' was up and drove right over there. She found Peggy in the bathroom covered in blood. She had slit her wrists. Clare bundled her into her car and got her to the hospital. Fortunately for Peggy, the cuts were pretty superficial, and she did not need to be hospitalized. Clare managed to keep the lid on the whole affair, but she had a long talk with John, telling him she thought that Peggy was sufferin' from depression and needed some medical help, big time. John was real considerate and persuaded Peggy to get some help. But, you know, Jen honey, that woman has never been the same since."

Betty drew a long breath after her long, harrowing narration and adopted an expression of world weariness and waited for Jenny's response.

"The poor woman," said Jenny, shaking her head in disbelief, "but tell me, Betty, how did you come to know about it?"

"Ha, that's my secret," teased Betty.

"Betty, you can't tell me an incredible story like that and expect me to believe it if you don't tell me where you heard it," demanded Jenny reasonably.

"Okay honey, but don't tell anyone else. The way I hear most things is through the staff that work for me. Y'know that the maids and the gardeners and the concierges and the like have a society of their own, and they like nothin' better than to gossip about what their employers are up to. It so happens that I treat my maid real nice, and she is only too willin' to pass on the latest gossip to me. On that night in particular, she was visitin' her cousin who cleans at the hospital and was there when Clare brought Peggy in. My maid knew she was a pilot's wife 'cause she'd seen her at a gatherin' at our house. My maid got all the details of what she'd done to herself from her cousin who'd been eavesdroppin' while she was cleanin'," confided Betty. "Anyway, can't you see that the poor woman is not in control of herself? She never did get over that bum. Look at her, she can't keep her hands off him. All her dignity is gone; what a waste," concluded Betty reflectively.

As the evening progressed, Peggy's conduct became increasingly embarrassing. She took every opportunity to hang on to Nikos, either by dancing with him or by managing to sit next to him on the sofa. Thankfully, before she was able to disgrace herself too much, Clare took control of the situation, managing to persuade Peggy to go upstairs and show her the new clothes she had bought on a recent trip to the States. Once inside the bedroom, Clare spoke to her sharply, "What the hell do you think you're doing Peggy?" she demanded. "It's supposed to be yours and John's anniversary, and you are practically throwing yourself at Nikos in front of everyone. Haven't you got any pride at all?"

"Oh hell, Clare," replied Peggy with a drunken slur, "I'm sick to death of pretending. I can't keep pretending that I'm a well-behaved, happily married woman when I am in love with Nikos."

"Peggy, get a grip on yourself," ordered Clare. "Can't you see what a fool you are making of yourself? Everyone knows that Nikos is the biggest womanizer around and the only woman he ever has any time for is Sherrifa. You must see that he has used you the same way that he has used all his other women. You're nothing more than another notch on his gun."

"No, no, Clare, you don't understand. When he's with me, it's magic. He makes me feel like a princess," whined Peggy.

"Oh for God's sake, grow up, Peggy. He only comes to you when there is no one else on the horizon. Why won't you accept it? He's told you himself that he is seeing other women," Clare argued.

"Yes, I know," said Peggy hysterically, "but you see, he only needs other women because he is still married to that cold wife of his. If he divorced her and married me, he wouldn't need other women, I would give him all the love he needs. Can't you see, Clare, I just can't pretend anymore."

"Shut up, you fool!" shouted Clare, slapping Peggy hard across the face. "We are all pretending. If we stop pretending, we stop playing the game. And if we stop playing the game, then we have no civilization, and we will be nothing better than animals. Think of your position. Think of what it would do to John if this came out. You would even harm your precious Nikos. Is that what you want?" demanded Clare. She did not enjoy taking such a hard line with Peggy but knew that it was required when it came to Nikos. She truly pitied her, knowing that Peggy was not like some of the other crew wives who thought little of jumping into bed with whoever was closest to hand if they were feeling lonely. Peggy had been faithful to John for as long as she could remember. *Probably that was why Nikos found Peggy so attractive,* reflected Clare. *Until that son of a bitch pushed his way into Peggy's life, she had been a good, happy, levelheaded friend. Now Nikos had reduced her to this* and she hated him for it. *If it's the last thing I do, I'll get Peggy right again,* she swore to herself. The slap across the face had brought Peggy to her senses. Clare plied her with strong, black coffee until she regained her senses. They later rejoined the party again without further incident.

Jenny was still chatting with Betty when Peggy and Clare came in. Jenny was relieved to see that Peggy was more in control of herself.

"It's nice that Clare is such a good friend to Peggy," remarked Jenny. "She seems to have sorted her out quite nicely."

"Yeah," retorted Betty cynically.

"I'm beginning to recognize that tone, Betty Bonner. It means that naïve, little Jenny has just misinterpreted the situation," observed Jenny caustically.

"You're beginning to catch on kid," said Betty sarcastically.

"Well, come on then, educate me," insisted Jenny.

"You're not exactly wrong to say that Clare is a good friend to Peggy, she is. They have been good friends for a long time. The only thing wrong with that was that Clare was a whole lot friendlier with John at one time than she was with Peggy," she drawled.

"You don't mean Clare and John were having an affair, do you?" enquired Jenny, trying not to look too surprised.

"I sure do, honey. That's the problem when folks see too much of each other. They start fallin' in love with each other's husbands and wives. Anyway, it didn't last long. Both of them felt so guilty about the whole darned affair that it soon fizzled out. Since that time, Clare has tried to make up for her little indiscretion by being a good and loyal friend to Peggy," informed Betty.

"Well, I am surprised. I thought the Gallaghers and the Lamberts were the model of propriety," commented Jenny.

"Honey, there are very few people around here who are the model of propriety. Pilots and their wives spend a whole lotta time away from each other, so temptation is always around. There's very few who can resist it when they are faced with another lonely night or day, especially here in the Middle East, where there is so little for folks to divert themselves with. The important thing, though, is to play the game well: We have to learn to have one life when our men are here and another when they are away. The trick is to never let one interfere with the other. 'Cause sure as eggs is eggs, there doin' the same thing themselves while they're away." Turning to look at Jenny, she could see that she had said too much too soon. So she quickly added, "Unless of course you are madly in love like you and Greg, and then things might turn out different."

Jenny absorbed Betty's comments with some disbelief. *Surely pilots and their wives were not bound to follow some kind of unwritten code of practice. That could not be what it was all about.* She thought about the intimate life she and Greg were making for themselves and felt reassured that their marriage would not follow the same pattern as the others. "Betty, if what you say is right, what about you and Chuck?" asked Jenny. "Do you and he play the game?"

"Ha," laughed Betty, "I guess I had that comin'. Well as a matter of fact, I have had some moments when I was younger, but that was a long time ago, and I don't recall too much about them. Y'see, I have never been the most glamorous or sophisticated of women. The men didn't exactly flock to my door, and them that did usually couldn't stand my unrefined attitude, y'know? As for Chuck, well, I know he must have had his moments, but knowin' men like I do, I had four brothers," giving Jenny a conspiratorial wink as if to confirm that she knew that all men were the same, "I told Chuck, after we got married, if your gonna do something behind my back, then that's the way it should stay. You can do your doin's outside, just don't bring it home to my doorstep. I don't ever want to hear about it. I guess that worked 'cause I never heard a word of scandal about him, and he has always treated me real well," she paused and drew a breath feeling that she had not quite done justice to Jenny's question. "But I kinda did get to know when he was meetin' someone 'cause when I would check his flight bag, he would have a whole bunch of condoms tucked away in there. Of course, I shouldn't have been pokin' around in his flight bag, but you know how it is, sometimes you just can't help lookin'."

Jenny drew a deep breath in readiness to ask Betty more about the prevalence of extramarital affairs among pilots, but thought better of it and exhaled with a long sigh. Betty caught Jenny's mood and decided to change the subject, discussing instead the intricacies of Arabic cuisine. Betty offered to teach Jenny some of the dishes that she herself had been taught by her maid. As the evening began to wind down, Betty felt obliged to ask Jenny whether she had been approached again by Nikos. "Honey, has that Nikos been botherin' you again since that other night?"

"I'm glad you asked, Betty. As a matter of fact, I received an apology from Nikos via Sherrifa the day after our dinner party," replied Jenny with a touch of smugness. "It seems that he has been under a lot of strain, his wife has been rather cold with him and all this has resulted in him acting a bit irrationally."

"Well there's a turn up for the books," commented Betty in a surprised tone. "It ain't often that Nikos will walk away from his prey, so there must be more goin' on than I figured."

"Betty, I don't want to sound rude or anything, but couldn't it just be possible that they are telling the truth?" argued Jenny. "I appreciate what you are trying to do for me, and I can see that Nikos is probably a philanderer, but in this case, I do feel that he made a mistake that he is genuinely sorry for. Why else would he go to the trouble of asking Sherrifa to apologize on his behalf?"

Betty could see that Jenny did not want to believe the things she was hearing from her. She also guessed that Greg could have put some pressure on her to comply with the wishes of those who are instrumental in furthering his career. Not wishing to put Jenny under any more pressure than necessary, she simply took her hand and said, "Jenny, all this is new to you now, and life might throw you a few curves. If things come up that you can't handle, you can always turn to Chuck and me for help."

"Thank you, Betty," replied Jenny, touched by Betty's sincerity, "I just hope everything will go well and I won't need to take you up on your offer."

"So do I, honey, so do I," agreed Betty in a doubtful tone.

As Jenny's life settled down into something approaching a routine, she began to feel boredom encroaching upon her. Apart from the Arabic lessons she was taking and the regular social outings with virtually the same circle of people, she had little else to occupy herself with. Greg had insisted that she should hire a maid because he did not want it said that his wife was doing menial work. Jenny had tried to argue the issue, saying their apartment was not hard to keep clean and she had plenty of time on her hands. However, Greg had been adamant and told her she was going to have a maid whether she liked it or not, and furthermore, they would soon be expected to give some small dinner parties at home and would need someone to help with the cooking. In the end, she gave up the argument and conceded to Greg's wishes, knowing that, in a way, he was right as all the other wives had at least one maid and often other household staff too. It would look rather miserly of Greg not to employ one. She also reflected that by employing a maid, it would make a very small contribution to easing the poverty of at least one family in the country. Jenny had been shocked at the dire straits in which the poor lived. Many of them were refugees who had been displaced during the protracted war in nearby Koudara. Nonetheless, she was ill-prepared for the sight of the ramshackle corrugated iron huts where they lived. Families of five and more would somehow manage to live together in the shacks that often comprised only one room with a divider down the middle. There was no running water and no sanitary facilities. Consequently, during the hot summer months, the refugee area was rife with cholera and dysentery. The plight of these people so moved her that she ventured to ask Greg whether he would mind if she made use of her nursing training by helping out at the University Hospital.

"What exactly do you mean, Jenny?" enquired Greg impatiently. "Are you saying that you want to take a job at the hospital?"

"Well, not a job that involves payment," countered Jenny. "Betty told me some of the foreigners over here that are attached to embassies, big businesses and so on have started a women's voluntary service at the University Hospital and are looking for people to help."

"For heaven's sake, Jenny, don't you ever mix with anyone except that fat cow Betty? She is a busybody, always sticking her nose in where it isn't wanted," snapped Greg unkindly.

Jenny bristled, hurt on Betty's behalf. "That's a very unkind remark to make about someone who has gone out of her way to be friendly towards me. I do see other wives too, but you know I'm so much younger than them all, and it's hard to find things in common. Besides, most of them have been friends for years, and it's difficult to carve a niche for myself with them. On the other hand, Betty is so much fun that the age gap doesn't even come in to it. Anyway, you are going off the subject we were talking about regarding me doing voluntary work at the hospital. You need to understand that it's very hard for me to sit around trying to create work for myself when there is a need for helpers at the hospital. What's more, it could be an opportunity to meet other wives unconnected with the airline and then maybe I won't have to spend so much time with Betty," she added somewhat maliciously.

Greg contemplated Jenny's request and conceded that it would be acceptable as long as she was doing voluntary work. He emphasized that he did not want to hear of any requests from her to take on paid employment. On some issues, he was very Middle Eastern in his beliefs. *No wife of his was going to be seen to take paid employment*, he reflected firmly. *However, it would look quite good for his beautiful young wife to be seen doing voluntary work at the hospital*, he reasoned. "Alright, darling, I don't mind you working there, but be careful not to get sick yourself," he cautioned.

"Don't worry about that; I will have all the shots I need. Besides, you forget I have spent quite a lot of time working in hospitals myself, so my immune system is quite used to all kinds of bugs," laughed Jenny, pleased with her triumph.

"Come here, you wicked, conniving female," teased Greg. "You won't always get your way that easily. Come here, I'll show you." Greg lunged at Jenny but she was too quick for him, and he went sprawling across the floor. "Just wait till I get my hands on you," Greg threatened playfully.

"You'll have to catch me first," shouted Jenny, running for the bedroom. Greg caught her round the waist and pulled her onto the bed. Jenny didn't struggle to get away from him anymore and allowed Greg to dominate their lovemaking. He was a little rougher than usual with her, but it did not detract from the pleasure that they both shared. She felt unusually aroused by the harshness of his kisses and thrusting of his muscular body. Usually, she tried to keep pace with Greg, gauging when he was about to reach orgasm and then let go so they reached climax simultaneously, but this time her body was arching in orgasm before she was able to exert any control on it. Her gasps of ecstasy and quivering body soon brought Greg to orgasm, and they fell back spent, surprised at the intensity of their passion.

"Thank you, darling," said Greg, gently pushing back a strand of hair that had fallen over Jenny's face. "It was so nice to feel you let go like that. Don't ever hold yourself back again."

"I didn't think you could tell that I was holding back," whispered Jenny breathlessly. "I thought that you really enjoyed it when we orgasmed together."

"Well, I certainly can't complain about that. You have a rare gift to be able to control your body the way you do. But, you know, feeling you lose control like that was incredibly sexy for me, and very, very satisfying," said Greg gently.

"If that makes you happy, I will be equally happy to comply," she said lovingly. Jenny chose this tender moment to broach a subject that had been nagging her for some time. Knowing that it was of a sensitive nature, she felt this was the right time to speak. "Darling, there is something that I want to talk to you about," said Jenny.

"What is it, love?" enquired Greg sleepily.

"Well, we have been married for about eight months now, and since we decided not to use any contraceptives, I'm a bit surprised that I haven't conceived yet. I wondered whether we ought to have some tests done to see if we have any fertility problems." Jenny felt Greg stiffen at her remarks and wondered whether she had been wrong to bring up the subject.

"I don't think we have any problems, and I don't want to hear you talking about going for tests again," he replied coldly. Greg got up and showered, leaving Jenny feeling rather hurt and confused. Greg was usually very practical about most issues, and she was not prepared for his brusqueness. She'd always loved working in the children's wards at the hospital and had been hoping that she would soon have Greg's baby. A child would help ease her loneliness when he was away flying and fill up her days. Most of all, a child would be the greatest gift of love that she could offer him. She lay for a few minutes, thinking of what had transpired and decided that, on reflection, she might have been tactless and wounded Greg's ego. She decided to drop the subject and be patient. Joining him in the bathroom, she put her arms around him and said she was sorry to have upset him.

"It's alright, Jenny," he told her stiffly, "but let's leave the subject alone. When it's time, things will happen."

"Yes, you're right. But do you know what?" she asked playfully.

"What?" he enquired, happy to leave the subject of conceiving a child behind.

"I'm starving, and there's nothing interesting in the fridge," she informed him.

"Well, what are we going to do about it?" he asked, catching her lightheartedness.

"Get some fast food," she said.

"Shall we go for a pizza?" suggested Greg.

"No, let's go to that little place that is famous for its falafel," said Jenny. They quickly dressed and went out into the still, warm night time air and drove to the poorer end of town where they bought their falafel sandwiches.

"Let's go and eat them by the sea," said Greg, "I always think food tastes better by the ocean."

"Yes, I know just what you mean," replied Jenny. They drove for less than five minutes to reach the coast and parked on the rough ground close to the shore. Opening the car door, the salty humid smell of the ocean rushed in on them.

"Mmm, I love that sea-weedy, briny smell of the sea," said Jenny inhaling deeply.

"Me, too," agreed Greg, "but if you don't give me my sandwich soon, I might just have to start nibbling on you."

"Here it is, enjoy," she offered. Biting hungrily into her sandwich, she asked Greg what the actual ingredients were.

"It is basically a mixture of ground chickpeas, ground lima beans, coriander and garlic, shaped into small balls and deep fried in olive oil. When they make the sandwich, they open

56

up the pocket of the Arabic bread and fill it with the crushed falafel balls and a traditional diced salad in a tahini and lemon dressing," he told her.

"Well, it is so delicious I could live on it without any trouble," she said.

"As a matter of fact, you probably could, since the combination of the wheat in the bread and the beans in the falafel form a perfect protein. What's more, the tahini is full of calcium from the sesame seeds it is made from. And the salad provides the daily requirement of fresh vegetables and, of course, bread also provides carbohydrates," he informed her rather loftily.

"How in hell are you so knowledgeable about food values?" demanded Jenny in a surprised tone.

"Well, my mother's a vegetarian. When she came over here from England, she was not a great meat eater anyway, but seeing the entire carcasses of animals hanging in the butcher shops put her off it all together. She did not force the rest of us to be vegetarians, but she refused to cook meat in the house. She told Dad that if he or the rest of us wanted to eat meat, we could go and eat it outside."

"Didn't that get rather expensive for you all?" enquired Jenny.

"Not really, because eating out is a regular event in the Middle East and is not really that expensive unless you go to the big hotels. However, mum did such wonderful dishes with pulses, fresh vegetables and cereals that we did not really miss having the meat. And she made delicious desserts, which I am just about ready for," he said lunging towards her, "Will it be you or the ice cream shop?" he teased.

"Mmm, ice cream, ice cream, please," she begged.

"That's what I like about you" he joked. "You're a really cheap date, the sandwich and the ice cream won't have even cost me half a dinar."

CHAPTER FOUR

Jenny's world widens

The next day Jenny set about making enquiries at the hospital about joining the voluntary service. Finding the number for the hospital, she dialed and got through to the switchboard operator, who then put her through to the appropriate section. The phone was answered by a woman with a strong Germanic accent, "Hallo, volunteers, how can I help you?"

"Oh hello, my name's Jennifer Youssef, and I heard you are looking for volunteers and I would like to offer my services," said Jenny.

"Your services vill be most velcome. My name is Mariella Sabat. I must first have you fill in a form and give you a little interview. When can you come here?" she asked.

"When do you want me?" asked Jenny.

"To tell you za truth, we need you right now. We are desperate for help at za hospital. Can you come down now and I will see you immediately?" said Mariella.

"I am on my way," said Jenny. "I'll be about twenty minutes if the traffic is good."

"Great, I vill see you zen, goodbye," concluded Mariella positively.

It took Jenny less than twenty minutes to arrive at the hospital as the traffic was unusually light. Locating the room assigned to the volunteers, she knocked on the door and waited for someone to answer. There was no reply, so she tried opening the door but found it locked. She decided to enquire the whereabouts of Mariella at the reception desk. Jenny had just set off down the corridor when a very out-of-breath woman shouted to her, "Hallo, hallo, are you Jenny?"

"Yes," replied Jenny, "are you Mariella?"

"Yes, yes, I am," she said breathlessly. I am so sorry I vas not there to greet you, but ve are really short of volunteers, and the hospital is very short staffed. I usually stay in the office and do the phone work, but I had to go and take some blood specimens from the ward to the laboratory before they congealed," lamented Mariella, her words pouring out twenty to the dozen. "Anyway, please come into za office and we can go through za formalities," she said, indicating a chair for Jenny to sit in. Mariella was a tall, striking Germanic blonde, whose classic beauty belied her forty-six years. She sized Jenny up in a glance and appeared happy with what she saw.

"Jenny, tell me why you would like to come and be a volunteer vith us?" she asked.

"Well, there are a few reasons, but I think the primary reason is that I have been told the hospital is short staffed and in need of help. More specifically, I feel I am well-placed to offer my services as I am a State Registered Nurse in England," answered Jenny honestly.

"Vot did you say!" exclaimed Mariella. "Are you really a nurse? It seems my prayers are answered. Za doctors are desperate for trained staff to help in za clinics, especially for Outpatients. I swear you were sent directly by za angels," she said dramatically.

"Please, Jenny, vill you just fill zat form for za hospital, and I vill get in touch vith my husband. He is a consultant in Gynecology and the head of staff, also. I vill ask him if it's all right for you to work in a professional capacity as a volunteer. Zat is if you don't mind?" gushed Mariella excitedly.

"No, I don't mind. On the contrary, I would welcome it as I have quite a lot of spare time to fill," answered Jenny.

"Say goodbye to your spare time, Jenny," laughed Mariella with a warning tone. "You vill be worn off your feet by za time we finish vith you here!" Mariella made an internal call and asked to speak to her husband. She was kept waiting for a few minutes before being put through, and then she launched into a quick-fire conversation with her husband in Arabic. Jenny tried to follow the conversation, but as usual, found that the classical Arabic she was learning was of little help when the colloquial Arabic was being spoken. However, she could almost read from Mariella's expressive face that her services would be warmly welcomed.

Turning back to Jenny after plonking the phone down firmly in its cradle, Mariella said, "I am sure you can guess how much you are needed here, and my husband vill be very grateful if you vould go to za emergency room and help out zere it you vould be so kind. I vill take you zere myself and introduce you as a new nurse."

Passing through reception, Jenny was introduced to the attractive receptionist who was also a volunteer. Jenny was not sure whether she was Arab or foreign until she spoke. "Hi, Candy," greeted Mariella, "meet Jenny, a new volunteer and, vould you believe, a fully qualified nurse!"

"Wow, that is good news. The doctors are going to love you," returned Candy in a soft Canadian accent. The phone rang shrilly, interrupting their introductions. Candy answered in fluent Arabic and calmly dealt with the situation.

"You can zee vhy ve have Candy helping in reception. She speaks Arabic so vell and is so calm vith the patients," Mariella said admiringly.

"Yes, I can see that," said Jenny. "I feel so inadequate, not being able to communicate in their language. I am taking classes, but they don't seem to be helping much."

"To tell you the truth, it took me quite a while before I could communicate with people here. It is a hard language to learn. Both Candy and I ver taught by our in-laws who refused to speak to us in English, even though they ver quite able to, until ve ver fluent in their language. It vas very difficult at first, but I thanked them for it afterwards," Mariella acknowledged.

"So Arabic will be your third language then?" enquired Jenny.

"Vell, fourth actually," she replied modestly, "I am Norwegian and ve ver required to learn both English and German at school."

"Well, I am really impressed," said Jenny. "I wish the English school system was more rigorous in teaching us foreign languages. Perhaps I might have been able to pick up Arabic a little quicker."

"Don't vorry," replied Mariella, "you vill soon pick it up. Maybe you can ask Candy to help you. She is always moaning that she does not have enough things to do in a day."

"That's right," replied Candy while putting the phone down, "I would enjoy teaching you the language. Since my divorce, I'm quite lonely. I only see my kids twice a week, and I really need to keep myself busy and keep my mind away from the negative."

At that moment, the head of Outpatients walked by, and Mariella grabbed him and introduced Jenny.

"Ah yes, your dear husband just phoned to tell me the good news," he told Mariella with a conspiratorial wink. Turning his full attention to Jenny, he intoned quietly to her, "I am Dr. Saeed, but I hope that you will call me Khalil. As you must have gathered, we are more than happy to have you working here, but there is one tiny problem. The government will not allow us to employ you as a nurse unless you have a permit to work and are paid a salary," he said in almost accent-free English. "Do not concern yourself about the work permit; we can arrange that very easily," he assured her.

"Oh, dear," said Jenny, "the work permit is not the problem. I'm afraid my husband won't like me working for a salary."

"Well, my dear," he said, his handsome face crinkling into a warm smile, "We rather anticipated that and came up with what we consider to be a solution. We propose to pay you a salary of one Kharjan dinar per year as your salary."

Jenny was both amused and relieved at his suggestion. She knew Greg could not object to such an arrangement. In fact, she could well imagine that he might take great pleasure in telling people that his wife earned only one dinar per year. "I think that's a very good solution and one that I think both my husband and I could live with," returned Jenny happily.

"In that case," said Dr. Khalil, "do you think I could steal her away from you both and take her through and introduce her to everyone in the E.R.?" Mariella and Candy both nodded their agreement. As Jenny and the doctor walked away from the desk, Candy shouted after Jenny to meet her for coffee in the staff cafeteria in two hours.

"Okay, see you there then," said Jenny, happy at finding a new friend so quickly.

The following two hours flew by, and Jenny had barely been introduced to any of the staff before her services were called upon. Cholera had really taken hold this summer, and patients were arriving at the hospital in droves. The overburdened medical staff in the emergency room had barely time to say hello to her. At once, Jenny offered her help which was immediately accepted. She worked with the worse cases, who were badly dehydrated, making them comfortable and setting up drips for them. The medical staff was impressed with her efficiency and more than relieved that she did not need supervision. All sense of time had departed from Jenny, and she was startled when she heard Candy's soft voice admonishing her for failing to turn up at the cafeteria.

"Come on, Jenny, if you don't give yourself a break every couple of hours you can be sure that no one else will," chastised Candy.

"I'm really sorry. I totally lost track of time," said Jenny apologetically, "but I must admit, I'm rather desperate for a drink."

"Come on," said Candy grabbing her arm, "I'll show you the way."

They arrived at the large cafeteria and were grateful for the coolness there. The central cooling was not very effective in Outpatients, due to the regular comings and goings of patients and staff through the outside doors, which let in the outside heat. Settling for a large glass of freshly squeezed lemonade, they began to chat with each other. Jenny found Candy very easy to talk to. She had no false modesty, despite her being such a striking, dark-eyed, raven-haired beauty.

"Are you married to an Arab or a foreigner?" enquired Candy.

"Well both, in a way, his name is Greg Youssef, and he's half English and half Arab. He flies for Kharja Airways," said Jenny.

"Well, well, well," exclaimed Candy, "it's a small world. My ex is also a pilot with Kharja Airways. Perhaps you know him, Captain Farris Sukkar."

"Yes, I have met him before. He's often at many of the functions that Greg and I attend," confirmed Jenny.

Candy's eyes reddened a little before she continued the conversation. "Yes, I can remember myself at some of those functions. They seem interminable don't they? That's one part of the divorce I don't mind," said Candy reflectively.

"Let's change the subject if it's painful for you Candy," suggested Jenny, sensing Candy's slight distress.

"No, no, let's not!" insisted Candy. "I think I should put you in the picture right away, and then you won't feel like you have to walk on eggshells every time we talk about subjects related to divorce and children, etcetera," she said with determination in her voice. "I met Farris when he was doing his pilot training in America. I was gaining work experience by working in the U.S. as an exchange student during the summer vacation. I was seventeen years old and he was twenty-eight. We fell in love right away and Farris proposed to me. There was rather a to-do-ment about it all from the family I was staying with in the U.S., who immediately contacted my parents. Of course, my parents were greatly opposed to my relationship with Farris in the beginning, but I guess they knew me well enough to realize that if they didn't give way, they were likely to have me run off with him. We were married in Canada, as a gesture to my parents, and then he brought me back here where his family made me very welcome and we were married again for the benefit of his parents. Before a year had passed, I was pregnant with my first child, Melissa. Of course the family was thrilled, but they also put pressure on me to have another child more or less straight away. Obligingly, I did, and I had Samira within eighteen months of Melissa. The family still kept pressuring me to have more children. I had not realized at that time how important it was for a wife to produce a male child. Well, to everyone's delight, Nicholas followed within eighteen months of Samira. Then, finally, the pressure on me lessened. But by this time I was constantly exhausted and rundown from looking after the children and our home, and I was always sick with some bug or other. Slowly, the relationship between Farris and me began to disintegrate." Candy took a deep breath at this point to compose herself again. "I was no longer the happy-go-lucky girl that he had married, I was underweight, haggard and ill-tempered. I didn't have any time for Farris, especially in bed, and it didn't take long before he began to look elsewhere for solace. Of course, his family was on his side, and if I'm truthful, there was good reason to be, since I was such an ill-tempered hag most of the time. The divorce was almost inevitable and, unfortunately, I lost custody of the children." Tears welled up in her eyes at this point, but brushing the back of her hand over her eyes, she quickly recovered. "I cannot complain about Farris. He is very good to me, he pays for me to have an apartment and gives me money to live on. More importantly, the children are able to see me this way. I knew that if I went back to Canada I would risk losing them completely. So here I am, twenty-three years old, feeling as if I have lived a lifetime," she concluded with sagacity that belied her years.

"Oh, Candy," Jenny whispered gently, "that is such a sad story. I hope that you don't blame yourself for it all. It seems to me that you were no more than a child yourself when you were married, and to have three children so quickly one after the other must have been a terrible strain." Jenny noticed that her sympathy was having the opposite effect on Candy than she had intended, as Candy's eyes were beginning to fill with tears. Immediately, Jenny changed her approach. "However, I must say, you have recovered well. You look the picture of health and don't show any trace of your ordeal," offered Jenny with a sweeping gesture towards Candy's face and figure.

Candy visibly brightened, agreeing that her health was much better now. "You know, in many ways, it is good to see the children on fewer occasions during the week. It gives me the opportunity to give them lots of treats without having to be the disciplinarian."

Jenny agreed that she could see the benefits attached to that arrangement and asked what she did with her time when the children were away.

"Well," said Candy, "that's one of the problems I have not yet overcome. There are too many hours in a day to fill on my own.

I do paint a bit, but even that is not enough. If you really want to learn Arabic, I will be more than willing to teach you, which will help fill some of my time," offered Candy eagerly.

"Oh, I would be really grateful," responded Jenny enthusiastically, "I'm going to hold you to it."

The days at the hospital soon became an integral part of Jenny's life. Greg did not object to the one dinar salary and, as Jenny predicted, he took great delight in telling people what salary she actually earned. In many ways, it was good for her that she was well-occupied at the hospital as Greg was being given longer and longer flights away from home as his experience grew. She and Candy became firm friends and spent many hours together. It was usual for them to go to Candy's house for their meetings because she didn't want to be out in case her children should phone her or make an unexpected visit. Often Jenny would spend the night at Candy's apartment if Greg was away, and they would chat late into the night. She learned much from Candy about the ways of the Middle East. Candy taught her the subtleties of preparing Arabic cuisine and regaled her with remarkable stories about other star-crossed lovers who had married against the wishes of their parents.

"Do parents really still arrange marriages for their children in this day and age?" asked Jenny incredulously.

"They certainly do," replied Candy. "For instance, Farris' cousin is of marriageable age and the family has drawn up a short list for her to choose from."

"And is she quite happy about that, to let her parents practically decide who she will spend the rest of her life with?"

"You would be surprised, although a lot of the kids get caught up in the 'love' thing when they go to Western universities. They are usually quite happy to let go of their lovers when their parents mention suitable candidates for marriage back at home.

You must remember that, over here, marriage is, in many ways, an alliance of mutual gain. In other words, it is of benefit to both the parties in some way, and usually to the families of the couple too."

"Well, how is it that both you and I married for love and our in-laws were quite happy to accept us?" Jenny queried.

"Well, if you consider that both Greg and Farris are airline pilots who travel frequently to the West, and who work closely with Westerners that hold important executive positions in Kharja Airways, you might concede that it is no bad thing for them to be married to foreign women."

"I do see your point, but I would hate to think that Greg was married to me only for the use I could be to him."

"I'm sure that in your case it is different, Jen, especially because Greg's mom is English too. But don't forget that since he's making his career in this part of the world, he will be subjected to the prevailing influences around him. He will be required to play the game according to the rules over here, or at least the unwritten rules."

"Why do I keep hearing about 'playing the game'?" asked Jenny. "Is there some major league game happening that I haven't heard of?"

"Well, I guess you could say that there is," replied Candy. "It is a devious game that everyone is aiming to win. Over here, people are so ambitious for their children to do well that parents sacrifice and scrimp and save to give their children the best education that they can afford. In return, the children work really hard and try to do their best by achieving good marks, etcetera. Then when droves of graduates come back home from university with their degrees and diplomas, they compete fiercely with others who are seeking jobs in the workplace. Obviously, there are not enough professional and executive positions to go around, so families will use connections and alliances to secure the best positions available. Thus, in many Middle Eastern countries, you will find an inordinate number of professionally qualified individuals without any immediate career prospects. In fact, I know of one PhD graduate who was unable to find work and set up a shoeshine stand downtown and hung his PhD diploma on a hook along with his brushes."

"Oh, how awful," exclaimed Jenny, aware of how hard it is to achieve a doctorate.

"Well, it is not all bad news. A high-flying executive stopped to have his shoes shined at that guy's stand and saw the diploma hanging there. He held a long conversation with the PhD guy and, on the basis that he was obviously intelligent but was not too proud to shine shoes, he decided that the PhD guy was exactly the kind of person he would want working in his company. Now the PhD guy has a great job, and his parents, who sacrificed everything they had for their son, have a lovely home bought by their son and are as proud as punch of him."

"Oh! How wonderful for them!" exclaimed Jenny.

"Yes, that was a great thing for that family, but normally the only way people can climb to the top of the ladder is by making alliances and generally toadying to those in positions of power. Hence, you have the game of social maneuvering."

"So does that apply to Farris and Greg also?" asked Jenny, who really could guess the answer.

"Of course it does, although the airline is a relatively new business here. There are lots of starry-eyed young men who are coming up through the air academy just living to become ace pilots."

"I guess you're right, but doesn't it mean that they compromise their integrity somewhat?" ventured Jenny.

"Well it does, but if they manage to 'keep face' while in the process, then it all becomes acceptable. You know, it's not unlike

Pareto and his 'Elite Theory.' He says the cream will always rise to the top no matter the circumstances. It's just another game of skill, and the most adept wins. It's just the final sorting process between competing individuals."

"Well, I don't like it," said Jenny. "It's not like that in England, and people can keep their integrity and dignity there."

"Oh, is that right?" Candy countered. "How many people get to university in England?"

"Not a huge number," answered Jenny.

"Well then, a different process is at work. Selection goes on at an earlier stage, and perhaps it's children who are told by their teachers that they don't have the ability to make it any further academically. I don't think there is a whole lot of dignity in that. And I don't happen to subscribe to the belief that only certain individuals are suitable for university. I think that any child, given a culturally nurturing environment to grow in, which is free of economic hardship, will be likely to make it to university and be a high achiever."

"Wow, that was a bit of a gob-full," said Jenny, reverting to her childhood colloquialisms. "I hadn't really thought that deeply about it, but I can see what you are saying."

"Since I started doing a correspondence course in sociology, I have begun to think deeply about quite a few issues," said Candy seriously. "Anyway," she said making an about turn, "I think that we are getting far too bogged down with weighty matters. Let's talk about something else. How are you getting on with your boss, Dr. Khalil?"

"He's an absolute dream to work for — kind, considerate and extremely well-mannered. His wife is a lucky woman", said Jenny with conviction.

"Oh, didn't you know? He lost his wife about eighteen months ago when she went to Koudara to visit her family. She got caught up in the uprising and was killed in a bomb blast."

69

"The poor man, was he terribly upset about it?" said Jenny rather shocked. "Yes, at first he was really cut up about it and had to take some time off work. But he came back after about two months with a new air of determination and has been alright ever since."

"He is really a lovely man, and so good looking. I imagine someone will be snapping him up before long."

Jenny looked over at Candy and noticed that her usually composed countenance was beginning to flush around the neck and cheeks. "Candy, does that unwarranted flush of cheek mean that I have hit a sensitive spot? Could it be that you are more than a little enamored of the dashing Dr. Khalil?"

"Well, I must admit to fancying him. He has been so kind to me. He offered me lots of help and advice when he heard of my situation."

"Yes, I have noticed that he finds every excuse he can to go to reception. I had not made the connection until now. I'm usually so busy that I don't notice things going on right under my nose."

"There isn't really anything in particular going on. He is very friendly with me and I am with him, but I don't want to push it. I think it's too soon after his wife's death for him to get involved. So I'm keeping the relationship on a platonic level, and he seems quite happy with that. But stay tuned for updates!" she added mischievously.

"I imagine he is quite a bit older than you. Does he have any children?" asked Jenny. "Yes and yes," replied Candy. "He is about sixteen years older than me, and he has two sons, one eleven and one thirteen. His mother looks after them while he is at work."

"It must be nice to have kids", said Jenny wistfully.

"Well, why don't you get on and have some," said Candy encouragingly. "That's a very sore point at the moment. If Greg knew I was talking about it, he would kill me, but I know that you are very discreet," she said looking over at Candy trustingly. Seeing Candy's nod of assurance, she continued, "Greg and I have been having unprotected sex now for around ten months, and I have not yet conceived. When I tried to bring the subject up with Greg, he became very hostile and refused to discuss the issue further. But I'm beginning to worry that something is wrong with me."

"Hmmm, that is unusual. Most of the time, the men want to produce an offspring as soon as possible to prove their virility and please their parents. Listen, I know what we can do. Mariella's husband is head of Gynecology. Perhaps we could ask her if she could arrange an appointment with him to see if all your plumbing is sound."

"That's a good idea. Let's ask her to have lunch with us tomorrow and discuss it," said Jenny, relieved that she could now address her problem.

"Now, Jenny Youssef, I suggest we get some sleep," admonished Candy, "or we will look like a pair of old hags tomorrow morning. It's already two forty-five a.m."

"Thank you and goodnight," said Jenny.

"For nothing, my pleasure, sleep tight," responded Candy.

The next morning, Candy contacted Mariella and arranged the proposed lunchtime meeting to discuss Jenny's problem. They met at two in the canteen. "Ya, I can see vhy you are vorried about going behind your husband's back about zis. But I also think zat you have za right to know vhat is going on vith your own body, if anything," said Mariella in a righteous manner. "I vill ask Nader, my husband, if he vould be villing to see you confidentially. I am sure he vill because he is indebted to you for all za hard york you have been putting in. The E.R. has really benefitted from your services." After a moment's thought, she added, "Don't worry about the confidentiality of the lab vork.

Nader's brother has a private laboratory, and he can do any tests zere himself."

"Thank you very much, Mariella, I really appreciate you going out of your way like this" said Jenny.

"One good turn deserves another. Think nothing of it. I have got to run now. Zey have got a panic in za laundry room. Zey are short staffed so I have to go and fold sterilized cloths for the za rest of za afternoon."

"Rather you than me," smiled Candy.

"Hmmm," said Mariella, leaving with a wry smile.

"Well that little problem looks like it's going to be solved," said Candy smiling.

"Yes it does, and I can tell you I will be relieved when I know the results. It has been bothering me more than I thought."

As predicted, Dr Nader was happy to help Jenny, although he would have preferred for Greg to be involved. Nader disliked the idea of secrecy; nonetheless, he was prepared to help Jenny because of her value to the hospital. They set up an appointment for late in the evening when all the clinics were closed. Jenny arrived with Candy and found Mariella waiting with Nader in his office. Mariella introduced Jenny. "You know Candy, of course, but zis is Jenny Youssef, angel of E.R."

"Your reputation precedes you, young lady. I am happy to meet you and hopefully be of service to you," acknowledged Nader in good English with slight Germanic overtones.

"I am pleased to meet you, Dr. Nader," replied Jenny.

"Please, just call me Nader. I am sure we are going to be friends, and we can do without all this formality," he said smilingly.

Jenny felt immediately at ease with this man who had a kind, fatherly air about him. She had been worried about how she would feel dealing with such a sensitive subject with him.

"Shall we go inside to the clinic? Mariella and Candy can stay here in the office and have a chat."

"That's fine," said Jenny.

Inside the clinic, Nader performed a routine check on her and asked how long she had been trying for children.

"You know, my dear," said Nader, "sometimes it does take a while before children come along, but as you know yourself, things do look a bit suspicious. I am sorry that your husband is unwilling to come along and have some tests. It would certainly help with the process of elimination."

"You know, I had not really considered that it could be a problem with Greg. He seems so strong and virile I had just assumed that the problem would lie with me, if there is one."

"You are not the first woman to have told me that. Women usually assume they are the ones to blame, never their husbands," he said, shaking his head as if to question why women were always so ready to take the blame for any deficiency. "Well, at least we will be able to ascertain whether or not you have any problems, but as far as I can see at this point, everything looks well. Nevertheless, we will wait for the results of the tests before deciding positively."

CHAPTER FIVE

Candy seeks love again

Jenny spent several nights with Candy before Greg returned from his London stopover. He returned in the early evening and seemed in a particularly good mood. "Hello, darling, how are you? Did you miss me?"

"Of course I did, but at least the time doesn't drag by the way it used to when you were away, now that I have a job to keep me busy."

"Yes, I think that, in retrospect, the hospital work was a good move," Greg conceded.

"Listen, darling," he continued, "I want to tell you some news. You may not be too happy about it right now, but it will be good for us in the long run."

"Well, don't keep me in suspense. What is it?" said Jenny, snuggling up close to him on their rather uncomfortable sofa that was bought by Greg for appearance rather than comfort.

"When I got in this evening, there was a message in my pigeonhole to go and see Hussein in his office. When I got there, he told me the airline is getting a new fleet of wide-bodied jets and that training will begin next month in the States for some of the crew. He told me that he and Nikos had been working out the schedule for the crew, and I have been selected to go on the first course that they are running. Hussein said he expects us all to work really hard on the course and expects no failures. He wants to impress the instructors with the quality of pilots that we have here in the Middle East. In other words, he expects us to pass with ease and to distinguish ourselves," finished Greg with a flourish and a large grin, indicating his eagerness to go and his immense pride to have been selected to be on the first course.

"I am really happy for you, Greg. You have done well to be selected for the big jets so soon after your command training. They must think very highly of you to send you on the first course. Who else will be on that course?"

"Well, of course, Hussein will be going, Geoff Lambert will be going and few more of the more senior crew that you have met, and there will be some of the more experienced first officers and flight engineers."

"I don't expect they will want any wives there will they?" asked Jenny hopefully.

"Darling, they did not, exactly, say no wives, but they are saying that it would be a good idea for crew to double-up in the quarters provided, either two or three to a villa, depending on the size of it. So I think it would be better for us if you stayed here while I go and study. I hope you don't mind," said Greg gently, not wishing to hurt Jenny by telling her that the company was actively discouraging wives from going with their husbands on the course.

However, Jenny was not prepared to give up so quickly. "Are any of the other wives going?"

"As far as I have been told, there will only be Sherrifa and perhaps Clare Lambert and, I think, maybe one more that I can't remember. But they are obliged to go for the sake of diplomacy. There will be dinners and so on that will be put on by Lockheed for the airline, and some wives have to be present for that. You do understand, darling, don't you?"

"I suppose I do," said Jenny, thinking of Candy's comments about playing the "game." "But I don't have to like it. When exactly are you going?"

"The first group of us will leave just after Christmas on the 27th of December, and we will be away for about six weeks."

"Well, at least you will be around for Christmas. Do you think you'll be off, or are you flying?"

"I had a quick look at next month's roster and, as far as I can see, I am coming in from a flight on Christmas Eve and then I'm off until we go on the course."

"Oh, that sounds good. We will have to do something special then," she said, her spirits visibly lifting.

"Whatever you want, my love, you shall have!" exclaimed Greg, happy to have sorted out the issue so easily. Some wives often protested about the long separations and almost demanded to go along with their husbands. He loved that Jenny was so compliant; she never kicked up a fuss about such things. "There is something else as well, sweetheart," he continued.

"Not more absences, I hope," said Jenny suspiciously.

"No, it's something that you are going to like."

"Come on, come on, tell me immediately or I'll scream!"

"Well," he said slowly to prolong the agony, "since I am going on the big jets, there is going to be a nice rise in salary, and we will be able to afford to move to a snazzier apartment, and you, Jenny, are going to pick it out while I'm away. I want us to have new furniture, the works, and I entrust it all to you."

"Oh, that's nice," said Jenny, brightening somewhat. "I will enjoy that. I can do it in the evenings when I finish from the hospital," she volunteered, feeling a little ashamed of herself because she did not really think that looking for a new apartment really made up for Greg being away for such a long time.

76

"You don't seem all that happy about it," said Greg disappointedly.

"I'm sorry, I'm just an ungrateful little so-and-so, but I would just rather be with you than picking out furniture."

"I know, sweetheart, but it is all for the best, you know. It is only a little sacrifice, and then things will get back to normal," he reassured her.

"I suppose so, but I'm really going to miss you. Six weeks is a long time."

"Yes, but think of all the fun we will have making up for lost time. In fact, let's start right away," said Greg, teasingly pulling her into the bedroom.

Greg was in such a good mood that it lifted Jenny right out of her slight depression. She decided not to worry about his lengthy absence until the time actually came. *After all,* she reasoned, *there were still a few weeks before he was to go, and she could leave her fretting until then.* Lying in Greg's arms, she felt relaxed and warm. Their lovemaking left them both feeling lazy. Neither of them had had dinner, but they felt too comfortable to move. The phone rang shrilly, next to the bed, bringing them sharply out of their soporific state. "Oh hell," said Greg, "who can that be? Doesn't the world know that we want to be alone."

"You get it," said Jenny. "The phone's on your side, and I'm not moving."

"Bitch," said Greg playfully. Picking up the phone, he heard Sherrifa's dulcet tones greet him in Arabic. "Congratulations, Greg, I heard that you have been selected to go on the big jets. You must be very pleased about that."

Greg snapped to attention, his former mood instantly evaporating. "Yes, I certainly am. I'm really honoured to have been picked, especially as I have not had my command for very long," he said with conviction.

"Well, they would not have picked you if you weren't up to the job. Now is your lovely wife there? I would like to talk to her."

"She's right here, Sherrifa, I will get her for you." Jenny was gesticulating that she did not want to talk to her, but Greg just ignored her and thrust the telephone in her hand. "Talk," he whispered forcefully to her.

Looking at Greg's face, Jenny knew she had better change her tune and be charming to Sherrifa.

"Hello, Sherrifa, how nice to hear your voice," she told her with as much sincerity as she could muster.

"Allo, Jenny, 'ow are you, chère? Eet ees so long since I have seen you. But I hear zat you are working at za 'ospital. You are really so sweet to do zat," she crooned. "I am 'aving a coffee morning for za wives next week and want you to come. Zat will be okay, ne cest pas?"

"Thank you very much, Sherrifa, I suppose the hospital won't mind if I take a morning off," said Jenny less than enthusiastically. Greg nudged her hard in the ribs, indicating she was saying the wrong thing. Thinking quickly, Jenny continued, "But there is nothing that could stop me from coming to one of your invitations. I would be delighted to come," Jenny enthused rather belatedly.

"Bon, I will see you at eleven then," concluded Sherrifa, who was aware of Jenny's slight reluctance in accepting her invitation but quite prepared to tolerate it as she needed Jenny's goodwill at present. *But not for long*, Sherrifa thought wickedly, as she replaced the handset in its ornate cradle whilst allowing herself to slip into a pleasant fantasy of how Greg would succumb to her charms when the time was just right.

Greg had the following two days off before flying to India for a four-day stopover. They took advantage of the cooler weather and went for some long walks by the seashore and played tennis at the sports club. Time seemed to pass in an instant in those two days and, all too soon, Jenny was back at the hospital in her familiar routine. It was a humid, cloudy day, and the heat in the cafeteria where she was lunching with Candy was becoming quite oppressive.

"Greg just told me he is going to be away for six weeks just after Christmas," said Jenny, fanning herself with a paper napkin. "He's going on a course to learn how to fly the new jets that the airline is getting."

"What a coincidence," said Candy, "Farris is going too. He told me just yesterday. He is really pleased about it."

"Yes, it is quite sickening. These men really get a buzz from it, but I'm not looking forward to six weeks on my own," protested Jenny.

"You know, you're not on your, Jen. You can stay with me whenever you want and for as long as you want to."

"Thank you, Candy, I will take you up on the offer. Greg has told me to look for a new apartment and to get it all furnished before he gets back. Would you like to help me to do that?" enquired Jenny.

"You bet I would. We can have some fun picking stuff out. It will help us pass the time," said Candy enthusiastically.

"You are such a good friend. I'm lucky to have you."

"Oh, think something of it," said Candy jokingly.

"I had better get back to E.R.," said Jenny. "Can I stay with you tonight? I can never bear to sleep alone the day that Greg leaves. The place always seems so empty."

"I know exactly what you mean," agreed Candy. "Of course you can stay. Perhaps we can go and see a movie tonight. I heard that there's a good one on at the Alhambra."

"Sounds good to me. See you later," said Jenny with a cheery wave.

Returning to E.R., Jenny was surprised to see there were no patients waiting. Dr. Khalil smiled at her and asked if she felt like having a coffee as it was unusually slow at the moment. "Well, actually, I have just had lunch, but I'm quite happy to go to the cafeteria for another quick one," she said with a smile, happy to spend a little time with the doctor.

"Why don't we have it in my office. I will ask someone to bring it for us. It will be cooler there. More importantly, there is something I would like to ask you about, and I would prefer to do it in private."

"That's fine," replied Jenny, wondering what it was he wanted to discuss with her.

"Come," he said, motioning towards the door of his office.

Once inside, he phoned the cafeteria to send two coffees down for them. Initially, they began to talk about hospital trivia. When the coffee arrived and the office door was closed, he began talking more seriously to her.

"Jenny, I want to ask you something of a rather delicate nature, and I'm sure I can rely on you to be discreet."

"Of course you can, Dr. Khalil. How can I help?"

"Well first of all, please call me Khalil when we're not on duty."

"Okay then, of course you can, Khalil, go right ahead," said Jenny, lightening the mood a little.

Smiling at her, Khalil began, "This is quite hard for me, but I want to ask you something about your friend Candy."

"Somehow that does not really surprise me," said Jenny with a smile. "I have noticed how many times you find reasons to go through to reception and make time to chat with her."

"Oh, I hope I'm not that obvious," he said losing his composure a little.

"Well not to everyone, but I think Candy might have noticed."

"That's what I want to discuss with you. Tell me frankly, do you think I stand any chance of getting to know her on a more person level?"

80

"Frankly, Khalil, I think you stand a very good chance of furthering your relationship on a personal level with her. However, I do think what you need to be sensitive about is the timing of moving forward," she said. "Candy is very concerned about starting a relationship with you so soon after the death of your wife. I believe that's why she's been keeping the relationship on a platonic level. She believes that you are happy with a platonic relationship too."

"Well at least that gives me some hope. I was beginning to think that Candy was trying to politely put me off her. She shouldn't be concerned about my departed wife. I have come to terms with that. No one can take her place, I will never love anyone the way I loved her, but I can move on. She was a very sensitive and loving woman of great intelligence, but I do not believe that she would have wanted my life to end with hers," said Khalil with conviction.

"I can't imagine that she would want that either," said Jenny sympathetically. "Would you like me to tell Candy about our discussion? Or shall I keep quiet about it?"

"I really don't mind if you tell her. It is quite normal in this part of the world for a third party to be called in to mediate in affairs of the heart," he said with lifted spirits.

"Actually, I'm going to stay with Candy tonight so I'll have the perfect opportunity to talk to her. I think that's what I will do," Jenny responded, gauging that is what Khalil really wanted her to do.

"I am really grateful to you, Jenny. Thank you so much for your help."

"Think nothing of it; I'm happy to be of help. Candy is a good, supportive friend to me, and I'm just glad to be able to do something that might bring a little more happiness into her life. She has been through a lot for her young age."

"Yes," responded Khalil, "that's one of the things that I admire about her. She has come through her hardships with courage and dignity."

Their conversation was interrupted by an urgent-sounding buzz on Khalil's pager. It was his nurse telling him of some casualties who were being admitted to the E.R. "Come on, Jenny, we had better get down to Emergency. There are some casualties from a road traffic accident coming in, and they sound pretty bad."

"I'm right behind you," said Jenny, snapping immediately into her professional mode. Khalil and Jenny were busy for most of the afternoon after their initial slow start, and she was more than ready to go off duty and meet Candy at the end of the day.

"Hi, Jenny," greeted Candy, "you look like you have been rather busy. I saw the road traffic accident come in. It looked pretty traumatic. Are they all right?"

"It was pretty bad, but there were no fatalities. I just wish people would follow some kind of highway code here. They seem to think that they are invulnerable when they get behind the wheel of a car. It's not until something like this happens that they begin to realize that they are as susceptible as anyone else."

"You're right," agreed Candy, "I wish they would stress road safety more on the television like they do in the West. If they would televise today's victims coming in, perhaps that would make them stop and think a little more. Anyway, I think you need to put work behind you. Let's see what time the movie starts and see if we have time to go and grab a bite first."

Taking a service taxi into town, they arrived outside the Alhambra Cinema to find that the next showing of the film would be in an hour and a half. "We have time to have a leisurely meal," said Jenny gratefully.

"Yes we do, and I'm ready for a break too. Where do you fancy going?" asked Candy.

"Well, what about going to Popeye's Pizza. They do the best pizzas in town and a good salad too," volunteered Jenny.

"That's fine with me. I'm a lifelong slave to pizza, anytime, anywhere," smiled Candy, leading the way into the popular restaurant.

Over dessert, Jenny decided to bring the conversation around to Khalil. "Dr. Khalil thought we were going to have a quiet afternoon today, so he asked me to have a chat with him in his office," said Jenny, unable to resist the temptation of provoking a little jealousy in Candy.

Candy looked up from her ice cream, trying hard to conceal her interest. "Oh yes, what did he have to say to you?"

"Quite a lot actually, and it was all concerning you," said Jenny with a smile. Turning her full attention to Jenny, Candy eagerly demanded to know what was said. "To put you immediately out of your misery, he wants to know if you are prepared to get serious with him."

"Really?" said Candy, looking visible shocked.

"He felt he needed to ask me to intervene since you had not been holding out any hope for him. He thought you were trying to reject him politely. However, I told him about the reservations you had about his deceased wife, and he wants you to know that he has come to terms with it and wants to move on with his life, preferably with you as a major part of it."

"Wow," said Candy unable to vocalize her emotions.

"If I didn't know you better, I'd think that you were indifferent to what I've just told you. 'Really' and 'wow' are not responses that I'd feel happy reporting back to Khalil with," said Jenny with an amused look on her face.

"Oh, sorry, sorry," said Candy, recovering her composure. "Look, don't report back with anything. I'll take over from here. You know how I feel about him, and I think it's time for me to let him know."

"Well, that's good news. I suppose it's only fitting that we go and drool over Zeffirelli's rehash of 'Romeo and Juliette' now. Come on, we have only five minutes to make it to the high street."

After spending a pleasant evening at the movies and talking late into the night with Candy, Jenny decided that even though Greg would not get home for another three days, it would be prudent for her to move back to her home in light of the recent developments with Candy and Khalil. Indeed, when she told Candy of her decision, she was met with no opposition. Jenny smiled a secret little smile, pleased with her part in bringing Candy and Khalil together.

Candy was prepared for Khalil when she saw him the next day at work. "Marhaba Khalil, how are you?" she greeted him in Arabic.

"I'm well," he responded. "It's so nice to hear Arabic spoken with that soft Canadian accent. I could listen to it all day."

"Since neither of us have all day, let me get right to the point," said Candy smiling, and for the first time, looking Khalil directly in the eyes. "Jenny told me about the conversation you had with her yesterday, and I want you to know that I am interested in becoming more personally involved with you. However, I have to tell you that it is not going to be easy for you to see me. As long as Farris is still supporting me and has custody of the children, I'm in a very vulnerable position."

Khalil looked at her with tenderness and told her, "I am aware of that and I will try my best to ensure that our relationship will not jeopardize you in any way. We'll find a way to meet and get to know each other better without the whole town gossiping about us."

"I don't know how that will be possible but I am willing to give it a go," Candy said with a smile lighting up her face.

"Well, we have one lucky coincidence. My cousin owns the building where you have your apartment and, at present, there is an empty apartment on the same floor as yours. I'll tell my cousin that I need to rent the apartment because I'm often late from the hospital and usually fatigued by traveling back home to the suburbs every night, which is, in fact, true. Then, my love, I can come and visit you whenever you are alone and feel like having some company. Is that too presumptuous of me, or shall I think of something else?" Candy thought hard for some time before answering, making Khalil worry that he had been too ambitious in his planning.

"No," she replied with a smile, "I might have thought it too presumptuous under other circumstances, but truly, I don't know how we can further our relationship any other way."

Khalil's handsome face lit up into a bright smile at Candy's response.

"I'll phone my cousin from my office right now. See you later, habibti." Candy smiled at the term of endearment that he had ventured to use with her. She replayed it in her head, *habibti means my love*. It seemed a long time since she had been anyone's love. She had imagined being in Khalil's arms many times. Now she could feel the sensuous feeling of anticipation rise up inside her. But this time, she determined, she was going to keep her head together and use her brain as well as her heart in this relationship.

Candy and Jenny went to their respective homes that evening. Jenny went to the emptiness of her apartment, where she made a simple meal for herself and curled up with a good fantasy book to lose herself in and escape the loneliness of being apart from Greg.

Candy returned to the sound of the phone ringing in her apartment. "Hello," she answered breathlessly and smiled as she heard Khalil's gentle voice welcoming her home.

"Darling, open your front door," he gently asked her. As she did so, the door of the vacant apartment opposite hers opened and Khalil stood grinning at her.

"How did you get in so soon?" enquired Candy.

"I phoned my cousin this morning, as I told you I would, and he was more than happy for me to rent the apartment. He also told me he had some furniture stored and he would furnish it for me if I liked. I told him that I was doing a night shift tonight, which I am, and would like to rest here before I go on duty. He got the place cleaned and furnished and even had my bed made for me. So here I am!" he answered, pleased with what had been achieved.

"Wow, what a cousin," said Candy in admiration.

"Well, let's say he owes me a few favours from our youth, when he was a terrible womanizer. I will tell you about it sometime. Are you going to be free tonight?"

"As a matter of fact, I know Farris is flying, and the children all have classes this evening so it's highly unlikely that anyone will be coming. However, it might be better to wait till nine o'clock before you come over because no one ever visits me after that time."

"That will be fine. I go on duty at midnight, so I'll grab a couple of hours rest now and come over at nine."

"Okay, I'll see you then."

Candy could hardly wait for nine o'clock to come. She busied herself tidying up the apartment and making some cookies before soaking herself in a heavily perfumed bath. At eight forty-five, she looked at herself in the mirror and was pleased with what she saw. Her long, dark hair fell softly round her shoulders, gleaming under the light. Her dark eyes shone with anticipation and her dusky skin glowed. At five minutes to nine, there was a soft tapping on the door. She ran to the door, forgetting her shoes in her excitement, and quietly opened it for Khalil.

"I couldn't wait any longer to be alone with you," whispered Khalil.

Candy felt the emotion rise in her at his words but struggled for composure. "Welcome, come in and sit down," she invited him. He sat down on the sofa, obviously expecting Candy to join him, but she needed some time to regain her composure.

"I was just fixing myself a drink. What can I get you?"

"Just a soft drink, please, juice or anything will do."

Candy reappeared with two freshly squeezed orange juices and a plate of freshly baked cookies.

"Here, have a cookie," invited Candy, sitting down next to him on the sofa.

"They look good. Did you make them? I could smell a lovely aroma of baking when I awoke. I imagine it must have been these delicacies that I could smell," he said, pleased that she had troubled herself to bake for him.

"Yes, I did make them. No one came to visit today, so I had a little time to spare. I thought you might enjoy them," said Candy hospitably. "Mmm, they taste as good as they smell," complimented Khalil.

They finished their juice in relative silence which broke the slightly formal air that Candy had being trying to preserve. The silence was more telling than words; it was electric.

"Candy, I can't be formal with you. The sight of you, the sound of you, the smell of you drives me wild," he said looking into her eyes.

Candy fought for control, knowing only too well what he meant. She felt the same way about him.

"Khalil," she said gently, "I feel the same way, but I'm afraid of the intensity of my feelings. Can we take it a little slower, please?"

He looked into her eyes again and whispered, "No," very gently as he pulled her towards him. Candy was lost to her emotions and felt powerless to pull away. She felt his strong arms around her and his mouth gently kiss her lips over and over, until their lips locked together in a fire of passion. They pulled the clothing off each other without restraint, kissing each other all the while. Khalil's hands explored Candy's slender figure as she let her hands run over his hard, muscled body. Their lovemaking was fevered. With each penetration, they both groaned with ecstasy, unsure of how long they could withstand the intensity of passion before climaxing.

Khalil whispered breathlessly to her, "Tell me when you are ready, my love. I can't hold myself much longer." The sound of his voice was enough to trigger her orgasm. "Now, now," she whispered, her words catching with emotion. They climaxed together, their bodies united in the fulfillment of their lovemaking.

"Candy, you are so beautiful. I could stay inside you forever. I can't believe the way I feel about you," he whispered passionately to her.

"Oh, Khalil, I have never felt this way. Just hold me close," she whispered. They lay together for more than an hour, just holding each other, their eyes locking, delving to the depths of the other's soul, feeling elated, as if discovering a treasure locked deep within each other.

Overcome with the intensity of their emotions, Candy was the first one to break their mood.

"Khalil, darling, it's eleven. I don't want you to go, but you are on duty at twelve," she said softly.

"I don't want to leave you. I only hope that I will be busy, then I won't have time to miss you," he said wistfully.

"If I wasn't on duty in the morning, I would come with you," volunteered Candy.

"I wish you could, but you need your sleep, but I'll tell you what," he said enthusiastically, "tomorrow morning, I will hang around for an hour or two after I go off duty and then we can have a coffee together before I come back to sleep."

"That will be nice, but we had better be careful what we say and how we look at each other or else tongues will start wagging, and we might find ourselves the latest topic on the hospital grapevine."

"Don't worry, angel, I would never do anything that would prejudice your position," he said seriously.

Khalil took a cool shower at Candy's apartment and hurried across the corridor to his new apartment to find a clean shirt. Candy kissed him goodbye and took a long warm shower before climbing back in bed. She found it hard to sleep at first but finally the physical exhaustion of their lovemaking took its toll and she fell into a deep, contented sleep. The next day, she could hardly wait to see Khalil again. She was at the hospital earlier than her shift required, hoping to sneak a little time with him. However, she was disappointed for he did not appear until the specified hour in the cafeteria. He carried his tray over and asked if he could join her. There was no hint in his demeanor of what had transpired the night before. Candy was a little confused but hoped that he was only playing his role for the sake of propriety. Candy was in torment for the rest of the day, wondering whether she had acted inappropriately with Khalil. Perhaps she had been too easy. She thought, *he probably thinks that I am a slut. Oh God, I must stop thinking this way as I'm not concentrating properly on my work.*

Lunch with Jenny did not help either. Candy could not bring herself to tell her of the previous evening's events because of the lecture she might get from Jenny for rushing things and because she did not want to share the intimacy she and Khalil had experienced.

She struggled to keep her emotions under control, knowing that she was vulnerable, as Khalil was the first man she had slept with since she had left Farris. *Anyway,* she resolved, trying to justify her actions, *if he did think of her in that way, she was surely entitled to the odd slip in moral conduct now and again. And if that was what it came down to, she could always put the whole incident behind her.*

The rest of the day went by easier after making her crude plan of action. However, on returning to her apartment building that evening, she felt a wave of nausea sweep through her as she saw a beautiful woman kiss Khalil gently on the cheek before leaving his apartment. Khalil acknowledged Candy by giving her a cursory nod and closed the door behind him. Candy rushed inside and pushed the door closed behind her. Standing with her back to the door, tears welled up in her eyes and she fought the nausea rising up within her. *Oh God, I am a fool, what have I done? Why did I think a man like Khalil would want someone like me? Of course he will have many women only too happy to throw themselves at him?* As she chastised herself, the phone rang shrilly in her lounge, forcing her back to normalcy.

"Hello, angel," said Khalil, "I have been waiting for you to come home. I have missed you so much."

Relief flooded through Candy at his words. "I have missed you too. You were so formal with me in the cafeteria, I was beginning to think that I had imagined last night," she replied.

"It was hard for me to be so distant looking at your lovely face and remembering what we shared last night, but I don't want to give anyone reason to gossip about you. Just remember our time begins here, where we can be alone. Will you be alone tonight?" he asked her, hoping he could be with her soon. He longed to be near her again.

"Yes, I will be after eight thirty. The children are stopping by to see me, and they always have their evening meal with me.

Come over at nine again, and then I'm sure to be free. Are you on duty again tonight?"

"I was but I have got someone to cover for me. There is no way that I am leaving you again tonight. You won't mind if I stay all night with you?"

"No, of course not, it felt very lonely for a while after you left last night."

"I will see you later then, my love," he whispered and slowly closed the phone.

Candy was happy to see her children and make them their evening meal. They spent a wild and happy time together, doing some artwork with her before their meal. "You look happy, Mummy," said Samira, "Your eyes are all shiny, and you have got red cheeks. Are you in love?" she asked innocently. "At school, they say you are in love when you have red cheeks."

"Do they really?" replied Candy. "Well, they are right: I am in love, with all of my beautiful children." Samira smiled, pleased with her mother's reply and glad to see that she was looking happier.

Candy looked at her children. They were indeed beautiful, and she missed seeing them every day. The first months had been the worst. It used to cut like a knife to be apart from them. As time went by, she learned how to insulate herself from the pain. She let reason take over, knowing they were very well cared for and they were in a totally supportive environment, which was far better than where they were before. When she and Farris had been together, it had become a living nightmare with fights and recriminations flying everywhere. Most of the time she was in tears, and the children thought that they were the cause of it. At least now, with the present arrangement, the children saw her as a whole and happy individual, with time to devote to them. They did not perceive themselves as the cause of great unhappiness between their mother and father.

"Children, it's nearly eight twenty and I think I had better clean you up before your uncle comes to collect you," said Candy, sad that they had to leave, but cheered by the thought of Khalil's visit a little later.

After seeing the children off, she cleared up the apartment and took a shower and dimmed the lights to give a soft romantic atmosphere to the lounge. Khalil arrived with a bottle of wine tucked under his arm. Putting it on the coffee table, he walked over to her.

"Come here," he said, pulling her into his arms, "I have missed you, and I need to have you near me again." Only too willing to oblige, she let his strong arms surround her, happily surrendering to her passionate emotions.

As they slowly released each other, Khalil said, "I thought we might have some wine tonight as I'm not on duty. Do you like Vouvray?"

"Yes, I do, I'm not really keen on red wines and Vouvray is nice and light."

"Are you hungry?" she asked him.

"Only for you, my love, I had a fairly good meal at around four o'clock and I'm not really very hungry." Khalil looked at Candy's profile silhouetted in the dimmed lighting and felt his heart give a tug. She was so sensuously beautiful. He loved the way she looked, how the light accentuated the curve of her rounded cheek and spun off into the contours of her face. He wanted to possess all that was her. He admired her so much that, on occasion, were it possible, he would gladly become her. He knew his inclination for passion, but what he felt for Candy exceeded that. She was a dimension that was, as yet, unexplored. He took her gently submitting body into his arms and covered her sweet face with eagerly anticipated kisses, both of them unable and unwilling to stem the surge of passion that engulfed them.

Their lovemaking was no less restrained this evening. Their very proximity to one another seemed to spark off a sexual desire that needed immediate gratification. The Vouvray was barely sipped, all else seemed trivial, "Your body is more intoxicating than wine," Khalil whispered to her as he kissed her burning thighs.

"Oh, please, join with me, I am so ready for you," she gasped, her body already undulating in anticipation.

They groaned with sheer ecstasy as he penetrated her. They moved together, feeling the heat and passion mount in one another until they fell limp, spent from the exhaustion of orgasm. After their passion subsided, they were both aware of their now ferocious hunger.

"Shall I make us a quick omelet?" enquired Candy.

"That would be lovely. There is something infinitely sexy about eggs. They seem to capture the essence of lovemaking," he replied.

"Mmm, I know what you mean. Do you like them spicy?"

"I wouldn't eat them any other way. I will bring the wine into the bedroom, and we can have a feast in here."

They consumed the omelet and wine, finishing off with the remainder of Candy's home-baked cookies. "I think that, in my whole life, I have never enjoyed a meal more," said Khalil appreciatively.

"Me too", agreed Candy.

Grabbing her, he playfully bit her earlobe and exclaimed, "Candy, Candy, you are so well named. You are quite edible. Is it your full name or is it short for something?"

"It's actually short for Cassandra. Back in Canada, everyone used to call me Cassie. But, after meeting Farris, I had to change it. When he tried to pronounce my name with his slight Arabic accent, it came out as *Gassie!* — which was not very flattering. What's more, when I came to live here, I found that even if folks did pronounce the 'C' in Cassie properly, my name sounded like a very rude Arabic word. Consequently, I am Candy," she told him with a straight face.

Khalil roared with laughter, knowing exactly what she meant, "You will always be Candy to me, nothing else sums you up so well," he complimented her.

Changing the subject abruptly, Candy asked Khalil forthrightly, "Who was that beautiful woman who you kissed when she left your apartment today?" She scrutinized his face, unable to keep her curiosity and jealousy under control anymore.

"Oh, that was Shakira, my cousin's wife. She and her mother had been doing a mammoth cooking session, and she was kind enough to bring me some of it to put in my freezer. I think they worry that I will starve if I don't go to my mother's every evening for a proper meal. You weren't jealous, were you?" he enquired, not entirely displeased that he had evoked the emotion in her. He wanted her to want him, the same way that he wanted her, passionately and completely.

"Well it did throw me a bit after your distant demeanor in the cafeteria. I thought I might have made an enormous mistake for a minute," she confessed.

He took Candy by the shoulders and, making her look him straight in the face, he told her, "Candy, promise never to think ill of me. I would never do anything to hurt you. Always come and ask me frankly about anything you need to know, and then there will be no room for suspicion to grow between us. If there is anything that you want to know now, please just ask me," he said with conviction.

"Well, if you can bear to talk about it, I would like to know about your wife," answered Candy.

"I can bear to talk about it now, although it was very difficult at first. Shadia was a lovely woman; she was a good mother to our children and a very loving wife. We knew each other from childhood. We both went to the same school in Koudara and virtually grew up together. Our families were close friends and hoped that we would want to marry without any prompting from them. We were, first of all, good friends who enjoyed each other's company. But when I went to England to study medicine, we really missed each other. On top of that, my family moved here to Kharja, and it became difficult to visit her. After I completed my internship in the hospital here, I was in a position to marry her, and both our families were delighted. After that, the children were born and only added to our happiness. I don't really know what more I can tell you, except her death was pointless, a pitiful waste of a beautiful individual. This war in Koudara has taken so many innocent lives on both sides. It's time they sat down together on the negotiating table and ended it. After all, not that long ago, all the people of different beliefs lived in peace together in that country. It was only the intervention of foreign governments that caused the division between them and has since unfairly intervened causing the war to continue for so long. Shadia is gone now, and I miss the comfortable life we used to share. She and the children were my world, but now all that is gone," he concluded sadly.

"Yes, I can understand your loss. It must have rocked your whole world," said Candy, remembering how she had felt when her world fell apart after the children were taken from her.

"Is there anything else you want to know?" asked Khalil.

"Yes, there is. When you talk of Shadia, I can tell how much she meant to you, but you never once said how much you loved her."

"I did love Shadia, but not in the way that I think you would be able to understand. She was my anchor, my stability, my family. When I was with her, I knew who I was. She represented my past, and until the bomb blast, my future. When she left my life, I lost all direction. I relied on her for so much. I was confused and scared, not knowing what to do. In the end, I could not function properly, and I knew I had to do something about my state of mind." He paused and squinted his eyes as if trying to recall something from a long time ago. "I remembered when I was at University in England, one of the professors used to tell us how, when he got bogged down with life, he would rent a cottage on the moors and spend the time there in isolation, trying to calm his mind down. He had no contact with anyone, not even a phone. I figured I needed something like that, so I got in touch with him and told him what had happened. He arranged for me to rent that same cottage, and I spent two months there trying to put my life together. The only contact I had with people was when I drove to the village to buy food and check my mail at the post office. I went through hell, but eventually I emerged sane at the other end of it. I came to accept what had happened to Shadia and rediscovered my calling as a doctor. I knew my sons needed a strong father figure to help them over the loss of their mother, and I was ready to face the world again."

"That is incredible. It must have taken a lot of courage to do that. I can't imagine what it must have been like."

"I don't know about courage, Candy. I think it is more courageous of those who pick up the pieces and carry on with life. All I really did was to run away."

"You underestimate yourself, Khalil. You may have run away from the physical world, but you faced your emotional turmoil head on, and you did it alone. There is nothing that will convince me that what you did was not courageous," she said while caressing his shoulder.

"Candy, can I ask about you Farris?"

"Of course you can, ask whatever you want."

"Well, can you just give me an outline of what went wrong? I know from other conversations we have had that you used to love him."

Candy told him of the troubles that she had gone through from having too many births, too soon and too young, and being too immature to recognize or address her problems.

"Couldn't Farris see what a strain you were under? Surely, he could have been more understanding," said Khalil.

"Well, perhaps he could have, and maybe it's difficult for you to understand, but pilots are not around that much, and when they do come home, they usually want the full homecoming reception. It got harder and harder for me to make time for him, or talk frankly to him, even when he had been away for a week or so. Usually, he was not home long enough to get into any meaningful discussions, and often when the time was right, he would be about to leave again. Every pilot's wife knows you can't send your husband out to fly burdened with domestic matters, so I was left to shoulder the burden all the time. In the end, I couldn't cope and Farris and I had lost the means to communicate without hurling abuse at each other. The love I had for him died a slow and painful death, as I came to hear of each knew mistress he took."

"Farris has lost a treasure, I wonder that he doesn't try to get you back," observed Khalil.

"I do think he regrets a lot of what happened between us and he has remained good friends. Occasionally, he hints at reconciliation, but I know that I could never return to what I left and that's what I tell him."

"Are you sure that you don't still love him?" asked Khalil possessively.

"There will be a part of me that will always love the romantic, young pilot who swept me off my feet when I was seventeen, but as far as my life now is concerned, I no longer love him," she said firmly.

"I am pleased to hear that. I don't want anything to come between you and I."

"Come between *us*," joked Candy, "just look at us. We are welded together so tightly in this single bed that even a pin couldn't come between us."

They both laughed, breaking the seriousness of their prior mood.

CHAPTER SIX

The hijack, Monique's fateful trip

The villa that housed Nikos and Monique commanded a remarkably good ocean view, being set on a slightly elevated piece of land close to the shoreline. The exterior exuded elegance and order, extending from the large well-tended garden to the imposing entre. The inside continued with the same salubriousness as the outside, however, it possessed a museum-like quality about it and a cold, pervasive air that often permeates stately houses and castles belonging to people who do not really live in them but merely pass through. The one exception in the villa was the small den containing a comfy, rather than stylish, suite and a complex electrical entertainment setup belonging to Roger, their twelve-year-old son. Together, Monique and Roger spent most of their spare time in this pleasant room. It was a room that had a happy, lived-in feel to it.

It was there that Monique was taking a morning cup of coffee and reviewing her imminent trip to the Gulf the following day. The French Cultural Centre had been fortunate enough to obtain the talents of some world-class opera singers and an Eastern European Ballet Troupe, and was staging a week of entertainment devoted to the performing arts. Monique had been sent a free, official invitation to the event because of the tireless work that she put in for the centre and was truly looking forward to the event. She had arranged for Roger to stay with a school friend for the week and had asked Nikos to get her the tickets for the flight. Nikos arrived that morning tired after a night flight that had been fraught with delays.

"Bonjour," she said politely in her native tongue, not wanting to incur his wrath before her trip tomorrow, "how was your flight?"

"Fatiguing," he replied in perfect French, "there were delays all along the route."

Did you manage to pick up my tickets for the flight tomorrow?" she enquired.

"Yes, they are in my flight bag. Going for week of whoring?" he asked rudely, unable to maintain a pleasant conversation with her.

"Please don't judge everyone by your own disgusting standards. Some of us have a higher moral imperative than merely servicing the base desires of the physical body. Along with others like me, I shall enjoy a week of soul-fulfilling music and dance."

As usual, he regretted making the snide remark. Monique rarely became ruffled, and her eloquence always left him feeling cheap. "I'm going to bed now. Any chance of a nice wifely screw to put me to sleep?" he said scathingly, unable to resist one last dig. Monique did not grace him with a reply, but simply resumed studying her itinerary and sipping her coffee.

Luckily, the next morning she experienced no problems with her flight arrangements. Often the flights were overbooked and concession tickets had to be off-loaded. However, today all was well, and she was welcomed to first class by the cabin staff. The French consul was already seated on board, and he greeted her enthusiastically, obviously looking forward to the event as much as she was. They spent most of the time on the flight discussing the week ahead, delighting in what they imagined would be the high points of the trip.

The flight was perfect and so was the week that followed. Monique enjoyed the freedom and distance from Nikos. She was able to be herself and not on her guard the whole time. She missed Roger, but had talked to him a couple of times in the early evening on the phone. He had assured her that he was having great fun with his friend and just hoped that she was having the same amount of fun. The week ended all too soon for Monique. As the day of her departure arrived, she hoped that the flight she was taking in the very early morning would be as hassle-free as the flight in. Happily all went well, and she got on the flight without any problems. She was again seated in first class. This time, she was directly adjacent to the galley and close to the cockpit. The cabin staff were polite and attentive to her. Most of them knew that Nikos was a womanizer with few scruples and felt sympathy for her. They respected the fact that she bore the indignity of Nikos' philandering with great dignity and always outwardly supported him.

As she settled herself in her seat, the cockpit door opened and Hussein strode out, purposefully, looking for the bursar. Sticking his head through into first class, he was surprised to see Monique sitting there. "Monique," he greeted her in English, "welcome on board, why didn't that husband of yours tell me you would be on the flight? I would have helped you through airport control."

"Oh, I suppose he was very busy with airline business," she replied in good English that was attractively enhanced by her French accent.

"Well, he should not have been too busy to forget about his wife's arrangements," he said sincerely, knowing that Nikos cared little for her welfare. "Look, I'm busy with the usual pre-flight stuff at the moment, but I would love for you to come to the cockpit after takeoff, and then we can have a good chat while the first officer takes over from me for a while," he invited.

"That would be very nice. I will see you in about forty minutes, yes?"asked Monique, her eyebrows rising questioningly.

"That will be perfect. I'll see you then," confirmed Hussein.

Monique sipped a welcome glass of orange juice before takeoff and occupied herself with a magazine until it was time to go up to the cockpit. Once they were airborne, and set on course, she called Mary, a bright, bubbly, Arabic hostess that she knew and asked her to see if it would be convenient for her to go to the cockpit. Mary returned right away, telling her that the captain would be happy to see her now, if she was free. Monique stood up, running her hands down the sides of the elegantly coutured skirt of her suit, trying to eliminate some of the creases that natural materials inevitably incur whilst travelling. Crossing the short distance between her seat and the cockpit, she tapped gently on the door and waited.

Hussein called for her to come in. "Sit down in the jump-seat at the back there, and I will swing round so that I can see you," said Hussein, unbuckling his safety harness.

"The view is so beautiful," said Monique, looking appreciatively at the panoramic view that the cockpit windows afforded her. "The desert has such wonderful hues before the sun gets high in the sky. I love the red and purple blend that it paints on the desert canvas."

"Yes," replied Hussein, nodding his head in agreement, "not everyone likes the desert-scape, but I think it has a stark beauty of its own." Before Monique had time to continue the conversation, the door to the cockpit burst open. It had been roughly kicked open by two men armed with guns, shouting orders in Arabic, one of them holding a gun to the head of Mary, the hostess. They had come up to the galley on the pretext of wanting a drink, and while Mary poured them some water, they grabbed her from behind. Panic-stricken, she had fought for composure but had noted, with relief, that the curtain separating the galley from the cabin was still drawn across and none of the passengers had been able to witness what had transpired. Should panic ensue, the immediate danger they were in would be increased greatly.

In the cockpit, one gunman, in a rough Arabic accent, ordered Hussein to change the aircraft's course and told him to head for a disused military airfield in the desert. Hussein replied that he could not do that without permission from air traffic control.

"Then get it fast, or she dies now," the gunman snarled, pulling Mary's head roughly to one side and aiming the gun at her temple.

Hussein leaned over to the radio and tuned to an emergency frequency apprising air traffic control of their situation.

"You are advised to comply," air control responded quickly. "You are cleared at twenty-six-thousand feet. This channel will be open for you at all times."

Hussein informed the gunmen that they had been cleared to proceed, and he would need to set a new heading. He spoke politely and evenly, without emotion, not wishing to provoke the gunmen more than necessary. They were already in a very agitated state and he, correctly, gauged that it would take little to incite them to further violence. Moreover, he was eager to appear reassuring to Monique under the extreme circumstances they were experiencing.

"Get on with it," the gunman barked at Hussein.

Shoving Mary roughly in the direction of the cabin, he growled at her, "You get back in the galley. Don't tell the passengers anything. I will tell them what is happening when I'm ready."

With Mary back in the cabin, the gunman was better able to see in the cockpit, where he spotted Monique sitting in the jump-seat. She was terrified but was managing to preserve a calm exterior.

"What's this foreign bitch doing in here," demanded the gunman, grabbing her hair and pulling her head roughly backwards.

Hussein felt an immediate urge to get up and defend the unwarranted, rough attack on Monique, but curbed himself knowing that as a foreign woman, she was potentially hostage material for them. He organized his thoughts quickly to try and bring her under the umbrella of his protection. He swiftly replied with great seriousness, "This woman is the wife of my brother, and he has entrusted her to my protection on the flight. Please do not harm her."

Hussein chanced that this traditional Middle Eastern code of conduct would not be lost on these men. As his sister-in-law, he would be expected to look after Monique as if she were his own wife whilst under his protection. Hopefully, these men would respect that.

The gunman grunted in reluctant respect of the custom and released her. "Tell her to keep her mouth shut then," he barked.

Hussein knew that Monique understood some Arabic and hoped that she had followed the conversation. "Monique, as you are my sister-in-law," he paused looking at her directly in her eyes meaningfully, "these men will allow you to stay here, but you must stay quiet. Do you understand?" Monique nodded, afraid to speak unnecessarily.

Thankfully, Hussein could see that she had grasped the situation and would go along with it.

Hussein ventured to ask the gunman who was giving all the orders, what was the purpose of this hijacking.

"Silence!" he screamed. "Fly the plane now. I will tell you what I want when I am ready."

Hussein returned to the control panel, concentrating deeply on his instruments. He indicated to the first officer and the flight engineer to do the same. He was determined none of them should inadvertently inflame the situation. The tension was high in the small cockpit, but Hussein's composure helped instill a measure of calm in all the crew. The new heading that he had been given was only about thirty minutes of flying time away, but Hussein was concerned about what would happen once they landed. He had no idea of what they were going to do with the passengers or crew, and he was aware that the temperature at the disused airfield would quickly become unbearable as the desert sun rose in the sky. There were many foreigners on board, who, like Monique, had gone to attend the arts festival in the Gulf. They would be ill-prepared to withstand the burning desert heat.

The hijackers' presence in the cockpit was stifling. They smoked foul-smelling cigarettes that made their breath acrid and joked crudely with each other, their raucous laughter piercing the ears of Monique and the crew. They frequently stared savagely into the faces of the crew at very close quarters without speaking, a measure that was effective in instilling fear in the recipients of such close scrutiny. To their credit, all of the crew was able to remain calm and efficient and avoid confrontation with the hijackers. The hijackers looked at their watches at regular intervals, and just before the descent, the head terrorist ordered Hussein to call Mary back into the cockpit. Hussein pressed the button to call the cabin staff to the cockpit, and within seconds, the bursar arrived in Mary's place. He had been fully informed of the hijack situation by Mary, and his hope was to spare her another ordeal with the terrorists. He intended to see if there was any way he could overpower them; he was well-built and had martial arts training. Upon seeing the bursar, the hijacker became agitated again and screamed at Hussein that he wanted the hostess and no one else. Hussein explained that the only way to communicate with the cabin staff without the danger of being overheard was to buzz them, and that is why the bursar had responded rather than Mary. Hussein immediately ordered the bursar to send Mary back in again. He could see that he was reluctant to comply, but Hussein insisted that he carry out the terrorist's orders, fearing the consequences for everyone if they were disobeyed.

Mary promptly returned to the cockpit ashen-faced but composed, looking directly at the face of the gunman for his instructions. "Tell the passengers that this aircraft has now been taken over by the liberating forces of the revolution of Koudara, and that if they value their lives, they must obey our orders. You will tell them to strap themselves in their seats and be silent. Go and do that now," he ordered, his voice ascending to a disturbing, fevered pitch. "My comrade will follow you into the cabin after you have spoken."

Mary returned to the cabin, sickened by the information she had to convey to the passengers. She made the announcement, first in Arabic and then in English and French. The passengers fastened their seatbelts and gradually fell into silent awareness of their grave situation. A wave of fear, which was almost tangible, swept through the aircraft as the gunman appeared. He walked up and down the cabin menacingly, aiming his small automatic repeat weapon at anyone who dared to look at him for more than a second. The passengers were terrified but silent. Fortunately, there were no children on board; such an early flight was not a very popular one with families. It was primarily used by businessmen, whose needs it served well as it arrived in Kharja at the beginning of the business day, giving them time to do their transactions and then return home to the Gulf on the evening flight.

In the cockpit, Hussein and the first officer were trying to get a visual fix on the old runway but, so far, had not been able to. Hussein was getting worried; there were only minutes to touch down. The hijacker, sensing Hussein's uneasiness, told him he would see some flares in about two minutes to guide him in.

Relieved, he continued on the glide-path, waiting for the flares to come into view.

The first officer interjected, "Captain, captain, I see them, ten degrees west, sir."

"Thank you, I have visual now, prepare for landing," responded Hussein. He landed on the old, bumpy runway that had been crudely extended by flattening the desert sand under the wheels of a jeep. The aircraft bumped and shuddered to a stop with sand flying in all directions. The head hijacker left the cockpit and shouted at the bursar to open the aircraft door. Outside, a jeep pulled alongside the aircraft with another armed man inside. He called up to the head hijacker, asking him what he needed.

"Bring a ladder so I can get all of them down from here," he told him.

His brief exit from the cockpit gave Hussein the opportunity to ask his crew if they were all right. They responded in unison that they were all in good shape, they too wanted to preserve a strong front in Monique's presence. Hussein turned around and looked at her. All he could manage to say, in a voice that threatened to break with emotion, was, "I'm so sorry."

"It's not your fault," she reassured him, struggling to keep her voice under control. She was shivering in spite of the heat of the desert. The effort of keeping a terrified silence and remaining still in the confined space of the jump-seat had taken its toll on her. The brief absence of the hijacker had allowed her emotions to surface and become evident.

The hijacker returned and ordered everyone out of the cockpit. "Climb down the ladder and go with my comrade," he ordered them.

The other gunman was waiting for them at the foot of the ladder. He was indistinguishable from the others in his quasi-paramilitary uniform, except for the fact that he was considerably taller and thinner than them. "Follow me," he shouted to them, his voice sounding less wired than the other two. He led them to a small wooden shack that appeared to serve as some kind of headquarters for the hijackers. Outside, there was a small electrical generator that catered to the demands of a small fan and other minor electrical necessities that were sparsely strewn about the hut. The other passengers and cabin staff were led off to a large building that had previously been used as an aircraft hangar. There were only about forty passengers, nine of which were women. The sun had not yet reached its zenith, and there was still some residual coolness from the icy desert night remaining in the large building, affording the hostages some relief from the sun. The hostages were still being held by the gunman who had been with them on the aircraft, ensuring their silence and complicity.

In the hut, where the aircrew was being held, the leader of the terrorists told Hussein to come back to the aircraft with him, leaving the tall, thin one to stay with the flight deck crew and Monique. They walked in silence to the aircraft, where the gunman indicated that he wanted Hussein to go into the cockpit. "I'm ready to tell you my demands now," he ordered in a surly voice. "Speak on the radio and tell them I want the release of all Koudaran prisoners from jail. There are four. And I want all the gold that was taken from them returned to us."

Hussein communicated these demands over the emergency frequency that was now being monitored at the highest level. There was particular concern over the European hostages. Kharjan authorities were anxious to prevent any kind of international incident arising over this situation as their relationship with the West had always been tenuous, and, at the present time, there were significant measures afoot to strengthen economic and diplomatic relations with them. The last thing that was needed, at this point, was a hijack from a quasi-paramilitary faction from the war-ravaged country of Koudara which borders Kharja. It would be hard enough for the authorities to convince the West that they had no complicity in the affair. Indeed, they themselves were finding it difficult trying to comprehend what these hijackers were actually seeking. However, when the authorities heard the demands conveyed by Hussein, the situation became clearer. Two months ago, four men had been stopped at the border trying to smuggle large amounts of gold out of the country and had been arrested and jailed and were pending trial. It seemed these men had been working for the liberating forces of Koudara and would have proceeded to trade the gold for arms had they successfully crossed the border with their consignment which had been stowed away in various parts of their trucks. They had been apprehended when the border patrol became suspicious of them. Their trucks, ostensibly carrying produce, had experienced great difficulty in ascending the hill leading to the border control. Consequently, their vehicles had been thoroughly searched and found to be laden with illegal amounts of gold to leave the country with. At the time, no one had connected them with any political faction. It was then determined that the men were smuggling for their own personal gain.

Initially, the Kharjan authorities were inclined to comply with the hijackers' demands and release the men from jail. However, after giving the issue deeper thought and consultation, and being mindful of the foreign hostages who were on board, the authorities came to the conclusion that they should distance themselves from appearing to support any particular faction in the Koudaran uprising. This was especially important because the West was heavily involved in Koudara both economically and politically and was, at present, trying to bring about a negotiating situation between the warring factions.

After Hussein had communicated the hijackers' demands, he was told by the authorities to stand by while the appropriate contacts were made. The hijacker seemed calmer after his demands had been conveyed. Sensing this, Hussein took the opportunity to try and make conversation. "I have family in Koudara. They have just about lost everything in this war, but they refuse to leave the land that they love. They pray for peace," he stated, showing some sympathy with the gunman's mission. Hussein had assessed the situation well. The gunman responded to this mild overture and told him that peace was what they all wanted, but they had waited for so long for the West to intervene that the only course left to them now was to fight for freedom. They began a cautious conversation. Hussein indicated his sympathy with some elements of the Koudaran situation without condoning the terrorists' methods. The gunman settled into the conversation and tried to justify to Hussein the wisdom of his actions. The hiss of the radio interrupted their conversation.

"This is control. We have conveyed your requests to the appropriate authorities, and they will respond within the hour."

The gunman responded angrily, ordering Hussein to tell them that he had enough water and food for his men but not enough for the hostages and that very soon the temperature in the desert would be climbing to the hundreds. They did not actually have the luxury of time on their side.

"I will convey that message to the authorities, standby," responded Hussein immediately.

The Karjian authorities were in the midst of fevered negotiations with foreign ambassadors, who were, in turn, negotiating with their respective countries. The status at the present was to stall the gunmen for as long as possible. However, with the knowledge that the hostages would be denied food and water, the situation had become much more serious, and action would need to be taken fairly quickly. Without water, the hostages would start becoming ill with heat stroke within one day followed by death shortly thereafter..

Hussein looked at the gunman and asked if he really intended to keep the hostages without water since there was enough water and liquids on the aircraft to supply them for about three days, if they were judicious in rationing it.

"Why should I give a damn about them? Do you think any of them care about what happens to us in Koudara? We can't even bring our children up decently — all they know is war and poverty."

"There are other Arabs on board who, like me, have family in Koudara and are actively seeking an end to the situation. Also many of the foreigners, that you claim to hate so much, are very sympathetic to your cause. Once foreigners come over here and get to know us and the way we think, they begin to understand us better, and they are often the ones that go back to their countries and educate others about our plight. Are these the people that you want to deny water to?" said Hussein with some passion, subtly allying himself with the gunman with his clever interjection of the phrase "our plight."

His ploy worked and the gunman began to relent. "What is your name?" asked the gunman in an almost mild tone.

"Hussein, Hussein Al Fayez."

"Hussein, I can tell that you are a good man, and for your sake, I will allow the hostages to have water. We will go together and tell your cabin crew to distribute some drinks now," he conceded.

At the small hut, the tall, thin gunman was ordered, by walkie-talkie, to accompany the crew and Monique to distribute drinks among the other hostages. The passengers received the drinks thankfully. The temperature had soared in the last hour, making them all feel extremely uncomfortable.

Hussein and the gunman resumed their conversation back in the cockpit, waiting for word from control. They did not have to wait long, as the authorities agreed to accede to the hijackers' demands. They said the prisoners would be freed but could not allow the gold to be released.

The gunman became agitated again. He seemed unable to make a decision. "Tell them I will let them know my answer in one hour," he told Hussein.

Hussein looked at him and seeing his agitated state, calmly asked him why he was hesitating.

"My orders were to get the prisoners released and also the gold. I can't accept this offer until I have spoken to command," he said gruffly.

"Let's get off the aircraft and speak to your superior on your radio," suggested Hussein, gradually taking command of the situation. The gunman looked troubled but decided that Hussein's suggestion was the best course of action. Arriving at the shack, Hussein was pleased to see that his crew was holding up well. But more especially, he was relieved to see that Monique was still looking outwardly composed.

The two gunmen spoke together for a while and agreed that they would get in touch with their base. Despite several attempts, their efforts to raise someone on the other end of the radio proved fruitless. Hussein ventured to ask what the problem was and why there was no one to answer them, given the enormity of the operation.

"I was told not to contact H.Q. unless it was really necessary," said the gunman in a tremulous tone, obviously losing his nerve now that the small band of terrorists appeared to have been abandoned, "but I cannot understand why no one is answering me now," replied the gun-man, becoming more perplexed.

"I must admit that it is strange for no one to be there," agreed Hussein.

"I will keep on trying every ten minutes," he told Hussein, trying to convince himself that everything would be restored in a matter of minutes. The crew was amazed to see the rapport between the gunman and Hussein, and how Hussein was slowly taking command of the situation.

The efforts to raise any response from the hijacker's base continued for some hours, but only proved to be futile. Hussein could see the hijackers' confidence was eroding, so he took the opportunity to work on their insecurities. "Shall we take a walk outside," he invited the leader.

The gunman complied, happy to have something else to do other than address a silent radio.

"Listen," said Hussein when out of earshot of the others, "this hijack is going nowhere. Your chain of command, for whatever reason, has broken down. You are not permitted to accept any offers that do not include the gold, so what are you going to do?" asked Hussein authoritatively.

The gunman was confused and no longer motivated to continue with the hijack without the support of his command leaders. The mental psyching up that he had undergone before boarding the plane was now being replaced by confusion and mounting terror as the reality of what they were doing began to penetrate his mind. He knew that the others in his small unit were to be engaged in a relatively small attack on the borders, from which they expected to return swiftly and without difficulty, but even so, he did not imagine that he would be left without backup on such a mission. He began to fear that things had gone badly wrong for his unit and now the fate of the hostages and the aircraft were left entirely in his hands. He began to shake visibly and was sweating profusely. In spite of having the other two gunmen with him, he felt isolated, and the thought that his command unit might be in trouble on their sortie left him in a state of panic.

Hussein seized the moment, "You can't continue, you know. You will gain nothing. I don't know what has happened to your unit, but they must be in trouble to have left you like this. If you wait any longer before releasing these hostages, some of them might die with the heat. There are some women, and how will it look if you leave them to die? What about your fellow Arabs who you're alienating? Let me talk to the authorities now and tell them that you are willing to release the hostages in exchange for leniency."

The gunman hesitated, trying to find a valid reason for continuing the hijack. Panic and confusion clouded his logic. Finally, he gave an apathetic nod to Hussein, wearily, releasing all control to him.

"Let's talk to your men and tell them to stand down from the hijack. I want to tell the passengers what is happening and distribute whatever we have in the way food and water to them."

The gunman just nodded, seemingly incapable of speech. The passengers, seeing the leader of the terrorists disarmed and fearful, became aware that Hussein was now in control of the situation, and began, for the first time, to have some hope of leaving the desert alive. After disarming the other gunman, Hussein told the passengers that their ordeal would soon be over and that the cabin staff would soon bring them whatever food and water was available. He advised them that, despite the conditions in the hangar being pretty uncomfortable, they were better off there than in the aircraft, which without ground power, had heated up to an extremely uncomfortable temperature inside. The passengers' relief was audible. They were happy just to be allowed to talk and walk around after sitting still for so long in the heat. Although their situation had been very uncomfortable, none of them had succumbed to the heat. Fortunately, the duration of the hijack had not been protracted; six hours had passed since they touched down in the desert.

After ensuring that the passengers were as comfortable as possible, Hussein returned to the small shack where the deck and cabin crew were still being held. The two terrorists accompanying him were now quite evidently unmotivated and compliant. Hussein appraised the situation inside and ordered the first officer to disarm the other hijacker and take all the weapons except one, and stow them securely on the aircraft. The other gunman was equally relieved to comply and succumb to Hussein's authority. For a fleeting second, Hussein felt pity for the confused and fearful men who stood before him. However, the moment he looked at Monique and saw the lines of fatigue that were now etched on her weary face from the ordeal, any feeling of pity deserted him. He ordered his flight engineer to tie up the terrorists and stand guard over them with the remaining weapon until they returned to the aircraft. He looked towards Monique, finally able to smile and reassure her. "Would you like to go and stay with the rest of the passengers? I think you might be more comfortable in there rather than on the aircraft or in here," he asked of her gently.

"Hussein, would you mind if I helped the cabin staff to serve the passengers? I really would like the opportunity to stretch my legs, and I would prefer to help if that would not be a problem."

Hussein looked at the bursar and raised his eyebrows questioningly. Before Hussein could voice the question, the bursar interjected.

"We would welcome Madam Stianou's help if she feels up to it."

"Well, there are no objections from the cabin staff, so you go right ahead," said Hussein, admiring the way that she had handled herself through the whole ordeal.

Hussein and the flight engineer escorted the hijackers to the aircraft and asked them to find a seat in the cabin, telling the flight engineer to take up a position next to the door and ensure that the hijackers did not attempt to leave the aircraft. Entering the cockpit, Hussein quickly contacted the authorities and told them that the hijack had been aborted and that he was now in control of the situation.

The Kharjan authorities were amazed and extremely pleased with the news of the gunmen's surrender and told Hussein to stand by for instructions. Turning to his first officer, Hussein sighed deeply as a warm sense of relief swept through him. He ran his hand over his face and eyes, showing for the first time the strain he had felt from the ordeal.

His first officer looked admiringly at him and told him "Well done, sir, I didn't think any of us would be getting out of here alive."

Hussein just nodded and took a swig from the remainder of the bottle of water that he always kept next to him in the cockpit. "God, that was disgusting," said Hussein, breaking the mood. "I forgot that this water has been standing for hours in the heat. I wonder how many amoebas were floating round in there?"

"Better not to think about it, sir," chuckled the first officer.

"Any chance of getting a fresh bottle?" he asked his co-pilot. "I'll check for you, sir." The first officer returned with a small tin of soda water.

"This is all we have, sir, the remains of the bottles of water are all fairly warm, but I found this stocked with some others in the bottom of the fridge. It has retained a small modicum of coolness about it," he smiled, happy to be able to have done something for Hussein. Hussein seized the tin and drank it with gusto.

The squawk of the radio drew Hussein's attention, and he turned to respond. It was Kharjan control, "Captain Al Fayez, you are commended for your actions. Your instructions are as follows: Keep the hijackers on board the aircraft, and let the passengers remain in the hangar with the cabin staff. Military helicopters have already been dispatched and are on the way to pick up the passengers and arrest the hijackers. You are advised to remain behind with your crew until all passengers have departed, at which time we will assess the condition of the aircraft and debrief you."

Hussein was unsure whether to let Monique go with the other passengers, since she had been in the cockpit and shared the ordeal of the crew. He knew she would be crucial to the debriefing. He explained who she was to the authorities and what her situation had been.

"Captain, we request that she stay with the crew if she is willing to," responded control.

In less than an hour, the military forces had landed their helicopters and begun ferrying the passengers to Kharja. The hijackers were taken into custody, leaving only the crew and Monique with the authorities on board the aircraft. "I am truly sorry for keeping you all longer than necessary in this overwhelming heat,"said one of the officials, "but we wanted to have an accurate as possible account of what happened and assess the state of the aircraft."

Hussein told them that he suspected that the only damage that might have been done to the aircraft was on landing. He'd noticed that a couple of the tires on the undercarriage were deflated. "Other than that," he told them, "with the provision of ground power and a towing vehicle, the aircraft should be able to take off, given that the fuel has cooled to a non-combustible temperature," he added.

"That sounds about right to me," said the official. "We will, of course, bring in another set of crew to bring the aircraft back. We have military transport waiting for you and your crew."

"Thank you, sir," said Hussein, thankful to leave the last leg of the ill-fated journey to someone else.

The debriefing was straightforward, although lengthy, and eventually the crew and Monique were able to board the military helicopter and relax for the remainder of the journey to Kharja. Hussein had seated himself next to Monique. He felt a great need to express his thanks to her for the way she had conducted herself during the most harrowing part of the ordeal.

"I really did not do anything," she told him. "I was honestly too frightened to move, and if I had been required to speak, I swear that nothing would have come out of my mouth. On the other hand, Hussein, I am really impressed and grateful for what you did for us all back there."

"I was just doing my job," he said modestly, "and I did not want to come back home in a body bag any more than anyone else. It is amazing how motivating fear can be," he concluded.

"Well, I think that there was more going on than just fear," she said with conviction.

Hussein reflected on that, and there had indeed been more than fear motivating him, although he would never admit it to Monique. During the whole ordeal, one of his overriding thoughts was to protect her. He could not bear the thought of anything hurting this lovely, vulnerable woman who has conducted herself with dignity and grace, while her husband has been shamelessly unfaithful to her. He had always admired her, but today, in the face of danger, he suspected that it was rather more than admiration that he had been feeling for her.

"How are you now?" asked Hussein.

"I am a little shaken still, but I imagine that a large cognac will do the trick," she answered, wondering why he was staring so intently at her.

"Nikos is away on a flight, isn't he?" asked Hussein, knowing very well that he was away for two more nights. "Will you be all right on your own?"

"Now that's a silly question, isn't it?" she replied, raising an eyebrow. "Surely you know that I will be better off on my own than with Nikos."

Hussein was startled by her frankness. He had never actually heard Monique say a bad word about Nikos before but understood perfectly the validity of her statement. Succumbing to an impulse, he asked her, "Would you mind if I visited you this evening, to check that the cognac worked? There will be a lot of work to do at the airport after all this, but I imagine that I will be free around ten. Will that be okay?"

"Yes, please do come, I don't mind at all. I will have had time to spend with Roger, and he should have gone to bed by then, and I dare say, I will be glad of the company," she told him, knowing that she was a lot more shaken than she was admitting to. She always felt safe around Hussein and welcomed his suggestion.

Feeling heartened at the prospect of spending the late evening with Monique, he settled into a quiet reverie of the dramatic events of the day.

Hussein, predictably, was delayed at the airport but managed to get away by nine forty p.m. by feigning extreme fatigue. He reached Monique's villa before ten o'clock and found her waiting on the veranda.

"Come and join me up here," she invited. "The evening is pleasantly cool, just right for sitting outside. What can I get you?" she asked. "I am already having the large cognac I promised myself."

"That sounds good to me," he replied, happy to see her looking more composed than earlier in the day.

"Roger has just gone to his room, but I promised him, that if you did not mind, he could come and see you for a short time before going to bed. He is very impressed with what you did and wants to be able to claim to have spoken to the 'hero of the day' at school tomorrow."

Hussein smiled and told her to call him come and join them. Roger plied Hussein with questions, wanting to have the ultimate story with which to impress his friends. After an hour of animated conversation Monique insisted that he should go and sleep, fearing he would not be in any fit state for anything the next day. Roger complied without argument. He tried to support his mother as much as possible as he was aware of the unhappiness that his father caused her to have and did his best to respond positively to her wishes.

"He's fine boy," offered Hussein. "You have done a good job raising him."

"Well, I am glad to have been able to do something right," she responded with a touch of sadness.

Hussein knew she was referring to her disastrous marriage. "Monique, I don't know everything about your personal life, but what I do know is that for as long as I have known you, you have behaved as the model of propriety. Whatever Nikos subjected you to, you have never shown it publicly, and you have never responded in kind. I think that deserves credit."

Monique looked at him sideways from under her long, sweeping eyelashes and said gently, "I think the same might be said of you too." Hussein was unable to answer, knowing the truth of her statement. Rather, he changed the subject. They talked for hours into the night, both of them more wired from their ordeal than they believed themselves to be.

"Don't you think that you should get some sleep?" asked Monique. "You will have to be up early for the office."

"I think that tomorrow, I am entitled to a morning off. There is no way I can sleep now. I can see that you are still wide awake. Would you mind too much if we talked some more? I am enjoying your company."

"No, I don't mind at all. I feel the same way, but I would be more comfortable inside. It is getting a bit chilly now." They moved inside, and Monique led him into the little den where she spent most of her time. She positioned herself on the big, comfortable sofa that was brightly adorned with throws made from large patchworks that she had made. Hussein intuitively understood that she was allowing him into her private space. In all the times he had been to the house, he had never been invited into this characterful den that was so clearly hers. Looking meaningfully at her, he asked if he might join her on the comfortable-looking sofa.

She patted the cushion beside her and told him, "Not at all, it's the most comfortable place in the whole house."

He sat down, sinking into the soft luxury of the sofa and resumed their conversation. However, once Monique had allowed herself to relax, she began to experience some delayed shock. Noticing this, Hussein felt his emotions stir, and he wanted to hold her in his arms until her pain and fear subsided. "You're shaking, are you all right?" he asked her gently.

"I think so," she answered in a small voice, "but I feel ice cold and I cannot stop shaking."

Hussein ventured to move close to her and slid his arm around her.

"Just let it all out, my dear," he said gently, pulling her around so that he could encircle her with his other arm. She felt immediately better with the warmth of Hussein's strong arms around her, but nonetheless, she could not choke back the tears that sprang unbidden to her eyes. She cried for some five minutes, all the time telling him how sorry she was for her loss of control.

"Don't worry, it's quite normal to be like this after what we have been through today," he said, enjoying the feel of her body close to his, wanting to make her hurt go away. He stroked her head gently, wiping the tears away from her eyes as if she were a child. Monique submitted to his ministrations until she felt able to regain her composure.

"Let me get you a cup of tea," he offered.

"No, I am fine now. I will make a pot of chamomile tea and perhaps a little cinnamon toast to fortify us."

"That sounds nice. Can I come with you into the kitchen?"

"By all means, I will even let you put the kettle on," she teased.

Hussein was happy to see Monique in good spirits again. He noted, with surprise, how happy he was to follow after her and share in the preparations of their light snack. He had not experienced this simple pleasure with anyone since he was a child and used to help his mother in the kitchen. Sherrifa had never lifted a finger to prepare anything either for herself or him in the whole duration of their marriage. It gave him a warm, satisfying feeling of mutual cooperation. They sat together in the kitchen to consume their small repast but found themselves still hungry.

"How about some grilled cheese sandwiches now?" suggested Monique. "Sounds great, let me slice the cheese for you." Their hunger finally assuaged, they made their way back to the den and sank into the comfort of the sofa once again, both of them becoming aware that there were tumultuous emotions arising between them that were seeking to be expressed.

"Do you know that it is four o'clock in the morning?" stated Monique, trying to insert some normality into this highly charged moment.

"Yes, I know, I really should be going, but I am very reluctant to leave."

"I will be all right now. You don't have to worry about me," she assured him, her heartbeat accelerating with tension of the emotion still between them.

"That's just my problem, Monique," he said tenderly, unable to keep silent any longer about his feelings for her. "I want to worry about you. Until today, I have always thought that what I felt for you was a mixture of respect and pity. But today, when I saw that you might be in danger, I was overwhelmed by my need to protect you from harm. My feelings have been running riot and they still are."

"Hussein, I think that tonight we both have sensed an intensity of feelings towards each other. I cannot deny that I enjoyed your arms around me, but I want you to understand that I can't allow myself to be swept away with the passion of the moment. I have lived to regret doing that before, but I have never given Nikos the chance to condemn my moral conduct. I don't want to start any kind of shallow or passing affair. I need time to know you and trust you before I allow my emotions to lead me anywhere."

Hussein moved close to her and embraced her, whispering in her ear, "Monique, I swear I will never give you a moment's doubt about the way I feel for you, or my intentions towards you. But I will happily wait as long as you like for your trust. Only please let me hold you like this sometimes."

Monique sank into the warmth of his embrace, happy and reassured that Hussein would behave respectfully and patiently with her. He did not try to kiss her, fearing that the intensity of his emotions might get the better of him.

Feeling the heat and passion of their embrace, Monique gently pulled away and took hold of Hussein's hand and kissed it gently in the palm, folding his fingers over as if to save the kiss inside. She told him, "My dearest, you must go now, but please come again and see me."

Respecting her wishes, he rose to his feet and took her hand again. Putting it to his cheek, he told her, "I will come again, as many times as you will allow me, and as often as I can."

With that, he left. Monique walked out onto the balcony to watch him pull out.

Looking upwards from the drive, Hussein saw her standing there and flashed his car headlights at her, wishing that she could see the kiss that he blew to her. "Sleep tight my beautiful Monique; I have been happier tonight than I can remember. Somehow, I will find a way to bring some happiness to our lonely lives."

He returned to his villa and crept into bed, falling quickly to sleep. However, the strains of the day had not been purged from him, and he woke up in a cold sweat two hours later after reliving the nightmare of the hijack in a vivid dream. He was relieved to see the early morning sun blazing round the perimeter of the heavy wooden window shutters. Darkness would not have been welcome in present state. Quickly recovering from his nightmare, he allowed himself the luxury of reliving his evening with Monique and fell back into a blissful sleep, waking at noon that day. He picked up the phone next to his bed and called Monique.

"How are you this morning, my love?"

"I am fine, and very happy to hear your voice," she responded warmly.

"How did you sleep?" he asked.

"Not too badly, it did not take me too long after you left, but I had to be up at seven to see Roger off to school. After he left, I decided that I needed some more sleep and went back to bed. In fact, that is where I am now, feeling truly decadent for sleeping in so late."

"Well, you have every reason for being there. We were up very late last night. I should have remembered that you would be seeing Roger off to school; it was very selfish of me. Please excuse my thoughtlessness." He had forgotten there was a world where loving parents personally take care of their children rather than having their servants do it.

"There is nothing to excuse. I knew very well that I had to get up at seven, and I was more than happy to stay with you. I did not want you to leave early either."

"It is so good to hear you say that. I was afraid that in the cold light of day you would forget about our evening and go back to our formal relationship," he smiled in relief.

"There is no chance of that. I do not enter into relationships lightly, and when I do, it is because I have a positive feeling about them. The only time you will see me behaving formally with you is when we are attending the interminable airline functions. But let us think of a sign that we can give to each other on those occasions so we do not feel isolated from each other," she suggested.

"Yes, let's do that. What shall it be?" he agreed happily.

"I know," she volunteered, "I am trying to grow a chamomile lawn in the garden and you can ask me how it is coming along. It sounds quite innocent, but it will remind us of our little meal last night."

"That's perfect," said Hussein, remembering again the pleasure of being with her in the kitchen, and eating with her. Reluctantly, they ended their conversation. Hussein phoned the airport, telling them he would be there in an hour. Going downstairs, he went into the kitchen and poured some coffee from the percolator and made himself a grilled cheese sandwich, as if to salute the one he had enjoyed so much the previous evening. As he prepared to leave, he encountered Sherrifa in the hallway.

"This is a rare surprise, seeing you at this time of day, but of course, you had a little adventure yesterday didn't you?" she drawled with mock admiration.

For a moment, Hussein was unsure of what she was inferring, concerned that she might be alluding to yesterday evening, spent with Monique. His mind quickly cleared, comprehending that she had no way of knowing his whereabouts, and even if she did, it would have been quite in order to visit Monique after the ordeal of the hijack.

"Yes, the hijack left me feeling exhausted. That's why I am so late going in to the office."

Hussein saw that Sherrifa wanted to hear more news of the hijack. Normally, she would have made her one sarcasm-laden comment to him and walked on, but today she lingered with a playful smile on her lips.

"I hear you are quite a hero," she said with a hint of true admiration.

"I did my best," he replied, not wanting to go into detail with her. However, Sherrifa was not about to let him go without gleaning firsthand information from him. The hijack was the talk of Kharja already and, as his wife, she would be expected to be fully informed of the events that had transpired.

"I imagine it must have been an ordeal for everyone," she pressed.

"Yes, but the passengers and crew withstood it very well. They all deserve credit," he answered, wishing she would leave.

"Someone mentioned that Monique was on board and that she was in the cockpit at the time of the hijack," Sherrifa continued.

"Sherrifa, you seem to know all the details of what took place already, as you usually manage to do, so if you don't mind, I need to get to the office."

She told him that she knew the overall picture but needed the details filling in, and pressed him again about Monique's role.

Reluctantly, he told her of Monique's part in the ordeal. "She did very well to stay calm and composed through it all," he commented, showing his admiration a little.

"I would have liked to see that, the French iceberg with ruffled feathers," she said unkindly.

Hussein bristled at the unnecessary comment about Monique. "I think her presence influenced all the crew. She maintained herself with dignity during the whole ordeal."

"Oh, how protective of you. If I did not know that you can no longer get it up, I might think that you were smitten by her. Although come to think of it, you would make the perfect couple, Madam Frigid and Monsieur Impotent," she laughed.

Hussein turned and left, unwilling to listen to any more of her unwarranted attack. "That's right, run off to the office," she shouted after him. "That's all you're good for."

Sherrifa was annoyed with him, and with herself. After hearing of the hijack and Hussein's fruitful efforts to bring it to an end, she had felt a renewed desire for him. The idea of him being a hero and the toast of the town appealed to her. She would have been very happy to share in his glory. And even though she did not fear any competition from other women, she was angered when he leapt so quickly to defend Monique. She was so unused to feeling the pangs of jealousy, that she was totally unaware of what they were. She was trying to ingratiate herself with him, but as usual, she had snarled back a vicious response to him which had alienated him even further from her. *Why did I have to let my mouth overrule my brain?* she lamented. *Never mind, I will get all the information from father. He should be privy to all the reports. Hussein, I will work on later.* She resolved to be kinder to him in the future and try and win him over again.

Later that day she phoned him at work, telling him sweetly that she had arranged a dinner party for all the deck crew who had been aboard the hijacked flight and Monique, to celebrate their heroism. Hussein knew that she was, in fact, doing what etiquette demanded of her, for the soiree would be the talk of the town with official photographs taken and television interviews snatched from the arriving and departing guests. However, it was not something that he welcomed in light of his new relationship with Monique. He had hoped to stay late at the office and call to see Monique on the way home.

"That's kind of you. Have you spoken to everyone?"

"Yes, they are all coming for eight o'clock," she told him in saccharine-laden tones.

"Okay, I'll see you later then," he confirmed.

Hussein immediately picked up the phone and dialed Monique's number. It rang for what seemed like an eternity; eventually, Monique's maid answered.

"I would like to speak to Madam Stianou. Is she available?"

"Just one minute, sir, who shall I say is calling?" she enquired politely.

"This is Captain Al Fayez," he informed her.

"Oh, yes sir, I will get her right away for you," the maid responded with admiration in her voice, clearly delighted to have had the privilege of personally speaking to the hero of the city. She rushed down to the garden where she knew Monique was working alongside the gardener. Excitedly, she told her that

Captain Al Fayez was on the phone for her. Monique put down her hand rake and walked quickly back up to the villa.

"Hello, this is a nice surprise, hearing from you again so soon. I was busying myself in the garden; it needs constant attention in this climate."

"How is the chamomile lawn doing?" asked Hussein smiling, trying out their secret code for the first time.

"The chamomile lawn is being well-nurtured. I am giving it a lot of attention so it will flourish in this dry climate," she said, joining willingly in the game.

Hussein was glad for this coded endearment. It was difficult to be intimate in the office with the possibility of being overheard by his secretary, and he knew Monique's maid would likely be listening to their conversation from a discreet corner. She, too, would want the prestige of being able to report firsthand information about the country's latest hero to her cohorts.

"I imagine Sherrifa has phoned you and invited you to dinner".

"Yes, she has. She was very charming, and asked me all about the hijack."

"I just wanted you to know that it is not what I had planned," he assured her.

"I did not think for a minute that it was. I know that Sherrifa is entirely the mistress of the house," and they both laughed at this understatement.

"Don't forget the chamomile lawn tonight," he reminded her, knowing that they would both feel strained under Sherrifa's scrutiny.

"I certainly will not. Take care till then."

Hussein felt dissatisfied with this last conversation he had shared with Monique, but he accepted that it was better than saying nothing before their meeting tonight. There was so much that he wanted to tell her. He wanted to reassure her that he would not use or abuse her, that it would be all right with him, that he was not like Nikos. That, somehow, he would find a way to make it all right for both of them. And, most of all, even though tonight it would appear to the world that he was Sherrifa's loyal husband, in his heart, he only wanted to be with her.

All the guests arrived promptly that evening; Sherrifa had thoughtfully sent her chauffeur to collect Monique so that she would not have to drive home alone, as Nikos was still away. Sherrifa went out of her way to make the evening pleasant, heaping lots of praise on the crew and Monique. The conversation was animated, with most of them wanting to dissect the intricacies of the hijack. Time passed swiftly and the guests were surprised to find it was already well past midnight. Hussein and Monique had no opportunity to exchange pleasantries as everyone's contribution to the evening's conversation was so interesting that it held the attention of all the guests and no pairing-off occurred. However, when it came time to leave, Hussein was able to thank her for coming, and took the opportunity to enquire about her chamomile lawn.

"It is doing very well. I managed to harvest some of the flowers and made myself a tisane with them. It was quite delicious," she said with a hint of mischief sparkling in her eyes. Hussein smiled at her elaboration, and asked if she would be all right going home with the chauffeur.

"I will be fine. It was very thoughtful of Sherrifa to think of sending him to collect and return me home," she said politely.

"Well, if there is anything you need while Nikos is away, just let me know," he told her, trying to think of something more to say to her that would delay her departure.

"That's so kind of you. Thank you very much, goodnight," she smiled formally.

Sherrifa was still being thanked by the first officer and his wife who were delighted to have been afforded an invitation to dinner with Sherrifa. It was almost worth getting hijacked for, they later reflected.

Noting Sherrifa's preoccupation, Hussein took the opportunity to walk to the end of the drive and watch Monique being driven off into the darkness. He wished fervently that he was the one driving her home.

After the departure of all the guests, Sherrifa turned to Hussein with a brilliant smile. "What an exhilarating evening," she purred. "I truly enjoyed it." Hussein had to admit that the evening had been pleasant and lively, and thanked her for her efforts.

"It was my pleasure. Shall we have a little more wine and talk some more," she said enticingly.

"I'm really tired actually and need some sleep," he said, feeling uncomfortable with her overtures of friendliness.

"Well why don't you let me unwind you with a nice massage," she offered seductively. He was unused to such attention from Sherrifa and did not welcome it, but neither did he want to risk another row with her, so he chose his words carefully. "I really appreciate what you have done this evening on behalf of the crew, and although there are few women more beautiful than you, I really must decline your kind offer."

Sherrifa seemed contented with his reply and told him to get some sleep. She resolved to break down his barriers slowly; she would get a little closer every day.

The following few days went by with Sherrifa being both seductive and charming to Hussein. He was thrown by her unwelcome advances but did not know how to reject her without causing offence and risking her volatile temper. Sherrifa, conversely, was enjoying the challenge of wooing her husband back again. His impartiality only made the game more exciting. Late one evening, she made her ultimate play for his attentions. Waiting until he was sound asleep, she crept into his room and slid silently into the bed with him. She ran her hands gently over his body and slowly down to his genitals. He startled awake, shocked to find Sherrifa in his bed.

"Sherrifa, what are you doing here?" he exclaimed.

"What does it look like," she replied, trying to coax his body to respond to her seduction.

She kissed him all over, pressing her naked body close to his, but she was disappointed by his lack of response, evident by his still-flaccid penis. Trying again, she slid down his chest and put his organ to her mouth, teasing it with her lips, gradually applying more pressure until she enveloped it entirely with her mouth. Hussein's body was not aroused by her attentions. He lay silent, not knowing what to say to her. However, words were not necessary. She moved away from him and returned to her own room. There, she reflected that it was a waste of time seducing him. He had clearly lost his ability to perform, and there would be no pleasure of conquest to be had with him. She would turn her attentions to more fertile pursuits. She let her mind return to thoughts of the charming and virile-looking Greg Youssef.

CHAPTER SEVEN

Chips begin to fall

Jenny awoke early, surprised to find that the apartment felt like ice. A sudden cold front had moved in and the temperature had plummeted. *Not surprising*, she reflected, *it is almost the middle of December, and it's common for weather fronts to move in at this time of year.* She rummaged through all the storage cupboards of the apartment in search of a small electric heater to provide herself with a little heat, but her efforts proved fruitless. She decided instead to have a hot shower and warm up that way. Jenny was not going to work that morning, as Greg was coming home from a flight in the late afternoon and she wanted to spend as much time with him as she could before he went to the States for his course. After her shower, she rifled through her stored-away suitcases looking for some warm clothing to wear. Seeing her warm clothing again made her slightly nostalgic. She had worn none of her warm, woolly clothes since she left England, *but still*, she thought *I wouldn't want to go back there again for anything. I love my new life with Greg far too much.*

Dressing quickly, she set off for the shops, and the first thing on her agenda was to find an electric heater to heat up their apartment, which proved much harder to find than she imagined. After much negotiating and bartering, she finally ended up with a metal heater that burned paraffin. Picking up the groceries for the next few days, she returned home to cook something special for Greg's arrival. Later in the evening, she planned to take him to see a new luxury apartment complex that was being built.

After a romantic reunion and dinner, she broached the subject with Greg. "Darling, you know that you asked me to look for a new apartment in your absence? Well, I came to hear of rather an exclusive complex that is in the process of being constructed. One of the doctors at the hospital mentioned it to me. It seems that a relative of his is the owner, who is not so concerned with making a fortune out of selling the apartments as he is in having good people living around him because he and his family will be living there too. I thought it might suit us quite well."

"It definitely sounds like a possibility. Any chance of seeing the place?"

"As a matter of fact, I set up a meeting with the owner for this evening, if that's alright with you. I only have to phone and confirm".

"Well, what are you waiting for?" said Greg good naturedly.

They arrived at the well-positioned site to find the owner waiting for them. Jenny introduced them, "Greg, meet Mr Fouad Jaffa."

"Just call me Fouad," said the owner, smiling and speaking in English for the benefit of Jenny.

"I'm Greg. This is a wonderful site for a building. It has an incredible view out to sea, I love the smell of the ocean."

"Yes, we think it's lovely. My family has had this piece of land for many years and now it has really increased in value. I've had many offers from building contractors to buy it, but I have been reluctant to sell. I always wanted to build a house here, but my wife felt that she would be too lonely since there are few houses close by and she has always lived in the town where everyone around is like extended family, constantly in and out of each other's houses. Then we came up with the idea of building a complex. There will be six apartments in all, each pair in a two-storey building of their own. As you can see, two of the buildings are finished, and the third one is going to be completed next month. Come and have a look round our apartment. We have already moved into the ground floor of this first building, and my wife's sister and family live upstairs." He led them into an elegant apartment, the marble tiling throughout was exquisite, and Fouad told them he had shipped it over from Italy. Both Greg and Jenny were more than impressed with the time and effort that must have been spent in creating such a wonderfully designed apartment.

"This is a beautiful apartment. Are all the others the same?" queried Greg.

"More or less, yes. Of course, we have added some of our own features in here for our personal pleasure, but apart from that, everything else is the same."

Greg looked at Jenny, who was smiling with evident approval. "We are certainly impressed with the apartment, but I don't know whether we can afford the mortgage on such a place," said Greg frankly.

"Don't think about that now," said Fouad. "Come and meet my wife, and we will discuss it over a coffee." Fouad called his wife who was upstairs with her sister. She was a sweet-looking woman, named Hilda and she fussed, good-naturedly, over her husband and her guests. Hilda's English was not quite as good as her husband's, but she managed to communicate very well. Jenny liked her immediately, and the feeling seemed to be mutual. Within minutes, Hilda called her husband to the kitchen, ostensibly to help her bring out some delicious-looking Arabic pastries while she carried in the coffee. But as soon as he got into the kitchen, she told him that she liked the young couple and was quite happy for them to buy one of their apartments if they wanted to.

"Are you sure, Hilda? They could be living here for a very long time, and you have to feel comfortable with them."

"Fouad, you know me. If I do not like a person within the first fifteen minutes of meeting them, I will never like them. And how often am I wrong?" she demanded in rapid colloquial Arabic.

He was forced to admit that she had been seldom, if ever, wrong about people. She had an uncanny ability to weigh up people very quickly and accurately in a very short time.

"Besides," continued Hilda, "she is a nurse, and my sister is pregnant again. It will be useful to have someone right here that has medical knowledge."

"Then I will make them an offer," agreed Fouad, who had also taken a liking to the eager young couple. Fouad and Hilda returned to the lounge with the refreshments and bright smiles on their faces. Greg guessed that their acceptability had been discussed, and by the look of it, approved.

"The value of these apartments is one hundred and fifty thousand dinars," he told them, while noting how their faces dropped. Fouad guessed that the amount would be out of their reach. "But, I am willing to negotiate an amount that you feel able to afford."

"That's very generous, especially as it will cost us a small fortune to furnish such a large apartment so as to do it justice. Our current one is quite small. We have calculated that we can afford an apartment of only around the seventy-five thousand mark, so I'm afraid that, sadly, we are not going to be in the running for this lovely place," responded Greg, gesturing towards the new apartment block under construction.

"Not necessarily, Hilda and I would like to have you living here, and for that, we are prepared to negotiate," persisted Fouad with a smile.

Hilda suggested that Jenny come with her into the kitchen while she did some cooking and leave the men to work it out between themselves. Jenny happily agreed, as the thoughts of moving into such a warm and friendly atmosphere as this heartened her. Their present apartment had little warmth about it, save that which Jenny had managed to create. Most of the time, she felt isolated from the community. Here, she would have the luxury of all modern conveniences, an unbelievable view of the ocean and a warm, friendly community. Indeed, it was more than she had hoped for.

Whilst they were in the kitchen Hilda taught Jenny how to make Ishta, a kind of cooked cream that is often used to fill small pancakes that are drenched in rosewater syrup and decorated with preserved rose petals.. "You need fresh cow's milk from za milkman," Hilda told Jenny in a motherly tone with a heavy English accent, "and then you keep boiling it and skimming off the skin on za top. After, you put it in za leetle pancakes and pour over sugar syrup and decorate."

"It sounds delicious," said Jenny, her mouth watering.

"Here, taste thees one," Hilda thrust the little stuffed pancake at Jenny. "Eet's called katyef bi ishta; eat, eat," she urged.

"Oh, that is divine," said Jenny, truly appreciative.

Fouad and Greg appeared smiling at the kitchen door, having come to a mutually acceptable agreement. Fouad had been more than fair. Greg was sure that Fouad was taking an enormous loss on the deal, but Fouad had reassured him that good friends could never be replaced by a fat bank account. Besides, he had made the condition that, should they ever wish to leave, they would sell the apartment back to him at the same price for which they had paid. That way, he told Greg, he might be able to make a profit if he sold again. Anyway, they both were in agreement that it was a good deal.

"I think zat you must have come to a good agreement, by za look on your faces," observed Hilda smiling brightly at her husband.

"Yes indeed, we have. Now we only have to decide when you are going to move in. Greg has left that up to Jenny," said Fouad, looking toward Jenny.

Jenny was overjoyed. She hadn't dared to hope that she might soon be living in this lovely apartment. She had been preparing herself for the worst so as not to be disappointed if the deal fell through. She felt like hugging them. As if sensing this, Hilda held open her arms and embraced her, giving her the customary congratulations in Arabic.

"Mabrouk, you are most welcome. You will be like one of our family now."

"Oh, this is wonderful," exclaimed Jenny. "How soon can we move in?"

"Well," said Fouad, "if you take the downstairs apartment, you can move in as soon as you like, as long as you don't mind hearing the workmen hammering away during the day as they put the final touches to the apartment upstairs."

Jenny looked at Greg, her eyes shining with anticipation. "I'm ready to move in right away. What about you Greg?"

"I do have five days off before my next flight. It would be as good a time as any to make a move. And it will be nice for Jenny to have you for company when I go away on my course."

"Don't you worry about Jenny. We will look after her when you are away," said Hilda kindly.

The next five days flew by in a flurry of packing up and unloading belongings. By the third day, Greg and Jenny had ferried a sufficient amount of their furniture to be able to move into their new apartment and spend the first night there. Although things still looked rather Spartan, Jenny felt that this was the real beginning of their life together. Choosing this apartment together meant a lot to her, as it was somewhere where they could both feel at home. That evening, Hilda rang their doorbell bearing a tray full of food. "Here you are. I know zat you are very tired, so I made you some dinner. Here, take it and enjoy."

"Thank you so much," said Jenny, touched by her thoughtfulness. "Please, come in." But Hilda was already walking away down the path, waving her hand behind her.

"Greg, come and see what Hilda has prepared for us."

"Mmm, that looks good," said Greg. "That's Molokhia. It's something like spinach, and it's cooked in broth and poured over layers of toasted pita bread, rice and chicken, then topped with a dressing of chopped raw onions and vinegar. I love it."

"Well, it sounds good, and I'm certainly ready to eat, wasn't it nice of Hilda to go to all that trouble for us."

"Yes, it is kind of her, but you know, most Arabic people are very hospitable, and Hilda and Fouad's goodwill typifies what is best in us Arabs — generosity and kindness. It is sad that our own cultural values have started to fade away since having to accommodate the Western world. Jenny looked at him, slightly surprised hearing him refer to himself as being Arabic. She had always felt that he acknowledged the English part of himself more. They sat and consumed their meal with appreciation. Jenny enjoyed its piquant taste and soon became used to the glutinous texture of the unusual leaf vegetable. Too tired to wash the dishes, they stacked them in the sink and showered before falling gratefully into bed.

Jenny snuggled onto Greg's chest, "Thank you for this lovely apartment. I feel that we are going to be so happy here. Greg kissed her, pleased to see her so contented. They made love almost sacredly that night as if to consecrate the new apartment as their own. The next morning, they surprised themselves by sleeping late. Mainly because the new apartment was so peaceful, they were far from all external disturbances, save the wheeling cries of the sea birds.

"We are going to have to get a reliable alarm clock, or there will be a few flights delayed, waiting for the captain to roll up."

"Yes, I agree, but I do feel truly refreshed after sleeping without noises from outside. Anyway, it's just as well I do, since we still have so much cleaning and unpacking to do."

"Didn't you ask the maid to come today and help with the cleaning?" enquired Greg, feeling that he had really done enough in the way of helping in the house. "I've arranged to have coffee with Fouad this morning and play trick-track."

"What's trick-track?" she asked.

"It's what you call backgammon."

Jenny made them both a light breakfast and embarked on the massive job of sorting and cleaning. Happily, her maid, Hala, arrived within the hour and took command of the situation. Hala, too, was delighted with the move. This well-appointed apartment would be much easier and pleasanter to clean than the old one. What's more, she was friendly with the maids who helped Fouad and Hilda and their sister's family, which would make the time she spent here more pleasurable.

Noticing that Jenny was looking fairly fatigued from the ordeal of moving, Hala told her, "You not do cleaning, Madam Jenny. You tired from working at hospital and moving. You go take rest, or go hairdresser," said Hala in her stilting pigeon English, knowing the hairdressers was the traditional place for sympathy and relaxation in the Middle East.

Jenny tried to object but Hala would not hear of it, telling her that cleaning was her job and not Jenny's. With some reluctance, Jenny did relent and decided that, since Greg would be with Fouad, she may as well take a much-needed trip to the hairdressers.

Leila was happy to see her, although she remonstrated about the fact that she had been neglecting herself again. "Look at zees split ends. We will have to give you a good trim and make za hair more healthy."

Jenny was happy to let Leila take her in hand, and even agreed to the luxury of having a pedicure. Relaxing in a totally blissful state of being, Jenny was brought quickly back to earth by the raucous tones of Betty Bonner.

"Well now, who've we got here? It's been so long since I seen ya that I can hardly tell it's you," Betty drawled in her strong Southern accent.

"Hello, hello, Betty," Jenny replied apologetically. "Honestly, I have been so busy with the hospital and moving to a new apartment that I have not seen anyone."

"It's okay, hun', I understand. In fact, that's why I told you about the job at the hospital in the first place. You were so low, havin' nothin' to do all day when that man of yours was away. I figured that ya needed somethin' to keep y'all busy. Anyway, I saw Candy just a little while back, an' she told me you were doin' fine."

Jenny had not really made the connection that Betty would know Candy from previous airline socials when Candy was still married to her pilot husband. It dawned on her that Betty, in her kindness, had probably thought that she and Candy might find a good friend in each other.

"Thank you for telling me about the hospital, Betty. It has made all the difference in my life, and meeting Candy was a bonus. She has become a good friend."

"I kinda figured that you two would hit it off. You both needed someone of your own age to hook up with."

"Betty, I was wondering whether you and Chuck are busy on Christmas Eve. I was hoping to arrange a dinner party for just a few of us. I am dying to show off the new apartment to our friends."

"Oh, honey, I'm sorry but the regal summons has been issued by that Sherrifa. I expect you will have an invite, too. It would have been real nice to be with y'all, but you know what trouble it would cause if we don't all show up for one of Sherrifa's parties."

"Oh," said Jenny dejectedly, "with Greg leaving so soon for his course, I had hoped that the Christmas period could just be spent quietly with friends."

"Well, you know honey, there are not too many of us old hands that would really choose to spend holidays with Sherrifa, but it's gotta be done. Like I told you before, that woman is mighty powerful. But listen, Jen, I'm plannin' a bash for New Year's. Why don't ya come on round for that? I know Greg ain't gonna be with ya, but that's no excuse for you sittin' at home."

"That's kind of you, Betty. I must admit I would welcome the company. I will try and be suitably merry for the occasion."

"That's the spirit. Why don't ya come over with Candy. I'm gonna invite her too."

"That's a good idea. If she's free, I will come with her," Jenny replied, remembering that Candy might well be otherwise engaged.

Jenny returned home from the hairdressers looking and feeling refreshed. She was delighted to find the apartment positively gleaming from ceiling to floor, and all the packing crates emptied. Hala had tastefully arranged everything in the lounge.

"You like, Madam Jenny?" she said, obviously proud of her morning's efforts.

"Like it? I love it. Thank you so much for doing all this work. How did you manage to finish all this so quickly?"

"Madam, after you go, I ask Captain Greg if I can call my sister to help. He say yes and we work together. This is big apartment, need much work. My sister, she need to work, she happy to work for you for half of what you pay me. Please madam, can she work here too? I ask Captain Greg, and he say it's up to you."

Jenny looked at Hala's imploring eyes and could not refuse her. After all, they hardly paid Hala a living wage. They could more than afford to pay both their wages. "Yes, of course she can," she said smiling.

At this, Hala called her sister, who was watching, concealed behind the lounge door.

"Come, come, Ranna, the madam she say you can work here too." Ranna came in delighted. Taking Jenny's hand, she wanted to kiss it, but Jenny gently pulled it away, embarrassed at her show of subservience. Jenny tried to treat everyone with respect and dignity, believing that everyone was created equal.

"Madam, thank you, thank you, for giving me work," she gushed happily, her English markedly better than Hala's. "You will see zat I will work very hard for you, and I am very good at za cooking. I will make special food for you. If you have dinner parties, I will make everything."

"That is a pleasant bonus, and I am sure the day will come when I need you to do the cooking. I have put off inviting Captain Greg's friends round for dinner because I've never cooked for more than four people. When I have been to dinners here, the hosts look as though they have prepared enough food for double the amount of people, and there are always so many different dishes. I have always felt so inadequate," said Jenny honestly.

"Madam, in this country, eet ees the custom to serve your guests very much food. We think it an honour for guests to come into our homes. You don't worry about inviting guests, I take care of everything."

"Thank you very much," said Jenny ,"and thank you for all your hard work today."

"You are most welcome," said the sisters in unison. "We see you tomorrow."

Jenny walked round the apartment amazed at how different it all looked now that it was clean and arranged. Even the modest furniture from the old apartment took on a new lease of life here in its new setting. She would enjoy buying new furniture, she thought, because it would help pass the time while Greg was away. At this juncture, Greg walked in, interrupting her thoughts.

"Hiya, babe, you look great, and so does the apartment. Hala and her sister worked really hard. They were eager to impress on us how Ranna would be indispensible to our needs. I more or less said that her sister could work for us too. Is that all right?"

"It's fine," said Jenny. "I'm quite happy for them both to work here. Ranna cooks too, which will come in handy for when we have parties. Anyway, she seemed to want the job badly."

"Yes, I believe they are trying to save up enough money for one of their brothers to go to university. Seems he's very bright."

"That's very good of them. People here sacrifice so much for their family," reflected Jenny.

"The family is the most important thing over here, Jen. Anyway, speaking of families, I forgot to tell you that we are invited to one of the leading ones. Sherrifa's invited us to dinner on the 24th. I accepted the invitation. Is that all right?"

"Well, I suppose that I don't really have any choice in the matter," she said grudgingly. "I saw Betty at the hairdressers, and she told me that no one refuses one of Sherrifa's invitations, on pain of death. I was a bit disappointed because I wanted us to have a dinner party here on Christmas Eve."

"I'll tell you what, why don't you make the dinner for the 25th instead?" said Greg enthusiastically.

"Oh, I really wanted to just be with you, since you leave on the 27th," she protested.

"Sorry love, we can't just be together on the holidays here. You'll find that many of the people who know us will come and visit and wish us well on the holidays. That is the custom here. You'll have to have a good supply of coffee and cakes to offer to the visitors," he informed her gently.

"Oh," said Jenny feeling rather naive, "I didn't know. Then perhaps I will have the dinner party on the 25th after all."

"Who did you have in mind to invite?" enquired Greg.

"I thought Betty, Chuck and Candy, and perhaps one or two of your friends from work."

"Jenny, if we give a party, we have to first repay those who have invited us. If it got around that we held a dinner and didn't invite people like Hussein and Sherrifa and Nikos and Monique, etcetera, it would be deemed an insult."

"Oh my god, I couldn't arrange a dinner fit for the likes of Sherrifa and company. I have never done it before, and it is sure to be disastrous," she exclaimed, genuinely terrified by the prospect.

"Listen, nobody is going to expect you to be able to live up to Sherrifa's standard. In fact, you should not even try to. All you need to do is be hospitable. Didn't you say that Ranna can cook?"

"Yes," she nodded.

"Well then, it's very simple. You leave all the preparations to Ranna and Hala, and you will be the gracious hostess. Then if anything does go wrong, you can always blame the help," joked Greg.

"I suppose that you're right," she conceded. "I had better send some invitations out."

Between making arrangements for the 25th and going to the hospital, Jenny was kept extraordinarily busy. For the first time since she arrived in the country, she did not miss Greg unnecessarily while he was away on his four-night stopover in London. Hilda popped by every evening to chat for a while, making sure that Jenny wasn't lonely. Her nights were peaceful in the new apartment, and the overwhelming loneliness that she used to feel in Greg's absence began to fade.

Ranna and Hala were delighted that they would be arranging Jenny's very important dinner party. The fact that Madam Sherrifa and Captain Hussein would be coming was a great honour. They were determined that everything would be as near perfect as they could manage. They took Jenny to all the best local places that they knew, to buy the food, and the rest they insisted they do themselves.

The evening of the 24th December came around quickly, and Jenny made a quick dash from the hospital to the hairdresser to be home in time to see Greg for a few minutes after he came home from his flight, and before going on to Hussein and Sherrifa's party. Greg was already home when Jenny arrived. "Hiya baby, your parents send you their love. They were at the hotel when I arrived in London. They drove down to bring all these for us," said Greg, indicating a huge bag full of presents.

"That was really nice of them. I had mentioned in my last letter that you would be coming to London, but I didn't expect them to bring all these. I imagine that they will have made a day of it, though, and visited all the shops," she said reflectively.

"Yes, that's what they said they were doing. It's good of them to send all this, but I had a hell of a time with customs. I'm afraid most of them have been opened a bit."

"Never mind, we can tape them up until tomorrow. You can do mine and I will do yours. I bought us a little plastic tree, and we can put them underneath it and open them in the morning."

"Okay love, whatever makes you happy," he replied with a slightly parental tone that Jenny chose to ignore. Greg looked at his watch. "We only have about half an hour before we need to leave for the party. I think we'd better get a move on. Has everyone accepted our invitation for tomorrow?"

"Yes, there will be twelve of us."

Good, have Ranna and Hala got everything ready?

"Yes, darling. They won't let me touch anything. They have even asked one of their relatives to take care of the drinks. He sometimes works in the hotel bars and is very good at mixing cocktails."

"Good, now let's get moving," ordered Greg.

"Yes sir, captain sir," said Jenny responding to his rather authoritarian tone.

They arrived at the party on time, along with several other guests, and were greeted effusively by Sherrifa and more formally by Hussein. Their sumptuous villa was filled to capacity with guests who stood chatting in all of the reception rooms. Somewhere, some vaguely Christmassy music was playing, but it was being drowned out by the sound of peoples' conversations. Later in the evening, the number of guests had reduced significantly, leaving mainly airline crew who Jenny was familiar with and Sherrifa's parents and some local dignitaries who held prominent positions in the country. She also noted that Hussein and Sherrifa's son was home from boarding school. A handsome young man of fourteen, with impeccable manners. Greg soon left Jenny and migrated to a group of other pilots who were deep in technical conversation. Jenny, unsurprisingly, found Betty and fell into conversation with her.

"Hi, Jen, seems like the world an' his wife are here tonight. There must be over a million bucks' worth of jewelry in this room alone."

"Hi, Betty, yes, I know what you mean. I feel quite underdressed, and yet when I left home, I thought I was dressed to the nines."

"You look just fine, honey. At your age, you don't need any sparklers to make ya look good," complimented Betty.

"Thank you, Betty, I like your outfit too. Is it new?"

"Yeah, it is. I found this real neat dressmaker downtown, an' she ran it up for me. It didn't cost me hardly anythin' either."

Sherrifa interjected at that moment. "Ladies, we are going to eat now. If you are ready, we weel go into za dining room," she told them in her attractive French-accented English.

They joined the rest of the guests who were heading towards the dining room. Jenny had never seen such a display of food before. It was a buffet that stretched the whole length of the room. On the table was every kind of delicacy imaginable, adorned with elaborate ice carvings. There was an audible "Ooh!" from most of the guest as they saw the table laden with its tempting cornucopia of delights.

After they had sampled the delicious spread, Betty and Jenny fell back to chatting again. Betty, astute as ever, had been watching the guests closely and had been making some observations.

"Jenny, have you noticed how relaxed Monique is this evenin'? Usually she is pretty uptight at these functions, wonderin' who her infamous husband is likely to be embarrassin' her with. Tonight, she looks radiant, and I notice that she has been talkin' a whole bunch with Hussein. He looks like he's enjoyin' himself too."

"Yes I must agree that she does look beautiful, but then again, she always does. I envy her tall, slim build and her golden-haired, classic beauty. I expect that she and Hussein have something in common after having gone through the hijack together."

"Yes, an' I gotta feelin' that it might have done just a bit more than that."

"Heavens Betty, you are always reading things into situations. Anyway, do you know any more details about the hijack?"

"Not too much, the authorities are keepin' real quiet about it. But it seems that the hijack failed because their chain of command broke down. On the day of the hijack, their headquarters had been the target of an enemy military faction and was destroyed. Those that were supposed to give instructions to the hijackers were killed, then the whole shebang just fell into shambles. Thank the Lord that Hussein is such a strong character and was able to gain the confidence of the gunmen or else there could have been a real tragedy happen."

"He has certainly won the undying admiration of all the crew and most of the people of the country. He's a brave man," Jenny concurred. Looking over to where Hussein was standing, Jenny noted he was deeply engaged in conversation with Monique in a small recess of the room. Hussein had been unable to visit Monique since their first encounter; they had only been able to communicate by telephone.

Looking deep into her eyes, Hussein told her, "I'm glad so that we can, at least, have the opportunity to talk together a little this evening. It seems an age since our first evening together. You look absolutely lovely tonight. I wish we were anywhere but here."

"I know, my dear, I have missed you too. I think more has transpired between us than we can comprehend. I would like to see you alone again soon," Monique invited.

"I will arrange something as soon as I possibly can, even if I have to alter the roster to do it. Let's go into the other room, as I can see that some of the guests have started dancing. At least if we dance, I can have you in my arms again."

They began dancing to the slow Latin rhythm that was playing. However, the temptation to pull close to each other was overwhelming. Hussein was squeezing her had so tightly that her fingers were turning white. Her very proximity aroused all his senses. He felt the rush of desire for her flood through him.

149

"God, Monique, I can't dance with you. I want you so much that the whole room will notice. I need to sit down somewhere." They danced towards a dimly lit area of the room where two chairs were situated, and unobtrusively left the floor.

"Monique, you have no idea how much I desire you. I feel like a young buck again. I just hope that you don't think it's disrespectful of me."

"No, my love, I can feel and reciprocate your emotions. I was overwhelmed too," she said gently, trying to control the flush she felt rising from her body to her face.

"Why did this have to happen now," lamented Hussein, "when I'm about to go away on the course for six weeks? Can I call you while I am away? I have a copy of next month's roster, so I'll know when Nikos will be flying and you will be alone."

"Of course, you can. I was hoping that somehow we might be able to keep in touch while you are away."

"Unfortunately, there will be no opportunity to see you alone before I have to leave, but at least, I can see you tomorrow at Greg and Jenny's dinner."

"Yes, with luck we can snatch a few minutes alone together like this," she whispered.

Sherrifa had finished her ministrations over the buffet table and was talking with Nikos, in the now-empty dining room. "Are you looking forward to your trip to the States? It is very close now, and are you still as keen on taking Greg under your wing?" Nikos asked her conspiratorially

"Oui, mon chère," she rejoined in perfect French, "what makes you think I would change my mind? Have you gone off the little English rose, perhaps?"

"Gone off her, my dear? I can hardly wait to get her charming little body into bed. I don't go near her, in case I say too much. She is very hard to resist, especially as she is so much in love with her dear husband. The challenge is going to be a new experience for me."

"Well, I think it is about time that she woke up to the real world, don't you?" Sherrifa said with contempt in her voice.

"Yes, Chichi, but I can't help feeling just a pang of guilt in being the one who is going to be responsible for bursting her bubble," he feigned remorse.

"Guilt only enslaves you and makes you miserable. Just play the game to win, and enjoy the spoils of victory," she countered with conviction.

Nikos did not need any persuading. He had little time for guilt himself, and like Sherrifa, he did not like to lose. He had learned early on in his life that unless he outsmarted his six siblings, he would be the one who came out worst of any situation. Being second youngest had left him in a vulnerable position. He was ousted from his position as the baby of the family when he was four years old, leaving him bitter and resentful towards his new baby brother. All his life, he had tried to compensate for the loss that he felt. He took the best of everything whenever he had the occasion, and at whatever the cost. Disillusioning Jenny would prove no barrier to his goal. He had only some slight doubts about Greg and his reaction to Sherrifa's overtures. It was obvious that he was no philanderer, but he was ambitious for his career to move in the right direction. Surely he would understand that Sherrifa was the key to gaining access to those in positions of authority. He himself had learned that years ago, but he had been deeply in love with her at the time of their affair. He questioned whether Greg would be willing to pay the price of success. Sherrifa was certainly beautiful and desirable, but he doubted whether Greg would be willing to jump to her tune every time she snapped her fingers. Nikos had not quite got the measure of Greg yet. *Well, only time will tell*, he reflected.

Shortly after twelve, the party began to break up. The 25th was a working day and many people had flights or offices to go to in the morning. On the way home, Jenny was unusually quiet.

"Are you alright, Jen, you're very quiet?" asked Greg, who was feeling particularly pleased with his liaisons this evening.

"I'm all right, but I am wondering how our dinner party is going to follow tonight's. I am feeling rather inadequate," she confessed.

"Jenny, no one will expect you to live up to Sherrifa's standard, believe me. They will just be happy to receive your hospitality," Greg reassured her.

Jenny allowed herself to be pacified by Greg's reassurances, but still in her heart, she was dreading the forthcoming evening, and there was something that she could not quite grasp that was niggling at the back of her mind that gave her a feeling of insecurity.

When the evening came, Jenny was surprised to find Greg's words to be true. All of the guests settled into the warm, unpretentious atmosphere of Jenny and Greg's apartment. Ranna and Hala had worked all day long to produce a buffet-table full of tempting food that was excellently cooked, bringing comments of praise from all the guests. They were lavish in their admiration of the splendid situation of the apartment and its well-planned architecture. Despite most of the guests having expensive villas, the design of them was not with the latest innovations that Greg and Jenny's exclusive apartment had been.

After dinner was finished, Greg asked Hala and Ranna to push back the furniture in the lounge so guests could dance if they wished. Those who did not were able to sit and chat in the reception room that faced the ocean. Jenny had borrowed some chairs from Hilda to furnish the room as they did not, as yet, have enough to fill all the rooms. As protocol demanded, Greg asked Hussein if he might dance with Sherrifa. "Of course, be my guest," he told him, seizing the opportunity to find Monique and spend a few quiet moments with her.

Nikos seized the moment to take advantage of the situation as well and invited Jenny to dance. "This is a lovely party, Jenny."

"Thank you, Nikos, you can't imagine how much I have worried over it."

"Well, let your worries be over now. Everyone is enjoying themselves, even Sherrifa," he said, unable to resist pointing out how she and Greg were enjoying a joke together whilst dancing. Jenny looked across and felt a pang of jealousy at seeing them dancing so happily together. They looked a handsome pair dancing stylishly to the beat of the latest disco music.

"Yes, she does look happy. I would hate to upset her in any way. She is such a prominent figure that it would mean immediate social death if she was not pleased at a function, I am given to understand."

"You are given to understand correctly. Sherrifa is very well-connected and as far as the airline is concerned, she is the one who sets the social agenda," he confirmed, then swiftly changing the subject, he made a play to ingratiate himself with Jenny. "Dear, Jenny," he began in a paternal gentle tone that belied his true intentions, "I hope you have forgiven me for that awful first night when we met. I have relived it again and again in horror many times. You and Greg are such lovely people that I would hate for you to still think badly of me."

"Oh, that's all forgotten about. I know how moody Greg gets sometimes when he has been flying on maximum hours. I think it goes with the job."

"Thank you, Jenny," he murmured. The music slowly faded at that point, and he decided to leave her while he was suitably restored in her good graces. He thanked her for the dance and moved over to talk to some of the other crew members.

Greg asked if Sherrifa would care to continue dancing, since she made no move off the floor.

"Yes, I am having a lovely time. Let's dance some more," she purred in Arabic. They continued to dance for some time together, with Greg enjoying Sherrifa's considerable charm and grace. When the bartender decided it was time to change the pace a little and put Julio Iglesias' latest ballad on, Greg felt unsure of whether to continue dancing, but since Sherrifa held up her arms expectantly, he became aware that it would be impolite not to continue. He was very cognoscente of her seductive presence near to him and pulled away slightly, not wishing to embarrass her.

"I just love this sensual music, don't you?" she said pulling him closer again.

"That man does have a bedroom voice, I must admit," he answered, allowing himself to be drawn close to her.

When the song had finished, Sherrifa thanked him for the dance and returned to where she had been sitting. Nikos soon joined her. "I see that you are starting the chase early."

"Oui c'est vrai, I think I am going to have fun," she said, almost purring with pleasure and anticipation. Greg's proximity had awakened a powerful lustfulness in her.

Peggy Gallagher came over and joined them. She talked for a while and then looked pointedly at Nikos. "Would you care to dance?" he offered, knowing that was what she had in mind. Peggy agreed and they took to the floor.

"I'm sorry that I haven't been to see you for a while, Peggy, but I have been flying nonstop."

"Not too busy to see that little tart of a hostess that fascinates you so much. Anyway, I just want to tell you that I have finally come to my senses and can see what an idiot I have been making of myself over you. I was foolish enough to believe all your lies; I really thought that we had a future together. Now I can see things for what they are. You have used me as a convenience, as you do all the women in your life. I have had a long talk with John, and we are going to try and build back our relationship. We had a good marriage before you came onto the scene."

"Is that why he had an affair with your best friend, Clare?" he said ruthlessly, unable to resist the chance to bring her down again.

"John told me about Clare, and I don't hold it against either of them. We all make mistakes in our marriages, especially in the flying profession. The important thing is that the marriage recovers from the blows that it takes. John and Clare have more than stood by me during my foolishness with you. Forgiving them was nothing in comparison to what they have seen me through. I can already see where you are headed with your next victim," Peggy said, indicating Jenny with an inclination of her head. "Can't you ever leave things alone?"

"Why should I leave things alone, when there is something out there that I want?" he said to torment her.

"Because some people have different values than you and because it is shameful to think of shattering that young woman's innocence. She loves her husband, just leave them alone."

"How long do you think she is going to stay so dewy-eyed about her husband? I don't know many marriages that can withstand the strain of our kind of life. They either break up very early or they learn to play the game," Nikos drawled sarcastically.

"Well playing the game almost cost me my life. Everyone that plays it takes a risk," Peggy shot back angrily.

"Yes, that's exactly what makes it worth playing," he told her, scorning her newfound fidelity.

"One day, Nikos, someone is going to bring you to your knees, and I want to be there when that time comes," she said. breaking free from his grasp.

"Never," he laughed, as she walked away in disgust.

Peggy returned to her husband, and Nikos to Sherrifa. "What was that all about?" Sherrifa enquired.

"Dear Peggy has dismissed me. She's decided that she no longer wants my services, claims that she and John are going to work at their marriage," he said with mock sadness.

"And I'm sure you are brokenhearted," she said in mock sincerity.

"I'm damn glad to get her off my back. It was fun in the beginning, but she became too obsessive in the end. It became a liability."

"Yes, it is good that she has cooled off. She was getting to be an embarrassment at social occasions. Good luck to her, at least she survived," said Sherrifa with unusual compassion.

The evening wound up congenially, with guests leaving around midnight. Jenny was relieved and delighted that the evening had gone so well.

"It was a good evening wasn't it?" she asked Greg.

"It was sensational. Everyone had a good time, and you were a great little hostess," he replied, picking her up and swinging her around. The sound of Hala and Ranna's voices broke their intimate moment as they entered the lounge. The two of them and their relative were ready to leave. "Madam, everything is clean in the kitchen. We come tomorrow and do cleaning. You not touch," said Hala.

"Thank you all so very much for making this evening a success. Take your time in the morning. Don't come too early; we all need a rest after today," said Jenny.

"You are most welcome," they responded in unison, and left chatting excitedly about the evening's event in the cool night air.

Greg and Jenny fell gratefully into bed and slept till late the next morning. Jenny was reluctant to get out of bed, feeling that if they stayed in bed for longer, it would somehow hold the day back a little. She was depressed at the thought of Greg's departure the next morning, and was dreading packing his infernal Samsonite suitcase, that she had come to hate so much. The packing proved to be an emotional ordeal for her. Each item of clothing they put in the suitcase made her feel like she was losing another small part of him. In the end, she could not hide the tears and the sense of abandonment she was feeling.

"Oh, Jenny, you have got to learn to be tougher than this. I am not going away forever, you know. It's only six weeks."

"I know, but to me, it will seem like forever. You'll be busy studying for your course and won't feel the time passing. But for me, the time is going to hang heavily."

"Look, you've got your work at the hospital, and Fouad and Hilda will look after you. It's not going to be as bad as all that."

"I know, I suppose I am being silly, but it's just this bad feeling I have. I can't seem to shake it off."

"Jenny, I think you're just tired after all the stress of the party and working so hard at the hospital. Maybe you should think of cutting down the hours that you work there. We will be expected to entertain more now."

"No, no, I couldn't do that. Without my work, I would go crazy when you are away," she told him truthfully.

"Well, I don't want to see you in this state when I get back, or I will insist that you give it up."

Jenny looked at him, feeling hurt by his insensitivity. She had never really broken down before in front of him, and she was surprised by his lack of compassion. "You could at least be a little sympathetic," she said accusingly.

"What do you want me to do?" he shot back angrily. "Tomorrow, I'm leaving to do a demanding course, and I don't need to be burdened with a neurotic wife at home that cannot cope."

Jenny ran out of the room, slamming the door hard behind her. *That was too much of an insult to take*, she thought, her depression turning into anger. Greg finished the rest of his packing alone, annoyed by Jenny's attitude. He stayed in the bedroom for some time after finishing the packing, studying the course manual, unwilling to face Jenny in her present mood. Jenny, still furious from the sting of Greg's words, decided to turn her anger into something constructive and went into the kitchen to make dinner, taking out her anger out on the pots and pans which she clattered with unnecessary force. Eventually her mood lifted and reason prevailed. *I am tired*, she reflected, *and it is thoughtless of me to send Greg off in this way*. Walking into the bedroom, she said, "Dinner's on the table if you're ready," offering him a bright smile.

Responding to her conciliatory tones, he joined her in the large kitchen.

"This is nice. What is it?" enquired Greg.

"It's shepherd's pie, but I have added some fresh tomatoes and some garlic to it to spice it up a bit."

"Mmm, well it's very nice," he told her, continuing to smooth her ruffled feathers.

"Greg, I'm sorry about before. Please don't worry about me; you know I'll be all right."

"That's my girl," said Greg brightening. "I'll be back in no time, you'll see, and we'll make up for lost time."

Jenny steeled herself the next morning, absolutely determined not to let her feelings show. She waved Greg off with cheerful smile and then returned to the bedroom and cried out all of her repressed misery. After regaining her composure, she got up and washed her face with cold water and reapplied some makeup and set off for the hospital. At lunchtime, she met Candy in the canteen and told her of the events of the past few days.

"It sounds like you have had a really busy time of it over the holidays," said Candy.

"Yes, it was hectic, but I just can't shake this bad feeling I have over Greg leaving."

"Yes, I know how it can be. I've experienced the same thing, in the past, with Farris sometimes. You shouldn't worry too much." Candy did not go on to mention the fact that when she'd had the bad feelings, it had turned out to be the occasions when Farris had been unfaithful to her. *Jenny*, she reflected, *did not need to hear that right now*, hoping to hell that it would turn out to be nothing. She decided that a change of subject was required. "Oh Jenny, Mariella wants to see you. It seems that your test results are ready."

"Great, at least I'll find out if everything in that department is all right." Jenny saw Mariella later in the day and arranged to meet her and Nader later in the evening.

At the appointed hour, Jenny presented herself at Nader's office. "Well Jenny, I am happy to tell you that there is nothing physical on your side that will prevent you from conceiving," said Nader with a beaming smile. "You have a clean bill of health. Without seeing your husband, I cannot venture any guesses as to why you have not yet conceived. But sometimes, these things do take time. You can tell your husband that I would see him in strict confidentiality, if you think it is appropriate."

"Oh, that's good news, but I'm not sure whether Greg would come for tests. But if the opportunity arises, I will try and convince him."

"Good, now just go and relax. Sometimes that's the best method of conception. Often when all the pressure to conceive goes away, then things just begin to happen on their own," he said reassuringly. Thanking them both for their trouble, Jenny left the hospital and drove back to the apartment.

Ensconced in her new luxury apartment, she put on the kettle and reflected on how much nicer it was here than in the previous apartment. She knew Hilda would soon be popping round to check on her and invite her to eat with them. Sometimes she was happy to share the evening meal with them, but tonight she wanted to be alone and collect her thoughts.

CHAPTER EIGHT

The betrayal, Greg and Sherrifa

Greg, along with the other crew members, had reached their destination by late afternoon U.S. time. Their West Coast desert location was hot and dry and its most prominent natural features were sand and an abundance of Joshua trees dotting the landscape. They got settled in the comfortable, small villas provided for them. Greg found that he was sharing with Farris, Candy's ex-husband. They were both happy enough with the arrangement, agreeing to study together as the course demanded. The course did not start for two days, allowing the crew to catch up with their jet lag and orientate themselves. A welcoming party had been arranged for them on the second evening. It was mainly male-dominated, except for some wives of the course instructors and, of course, Sherrifa and her small entourage. Greg and Farris, finding that they enjoyed each other's company, attended the reception together and spent a jovial evening with some of the locals who were quite curious about life in the Middle East. Wayne, a rather oversized instructor from Kansas, began asking them about their customs and habits.

"It sure is interesting to learn about how other folks live. We get pilots from all over the world coming here, and I try to learn a bit from all of them. Now tell me, don't you folks have all sorts of religions like Coptic and Maronite where you come from? What religion are you guys?"

Feeling that Wayne had been quite personal and blunt in his question, Greg and Farris exchanged knowing looks and, with a look of merriment in their eyes, decided to derail the conversation. "Now Farris, I never did ask you what religion you are?" enquired Greg with mock sincerity.

"Oh me, well I am a Samsonite. What about you Greg?"

"What a coincidence," answered Greg, trying hard to keep a straight face, "so am I. What about you Wayne, what's your religion?"

"Me, I'm a Baptist," he replied suspiciously, unsure of whether they were being serious.

However, it had the desired effect, and he refrained from asking such personal questions of them. Greg and Farris found that they had much in common and spent the rest of the evening joking and generally having a good time.

Sherrifa, noticing their jocularity, approached them. "Well, you two seem to be having a great time all by yourselves," she said, remonstrating with them slightly.

"Not really, but in the absence of wives and girlfriends, we have reverted to schoolboy level. I'm sorry, we had better behave ourselves," answered Greg.

"Yes, you better had, at least until the course is finished, and then it is a different matter," she said while pointedly looking at Greg. She walked away gracefully, but not before she had afforded Greg a long, meaningful glance.

"Wow," said Farris, "lucky you, I wish I was the one that got that look. She's a gorgeous woman and powerful, too."

"Yes, that's what makes her so dangerous. She's got Hussein right where she wants him, and she is more or less a free agent. Her Daddy adores her and will not hear a bad word said about her. And Daddy is one of the most influential men in our country," said Greg.

"On second thought, I would rather not be you. I'm too fond of my freedom, although I wouldn't mind trying to get back with my wife again. I regret messing that up."

"She sounds very nice. My wife, Jenny, talks about her. They work together at the hospital."

"Yes, that's right, Candy talks a lot about Jenny. They seem to be good friends. Perhaps we can all get together for an evening when we get back. It would give me an opportunity to work on Candy."

"Sure, whatever I can do to help," volunteered Greg helpfully.

The course was not too demanding for either Greg or Farris. They worked hard and well together and had a good grasp of the theoretical matter ahead of time. They were more than ready to take the exam, and both were rewarded with excellent results. Greg had called Jenny a couple of times from the States to see how she was doing, and planned to call her this evening to tell her the good news. They had to stay only another week and then they would be home again. He was feeling pleased with himself at how well the course had gone. In some ways, he had shared Jenny's misgivings about going away, and now that the end was in sight, he felt relieved that all had gone without a hitch.

The phone rang, interrupting his flow of thoughts. "Hello, yes?"

"Marhaba Greg, this is Sherrifa. I'm calling to congratulate you on your success," she purred in Arabic.

"Thank you very much, Sherrifa, it is very kind of you to think of me."

"Thinking of you is something that I don't find too hard to do," she said forthrightly.

Greg was aware of her inviting tone and chose his words very carefully. "Sherrifa, I don't know what to say. If you were any ordinary woman I could tell you how beautiful I find you and how pleasant it is to think of you, too. But you are one of the most powerful women in our country, we are both married and your husband is my superior."

"Greg, do not be afraid to approach me. Pleasing me can bring you great rewards," she said, allowing the unspoken threat to hang in the air, that displeasing her could bring about entirely the opposite effect. "Listen, Hussein has been invited to go and see some famous place of interest, which means he will be staying away overnight. I have declined to go on the grounds that I have a migraine. I will be all alone in the villa tonight and in need of some company. Can I expect you to come and be my companion?" she asked, knowing that he had little choice but to agree.

"Of course, Sherrifa, whatever you want. What time shall I come over?" he answered mechanically, knowing that he was at her mercy.

"Nine o'clock is good. I'll see you then." She replaced the handset of the phone, rejoicing that she had gotten her way with Greg. Her thoughts turned to the method of seduction she would use on him.

Greg stared dismally at the phone's receiver in his hand. *What am I letting myself in for*, he thought looking at his options. If she were any ordinary attractive woman, he might well have entered in a casual relationship with her just for the conquest. But Sherrifa was a different matter. He could not risk offending her. He knew he had little choice but to acquiesce to her demands, but what price would he have to pay? Greg had always been his own man, never allowing anyone else to call the shots, but all that stood to change now. *Well*, he thought, *there is little else I can do but leave things to chance.*

Farris walked in from the bedroom, interrupting Greg's thoughts. "Anyone interesting on the phone?" asked Farris.

"No, just one of the crew asking if we had any Arabic coffee," he lied, eager to keep Farris from suspecting what had just transpired.

"I hope you didn't offer ours. We only have enough to last a couple more days before we run out and we can't get any more around here."

"No, don't worry, I didn't," Greg replied casually, trying to hide the torment that was possessing him at this moment.

"Hey, let's take a drive into town today. I heard that there's a good Armenian deli where we can pick up some more coffee and stuff. Some of the crew found it the other day," offered Farris.

"Sorry, I really don't fancy a long, hot drive into town today. We can cut down on the coffee until we leave," he said in a preoccupied manner. Greg did, however, agree to shoot some pool with him at the recreation room to pass the time. One of the course instructors joined them and invited them to meet later on that evening. To allay any suspicions, Greg agreed to go along with Farris. However, when the evening came, Greg complained of feeling sick and told Farris to go without him. After Farris's departure, he phoned Sherrifa to confirm that everything was as planned for the evening. She told him that all was well and invited him to come over earlier if he was ready. He showered quickly and made his way over to her villa.

Sherrifa had ensured that the ambience in the villa was suitable for seduction. Satisfied that the heavily perfumed, dimly lit lounge was to her liking, she lay back on the sofa and put an expensive cigarillo between her lips, lighting it with a bejeweled lighter. She drew heavily on the sweet smoke and sipped from her equally expensive glass of red wine. The thoughts of the forthcoming evening were sending anticipatory sensations of delight through her whole body. She loved to feel this way.

The only bothersome thing threatening to spoil her evening was an uneasy feeling of guilt that had never quite left her since Nikos had voiced his slight misgivings about seducing the vulnerable couple. Within Sherrifa there was a latent capacity

165

for compassion and kindness, but from an early age, she had fought to repress such feelings, identifying them as weaknesses that would prevent her from attaining her goals. Ever since she was an astute child of seven and saw how wives were subservient to their husbands, she had reasoned that in order to be more than just an appendage to some man, she would have to manipulate those around her. If she gave way to pity and remorse, she would remain less than average in status, a position that was abhorrent to her. Until her brother was born, when Sherrifa was seven years old, she had believed that the whole world belonged to her. She had been the only child of wealthy, adoring parents who gave her anything her heart desired. However, when Ezert was born, she quickly learned that her elevated status had been usurped and that she would have to play only a supporting role to him. Her anger and disgust knew no bounds. She quickly learned the mechanisms of power that operated in the Middle East and found the best way to improve her situation. Her father, she found, was very susceptible to her charms, and she only had to do little kindnesses for him in order to win him over. She learned that pleasing him brought the rewards of his indulgence towards her. She spent her youth pleasing him with excellent scholastic achievements and social expertise. She became the model daughter for him, but him alone. Her mother, she had little time for, perceiving her as weak and accommodating. Her brother, she hated with a passion, and if she could ever do him a disservice, she did not hesitate to do so. For it was *he* who could move freely in their country with no restrictions upon him, it was *he* who could sow his wild oats around the world with the tacit approval of family and friends, it was *he* who had all the privileges of being a male, while *she* was a woman, who had all the same wishes and desires, but was restricted to the confines of her house, and houses of a few suitable friends in her country. She wanted the same freedoms that her brother had and the power that went with it. Her father was her passport to that power and, for him, and only him, she was prepared to be subservient. Taking another sip of her wine, she dismissed the slight guilt feelings, and succumbed totally to the warm glow of anticipation. Hearing the soft dingdong of the bell, she rose slowly to her feet and opened the door for Greg.

"Good evening, Sherrifa, you look wonderful this evening," he said appreciatively, looking at the silk dress that enticingly skimmed her voluptuous body.

"I'm glad you like it. I dressed for you this evening," she purred.

"I am flattered," responded Greg enthusiastically.

"What can I get you to drink?" she enquired with a seductive smile playing about her lips.

"Whatever you are having is fine for me." Filling a glass of wine, she indicated to him to sit down on the sofa.

Greg felt less uncomfortable than he had expected. Somehow in this seductive atmosphere, he felt removed from the rest of the world. Removed from guilt and responsibility, he soon relaxed and entered the mood of the evening that had been so carefully planned for him.

"Shall we dance?" he invited her, hearing the throaty, seductive voice of Jane Birkin singing "J'taime" on the FM station that Sherrifa was tuned to.

"Of course," she smiled at him, happy that he had the guts to pick up on her lead and take over the seduction. As the song progressed, they both quickly became influenced by the sensuous lyrics and the effects of the wine. Soon Greg's hands were travelling the entire length of her body as if they possessed a will of their own. Their bodies were swaying together almost in simulation of copulation.

"Come," said Sherrifa, indicating the way to the bedroom. "Let's go and have some fun." Greg followed her, only slightly losing the impetus of the passion that had arisen in him. Pausing at the bedroom door, Sherrifa addressed him, "Darling, I have to ask you one slightly inconvenient thing. You must wear a condom, since I am temporarily off the contraceptive pill."

"You don't have to worry about that," responded Greg. "I have a very low sperm count due to a childhood illness, and the chances of you conceiving are remote." He surprised himself by volunteering this information that he was usually so sensitive about. He had been unable to tell Jenny about it, fearing she would reject him for being unable to give her children. It was a secret that only few people knew, yet now he had volunteered it, as if sensing it was acceptable.

"Well, what a nice surprise, we can have all the fun of sex with none of the inconvenience of birth control," she replied, happy about the situation and storing the fact for possible later use. Something told her that Jenny did not know about this.

Sherrifa's reaction had a stimulating effect upon Greg, who never imagined a woman would find his lack of fertility a bonus. He was more than ready to make love to her. Sensing this, she pulled away a little, "No, mon chère, I have something special planned for you." Sherrifa was eager to make a lasting impression upon him. She wanted to hook Greg, not just have a passing affair with him.

"Just stand there and wait and watch." Standing in front of him, she unhooked her silk dress, letting it slide to her feet. She stepped out of it and stood before him in only a slinky camisole. Slowly, she walked over to the large bed where she slipped her hands through silken cords that she had previously tied to the four corners of the bed. She wiggled down the bed snaking her feet into the two cords tied to the foot of the bed, leaving her lying spread-eagled on the bed. The flimsy camisole had ridden up revealing the fact that she was not wearing panties. Smiling at Greg she told him, "Come and enjoy. Tonight, you can do as you want with me, and I will not do anything to stop you."

The spectacle of Sherrifa laying this way on the bed sent desire flaming through his body. He tore off his clothes, the urge to take this woman, to have mastery over her was overwhelming. Kneeling in front of her, he grabbed her hips and pulled her roughly upwards and jammed himself into her. Sherrifa gasped at the unaccustomed roughness but felt the pain mingle with pleasure in a new and exciting way. He pulled her back and forth as far as the bonds would allow him to, feeling an intense, animal-like pleasure in copulation without the need to consider the pleasure of his partner. Sherrifa was initially unprepared for such roughness, but with each thrust of his organ, unexpected sensations of pleasure shot through her body. Within seconds, she felt her body beginning to convulse in uncontrollable orgasm. She let out a deep-throated moan which filled Greg with an urgent need to climax too. He pulled her body closer, pushing into her as far as he could, succumbing to the pleasure of orgasm with a loud animal-like grunt. Falling on his elbows, he looked at Sherrifa, wondering whether his loss of control had been too much for her. She was lying with her back arched, trying to catch her breath. "Shall I help you out of those bonds?" he asked quietly.

"Yes, get them off me. I need to be able to move," she answered in a slightly abrupt tone.

"Was I too rough for you?" he asked her.

"No, no one has ever taken me like that. It was a new experience, and it gave me a different sense of pleasure."

"I am glad it pleased you. Seeing you lying there tethered left me with little control. The last thing I wanted to do was to hurt you." As Greg spoke, he knew he was lying. In that moment, when he saw her lying virtually helpless on the bed, he wanted not only to screw her but to debase her. He had to restrain himself from the urge to hurt her. It would have been easy to mark her beautiful skin. It was not a sensation that he was proud of, nor one that he wished to repeat. It had left him with an uncomfortable feeling of remorse.

"I am intrigued by the new feelings that I have experienced tonight. I'm sure we will try the bondage game again. But let's eat something now, as I'm very hungry," she said taking control of the situation again.

She slid into an expensive-looking dressing gown and threw him a toweling robe and led him into the breakfast room. She uncovered a tray of rye bread canapés topped with every kind of indulgent delicacy. "There must be something here that you like, come eat," she urged, noticing Greg's reticence.

"Thank you," he said, taking a canapé spread with pate de foie gras. He did not enjoy the feeling of a woman providing food for him, as it went against his nature. He was the one who wanted to be the provider, to watch the woman eat the food that he had bought. It was important for him to be in control. Greg fought with his feelings. He did not want to be here, yet to deny this woman what she wanted was to risk his career. Sherrifa, sensing his mood, began to speak of the airline. She was not prepared to let this man go. What she had experienced with him this evening had left her wanting more of him. There was something about him that attracted her in a way that she was unaccustomed. It was not just his obvious physical attributes. There was something more that she had not yet identified.

"Greg, you know that when we return, the airline will need more executive staff because of the arrival of the new wide-bodied jets. With your excellent record of achievements, I feel sure that Hussein will be considering you for a position."

"Do you really think so?" he responded eagerly. "I thought that I might be considered too young to take such a position, considering that I have not had my command for that long."

"True," she nodded, "the executive staff is usually selected from the more experienced captains, but we are moving to reduce the amount of nonessential foreigners in the company, as there are more of our nationals coming up through the ranks now. This leaves you well-placed for promotion."

"That's really great news. Thank you for telling me that," he said appreciatively.

"Well, if you want to express your gratitude properly, you had better come over here and show me," she told him, opening her silk dressing gown invitingly.

She was happy to have found Greg's weakness. Now she had a means of controlling him. Greg went over to her, delighted with the prospect of promotion. For that, he was prepared to dance to her tune. He could even get to like it. He perceived that she had some weakness for him physically, and he would be able to draw upon that. And if she enjoyed rough sex so much, he would have no trouble providing it for her. The mental image of her succumbing to him ensured his erection. Grabbing her hard, he pushed her onto the table top, sending the canapés flying to the floor. This time she was not passive. She entered into the dangerous game of pleasure and pain, biting him hard and digging her nails deep into his back. He responded in kind, but this time checking his responses the whole time to ensure that he did not do her any real harm. Their evening ended at three a.m. with Sherrifa promising to be discreet about their affair and him promising that the affair would continue when they returned home.

He crept into his villa hoping that Farris would be asleep. However, he was lying on the sofa, noisily cracking open sunflower seeds and munching the contents, whilst watching an old Western on the TV. "I thought you would be asleep by now," said Greg, annoyed that he had not been able to get in undetected.

"You look as if you have been mauled by a tiger," observed Farris, somewhat shocked by his disheveled appearance. "It must have been some night."

"You did not see me, okay?" said Greg, looking pointedly at Farris.

"I'm like the three monkeys: see no evil, hear no evil and speak no evil. But I'll tell you what, you should tell her to go easy on the perfume, because I surely can smell that evil," he replied humorously.

"Please, Farris, just keep your mouth shut about this. I don't want anything to get back to Jenny."

"Don't worry, your secret's safe with me. I don't envy your position, though. It's going to be hard for you jumping through hoops for her ladyship."

"Just leave that to me. I'll sort things out."

"Good luck," replied Farris and returned to his ancient cowboy movie.

CHAPTER NINE

Worlds are changing

Tomorrow, thought Jenny, *is going to be wonderful*, the seemingly endless days of waiting for Greg to return were over. She had missed him keenly. She had spent her time immersed with work at the hospital, taking on extra duties just to help pass the time between Greg's infrequent phone calls home. Now he was already on his way, and he would be arriving tomorrow afternoon. She had so much to show him, as she had bought several new pieces of furniture for the apartment. Hilda had insisted on coming with her to help, and had proved to be of great assistance in purchasing the furniture at a reasonable price. Hilda taught her that she should never agree to the first price that the seller came up with, and she should instead haggle until she brought down the price. In the beginning Jenny had felt cheap trying to argue about the price, but she had quickly come to understand that it was the expected way of buying here, and that you would be considered a fool if you did not bargain for the goods. Indeed, she came to see that it was part of the Arab culture, a practice that was enjoyed by both buyer and seller, with much celebration being made when a final price had been agreed upon. The apartment was greatly improved with its refurbishing. There were no more empty rooms, and everywhere had been graced by Jenny's tasteful touch.

It was three o'clock in the morning and Jenny was still wide awake. The imminence of Greg's arrival was making it impossible for her to sleep, and it had been ages since she had felt excited this way. *I must sleep*, she told herself, *or I shall not be at my best for Greg tomorrow*. Eventually, an hour later, she fell into a light sleep and woke at her customary hour of seven. A thrill of excitement shot through her, knowing it was only hours before Greg would be home. As she dressed, she decided to visit the hairdressers and pamper herself a little, so she would look her best for Greg.

"Hello, Madam Youssef," greeted Leila, happy to see Jenny again, "what can I do for you today?"

"I want to look beautiful. Captain Youssef is returning today, and I want him to see what he has been missing for all these weeks," stated Jenny with an unusual lack of modesty.

"Don't worry, madam, I weel do everything for you, and you weel see how beautiful you weel become. Do you have plenty of time?"

"Yes," said Jenny, "I have all the morning and half of the afternoon."

"Well, then I weel give you a whole day of beauty, ze epilation, ze massage, ze facial, manicure, pedicure and maquillage," Leila insisted, not unaware of the nice profit she would make from all of these treatments.

"That sounds wonderful. I'm all yours." *Being pampered seemed like a really good idea*, Jenny thought. In many ways, she had neglected herself during Greg's absence, feeling there was little point in doing much more than the basics to herself every day. Now her spirits had lifted, and she wanted to completely overhaul herself. She and Leila spent a pleasurable morning together. Leila devoted herself to attending to Jenny, letting her assistants deal with the other clients. However, in the early afternoon, two wives of prominent businessmen arrived and demanded Leila's services.

"I am very sorry, Madam Youssef, but I weel have to let one of ze other girls work on you for a while. It ees imposseeble for me to refuse to do what zees ladies want, or zey could stop attending my shop and zen my business is finished, you understand?" lamented Leila.

"I understand, don't worry, take your time. I am quite happy with one of the others." Jenny was a little disappointed to lose Leila's ministrations because her touch was particularly soothing and relaxing.

Leila left Jenny to fuss and fawn over the two women, spending the necessary amount of time on them that their status demanded. They were particularly animated, though Jenny could understand only snippets of their conversation as they were talking so fast in Arabic. When Leila returned to put the finishing touches to Jenny's makeover, she seemed a little quiet and withdrawn.

"You must be tired after all that fussing," offered Jenny.

"No, not at all," replied Leila obviously wrestling with some inner problem.

"Well, you look quite distracted. Is there some problem?"

"Oh, eet ees just those silly women. Zey are full of ze gossip, and zey were telling me zat Madam Al Fayez, who ees their friend, had talked to zem from America, and zey say she has a new lover."

In that moment, Jenny felt an overwhelming fear descend upon her, and she turned to ice inside. She struggled to maintain her composure and smiled weakly at Leila before saying, "Madam Al Fayez always seems to be the centre of attention. She always has something going on in her life."

"Yes, eet ees amazing zat she can get away weeth so much. She breaks all ze rules of our society, but no one ees powerful or clever enough to stop her," replied Leila, aware of the effect her words had on Jenny. The other women had been specific in naming Greg as Sherrifa's latest protégé, but Leila had stopped short of passing on that information to Jenny. However, she did feel that Jenny should be, at least, partly prepared for what she would eventually come to learn. She could not let Jenny greet her husband tonight in the firm belief that he had waited and pined for her, the way that she had for him. She loved Jenny's sweet and simple nature, but Leila also felt that it was time that Jenny was aware of the pitfalls around her. If she continued in her naive manner, she would be hurt worse. Leila felt badly about what she had said, but to have said nothing, she believed, would have been much worse.

"Let me get you a coffee," offered, Leila noticing that Jenny had turned rather pale.

"Thank you, that would be nice." Leila returned shortly with a steaming cup of Turkish coffee and presented it to Jenny. Normally, Jenny disliked the strong aromatic taste of it, but today, the strength and bitterness of the brew was just what she needed to bring her back to normal.

"Let us put ze finishing touches to zat beautiful face of yours and show zat husband of yours what a jewel he has got," said Leila, changing the subject.

It was three thirty p.m. by the time Jenny finished at the hairdressers. She drove home thoughtfully, trying to convince herself that whatever had been discussed at the hairdressers was very likely to be tittle-tattle for entertainment only. But she could not shake the nagging feeling that somehow Greg was involved. As she reached home and looked around their lovely new apartment, she felt reassured. What she and Greg had was something strong and solid like the new furniture and the cool marble walls of the hall. She decided to surprise Greg by driving up to the airport to meet him rather than wait for him to arrive home in the company crew bus. She had phoned Flight Operations, who told her that everything was on time for Greg's flight and to come to Operations to wait for him. By the time she set off for the airport an hour later, she had managed to reconcile her feelings. Until she heard it from Greg himself, she would trust in his fidelity. Today, she would allow nothing else to burst her bubble. She arrived fifteen minutes early, and the operations officer made her welcome and chatted to her in between talking over the radio. The flight arrived on time. She heard Greg's voice approaching operations and prepared to greet him. He was surprised to see Jenny waiting for him. He had forgotten just how lovely she was and was happy for the others to see his beautiful, obviously adoring, wife waiting for him.

Taking her into his arms for a kiss of greeting, he told her, "This is a lovely surprise. Have you been waiting long?"

"No, just about fifteen minutes, how are you, darling?" she asked him, her eyes searching his for any sign of betrayal.

"Fine, fine, look love, I just have a couple of things to do, so go to the car and I will be there in two minutes," he told her.

"Okay, darling, don't be long," she said with little expectation, knowing that a Middle Eastern two minutes could well become half an hour or even an hour.

Jenny walked outside to the car, and switched on the radio, settling in for a wait. However, within ten minutes she saw Greg appear at the door of operations, obviously still talking to someone, but making efforts to get away. He was inching out of the door bidding farewell, when Jenny saw an elegant bejeweled hand touch his arm. Biting her lip, she knew it was Sherrifa, but fought to maintain control. Greg turned and ran over to the car and jumped in. As Jenny pulled out, she saw a silhouetted Sherrifa in the doorway waving at them. Jenny forced a smile and a wave, and looked at Greg, who gave Sherrifa a military-style salute. "It must have been quite boring for Sherrifa while all of the crew were busy with the course," enquired Jenny, fishing for any available information.

"I don't think it was too bad for her. The resident staff's wives took her and the other wives to various places of interest, and judging by the excess baggage she had, she must have cleaned out most of the up-market stores in Los Angeles."

"Oh, that sounds reasonable," said Jenny, somewhat assured by his detached tone when speaking of Sherrifa. The rest of the journey home was spent in a pleasant exchange of news. On entering their apartment, Greg was delighted with Jenny's efforts. He approved of the new furniture, declaring that she has wonderful taste and would have to entertain more regularly now. After they had unpacked Greg's case and eaten dinner, Jenny curled up next to him on the sofa and began caressing him. Gently, he took hold of her hands and told her that he was really exhausted from the journey and needed some sleep.

"That's all right," said Jenny, who felt a little miffed yet understood that jet lag and fatigue often took their toll.

Greg got up and walked to the bathroom, grateful to be on his own. The pangs of remorse he was experiencing from his unfaithfulness with Sherrifa were making him feel wretched. Looking at Jenny's beautiful, innocent face was more than he could deal with right now. In the shower, he scrubbed himself until his skin almost bled. He felt that if he scrubbed hard enough, he would be able to eradicate all memory of his indiscretion. He vowed that he would somehow extricate himself from the impossible position he had got himself into with Sherrifa. He would tell her that he was not the man for her. This decision assuaged his conscience somewhat and left him able to face the prospect of being with Jenny again without guilt. Deep inside though, he was aware that he was only fleeing from the reality of what would most certainly take place again, but right now, he needed to be able to live with himself and his wife. *I must keep the thoughts of Jenny far removed from those of Sherrifa*, he thought. *Otherwise, I'm totally screwed.* Calmer now, in his newly reconciled mood, he was able to shout to Jenny that he was going off to sleep but was looking forward to waking up next to her in the morning.

Reassured, Jenny told him to sleep well and that she would see him in the morning. Settling down with a glass of wine, she tried to arrange her thoughts. She was loathe to admit it, but she had felt a definite suspicion of Greg ever since Leila had told her the news of Sherrifa's new conquest. Certainly, the protracted conversation between Greg and Sherrifa in operations had fuelled her suspicions, and his rejection of her advances this evening had surprised and hurt her a little. However, she reasoned, everything that had taken place could be explained away quite innocently, *Greg may not be the new protégé, the conversation in operations may have been purely social, and his rejection of me may have been due to genuine fatigue.* Still, the feeling would not go away, the feeling that something had taken place that would threaten her marriage. But she was at a loss to know what to do about it. *To confront Greg with it would be ludicrous and risk incurring his wrath. I can only wait and watch. Then if something is going on, I will be able to know for sure*, she reasoned. *Until then I can only go on as before, but at least if I'm aware of a potential situation, then I can prepare myself for it.* Having made this decision, she settled down with her latest novel and read for the rest of the evening.

Early next morning, Greg woke refreshed and happy to be home. He gently kissed Jenny awake and made love to her tenderly, treating her like a fragile doll. That is how he thought of her now, in comparison to the full-blooded Sherrifa, who could take him on as an equal. Jenny was the angel, sweet and caring, to be cherished. Sherrifa was the devil who would always be tempting and tormenting him. His guilt had been resolved in thinking this way, by viewing the two women in totally disparate ways. They lingered in bed after their lovemaking, catching up on the events that had transpired whilst they were apart.

Later in the morning Greg announced that he had to go up to the airport and see the Chief Pilot. "I'm hoping for some good news," he told her.

"Well, I will keep my fingers crossed," said Jenny, wondering what it could be about but not wishing to tempt providence by asking too much.

"Oh," said Greg, "you know that I stayed with your friend Candy's' ex-husband, Farris, while I was on the course. I thought that it might be nice if we invited them both for dinner, just the four of us. I understand that they are on good terms, and I think Farris would really like to get back with Candy. Maybe we can help them with that," he said brightly.

"I'll certainly give Candy a ring and ask her if she would like to do that, but I'm not sure that she will be ready for any reconciliation just yet. She was badly hurt in the past, and it took her a long time to rebuild her life," she said, knowing that Candy was so heavily involved with Khalil that any thoughts of patching things up with Farris would be inappropriate.

"Well, see what you can do, darling. I promised him that I would try to help," replied Greg, cognisant of needing to keep Farris as a close ally.

"Okay, what time will you be back from the airport?"

"I can't really say, but don't cook anything. We'll go out for dinner this evening somewhere special," he said smiling at her.

At the airport, Greg went straight to Hussein's office as requested. "Good morning, Greg," greeted Hussein, ushering him into his spacious office, "come in and sit down. How does it feel to be back home again?"

"Great, sir," he responded formally, knowing that Hussein kept friendship and business separate. "I understand that you wanted to see me."

"Yes, that's correct. First of all, congratulations on your achievement on the course. You performed better than anyone, well done."

"Thank you, sir," he responded, elated with the praise.

"I have watched your progress since you gained your command, and I'm very satisfied with your performance. Although it's unusual to give someone as young as you an executive position, I think it is appropriate. I'm thinking of appointing you as director of Safety and Standards. You have proved yourself to be very apt in matters theoretical as well as practical, and this job requires a good memory for facts and figures with the ability to apply it to the fleet. Would you be interested?"

"Yes, sir," replied Greg without hesitation and barely able to restrain his delight, "I'm more than willing to accept the post, thank you very much."

"Well then, you will have official confirmation by this evening, as soon as I get a letter typed up by the secretary. As you know, this is a new position, made necessary by the expansion of the fleet, so I'll need you to start fairly soon. Take a couple of days off to be with Jenny and report for duty on Sunday. Is that all right with you?"

"It is absolutely fine, sir," he replied, unable to repress a grin of pleasure any longer.

"Greg, there is something else, and this is off the record. My dear wife also thought that you would be a good candidate for a managerial position and made that quite clear to me. I want you to know that you would have been offered the post without her intervention," he told him seriously. Looking away from Greg, and fixing his eyes on the large blotter pad on his desk, he continued, "However, if you cross Sherrifa, I cannot guarantee how long the position will be secure for you. She has more influence than I do in this country." Greg did not know what to say. In those few short sentences, Hussein had shown that he was both aware that he and Sherrifa had had some kind of relationship and that he was virtually powerless to curb her. Greg respected and admired Hussein and immediately felt mortally ashamed of what he had done with Sherrifa.

"I'm sorry, sir," he stammered, not knowing what else to say.

"Don't be," he cut in, "you are not the first, and I doubt that you will be the last. Just go and do your job well and whatever else it takes." Hussein looked at Greg's distraught face and added, "Sherrifa and I lead separate lives. We live together only for appearances."

Greg nodded his understanding of what was being conveyed to him. "I'll do my best for the airline, sir. Thank you for your confidence."

Able to look Greg in the face again, Hussein smiled and ended their interview.

After Greg's departure that morning, Jenny phoned Candy at the hospital and passed on the invitation for her and Farris to come for dinner.

"Jen, it's kind of Greg to try and help Farris, but you know that I am very committed to Khalil, and he would flip his lid if he thought that I was having some sort of reconciliation dinner with Farris. Khalil has been asking about the possibility of us marrying, and I'm really tempted," said Candy excitedly.

"Oh, I'm really happy for you. When did all this happen?" responded Jenny enthusiastically.

"Well, Khalil has been suggesting it for a while, but I thought that it was too premature to consider, But as nearly three months have gone by since we began our relationship, I'm beginning to give it some serious thought. We do love each other, and I want to have someone of my own to be with. That way, I could still see my children and have a happy life too. The only problem is going to be telling Farris. He's not going to be too pleased about it, and he might make it difficult for me to see the children if I remarry."

"I understand how you feel, and I hope that you can convince Farris that you have the right to have a new life of your own. If I can help in any way, just let me know."

"Thanks Jen, I have to go. I've got some patients waiting."

Jenny put down the receiver, thinking that it would be a terrible shame if anything came between Candy and Khalil. She started towards the kitchen when the phone rang. Jenny was annoyed to find that it was Sherrifa.

"Allo chèree," she purred in her Anglo/French accent, "ow are you? Eet 'as been so long seence I saw you."

"Yes, hello Sherrifa," she said remembering to be polite, "how was your trip to the States?"

"Eet was rather boring, I am glad to be 'ome. Chèree, I am phoning to invite you to a leetle soiree tomorrow evening. I know zat Greg is not flying, and I believe he might have something to celebrate, so I weel expect both of you, yes?"

Jenny resented the fact that Sherrifa always seemed to know more about Greg's movements than she did, but she swallowed her indignation and told her they would be delighted to accept her invitation. Jenny stormed off to the kitchen to make herself a coffee, more for something to do than for the need of a drink. She clanked the cutlery drawer viciously, wishing it were Sherrifa's head she was beating. *Why can't that woman just mind her own business and leave us alone?* Jenny's suspicions were surfacing again, and she did not want to have to deal with them. She abandoned the cutlery drawer, deciding to go over to Hilda's for a coffee, knowing she would be welcome and could get her mind off things pertaining to the airline and everyone connected with it. She scribbled a quick note for Greg, saying where she was, and left.

On Greg's return, he collected Jenny from Hilda's and told her the good news of his promotion. "That's wonderful," she cried while hugging him tightly. "I know it's what you wanted. I imagine that I'll see even less of you now though."

"Well, it will mean that my days off are spent at the office, but I'll be home in the afternoons, and I'll be able to pick and choose my flights to some degree. But we will have a nice fat salary at the end of the month to compensate," he said grinning broadly.

Jenny thought that she would rather have more of Greg than the extra money and prestige, but restrained herself from saying so, not wishing to spoil his obvious pleasure.

"Did you talk to Candy? It would be nice to go out and celebrate with them this evening."

"Yes, I did, love, but I'm afraid that she's not really interested in reconciling with Farris. She said no."

"Why, what's stopping her?" he almost shouted. "I'm sure that they could make a go of it if they get back together. Convince her that she must come."

"Darling, it isn't as simple as that," said Jenny almost timidly.

"What's the problem then?" demanded Greg.

"It is not really a problem, but if I tell you, will you keep quiet about it?"

"Sure, I promise, tell me what it is," said Greg, curious to know what was going on.

"What it is," said Jenny, careful not to paint Candy in a poor light, "is that Candy has met someone else. She's in love with one of the senior doctors at the hospital, and they are planning to get married. So that, in a nutshell, is why she isn't interested in reconciling with Farris."

Greg raised his eyebrows and gave a low, whistling exhalation of breath. "Well, Farris is just going to love that," he said with a note of sarcasm. "Would you like to invite someone else to go out with us this evening and celebrate then?"

"Not really, I'd like it to be just you and I," said Jenny firmly.

"Alright, love, if that's what you want."

Jenny went off to the kitchen to make them a sandwich for their lunch, happy that she and Greg would be going out for dinner alone. It seemed a long time since they had done something special on their own. In the distance, she heard the phone ring and Greg answer it and start speaking rapidly in Arabic.

"Who was that?" she enquired as she carried in the sandwiches.

"It was Farris asking if Candy would agree to see him tonight."

"What did you tell him?" she asked, curious to know Farris's reaction.

"Oh, don't worry about it, it's taken care of. Let's have lunch."

Jenny was content to trust in Greg's ability to handle the situation and settled down to eat her lunch.

In the hospital reception, the phone rang out shrilly, disturbing the relative quiet that sometimes descended during lunchtime. Candy, startled in surprise, had been on the verge of switching the phone through to the operator and leaving for the cafeteria. "Hello, University Hospital, this is reception. How can I help you?" she said competently in Arabic.

"Hi, Candy, this is Farris. I need to see you urgently. Can I come over this evening?"

"Are the children all right?" asked Candy, alarmed by his tone.

"The children are fine. It's something else, and I'll come over at seven if that's all right with you."

Candy did not really want to see him this evening. Khalil was coming over, and she did not want anything to get in the way of their plans. Since Farris had been away in the States, she had experienced a new kind of freedom. Without his frequent phone calls and visits, she had felt like a free agent. Now that he was back and demanding to see her again, she was resentful that he was demanding of her time. However, for the sake of the children and the fact that he paid her rent, she felt unable to refuse him. "Sure, come over at seven and we will discuss whatever it is."

After she put down the receiver, she phoned through to Khalil and told him that Farris would be coming over this evening, so they would not be able to have dinner together as planned.

"Don't worry, darling," he told her, noting the disappointment in her voice, "We can have a late supper together to make up for it. I'll bring something tasty for us to eat. You know dear, I think the time has come for us to take steps to get married, that way we can ensure our privacy and respect."

"Yes, I think you are right. I won't keep you waiting any longer. I know my own mind and trust that you do too. I'm ready to get married to you now," she said determinedly.

"That's wonderful. I'm going to start things in motion," he said elated that she had finally agreed to his proposal.

The rest of the day flew by. Candy quickly tidied up the apartment before Farris's arrival, and poured herself a drink. He arrived shortly afterwards.

"Hi, Candy, I missed you while I was in the States. Being so far away from you gave me time to think about our relationship, and that's what I want to talk about this evening," he said, looking directly into her eyes.

"Oh," replied Candy, at a loss for the appropriate thing to say.

He put his arm around her and guided her to the sofa. "Listen, in the past I was not the most sympathetic or considerate husband, especially after we had the children, but I've come to understand that in spite of all the acrimony we went through in the past, I still care for you a great deal. I accept that most of the fault was on my part, and I want to have the chance to make it up to you. I want us to get back together again."

Candy was stunned at his words, as this was the last thing she had expected. She felt gratified that he had finally accepted his share of the blame for the breakup, and had this conversation taken place a year earlier, she might well have been tempted to return to him. But in the past twelve months, she had grown in self-confidence and begun to feel like a whole person again. Now that she had met and fallen in love with Khalil, she could not entertain the idea of going back to Farris. She chose her words with care.

"Farris, there is no doubt that a few years ago I loved you with all my heart, but in many ways, I was immature and couldn't handle the stresses and strains of being a wife and mother, especially a pilot's wife. Since we've been parted, I was forced to become independent and learn to live alone in a country that is not my own. I've had to learn to be strong and face my weaknesses. You, on the other hand, have been able to come and go as you like and lead whatever kind of life you chose. I have been desperately lonely living this way, with only the children's company to look forward to. I've had very little chance to meet and mix with anyone except those I work with. It has been a great struggle for me living this way, but I learned to accept it. However, in the course of my work, I have met someone who cares deeply for me and wants to marry me. I love him too, and although it may seem totally inappropriate now, I would like to think that you will not oppose me in any way." She looked at Farris's face, and noted that he did not seem surprised by her announcement.

"Candy, I still love you and I can offer you as much as this other man. Won't you reconsider?"

"You hurt me so much, Farris, especially with all the other women you had. I don't honestly think that I can put that behind me. I believe that with Khalil, I can find happiness and stability. He will be around all the time, and I'm sure I can trust him."

"What makes you think some doctor is going to be any more faithful than a pilot?" he asked, unable to keep the sarcasm from his voice.

"How do you know he is a doctor?" demanded Candy.

"Your dear friend Jenny's husband told me. See how much you can trust people?" he said maliciously.

Candy quickly reasoned that Jenny might have found it necessary to tell Greg about Khalil, due to the refusal of the proposed reconciliatory dinner. "I imagine that Jenny will have told him because I refused the dinner invitation for tonight. He would have needed an explanation. I'm surprised at Greg. Jenny trusts him implicitly, and she would not have expected him to mention anything to you."

"Well, you shouldn't be surprised. Greg is no more trustworthy than most of us," he said maliciously, wanting to blacken someone else's reputation in his anger at being rejected.

"What do you mean by that?" asked Candy, already suspecting the answer she would receive.

"I mean that Greg is no saint. He's been putting it around in the States, and with no lesser person than the wife of the Chief Pilot, Sherrifa," he said with venom.

"Oh God, no, why did you have to tell me that?" she said, knowing the pain that Jenny would feel when she found out, as she surely would.

"I told you only to point out that we are all likely to go off the rails sometimes, but it doesn't mean that everything has to break down. People patch up their marriages and start again, especially people like us who are always away from our homes. It can get lonely for us too, and sometimes you take comfort where you can get it."

"Well, I believe there is another way. I think I have found a man who is prepared to be faithful to me alone, and I'm ready to take a chance with him, in spite of everything I know about men and their weaknesses," she said emphatically.

Farris looked at Candy and knew there was little point in continuing. He could see by her face that her mind was made up. He had tried everything he could think of, including the cheap shot about Greg, in hopes of making her change her mind, but he had to accept that she would not be coming back to him. In many ways, he could not blame her. He had neglected her badly after the children came along. Now he would have to accept that she would be another man's wife. He was hurt, but not to any great extent, it was more of an ego-bruising. There would always be another woman to console him, and that was probably his greatest weakness. Although he had fallen hard for Candy when she was little more than a young school-girl, the magic began to wear off when she became bogged down with the responsibility of the children. Seeing her independent and strong again had brought back some of the old feelings that he'd had for her and an admiration of her courage. He decided to lick his wounds and move on.

Khalil heard Farris leave, and lost no time in going over to Candy's apartment. "You look a bit shaken, are you all right?" he asked concerned.

"I'll be all right in a while. It's just that Farris has asked me to go back to him."

Fear rose in Khalil's throat at her words. He had dreaded the time should ever come when her ex-husband would ask her to come back to him. She had told Khalil how much she had loved Farris when she was young. He could only pray that the love they now shared could stand this trial. He steadied himself and faced her. "What did you tell him?"

"I told him that I couldn't think of going back to him and that we were seriously considering marriage." Khalil exhaled audibly, relieved that she had rejected Farris and told him of their intention to marry. He could not have borne to lose Candy now. She had become so precious to him, and he loved her with a passion that constantly surprised him. "Thank God, if I lost you, I don't know what I would do," he told her tenderly.

Candy, touched by his words, embraced him warmly, "Don't worry, I will never go back to Farris. What I felt for him pales in comparison to what we share. I was very young then and driven by the urgency of youth and ignorance. Now that I know myself fully, I can say with much more certainty that I'm ready to enter into a permanent relationship, based on love, mutual respect and consideration. I love you, Khalil, and I want to spend the rest of my life with you."

"I will never give you any cause to regret your decision if it is within my power. I will be the best husband that I can be." He paused briefly and asked concernedly, "Do you think that Farris will stand in our way?"

"It's hard to tell at the moment. He is more than a little annoyed at not getting his way with me. He has said nothing at present to indicate that he might object, but let's wait until he has had time for things to sink in."

"Yes, I suppose it is early yet. You are still looking a bit troubled, darling. Is there something else?"

"There is, but I don't know how justified I am in telling you this. Farris was trying to point out how even the most seemingly faithful of husbands can go astray, and he told me the last thing that I wanted to hear." Candy hesitated, not sure if she should divulge the information that Farris had forced upon her.

"Come on, we are going to share our lives together and anything that troubles you is going to worry me too. You know that you can trust me in everything."

She looked at him knowing instinctively that he would do his best for her. "Well, what he told me was that one of the airline crew members who was in the States doing the training began an extramarital affair with Sherrifa Al Fayez. That person is Greg, Jenny's husband."

"Oh, that is bad news, and it puts you in a very awkward position," he said with obvious sympathy.

"Yes, I'm painfully aware of that. I have a strong feeling that it is the truth and not just a malicious story."

"Let me make some discreet enquiries," said Khalil helpfully. "If it turns out to be true, then we will discuss the matter again and decide what, if anything, we should do."

"That sounds good to me," she replied, happy to have had a portion of the unwelcome burden taken off her shoulders. At least for now, she could continue as normal, just being Jenny's best friend.

Jenny and Greg went out alone that evening to celebrate Greg's promotion. Greg went out of his way to make the evening pleasant for Jenny, especially since he knew he would be facing Sherrifa the next evening. Jenny returned from their evening with renewed confidence in Greg, dismissing her earlier suspicions as being simply her own insecurities.

They lay in bed late the following morning, enjoying the freedom from work. They were only disturbed by Hala and her sister letting themselves in with the key that Jenny had given them. "I'm not entirely sure that it's a good idea for them to have a key," commented Greg, worried about the possibility of their overhearing any private phone calls from Sherrifa.

"Well, I do trust them both completely, and it would be difficult for them to do their work if there is no one around to let them in," interjected Jenny on their behalf.

Greg sniffed and let the subject drop, not wanting to make an issue of it. The women were entirely trustworthy and he guessed it would be unlikely that Sherrifa would risk any private phone calls to the house. She, more than anyone, knew the rules of the game.

"What would you like to do today?" asked Jenny, changing the subject.

"Whatever you want to do is fine with me," he told her with a smile. Guilt was beginning to cloud in on him again, with the thoughts of seeing Sherrifa again tonight. It was going to be unpleasant for him having Jenny in the same room as Sherrifa.

"Let's go for a long walk on the seashore to wake us up and then go have lunch at Popeye's Pizza. Then we can come back and have a rest before we go to the dinner this evening. How does that sound to you?"

"It sounds mostly good to me. Let's do it," said Greg as he brightened at the thought of a walk in the fresh air, far away from Sherrifa and her manipulations. Their day flew by all too soon, and while they were dressing for Sherrifa's soiree that evening, Jenny noticed Greg had become more and more sullen. He put it down to residual jet lag and decided not to comment upon it. They arrived at Sherrifa and Hussein's villa promptly as expected. Sherrifa received them both with much ceremony, kissing them both as if they were long-lost friends. They went inside and found the usual senior members of the air crew who had also just arrived. The evening was, more or less, a celebration of Greg's promotion, although Sherrifa pronounced that it was also to see everyone again, since she had missed them all when she was away in the States. Jenny was happy to see Betty there and spent the greater part of the evening talking to her. They were deep in discussion when Jenny looked over to the recently deserted buffet table and caught sight of Greg and Sherrifa talking. She could see by Greg's face that he was not too amused by something Sherrifa was saying.

"Are you enjoying your evening and the promotion?" she asked him, expecting a grateful answer.

"I appreciate the trouble you have gone to on my behalf, but it seems that I would have had the position anyway, according to your husband."

"Is that what he told you?" she answered, her face clouding somewhat.

"Yes," he replied, "I felt like dirt when he told me. Don't you feel any shame knowing that your husband is aware of what's going on?"

"About as much shame as you felt when you were screwing me on the table back in the States," she shot back at him. "He is a free agent. I don't enquire about his affairs. We are married for conveniences' sake only."

"Maybe, but you don't have to face his lovers the way you are making him do with me."

"Don't be too sure of that," she told him, nodding over to where Hussein was standing deep in animated conversation with Monique.

"Oh," said Greg, quickly getting the gist of Sherrifa's insinuation, "I had no idea."

"Neither did I till tonight, but there you are, just goes to show that we all have our little weaknesses." Sherrifa had watched Hussein closely all evening. She could tell by his whole manner that he had been looking forward to this evening, but she did not know why until Monique and Nikos arrived. There was no doubt in her mind that something was going on between them when she saw them together. Obviously, they had missed one another during Hussein's stay in the States. It was written plainly on both their faces.

Sherrifa seized on the moment, "So, when are we going to meet again?"

Greg squirmed uncomfortably, "I don't know, it will be difficult now that I'm working at the airport every day and not flying quite so much."

"No darling, you have got it all wrong," she drawled. "Working at the airport makes it easier for you to see me. I'm looking forward to some interesting mornings. I will call you at your office when I am free."

She walked provocatively away from him to entertain her other guests, leaving him fuming at the way she had treated him. Never in his life had a woman played with him like this. Moreover, he was infuriated by the fact that he was powerless to stop her. She had him by the proverbial balls.

Hussein and Monique spent the whole evening gravitating back and forth to each other, reluctant to part for long after their recently enforced separation. There was little doubt in either of their minds that they wished to go forward with their relationship. The only question was when. "I understand that Nikos will be on the next course to the States. When will that leave?" enquired Monique.

"Next week, will you be free to spend some time with me then?" asked Hussein, anxious to be alone with her again.

"Of course, just let me know when, so that I can arrange for Roger to stay overnight with his friend."

Hussein looked at her questioningly. They had not actually spoken about sleeping together, but it was obvious from Monique's words that she had made the decision. "Are you sure that you are ready to do this. I don't want you to feel pressured. I can wait."

"I do not feel pressured, and we can't deny what we are both feeling any longer. God knows where it may lead us, but I want to go ahead," she told him, looking directly into his eyes, allowing her feelings for him to show.

Hussein smiled at her, unable to disguise his pleasure. He had missed her while he was away and had only managed a couple of unsatisfactory long-distance phone calls to her. "I'm sure that wherever this leads us to won't be bad. I can hardly wait to be with you again."

"I think we had better circulate a bit, or people will be noticing us," said Monique, afraid that they were being a little too obvious for respectability.

"I don't really care, but I will for your sake," replied Hussein truthfully.

Hussein looked over at Sherrifa to see if she had picked up on their intimate conversation, but she was busily engaged laughing with Nikos.

"So you have finally got your man then," Nikos observed.

"Yes, but I am not sure for how long. He is uncomfortable about deceiving his little Jenny."

"But it did not stop him from succumbing to your charms, Chichi."

"He is different from the others. I don't really understand him. The only real hold I have on him is that he's ambitious and I can affect his future. Other men usually just fall in love with *me*.

I am used to having the upper hand in everything and calling all the shots. Tell me, Nikos, am I losing my looks?"

This was the first time in their long association that he had ever seen Sherrifa doubt herself. "By no means, chèrie, you are still as lovely as the day I fell in love with you. You don't have to worry about that for many years yet. But, tell me now, what is happening with Jenny? Is it time for me to make a move on her?"

"Well, I have made Greg's indiscretion known to some of my friends, who were only too happy to pass the gossip on to dear Jenny's hairdresser who, I imagine, will give her some hint of what is going on. More than that, I cannot really do anything as I promised Greg that I would be discreet about our affair."

"Perhaps then, I should start coming in to the picture a little now. There isn't much time left before I go on the course. I'm leaving on Tuesday."

"Yes, I think it's the right time now, and if she doesn't already know about Greg and me, I will make sure that she does before your return, darling."

"Thank you, Chichi, I have waited a long time, and now I am starting to become impatient."

Nikos walked over to where Jenny and Betty were sitting and joined in their conversation. When a suitably slow piece of music started to play, Nikos asked Jenny if she would dance with him. Joining others on the dance floor, Nikos deftly swirled her round to the music.

"You must be very proud that Greg has been given a position with management," he said to Jenny, fishing for any clues as to the status of their relationship.

"Well, to tell you the truth, he is probably more excited than I am, since it means that I will spend even more time without him."

"That *is* the price of success," he joked with her, "but seriously, if you have any problems, don't hesitate to call me. Now that

Greg is going to be away more often, you might need help with things. I know that this part of the world is very male-oriented, and you can rarely get anything done without a man around."

"Thanks, Nikos, I know what you mean. I have had trouble getting people to listen to me, especially workmen and delivery people, but I'm fortunate enough to have wonderful friends living next door who take care of all that side of things while Greg is away."

"Well, if you need anything at the airport, just think of me as Greg's deputy when he is away," he smiled, revealing his perfect teeth contrasting against his handsome tanned features. Jenny had to admit to herself that he was an extremely good-looking man with considerable charm. She could understand why women found him irresistible.

"Thank you, that is very kind," she answered, blushing slightly at her admiration of his looks. Nikos returned her to Betty, fully aware of the impression he had made upon her and only slightly miffed by the fact that Jenny was evidently still on good terms with Greg, unaware of his dalliance with Sherrifa.

"I don't like it when that son of a gun, starts smarmin' round. It means he's up to somethin'," observed Betty.

"Betty, you are so suspicious. He was just being polite."

"Well, I'm tellin' ya, he's up to no good, mark my words."

The evening came to a reluctant end around two a.m. with a fair amount of the guests wishing that time would hold back a little longer so they could remain in the proximity of their desired ones.

By the following Tuesday, Greg was installed and working in his new office at the airport, and Jenny was back at the hospital.

Nikos was on his way to the States, leaving the way clear for Hussein to call Monique, who was having lunch in the den when the call came.

"Hello, darling, are you free to talk to me?" enquired Hussein.

"Hello, yes, I'm all alone. I have been waiting for you to call. How are you?" she answered in attractively accented English.

"All the better for hearing your voice. I have missed you so much while I was away."

"The same is true for me. I'm looking forward to seeing you so very much."

"When will it be convenient for me to visit you?" asked Hussein, his heart skipping a beat at her affectionate response.

"Roger is staying over with his friend all this week, so it is your choice."

"I'll be there this evening," he replied without hesitation. "I can't believe I am going to be with you again at last. I'll be there at nine o'clock. Is that all right?"

"Yes, it's fine. I am looking forward to that, au revoir, darling."

Hussein was filled with anticipation all day; it seemed as if the evening would never arrive. For the first time in many years, he was eager to get out of the airport and back to something that was more important to him. Leaving the airport at seven, he went home to shower and change. Happily, he did not encounter Sherrifa, and he was on his way by eight o'clock. He arrived outside Monique's villa at eight twenty, and debated whether to stay in the car until their appointed hour. After five minutes, he gave in and pulled into the drive. Looking towards the balcony, he saw Monique standing there smiling down at him. She was dressed seductively in a silk, ivory negligee showing from beneath the opened, matching silk peignoir. Hussein paused to admire her beauty. With her auburn hair cascading round her shoulders, she looked like a medieval princess waiting for her knight to rescue her from her lofty tower.

"The door is open. Please lock it before you come up, darling," she told him in the soft, accented voice that he had come to love.

"Yes, of course, I'll only be a moment." Hussein was with her in seconds. "You look so beautiful," he told her, putting his arm around her waist and pulling her gently towards him.

"It's all for you," she told him as he closed his lips over hers. "Let's be comfortable. Shall we go to the bedroom?"

"Whatever you want my love," he told her, his voice hoarse with emotion.

She led him to the guest bedroom rather than any that were in use. She wanted their union to be new and untouched by any of the events that had taken place in the other rooms. Here, they could create something uniquely their own. Deftly, she unfastened Hussein's clothing while he gently slid her negligee off her shoulders. Standing together naked, holding each other, they enjoyed the pure sensuousness of the moment. Hussein lifted her gently onto the bed, admiring her physical beauty. Her hair framed her softly curving face, with all traces of the iciness that often played upon it gone. Her body was vibrant with anticipation, and his passion for her threatened to overpower him. Restraining himself, he moved gently down on her, letting his hands travel the whole length of her body, kissing her passionately on her lips and body. Instinctively, they found each other and began making love gently and provocatively. They rocked together on slowly undulating waves of passion, reluctant to release the self-gratifying passion that could burn out so quickly. Their bodies trembling from the sheer ecstasy of their union, they fought to prolong the moment of ultimate orgasm. Wanting to be together this way forever, swirling in a sea of loving, ecstatic sensations far from the cruelty that their spouses subjected them to. Their union became too intense for Monique to bear. Beyond all control, her body trembled into orgasm. Feeling her tighten around him was the trigger that Hussein was anticipating, so he too allowed himself to achieve orgasm, with both of them spent from the sheer intensity of their feelings.

"Darling, darling," exclaimed Hussein, "this is so incredible. You are beautiful, adorable, and you are everything that I admire and want."

"What we have shared is truly wonderful," she answered him, "and you are all I could ever hope for."

They spent the whole night locked in each other's arms, waking early in the morning to fulfill each other's needs once again. Indeed, Hussein spent every night that week sleeping at Monique's, their love for each other deepening by the day.

Shortly before Nikos was due to return home, Hussein told her in a serious manner, "Monique, what we have together is so very special. I'm having great trouble reconciling myself to the fact that Nikos will be coming back, and that he is married to you."

"We are married only in name, nothing more. You should not worry darling," she told him earnestly.

"I know that, but somehow it doesn't help. I want to be the one with you, to escort you to the interminable functions that we have to attend. I want it to be me who goes to bed with you at night and kisses you good morning every day."

"Do you not think that I want that too, dearest? But in reality, what chance have we got? Your wife calls the shots and could bring you down very quickly if you cross her. You know that she does not want a divorce for she can get away with the lifestyle that she desires while she has you as the foil. I think we must continue the way we are now, taking our happiness when and how we can, whilst we continue with our obligations," she told him stoically.

"There is a way, but it will be a little difficult and mean accepting a much lower standard of living. I was thinking that I could resign and try and join another airline somewhere else, and you could join me. We would not have the same kind of money, but we would have each other," he said with some desperation.

"I don't care about the money. I left more money than I could ever dream of when I, so foolishly, married Nikos. I would go anywhere with you, but you know that Sherrifa would take her revenge on your family. Social disgrace and exclusion in this country is unbearable. You know that you could not do that to them."

"Monique, believe it or not, for you, I think I could even do that." Seeing her about to protest, he quickly interjected, "But I know that you are a person of moral integrity and principle, which is one of the many qualities that I love about you, so I suppose you are right. Nonetheless, I feel that what I have to offer you, as things stand now, is so inadequate," he concluded sadly.

Monique took him in her arms, "Listen to me, there is nothing inadequate in what you offer me. The love we share, the passion we share is beyond words. It fills me completely. It makes my mornings happy. When I wake up and think of you, I have purpose and joy in my day. Whatever I do, it is better because of you. You give me much more than you know. If we are patient, I am sure things will work out. Let's just take one day at a time for now."

Hussein looked at her in admiration. She had eased his mind and made him feel like a king with her loving words. "I love you, Monique, and I swear that one way or another I *will* make a life for us, and our respective children, where we can be free from those that hurt us."

CHAPTER TEN

Jenny's heartbreak.
Nikos and Sherrifa play the odds

"Jenny, I have something to tell you," said Candy, unable to disguise her pleasure.

"Mmm, what is it?" said Jenny, looking up from her cafeteria lunch that she was particularly enjoying. "Oh-oh, I can see that it's something important and something that you are pleased about, judging by the soppy grin on your face."

"You are so right. Khalil has asked me to marry him, and I have agreed," she told Jenny beaming.

"That's wonderful," said Jenny, shrieking somewhat. "I'm so pleased for you both."

"Shhh! I don't want the whole hospital to know. We're keeping it a bit quiet until we have sounded out Farris in regard to the children."

"Do you think he'll be difficult?" asked Jenny, immediately sobering.

"It's hard to say. He asked me to consider a reconciliation the other day. I refused and told him about Khalil."

"How did he take it?" asked Jenny apprehensively.

"Not too well at first, but when I reasoned with him, he calmed down a bit. Khalil is going to ask some friends who are influential and who also know Farris' family to intercede on our behalf. With any luck, it will all turn out well."

"I certainly hope so. You have had your share of misery. You deserve a good life with a man who will take care of you and be with you all the time," said Jenny with a hint of introspection.

Candy was quick to pick up on a mood and asked her, "How is it going now that Greg is in his new position?"

"Truthfully, it's worse than before. Even though I know he's here, I don't get to see him much at all, much less than when he was flying,"

"Oh, Jen, I know how it can be. Just hang on in there, and things will pick up," said Candy sympathetically, hoping she was hiding the damning information that she knew about Greg.

"It is not just that, but ever since Greg came back from the States, he is not the same."

"You just need to get used to him again, Jenny. He was away for quite a spell. Sometimes it takes a while to tune in to each other again."

"I wish it was just that, but there's more. I've had this suspicion that Greg is having a relationship with someone. I have tried to dismiss it, but there are clues here and there that all add up to the same thing. The worst of it is that I believe Sherrifa is the one he is involved with."

Candy was dreading this subject coming up, and she chose her words carefully. "Jenny, I have been through this in my marriage, and I know the agony that you are going through now. There is only one way to deal with this and that is to speak to Greg and tell him of your fears. No one else is in a position to clarify the situation other than him."

"You are right, but I'm truly afraid of what I might hear," she said honestly.

"Well, the choice is yours, live with the doubts or confront the situation," stated Candy bluntly.

Jenny resolved to speak with Greg that evening. She had been tormented by her suspicions long enough. That night, after they had finished dinner, Jenny asked Greg if they could have a serious talk. He felt a tingle of discomfort at her words, instinctively knowing that she was about to confront him with his misdeeds. "Is it really necessary, darling? I'm really tired," he countered, trying to avoid the issue.

"Yes, it is really necessary," she insisted, refusing to be sidetracked.

"Fire away then," he responded casually, trying to evade her serious demeanor.

"Greg, I have to talk to you so that I can come to terms with suspicions that I have that are continuing to mount. This is not going to be easy, and I ask that you be honest with me. From various sources, I've been given information that has led me to suspect that you have become involved with Sherrifa. I've tried to put my suspicions into perspective, but every time I do, something else starts them off again. Whether it is a remark from the hairdresser, or me observing the two of you talking together, even the way she speaks to *me* makes me suspicious. Please, Greg, if there is something going on, tell me. I would rather know and come to terms with it than be kept in the dark."

Greg studied her face, carefully looking for clues as to what he should tell her. Every sense he possessed told him that the truth would be the best option, and knowing her the way he did, he decided to go for broke and tell her everything. He fixed his eyes to the floor, unable to look at her face, and began to tell her of what had transpired with Sherrifa. His words cut through her like a knife. She felt a pain so intense that she thought she would have a seizure. She sank back in the sofa, trying to maintain her composure. Tears stung at her eyes, her breath felt like it was being squeezed out of her body. Leaning forward, she snatched a glass of water that was sitting on the coffee table and gulped it down, trying to stem her rising emotions. Finally, Greg came to the end of his sordid confession and looked at Jenny. He was shocked at the devastation in her eyes. He felt as if he had brutally wounded some small, trusting creature that was in his care. "Oh God, Jenny, please forgive me. I should not have done it, I know, but you know how much power that woman has access to. If I displeased her, she would have made life difficult for both of us."

"Oh please, don't try and tell me you did it for us. It simply won't work," she retorted, disgusted at his attempt to whitewash the situation. *Even if there was truth in what he was saying, he could have spared me that*, she thought.

"Jenny, Jenny, believe me I am not trying to get out of it. I am truly sorry for what I've done, more sorry than you will ever know. I just want you to forgive me. I can't bear to think that I have hurt you like this, and I could not bear it if you left me."

"You should have thought about that when you were screwing Sherrifa," she said venomously. "I don't know how to deal with this right now. I had secretly hoped I was simply being neurotic. I hadn't really prepared myself for this. I need some time on my own, to sort things out."

"Take as much time as you like, darling. Look, I'll go and stay with Farris until you have sorted things out," he volunteered immediately, feeling that separation would probably be fairer on her, and hopefully give her a chance to miss him. He knew the extent to which she loved him before this, and his ego was just large enough to believe that she would stay even in spite of what he had done.

"Thank you for that small consideration, I would be grateful for the space."

"I will go right now, darling. I'll just get some of my stuff," he said to placate her. He was eager to remove himself from her presence. He could not bear the guilt and recriminations, and it would be more pleasant for him at Farris', and he would be able to take advice from him on how to best handle the situation. Jenny watched Greg drive away from the apartment, and she found her usual gentle nature being challenged by an inner voice that demanded retribution. Her pain was turning into anger. *Yes, you bastard, dump your dirt and then go and fly away. That's the way it is with you fly-guys, never around long enough to confront or deal with a situation. God*, she thought, *I am so bloody angry that I feel like smashing every ornament and dish in the place.* She went to the cocktail cabinet and poured herself a large neat brandy. Gulping it down quickly, she tried to come to terms with what he had told her, but somehow, her mind refused to accept the facts. She sat there for about two hours in a state of emotional conflict before the tears came. She cried bitterly for the betrayal she felt and for the loss of trust. *Never*, she though, *will things ever be what they were. Whatever happens now, Greg will never, ever mean the same to me again. I can't love him in the same complete and trusting way I did before*. Engulfed by loneliness, she picked up the phone and rang Candy's number, fervently hoping she would be there. She was more than grateful to hear Candy's soft voice answer the phone. "Candy," she said, her voice striving for normalcy, "are you free to talk to me now? I confronted Greg this evening and ..." her voice choked up, leaving her unable to finish the sentence.

Candy did not need to hear the rest as she could hear the pain in Jenny's voice. "Jenny, I will be with you in about half an hour and we will talk then. Or would you rather come here?" she asked, suddenly wondering whether Greg was there with her.

"No, please come here," she said breathlessly. "I'm not in any fit state to go anywhere. Thank you so much, Candy."

Candy turned to Khalil, who had been pouring a drink for them both, and told him what had transpired.

"Candy, take an overnight bag with you, and I'll drive you over to Jenny's. I don't like to think of you driving on your own at this time. And if I can help in any way, just let me know," he said with emphasis.

Candy was grateful for his offer of help. She hated driving at night, especially since the area where Jenny lived was very poorly lit, having only recently been developed.

Candy arrived at Jenny's within half an hour and, on seeing her crumpled face, threw her arms around her to give her comfort. Jenny sobbed again, grateful for Candy's supportive shoulder.

"Come on," said Candy encouragingly, "what you need is a large mug of hot chocolate and a box of tissues, and then you can tell me the whole story."

Jenny felt much relieved after Candy's arrival and managed to gain control of her emotions. Sobbing all the while through the sad tale, Candy just listened without commenting until the entire story had been told, giving no indication that she had already heard about it via Farris.

"I feel so betrayed. I never imagined that he could be so disloyal," said Jenny, catching her breath.

"I know how hard it is; I've been there myself. You just need some time and space to heal at the moment," she told Jenny sagely.

"Yes, thank God that he is out of my sight for a while. I truly feel that I might do him physical harm if I had to be in close proximity to him. He went to stay with Farris, you know," added Jenny, feeling that Candy should be aware of this.

"Yeah, it doesn't surprise me," responded Candy. "It seems that they became quite close while they were in the States. I only hope that Farris will give him some good advice. But what you need now is a good night's sleep, which I know is going to be a little hard for you tonight. Khalil sent these mild tranquilizers for you, to help you through the next few nights. He was there when you phoned me, and I hope you don't mind that I told him about your suspicions. He sent these tablets in case of the worst."

"God no, I don't mind. I am only too happy for him to be in the picture. It will save a lot of explaining at work, and I do appreciate his concern for me," Jenny assured her.

"I'm going to stay with you tonight and for as long as it takes to get you on your feet again," insisted Candy.

"Thank you, I really appreciate that. I imagine that a couple of nights should do it."

The tablets that Khalil had sent for Jenny were effective in putting her to sleep, although she did wake with a throbbing head the next day. Candy fussed over her and made sure that she ate properly and gave her plenty of time to talk everything out. She was happy to see that as the day wore on, Jenny seemed to grow in resolve, all traces of her devastation of the previous night had evaporated. Candy began to think that she had underestimated Jenny's emotional strength. She could see that she was fighting back the negative emotions that had previously engulfed her and replaced them with positive planning. She was already debating the possibilities of continuing with her marriage or not. But she was doing it in a mature and sensible way.

"Jenny I'm so glad to see you facing up to the situation this way. You are doing a lot better than I ever did when I was in a similar position," she told her with admiration.

"You know, Candy, I really thought I could carry off the perfect marriage, that if I only believed in him and showed him the genuine love that I felt for him, everything would work out well. I was going for the fairy tale. But underneath all this, I have found a very pragmatic side to me that has surfaced. It has taken this bombshell for me to discover my strength. What is hard for me to face is the betrayal, but now that I can see Greg without the distortion of rose-tinted spectacles, I can deal with the situation practically. He will never, ever have the chance to hurt me this way again. All I need to do now is to sort out whether I can live with him knowing what he is capable of. Ever since we married, Greg was the one to call all the shots in our relationship. The way it stands now, with him wanting me to forgive him, I will have the upper hand. I have to give the issue a lot of thought, but whatever happens, he will never again hurt me this way," she said emphatically.

"I can see that you have the situation summed up quite well, but do give yourself time to heal," advised Candy. "Blows like this are not easy to take."

"I know that, but through my nursing career I have learned to have a strong sense of self-preservation that serves me well in times of crisis. Besides, on a different level, I really want to have children before I am much older, and since I'm not likely to find the fairy tale with anyone else, I might as well consider facing the future with an errant husband."

"Jenny, I don't think you should give up on the fairy tale so easily. There is always the chance that there is someone else out there, unconnected with the world of flying, that might make an ideal husband for you and be able to give you the faithfulness that you deserve. You are still very young. There is plenty of time for you to find someone else. I say this because what I have now with Khalil is better than I could ever have hoped for. Not all men have the same set of values. I really feel safe and protected with him. He is open and honest, and from what he has told me about his former marriage, it is obvious that he was no philanderer," she argued forcefully.

"Yes, I imagine that is all true, and quite right for you, but perhaps not for me. I strongly doubt that I will ever fall for anyone the way I fell for Greg. No matter who I meet, any relationship would be subject to doubts, so practically speaking, it all boils down to being the devil you know rather than the devil you don't," she reasoned.

Candy was unable to argue with Jenny's personal brand of logic, so decided to change the subject. "Do you think that you will feel like coming in to work tomorrow? I was able to find someone to cover for me today, but I must go in tomorrow as there is no one else available to cover for me. I don't want to push you, but if you think you are up to it, work might be just the thing to keep you going right now."

"I agree a hundred percent. Nothing can be served by sitting on my own other than self-pity, so I would rather be busy and leave my feelings to sort themselves out," she concluded.

Jenny was as good as her word and threw herself into her work for the next few weeks, only allowing herself the time to think of her problems when she had finished a hard day's work. Greg phoned her several times during this period, each time telling her how much she meant to him and would she please forgive him. She refused to be rushed in to any kind of decision before she was ready and told him the same.

Since Greg's departure from the apartment, Sherrifa had made contact with him and summoned him to her villa one morning. He had no sense of what he had to offer her. He was consumed with rage over the way she had manipulated him. Nonetheless, he turned up at her villa as requested, not wanting to rock the boat more than necessary at the moment. The last thing he wanted was to lose his career prospects as well as possibly losing his wife.

"Marhaba, stranger, come in," she purred seductively in Arabic at him from the steps of her villa. "It seems such a long time since I saw you."

"Marhaba, Sherrifa, a lot has happened since I last saw you. I think we should discuss it."

Sherrifa was slightly alarmed at the tone of his voice, warning bells started to ring in her head. She had started to fall for this man in a way that she was unaccustomed to, allowing herself to daydream about him almost daily. It had cost her considerable effort of will not to have called him before this, but she was struggling for control in the relationship. She could feel that whatever was going to be discussed would not benefit her.

They entered the lounge, and Greg refused her offer of refreshments and got straight to the point. "Sherrifa, in many ways you engineered our relationship, and although I freely admit that I was more than willing to be with you, you assured me that you would be discreet and keep things quiet. Somehow, Jenny has come to know about us, and as I have said nothing to anyone about it, I can only conclude that you must be the source."

Sherrifa was unsure how to handle the accusation and she did not want to further alienate Greg.

"Oh, Greg, I'm so sorry that poor Jenny has come to know about us. The last thing that I wanted to do was to hurt her."

"*Yes, me too*, but that does not answer the question of how she came to find out about us," he said challengingly.

"Darling, I really can't imagine how it happened. I have not told anyone. Perhaps someone saw us together?" she said thinking quickly. "What about Farris? Weren't you sharing a villa with him? Maybe he could have figured out what was going on."

Greg had considered the possibility of Farris letting something slip, but on balance, decided he could trust him. However, he had not thought of the possibility of someone actually observing them. "I suppose that it is always possible that someone did see us together, or at least me creeping out of your villa early in the morning. But the fact still remains that Jenny has found out about us, and that means our relationship is going to have to end if I stand any chance of getting her back."

Sherrifa felt events slipping out of her control. She had underestimated the strength of Greg's feelings for Jenny, and she had not expected to have found herself so infatuated with Greg. She struggled to maintain a cool exterior. "Listen, I can appreciate how you are feeling, and I am in sympathy entirely. What we need now is some time for things to cool down. It seems such a shame to finish our relationship so prematurely," she reasoned.

"No!" he snapped, "I'm simply not prepared to lose my wife over this, Sherrifa. To you, I'm just another amusement, a toy to entertain you for the moment. Jenny is the one who I want to spend the rest of my life with. She will be there for me when you have long since lost interest. I've had plenty of time to review things while I've been on my own and have come to know how much Jenny means to me. I understand that you have gone out of your way to help me get a good position with the airline, and I appreciate that. But if you want to bring me down over this, so be it. I'm even prepared to leave the country and work for a foreign airline. I have some connections in the States, and I believe that I could find work there. I know for a fact that Jenny would follow me there, if she still wants me back. I'm not the kind of man who can be at someone else's beck and call. What we had was exciting, a fantasy, but that is all. We have no future."

Sherrifa felt her head spinning and nausea rising in her throat and she fought to keep it down. Taking a large breath of air, she managed to smile. "Greg, do you think I am so petty as to try and destroy you because of this? You do me a disservice, and besides, it is well known that you deserve the job, and would have got it anyway without my intervention. I don't want to hurt you or Jenny. On the *contrary,* we will continue as friends. When things cool down, I will talk to her and tell her how sorry I am," she stated in a conciliatory tone.

"Thank you for that, Sherrifa, I can use all the help I can get at the moment," he told her, relief flooding over him.

He stood up to leave, and she walked over to him and gently kissed him on the cheek. "Take care, my love," she whispered tenderly to him. Watching him pull out of the drive, she felt the nausea engulf her once again, but this time she was unable to fight it off. She ran quickly to the bathroom and vomited repeatedly. For some time afterwards, she sat in confusion, staring motionlessly out of the window of her elegant salon, trying to comprehend what had happened and how she had been maneuvered into a position of submission. Never had anyone outwitted her, never had anyone come close to it. Now this man, with one stroke, had brought her to her knees, and she found the experience unbearable. Worst of all, she was suffering the agony of unrequited love. She had been so positive that he would become besotted with her, as others had done, that she had allowed her feelings to dominate her reason. Slowly, she brought herself under control and began the task of reconstruction. She would salvage this relationship somehow. She had never wanted a man like she did Greg, and she would find a way back into his affections by some means. She would not be beaten. And as for that bitch of a wife of his, she would destroy her, crush her, like an ant, underfoot. *No one*, she thought, *will bring me to my knees.* She would begin work on Jenny very soon, she decided. She would tell her how sorry she was for the dreadful thing that had taken place in a moment of weakness between her and Greg. Then she would systematically break her with every device she could lay her hands on. She would drive the poor, little, innocent girl right back to where she came from. Sherrifa felt fully restored after deciding on this course of action.

213

Jenny's emotional stability returned after a while, and she felt able to face Greg again. This time, she was in control of the conversation, telling him she had given their relationship much thought and was prepared to take him back, but only on her terms.

"Oh, Jenny, thank God, I'll do anything you want. I never knew how much you meant to me until all this happened," he told her fervently.

"It won't be easy," Jenny cautioned. "I still need some space and time to learn to trust you again."

"Believe me, I'll never give you cause to doubt me again," he insisted.

It was some time before Jenny could begin to function normally around Greg again. Their relationship had so significantly changed that it was like living with a stranger. His whole attitude had changed towards her; he gave her more attention than before and listened to her opinions with interest. He phoned at regular intervals through the day as if to reassure her of his continued fidelity. Eventually, her confidence and trust began to creep back, and she decided to let him return to her bed again. She would try, once again, to broach the subject of having children with him. This time, she would insist that he have a checkup to see if all was well with him. That evening, she approached him, "Greg, there is something that I have to tell you, and there is something that I want you to do for me," she announced with determination.

"Just tell me what it is, and I'm sure that we can arrange it," he told her with a lazy smile.

"To come right to the point, a while ago I had a medical examination at the hospital because I was afraid that I might be infertile. The results showed that I was alright and that I should be able to conceive normally. However, the doctor said it was necessary for you to have tests in order for him to have a balanced perspective as to why I'm not conceiving after all this time. I would like you to take the tests so that we can take the appropriate action," she concluded.

Greg's stomach churned. He knew she desperately wanted children, and to admit that he had kept the truth from her on top of all that had transpired would be too much for her to take. He decided to take the opposite course of action, which was to undergo the tests and feign surprise at the negative results and hope that Jenny would stay with him anyway.

"Of course I'll take the tests, Jen. I know how much you want a baby, and I don't want anything to stand in our way," he said, evading her eyes.

"Greg, you do want children too, don't you?" she asked, noticing a strangeness in his tone.

"Of course I do, nothing would make me happier," he replied with honesty. He would be more than happy to have children of his own, were it only possible.

"Well that's settled then," she said happily. "I'll set the appointment up for as soon as possible."

With subtle manipulation of the flying roster and feigned urgent work requirements, Greg was able to put off taking the tests right away. He knew he would have to face the inevitable before long, but right now, he was happy to let things ride.

Meanwhile, Sherrifa had taken the opportunity of visiting Jenny at her home while Greg was away on a flight, and she made an abject apology for what had happened with Greg. Jenny found it nauseating but for Greg's sake was polite.

"You know, chère, in our 'usbands' line of work, these theengs go on all ze time. We as wives 'ave to be very understanding," she effused with an affected air of wisdom.

"So I'm given to understand," Jenny replied shortly, trying hard to swallow her loathing of the woman.

"I am so glad zat you 'ave both been so sensible as to put thees leetle indiscretion behind you. In a year or two, eet weel be as eef eet never 'appened."

"Yes, I imagine that will be the case. By then, Greg and I hope to have started a family, and all this will seem very small in comparison," said Jenny firmly and venomously.

Sherrifa could not believe her luck. Jenny did not know of Greg's impotence, and now the darling girl had given her all the ammunition she needed to destroy her. She did not allow the moment to grow cold.

"Darling Jenny, no, no, thees ees too awful for me. Oh, what must I say? I theenk I must say nothing," she said, her hands dramatically flying to her cheeks.

Alarm bells started sounding in Jenny's head, coupled with a great annoyance at Sherrifa's dramatic behaviour. "If there is something that you know and you are attempting to keep it from me, I suggest that you come right out with it," Jenny said challengingly.

"Chère, chère, how can I do thees to you? I cannot hurt you twice. You weel hate me forever, and I came here to try and restore our friendship," she simpered.

Jenny looked her straight in the eye, and her whole demeanor demanded a response. "I am waiting for an answer, and you can cut the act." A glimmer of respect for Jenny rose in Sherrifa's breast for a split second, but she could not wait to come in for the kill.

"Oh, my poor Jenny," she told her continuing with her mock sympathy, "Greg did not tell you zat he cannot have ze enfants. Eet ees because of some childhood illness. I am so sad zat I have been ze one to tell you zis news," she said while inwardly relishing the moment.

Jenny was reeling from the disclosure, and she was sure it was the truth. Struggling to maintain her composure, she did not wish to give Sherrifa the satisfaction of enjoying her victory more than necessary. "Thank you for telling me that, Sherrifa. At least we can now make the appropriate arrangements for adoption. That was always our fallback position."

Sherrifa looked at Jenny with admiration. She was holding her own well, better than she ever imagined that she would be able to. She found her quite inscrutable, and the devastation she had imagined did not appear on Jenny's face. She was still in control. "Oh darling, I am so glad zat eet ees not a problem for you. I hope zat we will continue weeth our friendship, like before."

"Just like before," said Jenny with a false smile, "and I must ask you to excuse me now because I am expected at the hospital."

"Of course, chère, I have heard of the wonderful work zat you do there. You must not keep zem waiting. I weel be in contact weeth you soon, adieu."

Jenny escorted Sherrifa to the door, determined to stay in control to the last minute. She even managed to walk outside with her and wait until Sherrifa's chauffeur drove off without showing a glimmer of the hurt that was churning inside her. Returning to the apartment, Jenny expected the tears to come, but strangely, there were none. It was as if something inside her had shut off. Somehow the pain inside refused to be channeled into tears, so she sat down and began to think constructively. If she faced Greg with his dishonesty now, she knew their marriage would not withstand a second blow so soon after the first. She thought, *Do I want this marriage or not? Would I be content without my own children for the rest of my life? Can I trust Greg ever again? Can I ever love him enough again?* The questions just rattled around in her head without any solutions presenting themselves. Suddenly, out of the blue, she knew what she wanted to do more than anything else: She wanted to go back to England. Back to where it was safe and predictable, where she could hear the "no nonsense" tones of her mother remonstrating her for acting in haste and letting her heart rule her head, and see her father nodding in agreement. She picked up the phone and dialed Nikos' office. His secretary answered.

"May I speak to Captain Stianou, please?" she enquired firmly.

"Who shall I say is calling?" asked the secretary a little doubtfully, knowing that Nikos disliked being disturbed by his female admirers at work.

"This is Captain Greg Youssef's wife," she said insistently.

"Just hold one moment," the secretary replied a little resentfully. The secretary buzzed Nikos and told him who was on the line.

"Put her on right away," he told the secretary sharply. With a vicious slam of the phone switch, she put Jenny through.

"Jenny, dear, how nice to hear from you. It has truly brightened my day up. How can I help you?" he said invitingly, anticipating the thoughts of working this moment to the maximum.

"Nikos, I need a ticket to England on the next flight. Greg is away, and I can't wait until he returns. There has been a small emergency at home," she lied convincingly.

"That's no problem, Jenny. I can get you on a flight this evening if you don't mind going on another carrier," he told her obligingly, wondering what emergency required such immediate attention.

"No, I don't mind going on another carrier at all. That will be fine," she replied, rather relieved she would not have to encounter any familiar faces of the cabin staff. What she needed now was distance.

"Listen, Jenny, I don't know what the problem is, but if there is anything I can do to help, please let me know. I'll bring your ticket this afternoon and drive you to the airport and put you on the flight," he said sympathetically.

"Thank you, Nikos, but I could take a taxi to the airport. If you leave my ticket up there, I can just collect it at the desk."

"Absolutely not," he told her, not wishing to let a chance like this slip through his fingers, "I will not hear of it. How could I possibly face Greg if I had not seen you safely onto the aircraft myself. I will be there at four. That will give us plenty of time to get the airport and check in."

"Thank you," said Jenny, rather relieved to have someone take all the hassle out of the travel arrangements. All she really wanted to do at this point was to pack and leave. The following hours were spent gathering her belongings and telling Fouad and Hilda that she had been called away on an emergency to England. She also phoned Candy to tell her that she was leaving. "What is going on?" asked Candy, surprised at Jenny's sudden decision to leave.

"Candy, I just can't talk about it now. I'm going to England, and when I have sorted myself out, I'll write to you from there," said Jenny emotionally.

"Okay, Jen, I think I understand. Just take your time and heal those wounds. I'll tell the hospital that you have gone back home for a while because of an emergency there."

"Thanks, Candy, take care and hold on tight to that man of yours. There are not too many good ones left."

Shortly after she put the phone down, the front door bell chimed. It was Nikos. "Is it that time already?" asked Jenny with a smile.

"Yes it is, although I admit to being five minutes early. Are you all right Jenny?" he enquired with a concerned look on his face, determined to find out what it was that was causing Jenny to take flight so suddenly. "I hope that it is nothing serious with your family that causes you to leave so suddenly."

Jenny felt uncomfortable under his scrutiny, but decided to go for a lie. "Well, I received a telephone call from my mother this morning, and she said my father was going into the hospital tomorrow, and I want to be with her as she is getting older and is less able to manage things out of the ordinary." That is also what she had written in her letter to Greg, and there was a grain of truth to it. Her mother had written to tell her that her father was going to have some minor surgery done on his hand this week, but certainly nothing so serious as she was implying.

"Oh, how considerate of you," Nikos told her. "You must let me help however I can."

"You can't really do more than you are doing Nikos, and for that I am very grateful," she said.

"Well, where are your bags? We should be leaving now if you want to catch that flight."

Nikos was not convinced by her story; he was too good a liar himself to be taken in by her performance. He made a mental note to talk to Sherrifa this evening to see if she could throw some light on the subject.

Nikos ushered Jenny through the airport with ease. His position in the airline ensured an uninterrupted passage through all the gates. He even sat with her in the first-class lounge until her flight was called, and he requested to come on board, where he introduced himself and Jenny to the captain and asked him to look after her on the flight. Jenny felt like royalty, and the cabin staff and crew went out of their way to make her comfortable. She had no idea that Nikos was held in such esteem at the airport.

Jenny phoned her parents when she reached London and told them she would spend the night at a hotel at the airport and arrive home the following day. Her parents were surprised at her sudden arrival but did not press her too much on the reasons why. They were just glad they would see her again, as it had been so long. After an easy train journey to the north, she arrived home to a warm welcome from her parents. The next few days were spent sitting with her mother listening to all the news of friends and family. It was only then that she confided to her mother the reason why she had arrived home so unexpectedly. Her mother found it difficult to comprehend the kind of life she was living in the Middle East, but she did tell her that she had done the best thing in coming home to sort herself out. She knew better than to offer any direct advice to her. From long experience, she knew that with just a word of consolation and support, Jenny would eventually solve her own problems, and to offer her opinion would be counterproductive. Indeed, both her parents gave her time and space to sort herself out, whilst giving her a pleasant and loving atmosphere where she felt safe. Whenever Greg called Jenny, they greeted him warmly, but maintained the charade of her father's illness before passing the phone on to Jenny. Jenny continued with the facade right up to the last minute of her stay in England, never letting Greg guess what she had found out from Sherrifa. Spending her time in England, taking long walks and involving herself with her own family, she finally came up with what she considered to be the right decision concerning Greg. Her raw emotions had settled, and she now felt inwardly calm and was ready to face the world again. It had been wonderful at home, with its calm predictability, but the lure of the Middle East was calling her, and she had unfinished business to settle. Knowing her own inclinations better, she understood that predictability and security were not right for her at this time in her life. She had become so embroiled in the customs and culture of the Middle East that it felt a part of her. Jenny had come to understand that she needed the stimulus and challenge as well as the appreciation that she received from working at the hospital in Kharja. Even more, she needed the fire and passion of the people, no matter how unorthodox they had appeared to her initially. In her reflections, she believed that she now understood them, seeing clearly, a kind of truth underneath the frantic scrambling for power and prestige. She wanted to return to Greg, though she no longer loved him in the immature, adoring and impractical way that she had before. Now she could take him on with all of his faults, even the fact that he had hidden his inability to have children, she was now able to understand. She felt sure that he would agree to adopt a child if she returned to him. The time had come for her to leave England and return to the life she had run from in the Middle East.

After Jenny's hasty departure from Kharja, Nikos wasted no time at all in contacting Sherrifa. As soon as Jenny had departed, he had driven to Sherrifa's villa and filled her in on what had transpired.

"C'est marvellieux, what good news you bring me, chère Nikos," she said, her face lighting up at his words. "Now nothing will stand in my way of having Greg." She began telling him of her visit earlier in the day and how she had dropped the bombshell of Greg being infertile.

"Chichi, that is fine for you, but it looks like I have lost my chance of ever getting Jenny. God knows where she is in England, and it would be impossible to carry on an affair from such a distance. It is so unfair, and I could almost feel her falling into my web," he told her in an injured tone.

"Oh, darling, I am sorry, but it cannot be helped. I will find a way to make it up to you. You have so many opportunities with women, and you will not pine for her long," she laughed.

You are wrong this time Chichi, he thought. Jenny was the object of many of his fantasies. He had dreamed of her. She represented the unattainable, thus she was in a different class to the other women who were so eager to share their charms with him. Jenny would be a conquest, not a walkover. He wanted her with an intensity that surprised him, and now he had to face the prospect of losing her without even having the chance to win her. He finished off the drink that Sherrifa had poured for him and left, not wishing to allow the anger he felt at this moment towards her to become apparent. She was still his meal ticket, and as such, he did not want to upset her in anyway.

Sherrifa was delighted at the events that had taken place on the day she faced Jenny. Her day had gone from good to better. *Now*, she thought, *I have a second chance with Greg, and I am not going to blow it.* She decided to give the situation time to cool off.

After a month, she phoned Greg to ask how he was, and indeed how Jenny's father was. Greg told her that he sounded to be recovering and thanked her for her concern.

"So, Greg, when can we expect Jenny to return?" she asked sweetly in Arabic.

"I am not sure at the moment, but the way things sound, it may well be soon," he told her frankly.

She was not pleased with Greg's reply. She had figured that Jenny would be departing from the scene permanently after her bad experiences. "Oh well, do be sure to let me know when she is returning. I will have a little soiree for her," she said, just managing to maintain a civil tone. She was angry, and Jenny was the object of her anger. *Who does she think she is, messing up my plans, trying to outmaneuver me? If and when she comes back, nothing will stop me from destroying the irritating little bitch.*

CHAPTER ELEVEN

Reconciliations, revenge and political turmoil

On the day of Jenny's return, Greg tried hard to adjust the flying roster so he could pilot Jenny's flight back to Kharja. However, despite his best efforts, he had to settle for entrusting her to Farris, who was operating the flight. Greg instructed him to take Jenny out to dinner in London and ensure that she had a good seat on the aircraft.

Farris enjoyed meeting Jenny. He found her pleasant company and went out of his way to make her feel comfortable. It also assuaged his conscience a little for disclosing Greg's indiscretion with Sherrifa to Candy. Although he knew Candy would have been very discreet about it, his disloyalty was still preying on his conscience.

The following morning, Farris escorted Jenny through the airport to the departure gate, where he discovered that a government delegation had decided to return home at the last moment and had taken over most of the seats in first class. "Sorry, Jenny," said Farris, "it's going to be fairly crowded in first class. They can still fit you in, but you will have to sit next to someone."

"That's no problem at all. Don't worry about it," she told him. "In fact, it might be nice to have some company next to me." Often first class was pretty empty, and she would spend the whole flight reading and only having the odd chat with the crew.

"Okay, then I'll have to leave you now. I have to get back to the aircraft and finish off the checks with the first officer. It will not be too long before the flight is called, and I'll see you on board," he said, taking amiable leave of her.

"That's lovely, and thanks for all your help. See you later."

When Jenny boarded the aircraft and was shown to her seat, she found that there was already a man of around thirty years sitting in the window seat. She could not help but notice his tall, angular good looks. He looked up at her with unusually beautiful green eyes and smiled. "Good morning, would you care to have the window seat?" he enquired genially, with something of an American inflection to his voice.

"No, I'm not bothered where I sit. Please stay where you are," she responded politely. She settled in, stowing her hand luggage and getting her reading matter out on the armrest next to her. Her travelling companion glanced at her book and remarked that he had read some of the author's other works. They then fell into a pleasant conversation critiquing some other books that they had both read. Jenny was quite entertained by his easygoing, jovial manner and soon felt comfortable with him.

"Since we have read so many of the same books," he told her, "don't you think it is time that we introduced ourselves? My name is Talal Khouri. May I have the pleasure of knowing your name?" he asked with gallant charm.

"Yes, of course," she responded, trying hard not to show how attractive she found this man. "My name is Jennifer Youssef. I'm very pleased to meet you," she said with a smile.

"*Jennifer*," he repeated, "I have not heard that name before. It is very nice but much too serious for someone as lovely as you are. Will you permit me to shorten it to something less formal? What do your friends call you?" he asked.

Jenny was surprised by his forthright behaviour. Usually Arabic men were very reserved when meeting women. But his easy charm was very appealing, and she found herself responding to him. "My friends either call me Jenny or Jen."

"Hmm, now that does not sound right either. We must think up something else that will be more suitable for you," he persisted.

Jenny was amazed by the audacity of this man who had met her for approximately thirty minutes, yet was already getting quite familiar and personal with her. "Well, you had better think of something, or you'll have to call me, *hey you*, for the rest of the flight," she told him with laughter threatening to break through her usual formal demeanor.

"I could never call beautiful Jennifer, *hey you*. It would be an insult to your beauty," he told her, with remarkable sincerity. "What did your parents call you when you were a little girl and they wanted to spoil you?" he enquired.

Jenny looked at him with disbelief. She had never had anyone come on to her so strongly before, and she felt that she should make it clear that she is a married woman.

"I think I should tell you right now that I am married," she said.

"Yes, I am aware of that," he told her. "Your surname kind of gave it away, plus the ring on your finger. But I am a person who believes in destiny, and whatever stroke of fortune sent you to share this seat with me, I give my thanks to. You will think me crazy, but the second I laid eyes upon you, my heart was lost to you. I never question feelings such as this. I just act upon how I feel," he told her, speaking with considerable warmth.

Jenny felt her own heart leap inside her breast at his words. She was stunned to acknowledge the same feelings. "Talal, this is madness."

"How sweetly you say my name. I will never forget that this was the first time you used it. Now tell me what your parents called you."

Jenny smiled at him with some embarrassment, "Well, they either called me Jenjen or Jenny wren."

"Jenny wren, now that sounds more promising. But tell me first what is a wren."

"A wren is a very small, brown bird, once seen on the old coinage of Britain."

"That will do nicely. That will be my special name for you," he said softly.

"You cannot call me that in front of people," she told him seriously. "It would sound really ridiculous."

"I have no intention of calling you that in front of people. It is what I will call you in private when no one is around," he said with sincerity.

"How can you say that when you know nothing about me? How do you know we will ever see each other again after this flight?" she asked with growing incredulity.

He reached over and took her hand and looked into her eyes, "Tell me, sweet Jenny, that we will never see each other again." She looked into his intense green eyes and found it impossible to answer him. "You see, Jenny, you cannot deny what has happened between us today. We will see each other again. Nothing will keep us apart."

Jenny looked at the floor, unable to stand the intensity of his gaze, trying desperately to understand everything she was feeling at this moment. Fortunately, the cabin staff arrived with drinks, giving her time to collect her senses. She took the complimentary glass of champagne, hoping it would return her to normalcy. Talal, she noticed, took only tomato juice.

Looking at her, he raised his glass and said, "To our future, my Jenny wren." After this solemn moment was acknowledged by both of them, Talal continued, "Jenny, tell me, do you have children?"

227

"No, I don't, do you?"

"No, I'm not married. How do you spend your time when you are in Kharja?"

"Well, as my husband is an airline pilot, I spend a lot of time alone, so I work voluntarily as a nurse at the hospital when he is away."

"A nurse, yes, I can imagine that. Is your husband piloting this flight today?" he asked with a little concern tingeing his voice.

"No, no, Greg is not on board today. He will be meeting me when we land."

"Well, at least we'll have a few hours together," he said with relief in his voice.

"You have been asking all the questions, so now it is my turn. What are you doing on this flight? Do you travel a lot?" she gave him a warm smile.

"I am just positioning to Kharja so I can rendezvous with a group of tourists from the States who want to visit the holy land and the surrounding areas of historical interest. My family has a travel agency, and I travel mostly between the States and the Middle East as a tour guide for them."

"That must be interesting, meeting so many people," she said.

"Yes, it is. I have always enjoyed meeting people, but never so much as the person I have met today," he told her tenderly, tilting his head down and around so that he could look into Jenny's lowered, embarrassed eyes. "Don't be embarrassed, Jenny. I am only speaking the truth. You know it, I am sure. Can't you feel the electric current sparking between us?"

Jenny just nodded, unable to deny the strength of the attraction between them.

Recovering, she continued, "Where is your base then?"

"Well I don't really have one, but I was born in Koudara and still have family there. I also have many relatives in Kharja, in fact. That reminds me, which hospital do you work at?" he enquired.

"The University Hospital," Jenny responded.

"I have a cousin who is a doctor there. His name is Khalil. Do you know him?"

"Know him?" said Jenny laughing. "He is my boss at the hospital. I work for him in the emergency room. What a small world!"

"What a lucky coincidence," said Talal jubilantly, "at least that is one point of contact for me when I want to get in touch with you. This is destiny at work again." Their conversation was interrupted at this point by Farris, who had come to check that Jenny was all right.

"Well, I see you have found someone to chat with," he said, quickly sizing up the intimate air that had arisen between Jenny and her companion.

"I'm Captain Farris, and I'm a good friend of Jenny's husband. He's entrusted her to my safe-keeping until we land, where he will be waiting," he said pointedly, observing that this man and Jenny were getting far too comfortable for his liking. The last thing he wanted to do was let Greg down again.

"My name is Talal Khouri, pleased to meet you. And please don't worry about Captain Youssef. I will ensure that Madam Youssef has as pleasant a flight as possible. We find that we have many literary interests in common," he replied with such diplomacy that it diffused the situation. Farris turned to Jenny feeling somewhat reassured and told her that he had already spoken to Greg at base and that he was looking forward to meeting her when she landed.

"That's kind of you to tell me, thank you Farris," Jenny replied, wishing fervently that he would go back to the cockpit. She felt that he was intruding on the precious little time that she and Talal were sharing. However, she managed to keep a pleasant and polite countenance, remembering Betty's words about 'always playing the game.' Now she understood, *keeping face is everything. No matter what you are feeling inside, don't let the world know.* She had also noted how well Talal had played *'the game.'* She admired his handling of the situation.

"You handled that situation well, Talal. I think Farris was rather alarmed at how we seemed to be getting along," she told him with a smile.

"It's a gift I have. I never let people guess my true motives; it's too dangerous," he replied with some solemnity.

Jenny felt her emotional guidance system give a warning and swiftly responded to Talal, "In light of what you have just said, it makes me rather wary about believing everything that you have said previously about me."

"Oh, Jenny, Jenny, no, no, *no*, I was not alluding to you. You have taken me out of context, and I should not have been talking without thinking," he said earnestly. "Jenny, just look at me: Do you think that my motives are less than honest with you? If you do, I am prepared to walk away from what we might have right now, rather than have you doubt me."

She looked into his hypnotic green eyes that implored her to believe him. "No, you don't have to do that," she told him, putting a hand on his knee as if to restrain him. "I do believe you, but you must agree that what we are embarking on is ill-advised."

"It may be ill-advised, it may be absolutely crazy, but it is still happening. Do you want to just let this opportunity slip by you and go to your grave wondering what it would have been like if only you had experienced this romance with me?" He paused, looking intently into her eyes. "I don't think you are that kind of person, Jenny. Your eyes tell me that you have a liking for fire and excitement. I don't want to lose this magic, do you?" he said perceptively.

"You are right, Talal. I don't want to walk away from this," she said with unaccustomed veracity. "I do like fire and excitement, and looking at you, that is what I see. And what I feel is an incredibly strong attraction to you. It feels like a supercharged lightning bolt blazing between us."

Talal gasped, the passion of her words had sent his senses soaring. "Oh, Jenny" was all he could whisper at that moment. They spent the remainder of the flight in intense conversation, feeling that they must make the most of the time they had together. Neither one could commit themselves to a time when they could be free to meet one another. Talal had told her to leave everything to him and never to doubt that he would find her and they would be together again.

During the landing, a feeling of sadness fell over Jenny, knowing that, in minutes, they would have to return to being virtual strangers. Experiencing the same emotion, Talal looked into her eyes and told her that this was not goodbye. As they touched down, he leaned over and kissed her tenderly on her lips. Jenny felt her heart race, and if she could have turned back time, she would have done so unhesitatingly. She struggled for normalcy as the aircraft taxied in. As soon as the steps were brought to the aircraft, Greg leaped up them two at a time and came aboard. Sticking his head through the cockpit door, he gave a mock salute to Farris and asked if everything was alright.

"Everything's fine. Go and get your wife," he told him with a friendly grin.

As Jenny saw Greg's smiling face coming towards her through the cabin, she felt a stab of guilt at her disloyalty.

"Welcome home, Jen," said Greg while embracing her. "How was the trip?"

"It was a very smooth trip. We were lucky to have clear weather most of the way, and all the crew were really helpful," she said, trying hard to conceal her uneasiness.

"Well, come on, let's get you through customs and back home," he said, picking up her hand luggage.

Talal had turned his face to the window and pretended to be engaged in watching something outside. He could not bear to see her leave on the arm of another man. He felt no shame in what he had done; he was an unconventional man who lived for the moment. He disregarded many of society's conventions, living greatly by the dictates of his instincts. Watching her leave the aircraft, he swore that he would be back to claim her. The feelings he had experienced from the moment he had met Jenny were far beyond anything he had ever before felt.

Greg hurried Jenny through the formalities of the airport and claimed her luggage, which Farris had thoughtfully sent through with those of the crew. Within less than half an hour, they were already on the road back to their apartment. Greg was in good spirits, delighted that his wife was back with him. This time, he would ensure that nothing would take her away from him again. He had already taken steps to ensure that they could start off on a new footing. Jenny had regained her composure, and the events on the aircraft were beginning to recede into the background. She even began to doubt what had taken place; it had all taken on a dreamlike quality. In the clarity of her present situation, she decided that it would be better to put the whole experience behind her, only to perhaps relive it in moments of indulgence. She owed it to Greg to try and rebuild their marriage.

Greg whisked her out of the car and into the apartment, flamboyantly throwing the front door open to reveal a welcoming party of Candy and Khalil, Mariella and her husband, Betty and Chuck, and Fouad and Hilda. Jenny was both stunned and touched by the thoughtfulness on Greg's part. *He must have gone to quite some trouble to set this up,* she thought. Hala and her sister were both there supervising the cooking and drinks, beaming in delight to see her again.

"Madam Jenny, welcome home. We hope you like the party. You enjoy everything with your friends. We will take care of all things," Hala said as they were fussing around her.

"Oh, I'm very happy to see all of you. It is so kind of you all to come. I have missed you all so much," she said, feeling tears stinging the back of her eyes. It was wonderful that Greg had arranged a party truly for *her*, with people that she considered her friends. The evening was a success, with everyone feeling comfortable and enjoying the easy atmosphere that pervaded. It ended convivially at around midnight. Hala and her sister remained and worked for about an hour to clear up before leaving Greg and Jenny on their own. Invigorated by the evening, Jenny and Greg made themselves another drink and sat down together in the lounge.

"Thank you for tonight, Greg. It was a wonderful surprise, and I appreciate the trouble you have gone to for me," she said, smiling at him.

"It was more than worth it. Nothing is too much trouble for my lovely wife. You have no idea how much I have missed you. Jenny, there is something that I want to tell you and I think that now is as good a time as any. I want to be honest with you about the chances of our having children," he said seriously. Jenny knew what was coming but decided to pretend that she knew nothing on the subject. In light of the evening, Jenny could not really be angry with him, and besides, she had already reconciled herself to the situation.

"Go ahead," she told him, inviting a response.

"Jenny, I should have told you this before, but I don't think it is at all likely that you are going to conceive. I had a childhood illness that left me with a very low sperm count. But in your absence, I contacted Candy who put me in touch with Mariella's husband. I had an examination and had some tests with him, and he confirmed that I have a low sperm count. However, he was very helpful and told me of a new treatment that could possibly help. I'm quite happy to go through with it," he said with determination.

"Well, Greg, I'm not as surprised as you might think. I had my suspicions for some time that all may not be well with you, especially as you were so touchy about the subject. I've had a lot of time to think while I was in England, and I have returned here because I want to make our marriage succeed in spite of what has happened. Having children is important for me, but whether they are children that we have conceived together or whether they are adopted does not matter much to me. I hope you will agree to adoption if your treatment does not work?"

Greg was happy that she had taken his revelation so well. He had not really considered the prospect of adoption but was willing to go along with it if it was what she needed. "Jenny, if you need children and I can't give you them, then we will adopt. I want to save our marriage too."

Greg reached over and embraced her. It was the first really intimate moment they had shared since Greg's unfaithfulness, but now Jenny was emotionally ready for this. She responded to his embrace happily and allowed him to lead her to the bedroom. He lifted her onto the bed and began taking off her clothes, kissing her and caressing her all the while. He slipped out of his clothes, and they began to make love slowly as if wanting to prolong their reunion. For Greg, it was a gratifying experience, as he had been tortured by the thoughts of his infertility. Now with Jenny knowing everything, he could relax and enjoy their lovemaking without that shadow hanging over him. Jenny too noticed the difference in their lovemaking. It was less intense, more relaxed and intimate. They both slept soundly after their night of reconciliation and reunion. They were awoken by the phone ringing early next morning. Greg answered it; it was the hospital asking for Jenny. He passed the phone over to her. "It's for you," he said sleepily.

"Yes, Jenny Youssef here, how can I help you?" she said, trying to wake herself up. It was one of the receptionists, who told her that there had been a bomb blast. It had been planted on a bus that was travelling through a small village on the country's borders, and there were many casualties. They were bringing in the wounded to the University Hospital and urgently needed all the staff available and asked Jenny if she would come. "I will be there as soon as I can," she told them.

Greg looked up at her, sensing the urgency in her voice, and asked, "What's going on?" She quickly replied, "There's been a bomb blast in a small village on the borders, and there are lots of wounded. They need me urgently at the hospital."

"You must go at once. Do you want me to take you?" Greg asked in a concerned voice.

"No, I will drive myself.

"If I can be of assistance in any way, just give me a call at the airport."

"Thanks, darling, I don't know what the situation is, but I will keep you posted."

Jenny was at the hospital within half an hour. The emergency room and corridors were crowded with seriously wounded people. There were men, women and children. Jenny had never experienced anything on this scale before. "Thank God you're here," shouted Dr. Khalil across the emergency room floor. "It's utter chaos here, and we need as much help as we can get. Can you attend to those who have not been seen by a doctor yet and make them as comfortable as possible? The operating rooms are already full with the most serious cases. We'll have to leave those that don't have any hope of making it. It is an appalling situation," said Khalil sadly.

"I'll go at once," she told him, not wanting to waste time by talking unnecessarily. She returned to the corridors where Candy had begun talking to the wounded and trying to reassure them.

"Thank heavens you are here, Jenny. Can you check these people over and see who needs immediate attention?" she said, happy to have someone with professional medical knowledge to help her. The hospital staff worked nonstop through the day, and only by late afternoon did the pressure ease off a little. They'd managed to send some of the wounded to the smaller, private hospitals in town and were now left treating the less seriously wounded. Jenny was putting up an intravenous drip for the last patient, when she was aware of someone entering the room.

"Hello, Jenny wren," said a whispered voice behind her. Jenny froze on the spot, knowing exactly whom the voice belonged to. Slowly turning round, she saw Talal standing there, his right arm in a sling and light shrapnel wounds on the right side of his face.

"Oh my God, Talal, what happened to you?" she asked in alarm.

"I was caught in the blast. Fortunately, I'm not too badly hurt, just a shoulder wound. I was helping with the wounded back in the village and arrived here about two hours ago. They patched me up in outpatients. They told me that you would be about finished by now. Will you come and have a coffee with me?" he asked, his green eyes imploring her to come.

"Yes, I will come. I really need a sit down," she said matter of factly, trying to diffuse the electric current that was pulling her towards him again. In the cafeteria, Jenny asked what had happened in the village.

"There was a bomb planted in one of the wagons that brings fresh produce into the town. The villagers are nearly all farmers with small holdings whose livelihood revolves around selling their produce to the bigger towns in the area. They all gather at the market early in the mornings to load their produce for sale, and often the whole family will help. When the bomb was planted, it was calculated to do the most damage and cause the most casualties. It was a cluster bomb," he said, his voice trailing off sadly.

"Oh, that's awful. Who was responsible for it?"

"Almost certainly it is the extremist wing of a militant political party in Koudara. They claim that the village was giving refuge to terrorists making their way over the borders and performing acts of sabotage. They feel that they were justified in their actions."

"What have women and children got to do with that?" asked Jenny indignantly.

"I know what you mean, but when men go out to fight, it is with the knowledge of their wives, and there are many women who ardently support the terrorists' cause and actively encourage their menfolk to go and fight. They also bring up their children to be militant too," he told her frankly.

"Oh, I didn't know that, I always thought that the peasant Arab women were very subservient to their husbands."

"Well, they may well appear that way to world, but through strong alliances with other women and their families, and the great influence they exert over their children, the women manage to hold a significant sway over their men."

"In that case, I applaud them, but I still think that women with children to raise are unsuitable targets for saboteurs," she said emphatically. Their conversation was interrupted by the arrival of Khalil and Candy.

"Talal, how are you? It's good to see you again. I wish it was under better circumstances," said Khalil, embracing him with a customary kiss on both cheeks.

"Hello, Khalil, it's good to see you. I see that you only employ the most beautiful of staff," he said, looking at Candy and back over to Jenny.

"Talal, meet my fiancée, Candy."

"Well, this is wonderful news, congratulations," said Talal, obviously surprised by the announcement. "When did this all take place?"

"We announced it to the world last week, after settling the question of access to Candy's children from her former husband. Fortunately, his family has been cooperative so we are planning our wedding for later this year."

Jenny already knew their engagement had been announced, but being tactful, she refrained from asking about how Farris and his family had taken it. She was delighted to hear that no obstacles were going to be put in their way.

"Do you mind if we join you for coffee?" asked Khalil, obviously expecting a positive reply. Instead, Talal fired off a long statement in Arabic that Jenny could not catch, causing Khalil to change his jovial expression. In response to Talal's request, he did a complete about-turn, telling them that on second thought, he and Candy had better take advantage of the coffee break to deal with some pressing matters that needed their attention, and he would look forward to seeing Talal on another occasion.

"Did you ask him to leave?" Jenny asked Talal perceptively.

"Yes, I don't have much time, and I want to spend as much of it as I can with you," he said earnestly.

"Talal, I have to be honest with you, after the flight yesterday, my husband went out of his way to reconcile our former differences. Although I am very attracted to you, I still have strong feelings for Greg. Right now my mind is in turmoil, and I think that I owe it to Greg to try and make it work," she said with honesty.

"Jenny, you owe nobody anything. I don't know what has gone on between you and your husband in the past. That is just history. Now, is what is important. Now, we can look at each other and know that love and passion are pulling us together. You have no children to keep you together. All you have to do is to walk away from him and be with me," he said, reaching for her hand.

Feeling overwhelmed by his intensity, Jenny slowly pulled her hand out of his. "Everyone will notice if you show me any affection here."

"I don't care, Jenny. I want everyone to know that I am claiming you. I want you so badly."

"Please don't, Talal, I am overwhelmed by my feelings towards you, but I can't take things at this speed, so just give me a little space and time to arrange my thoughts. I know so little about you. I can't base any kind of future on a few hours of knowing you," she reasoned with him.

"You know that I love and want you. You know that you feel the same way too. Whether you are married or not doesn't really matter, whether there is a question of a future together or not doesn't really matter. All that matters is that we have these feelings for each other now. They are not going to suddenly disappear. Life is not long enough to deny the feelings we share," he said passionately.

Jenny's head was spinning with his words. If she did not have a strong sense of propriety, she would have walked away with him now. She had never felt so intensely attracted to anyone before, but common sense prevailed. "Talal, give me some time and space. I cannot deal with this now. I can't deny my feelings for you, but I am not ready to throw caution to the wind and possibly regret my actions for the rest of my life," she told him with as much sincerity as she could muster.

Talal saw that he would not win the day and decided it would be better to give her some time, rather than pushing her any further and risk losing her forever. "Jenny, my love, I have to leave now. You will be forever in my thoughts, and I will return to be with you soon. Part of you is already mine; I can feel it." Standing up, he pulled her to her feet, embracing her and kissing her on both cheeks in the customary Middle Eastern manner. With a wave to Khalil and Candy, he left.

Jenny left the cafeteria immediately, not wishing to face Khalil and Candy's inevitable questions. Outside the hospital, she ran to the security of her car and drove home, trying to make sense of her feelings. As she entered the apartment, the phone was ringing, and it was Greg. "Hiya, honey, I have been trying to track you down. I phoned the E.R. a while ago, but they told me you had left."

"Yes, the rush is finally over, and we dealt with the last of the patients about an hour ago. It has been truly horrendous," she said, happy to hear his familiar voice.

"You poor thing," he said sympathetically, "listen, don't cook anything tonight. I'll bring something in for us on my way home. Go and have a long soak in the bath and relax now, sweetheart."

"Thanks for being so understanding, love," she told him appreciatively.

"It's the least I can do, I'll be home in about two hours," he told her anticipating, with pleasure, sharing their first evening alone since her return.

Jenny enjoyed the tranquility of the apartment after the trauma of the day. Her aching muscles began to relax in the warm, soapy water of her bath, and she closed her eyes to let all the tension ebb from her. The next thing she remembered, Greg was bending over her and kissing her into wakefulness. "Oh, good heavens, I must have fallen asleep in the bath. I have never done that before in my life," she said, surprised by her actions.

"Don't worry, it happens sometimes when you are exhausted. Whenever I have done a long-haul flight, I always call the first officer when I get in the tub and tell him to give me a ring in half an hour just in case I slide into unconsciousness. It's one of my quirks," he said, helping her to her feet and wrapping her in a big towel.

The sleep had restored Jenny's energy somewhat, allowing her previously raw emotions to settle down. Again, her encounter with Talal had receded into a safe dream world, completely unconnected with her present reality. She was glad to have Greg's strong arms supporting her, reinforcing normality again. She put on her dressing gown and sat down to eat the meal Greg had brought in. It was the first food she had eaten all day other than a sweet nut pastry that she had grabbed from the kitchen table before she left for the hospital that morning. As she ate, she began to feel better. Her head, which had begun to pound after coming out of the bath, settled down. She felt glad to be home with Greg, being her normal self again. After dinner, Jenny brought Greg up to date with the news of the bomb blast.

"It has been the talk of the airport," Greg told her, "and feelings are running very high. "People are outraged at the killing and wounding of old men and women, mothers and children. There was simply no need for that; it was an act of savage barbarism."

Jenny thought of Talal's response, when she'd uttered the same protest. Although she understood Talal's logic and cynicism on the subject, she could not find it within herself to agree with him. Rather she echoed Greg's feelings and decided not to mention what Talal had said. They continued to discuss the day's events at length before retiring to bed. Jenny fell into an exhausted sleep, waking to find that she had slept in late and that Greg had crept out without waking her. She found a note on the kitchen table saying he would see her in the evening and urging her to take the day off work to recuperate. She appreciated his thoughtfulness, but she felt rested enough to go in to the hospital, knowing they would still be hard-pressed for staff, due to the influx of patients yesterday. After making a light breakfast for herself, she left for the hospital.

Sherrifa, hearing of Jenny's return, called Nikos to her villa that afternoon. He arrived punctually, bringing her a large bunch of roses. He had perceived that she had been in a very depressed state of mind lately and wanted to ensure that he stayed in her good graces. "Bon jour, Chichi, these are the only things that come anywhere close to mirroring your beauty."

Sherrifa took the roses and offered her cheek to be kissed. "Merci, come and sit down. We need to talk." Walking into the lounge, she called her maid to bring them coffee. "Nikos, things have gone badly for me with Greg, and I believe that I have lost him entirely. Jenny has returned, and he is not prepared to do anything that might risk their relationship," she paused, unaccustomed to having to admit defeat in any way.

Nikos went over to her and put his arms around her to console her. He found it unsettling that she was practically admitting defeat. He always admired her ability to turn situations to her advantage. Seeing her like this evoked sympathy in him. She was his kindred spirit, and he did not want to see her like this. "Chichi," he whispered, "he is nothing. Forget about him. He is not worthy of you. He is a fool to turn away from you. Doesn't he know the harm that you can do to him?"

"He is well aware of what I can do for him, and he is even prepared to walk away from here and work abroad. That is the galling part of it. He would leave everything he has here, and all that I can bring to him, for that little English whore," she said, trying hard to maintain her composure.

"Listen, Chichi, we will find a way to solve this. I never had the opportunity of working on Jenny. Perhaps with the right kind of persuasion I can lure her away from Greg. When he comes to hear of Jenny's disloyalty with me, he might just re-examine his position and find that you are the better choice."

Sherrifa seemed a little heartened at this. Her situation would certainly be improved if Jenny did not look so squeaky clean all the time. *If Greg sees her with a tarnished image, he would certainly be amenable to my charms again*, she thought. "Nikos, mon chère, I think your plan might have some merit. We should consider how best to put it into action."

They planned a series of formal occasions that Greg would be obliged to attend because of his position at the airport. Jenny would be expected to accompany him, and it would be during these occasions that Nikos would start to move in on Jenny. By the time Nikos left Sherrifa, she was feeling in much brighter spirits. She would now have another chance with Greg, and this time she was determined that nothing would go wrong. *Jenny would be crushed under her foot and discarded*, thought Sherrifa. *She does not belong here, and I will enjoy watching her crawl away with her tail between her legs.*

CHAPTER TWELVE

Brutality and blame, Monique, Hussein and Nikos

Jenny arrived at the hospital slightly late that morning and worked solidly until lunchtime, helping out on the wards when things got slow in the E.R. At two o'clock, Candy came looking for her to have lunch together. "Just give me five minutes, and I will be with you," said a smiling Jenny, happy to have some time with her friend again.

"It's so nice to have you back at the hospital again, Jenny. We have all missed you. Did you manage to come to terms with everything?"

"It wasn't easy and it took me some time, but I think that I have come to terms with things now. Being back in England was wonderful at first, but after a while, I began to miss the Middle East. That was quite a revelation!"

"Yes," said Candy, "I know how it is. This place gets into your blood after a while. Somehow, you can never go back to being content with the way you were before. What about Greg, have you truly forgiven him?"

"I wouldn't say *forgiven* is the right word. I think it is fairer to say that I have re-appraised our relationship. Once I got over the pain, I was able to think clearer and take into consideration how the system works here. Then I was able to understand how he could have been compromised into the situation. It still hurts to think of it, but Greg has been so considerate and caring that it has made coming back easy for me. I have lost a lot of my idealism, and hopefully we can both move on in a more mature manner," she said with determination.

Candy looked at her with admiration, knowing how hard it is to lose your ideals about love and life. She could see that Jenny had matured and was ready to be more pragmatic about her future.

"I'm so happy that you have resolved your feelings and have a new perspective on life here. It's hard enough adapting to the customs and culture of the country, but adapting to the elite culture of the airline is a mammoth task. In the end, it defeated me, but I believe you and Greg can make it work if you both put in the time and the effort," she said with sincerity.

"Well, I know one person that is not going to be rooting for us and that is Sherrifa. She is going to be waiting to pounce the moment either Greg or I slip up," Jenny said philosophically.

"That's for sure," rejoined Candy. "The best thing is to avoid her as much as possible."

"Avoid her? I wish I could. You know she calls all the social shots, and, in reality, Greg cannot afford to miss these functions where much of the business is done for the airline. He has to be there, and I would not be happy for him to go alone."

"Yeah, I can see your predicament," Candy acknowledged. "It's going to take all of your tact and diplomacy to face Sherrifa again after what happened."

"Yes, and you don't know the half of it. When Sherrifa came to say how sorry she was about the whole affair, I happened to mention that Greg and I would soon be having children and that I would be too busy to even remember his fling with her. Unfortunately, she had possession of knowledge that I didn't, and did not hesitate to use it as a weapon to push me even further away from Greg," she said hesitantly, remembering the pain of Sherrifa's disclosure.

"What was it?" asked Candy gently, sensing Jenny's vulnerability.

"For whatever reason," she said, trying to shrug off the mental picture that was trying to imprint itself on her mind, "Greg had told her that he was infertile and that he was unable to father children. Greg has told me since that he was afraid that he would lose me if he told me earlier in our relationship, and that is why he stayed silent about it." Jenny looked down trying to compose herself. She had thought she would be able to talk about this with Candy without undue emotion, but Sherrifa's actions and Greg's deceit still rankled her. Jenny was beginning to understand that she needed more time before these issues could be quietly laid to rest.

"Oh, Jenny, that's awful. I didn't imagine that even Sherrifa could stoop that low. No wonder you left in such a hurry. It was a double blow. How do you feel about the possibility of not having children?" asked Candy concerned.

"Well, as you probably know, Greg has had a fertility examination and the doctor has told him that there is a possibility of increasing his sperm count. So children might not be out of the question altogether. Then there is the option of adopting, of course. Either way, I want to have children," she said positively.

"And Greg?" queried Candy.

"He doesn't mind. He says he wants me to be happy. Now that the knowledge of his infertility has come out, he seems a lot calmer and more open about things."

"Yes, some men really feel that their whole manhood is at question if they have an infertility problem. They feel that they must preserve an aggressive, macho image in order to compensate," said Candy sagely.

"I can understand it, I suppose, with Greg. He knew that I desperately wanted to get pregnant, and his inability to oblige must have put him under a lot of pressure. Why couldn't he have just told me?" she lamented.

Candy looked searchingly at Jenny and asked her, "If he had told you before you got married that he could not father children, would you have still married him?"

Jenny took a minute to consider Candy's question. "You know, I'm not sure that I would have. I have always imagined myself with children, so perhaps I might have turned him down. In truth, I don't really know. But I understand your point."

"Although it was totally deceitful of Greg to keep the information from you, you can see his motivation. He could no doubt tell, in the same way that I can tell, how important children are to your life, and he did not feel that he could take the chance of being honest with you, if he hoped to keep you," Candy recounted, hoping she was clarifying things for Jenny.

"Well, I had better concentrate on the here and now, since we can't turn back the clock," said Jenny smiling.

"Speaking of the here and now," said Candy, her curiosity blatantly showing, "what were you doing yesterday with Khalil's cousin? And what was so important that he had to shoo us both away so he could talk to you alone?"

"Hmm," said Jenny, clearing her throat in a slightly embarrassed manner, "his name, as you know, is Talal. It so happened that I was sat next to him on the flight back. We got quite friendly," she said, trying to make light of it.

"Jenny, this is Candy you are talking to. Your lack of composure and flushed cheeks yesterday were not entirely due to the horrendous day we had. And that handsome Talal was looking at you with such intensity there had to be more to it," she insisted.

"I'm ashamed to tell you about it, but from the minute I laid eyes on him, I was very attracted to him. That's all it would have been if we had not got to talking. It seems that he felt the same about me; it was like there was an electrical current running between us. By the time we landed, I was agreeing to see him again when he was in town. I really don't know what came over me. Then yesterday, he was injured and turned up in the E.R. I could hardly refuse to have coffee with him in light of all that had transpired," she said slightly defensively.

"Jenny, calm down! I'm not judging you. I'm only curious. I asked Khalil about Talal yesterday, but he fobbed me off with some inadequate excuse, so I'm asking you."

"You may not be judging me, but I'm judging myself. I cannot understand how I could have let myself behave like that," she stated, looking firmly down at the ground with her cheeks flaming.

"Jenny, you are flesh and blood, and even the most controlled of us can be caught off-guard sometimes. You cannot punish yourself for something that hasn't happened. Just make sure that it doesn't go any further."

"That's what I was trying to tell him yesterday, but I'm afraid that I wasn't very convincing. And what's more, I still feel really attracted to him. I have honestly never felt this way before. Even when I first met Greg, the attraction was not this strong, and I was nuts about him until the Sherrifa thing," she said with considerable honesty.

"Jenny, your wounds are still raw, and it is understandable that part of you still rages at Greg for his infidelity. It will take time before your emotional life settles. Be kind to yourself and stop trying to be so perfect," she said gently.

"Do I seem as if I am trying to be perfect?" asked a shocked Jenny.

"Well, you do seem to try and put everything in neat conformist packages and file them away. I never see you taking chances and losing control for even a minute," she replied honestly.

"I'm amazed. I didn't think that I came over that way at all. But I suppose I do conform. The truth is that I'm too afraid not to, and I panic if things are not under control. Those neat little packages are my security. If I take them away, I'm lost," she said reflectively.

"Jenny, try letting go a bit, relax and enjoy life now. Forget about Talal. If he turns up again, worry about it then, but don't bog yourself down with unnecessary troubles," suggested Candy.

"Yes, you're right, I know. I will make a concerted effort to wind down a bit and take life as it comes."

Jenny returned to the E.R. feeling decidedly better after unburdening herself to Candy. Later, after finishing work, she was looking forward to relaxing with Greg in the evening. Things had been hectic since she'd returned. Tonight, she would be the one who took care of Greg.

On his return home, Greg was happy that Jenny was there waiting for him with a home cooked meal ready for them to eat. He took her in his arms and told her how much he had missed her being there for him. "When you were away, this apartment seemed like a mausoleum. I never understood that it was you that lit the place up and made it feel like home," he said while nibbling her ear.

"Aha!" she said playfully. "Does that mean that I have the upper hand now?"

Greg looked at her seriously and said, "From now on, you are the one who will call the shots. Whatever you want, you can have. Just never leave me again."

"Oh, Greg, let's make it work this time," she said, moved by the emotion in his voice.

"I'll do everything in my power to keep us together and make a comfortable life for us," he answered honestly.

After eating dinner and discussing the highlights of their day, they moved into the lounge with the remainder of the bottle of wine they had consumed over dinner. "Jen, there is a function at the Marriott at end of the week that I'm obliged to attend. Some executives from foreign carriers are here to discuss sharing some routes and pooling passengers. All the usual crowd are going to be there, and I will understand if you don't want to come. But I'd really like you to be there," he concluded, looking searchingly at her.

She hesitated a moment before answering, and then told him with strong conviction that she too wanted to be with him, and that she was quite capable of facing up to Sherrifa. "Does anyone else know about what happened between you and her?" enquired Jenny tentatively.

"I don't think so, love, but there's a good chance that Hussein knows, but he's too much of a gentleman to let it show."

"Well, that's settled then," she said. "We'll go on with our lives as before."

The evening of the function, Jenny went to great pains to look her best. She took half a day off from the hospital in order to have a complete beauty makeover with Leila. Leila was delighted to see Jenny back again. She had heard through the executive wives' grapevine that she had left. She really had not expected to see her return. But she soon came to understand that she had underestimated Jenny. From the gossip in the salon, Leila had ascertained that Sherrifa was no longer in control of the affair anymore. Now she wanted to pamper Jenny and show her how welcome she was here.

While Leila was manicuring her nails, Jenny said quietly, "You knew it was my husband, didn't you?"

"Yes, Madam Jenny, I did," she answered, seeing no point in lying. "Tell me, how many other people know about it?" asked Jenny, trying to ascertain the extent of her humiliation.

"Madam Jenny, first let me tell you zat I said nothing to anyone. But from ze friends of Sherrifa's, zere ees maybe four or five of zem zat would know and who would be eenterested. Zere are many women here who do not like Sherrifa. Zey theenk zat she ees a bad woman. But zey cannot say anytheeng about her because her father ees so powerful. Don't worry about what people theenk about eet. Zey weel respect you for coming back to face her again. Even zose four or five women are amused zat Sherrifa was put down by an Eenglish girl. But Madam Jenny, you must be very careful because Sherrifa weel not let you live peacefully. She weel be at your back za whole of za time."

"I know that, Leila, but I'm ready to face her. When I went back to England, I had enough time to think things out, and I now know that I want to be here, trying to make my marriage work. My husband is sorry for what he did and wants to make amends. I am not going to let Sherrifa spoil my chances of happiness," she said emphatically.

"Good, I theenk zat you weel be okay. You are much stronger zan before, and I weel help you eef I can. Eef I hear anything, zen I weel tell you, yes?" she told her, eager to help.

"Thanks, Leila, I appreciate that. I think I'll need all the help that I can get," she told her smiling. The rest of the afternoon went by in a pampered haze for Jenny. She relaxed in the sheer pleasure of Leila's ministrations. By the end of the afternoon, she looked stunning.

She and Greg arrived in good time at the Marriott, where the Gallaghers, Lamberts and, surprisingly, the Stianous were already gathered. Greg mentioned to Jenny that it was unusual for Nikos and his wife to arrive early as they usually came with Sherrifa and Hussein's entourage. Both Greg and Jenny were warmly received by everyone. All asked courteously about the health of Jenny's father. She felt rather a fraud while elaborating on her father's ill health. However, in order to save face, it was necessary. Both Nikos and Greg had told the others that she had made her hasty departure because of her father's illness. She assured all that he was in good health now. Greg looked at her admiringly, thinking that she was coping with the situation well. Watching her now, he saw that she had matured and seemed more than able to hold her own against everyone. Her ultimate test would be when she faced Sherrifa, and he only hoped that she would handle herself as diplomatically and adeptly with her.

During the period before Sherrifa's arrival, Nikos lost no time ingratiating himself with Jenny.

"Jenny, Jenny, how nice it is to see you so happy and well. We have all missed you so much," he said, trying to raise his voice to be heard above the noise of the band that had just begun to play. "And since I have not seen you for so long, I must insist that I have the pleasure of escorting you for the first dance. That is, of course, with Greg's permission," he added. Greg smiled and nodded his approval. Jenny was happy to oblige Nikos since she felt somewhat in his debt for all he had done for her when she had left. They were the first ones on the dance floor, and they looked to be an extremely handsome couple as they swung in tune to the music. The sight of them encouraged others to the dance floor, and soon they were lost from view of the others.

"Jenny," he said her name gently and warmly, "I'm so glad you have returned. I was so worried about you when you left that day. I know you must have been worried about your poor father, but I could not help feeling that there was something more that you were not telling me. Is everything all right now?"

252

he enquired, sure of his footing, having been fully informed of everything from Sherrifa.

Jenny was unsure of how to answer him, and she wondered whether Sherrifa had been callous enough to have discussed matters with Nikos. She opted for caution. "No, no, there really wasn't anything more. It's just that I don't handle crises too well when they concern people who are close to me," she answered ambiguously.

"I can understand that. I am not too good at handling crises of a personal nature either. But promise me that you will always look upon me as a friend if you need help again. Life was very dull while you were away, and I don't want you to run off without me knowing. Your beauty brightens up our little social circle, and you have become very dear to many of us," he said flatteringly.

"Now, now, Nikos I'm going to get a swelled head with all these compliments," she teased.

"It is nothing more than the truth," he countered.

Jenny just smiled and accepted the compliment. After a moment of silence, he looked at her and stroked her cheek softly with his fingers. "Jenny, you really are an incredibly beautiful woman, and I envy Greg so much. If only you and I were free, I would pursue you until you gave in to me," he said sincerely.

Jenny was thrown by his unaccustomed tenderness. As he moved closer to her, she felt the heat of his body and the sensuous tingle as he whispered in her ear. For a second, she could have given way to his seductiveness. Sensing the honesty of the moment, she did not want to rebuff him unkindly, so she told him that it would be easy to fall for his charm. But unfortunately, they were both spoken for. Nikos seemed happy with her answer and escorted her off the floor at the end of the dance.

"I thought you two were never coming back," exclaimed Greg jokingly. "Well, Jenny has been away for a long time, and you cannot blame me for making up for all the dances I have missed," responded Nikos.

As was usual when Sherrifa enters a room, a slight buzz of interest filters amongst the guests and all eyes turn upon her. Tonight was no exception; she looked breathtakingly beautiful. Sherrifa was dressed for the part, as she was wearing a designer cocktail dress of royal blue that clung to her voluptuous figure and offset her skin tone magnificently, giving her an iridescent glow. Her beauty was undeniable. Jenny was the only one in the room who could compete with her. Their entourage moved to the table amongst a bevy of waiters fussing to and fro around them. Sherrifa arrived at the table with Hussein at her side, enjoying the prestige that was afforded them, and sending unspoken messages to those gathered that she was a significant force to be reckoned with. Seeing Jenny sitting at the table, her first reaction was of anger and loathing. However, no one, except perhaps Nikos, saw the fleeting look of contempt flash across her face. Immediately, she walked over to where Jenny was sitting and greeted her effusively. "Jenny, Jenny 'ow wonderful to see you chèrie. We 'ave all missed you so much. Eet ees so good to 'ave you back 'ere again." Jenny bristled inside at the sight of this woman who was capable of so much evil, but equally as adeptly as Sherrifa, she smiled her brightest smile and assured her that she was delighted to be back and had no intention of leaving again in the near future. The evening continued smoothly with Jenny keeping pace with all of Sherrifa's velvet clawed remarks, and it was considered a success by all the business people both socially and financially.

The following day, Nikos dropped by Sherrifa's villa on his way to work. The maid answered the door, and he asked whether Madam Sherrifa was awake yet. He heard Sherrifa's distinctive voice coming from the lounge, telling him to come in. "Bon jour, Chichi, I did not know if you would be awake yet, but I wanted to update you about last night," he said cheerfully.

"Bon jour, Nikos, I had a terrible night. I was up even before Hussein left this morning. I only slept for about two hours, and I had horrible nightmares. I dreamt that my teeth and hair were falling out, and I woke up crying," she wailed miserably.

"Poor, Chichi," he responded sympathetically, taking her into his arms. Sometimes he perceived her as a child in need of reassurance. He held her comfortingly until she pulled away. "Chichi, you should not worry about silly things like that. Last night, our American friends told me that you were one of the most beautiful women they had ever seen. You looked magnificent, and no one could compare to your beauty."

"Don't tell me they didn't mention sweet Jenny," she shot back maliciously.

"They are used to her kind of superficial beauty, as they see it all the time where they live. You are the one who is special," he lied convincingly. In truth, they had mentioned both women, saying they represented the best of East and West. But he was not about to tell that to Sherrifa and risk her wrath. She seemed placated by his words, so he continued, "I had some luck with Jenny last night. I thought that you would want to know. She seems to be warming to me. I made a play for her, and she did not seem unwilling at all. Rather, she was quite playful, saying that if we were not both married, she would be tempted," he said smiling, unable to conceal his pleasure in finally eliciting a promising response out of Jenny.

"That's good, but don't move too quickly," she warned. Despite being confident of Nikos' prowess with women, she could not help feeling that Jenny might not succumb so easily. "I am sure that you will be able to win her over, but don't spoil it by rushing things."

"I will try to take my time with her, but I can already feel her giving way. I can hardly wait to have her," he confided.

"Well, when you do, just use her and throw her away. Don't get emotionally involved with her. I want her out of my life forever," she said aggressively.

"Don't worry, Chichi, other than you, there has never been a woman that I would change my life for." He took his leave of Sherrifa, gratified that he had been able to make her a little happier than when he first arrived.

Discreetly watching him leave, she noted what a good friend he was. She was rarely as low as she had been in the past few months, but he had stood by her. In truth, he was the only true friend she had whose shoulder she could cry on. Hussein was not interested in whether she had slept or not, or if she was feeling depressed. Besides, she was almost certain he was having an affair with Monique, although she had not mentioned it to Nikos. She knew that he would not take it lightly, and she did not want to upset any of the plans they had made. She wanted no diversions; she needed Nikos' full attention. *Oh God, Greg, what have you done to me?* she lamented. Ever since they had been together in the States, she had not been the same. She had not experienced these feelings of longing for any other man. Her thoughts went back to the previous night. It had been a torturous evening for her. It had cut like a knife watching Greg look at Jenny with love and admiration whilst trying to avoid making eye contact with her. She knew that deep inside him, somewhere, there was a part of him that was attracted to her, but he was refusing to acknowledge it. Somehow she had to unlock that door inside him and get him back. Walking away from the window, she resolved to get herself back on form again. She wasn't going to let some little nurse come between her and the thing she wanted.

Nikos drove away from Sherrifa's villa in high spirits, convinced that now was the time to move in on Jenny. He decided to make changes to the roster to ensure Greg would be away flying for most of the month, and when little Jenny was at her loneliest, he would appear like a knight in shining armor. It was foolproof, as it had worked with every other wife he had seduced before, and it would work again now, he was convinced.

Hussein was in his office debating whether he should phone Monique right now or wait a little longer. He guessed Nikos would be on his way to work, but Hussein decided that he had better wait until he actually saw him in his office before he risked calling her. He did not want to put her in an awkward position with Nikos. Hussein was eager to talk to her, as the evening before, he had not even had the opportunity of having a dance with her or to tell her how much she meant to him. Within minutes, Nikos stuck his head around Hussein's office door and asked if all the flights were under control. Waving him off with a hasty OK sign, he lost no time in phoning Monique.

"Hello, are you free to talk to me?" enquired Hussein.

"Just give me a moment, and I will go to the extension in the den," said Monique, delighted to hear Hussein's voice. Picking up the extension in the den, she ran back to close the line in the entrance where she had first picked up the phone, slightly anxious that her maid might overhear their conversation.

"Here I am, darling," she said a little breathlessly, "I am more comfortable in here to talk to you."

"I am so sorry that I did not have a chance to dance with you last night, my love. It was an important deal that we were making, and I wanted to ensure that they agreed to our terms," he said apologetically.

"Of course, I don't mind. I understand fully. Besides, all I had to do was to look in your eyes to know how you were feeling," she responded kindly.

"You are wonderful, darling. How I wish we could be together all of the time. I have missed you so much. It has been twenty-three days since we were together, and Nikos hasn't any overnight flights for the rest of the month."

"I know, darling, I feel the same way too, but there is very little that we can do but wait. I am not afraid of waiting, are you?" she asked

"No, of course I'm not. What we have will stand the test of time. Neither of us are teenagers. Although I admit to feeling like one when I am around you and smell your perfume. You drive me wild with desire."

"Mmm," she responded enthusiastically, "I know exactly what you mean. The feeling is entirely mutual. One day, darling, I'm sure things will work out for us, and life will give us a chance of happiness together. Oh how I long for that day," she sighed, wondering what could possibly free them both from their respective burdens. "It was nice to see Jenny back again last night, Greg was looking so despondent while she was away," she said, changing the subject abruptly.

"Yes, I agree. She seems to be a very sweet person. I have heard that she works very hard at the hospital and is very well-liked there. I only hope that Greg appreciates what he has got in her," he said philosophically.

"Why do you say that? Does Greg mess around behind her back?" Monique asked in surprise. She had pegged Greg as a fairly reliable man, not likely to be interested in extramarital pursuits.

"Unfortunately, my love, Sherrifa has taken a shine to him, and he might have some problems staying out of her reach. At a guess, I would say Jenny's recent absence was due more to her finding out about Greg's infidelity than to her father's illness. But I must say that he was much more attentive to her last night than in the past. Possibly being alone made him see what he stood to lose."

"I'm so sorry to hear about that, darling," she said sympathetically.

"Don't worry or think that Sherrifa bothers me personally. As far as I'm concerned, she is my wife in name only. Other than that, she can do what she likes. It is only her capacity to cause pain to the innocent parties in her affairs that bothers me," he said sincerely.

"I know what you mean. In fact, I was wondering whether Jenny might be Nikos' next target. Seeing him dancing with her last night, I could detect all the usual signs. I just hope she will not fall victim to him," she commiserated.

"Indeed, I had wondered the same thing too, but I didn't want to embarrass you by mentioning it."

"Don't worry about embarrassing me. Nikos took care of that a long time ago. I am immune to his philandering, but like you, I hate his capacity to hurt decent people."

"Let's just hope they can both withstand the pressures they are likely to encounter from our respective spouses." The door opened in Hussein's office, and he asked Monique to hold for a moment while his secretary brought next month's roster in for him. "Darling, that was my secretary, and I told her to bring me the new roster as soon as it was completed. From what I can see here, Nikos has no night stops at all for next month. That means another month without being with you. He does have a Gulf flight in two days' time, though, when he leaves at about two o'clock in the afternoon and does not land until eleven in the evening. Would you think me too demanding if I asked if we could be together then? I am missing you so much," he said tenderly.

"Of course I wouldn't, I'm missing you in the same way. I will arrange for Roger to stay with his friend after school, and we can be alone for a few hours. I can't wait to see you," she said brightly, happy at the proximity of their next meeting. She had been steeling herself for the possibility of a long wait.

"I will call you tomorrow, darling," he told her, feeling similarly brightened.

"Au revoir, mon chère," she whispered in her native tongue.

For both Monique and Hussein, the two days seemed to drag on for an eternity. When finally the day came, they were both filled with eager anticipation. Hussein waited at the airport until Nikos' flight had taken off and then phoned Monique.

"The flight has left, darling. Is it alright for me to come to you now?"

"Yes, everything is taken care of and I'm alone here. I am so happy we can be together for a while," she whispered to him.

"I am leaving right now. I'll be with you in about twenty-five minutes." Hussein sped down the highway, which was virtually deserted, as most people were at home eating lunch or settling down for their afternoon siestas. He reached Monique in less than twenty minutes. Opening the door to him, she reprimanded him, "Darling, no matter how much we want to be together, please don't drive at that speed down the highway. I want you here in one piece, not in pieces. You are so very precious to me," she whispered, closing the door behind him.

"I know, I'm sorry, I wasn't thinking. I just wanted to get to you as fast as I could," he replied apologetically.

"Would you like a cool drink?" she offered.

"You are all the drink I need," he said, lifting her in his arms, sweeping her upstairs to the guest room, which they had made their own. Laying her down on the bed, he admired her sensual beauty. "You are so beautiful, Monique. I am the luckiest man alive to have you," he whispered.

"I am also lucky to be loved by such a fine man as you," she replied, pulling him down on top of her, "and to have such a wonderful lover." Her words sent flames of passion shooting through him. He pulled off the simple cotton shirt she was wearing and began to kiss her passionately on her shoulders and breasts. She closed her eyes and enjoyed the blissful sensuousness of his fiery kisses. Her breathing became heavier as she thrust her head back. Her lips parted as she gasped in pleasure of his searching touch. Her whole body was burning with desire for him. She pulled off his shirt and trousers, eager for him to unite with her. She stroked his hard, tensile body, enjoying the sensation of his rock-hard penis touching her belly. In seconds, their bodies were joined together in ecstatic union. Sighing and gasping, they rocked together in fevered abandon. He wanted to speak to her as they made love and tell her how he felt when he was inside her and so close to her, but his passion was so great that he could not speak. As if sensing his words, she responded by arching her back and bringing them even closer together each time he thrust his penis inside her. She moaned as she felt the beginning of an orgasm triggering inside her, and she felt him push deeper and deeper inside her as he began to climax. Arching and gasping, she lost control of her body, together their union found ultimate gratification. Slowly their passion subsided, both feeling that they had experienced something magical and unique.

Nikos' flight had taken off on time, without problem. However half an hour after leaving base, the aircraft developed a technical problem. Nikos ascertained the extent of the problem and contacted base. "This is flight KA 202, Captain Stianou, I have a technical."

"What is your status?" enquired base.

"Err, I have a borderline no-go item, it should not be a problem. We can have it fixed in the Gulf, request permission to continue?"

The dispatch officer quickly phoned the V.P. of operations to get clearance for the flight to continue. Returning to the mike, the dispatch officer contacted Nikos again. "That's negative, captain, sorry. Due to having a member of the royal family on board, I have been advised to tell you to return to base."

"OK, will comply," returned Nikos. He had suspected that might be the response. The airline had to be particularly vigilant in matters of security around the royal family. He sent for the bursar to inform the royal family member of the situation and then made an announcement to the other passengers.

After landing, Nikos prepared himself for an hour's wait until the snag could be fixed. He informed operations of his whereabouts and settled down in his office with a newspaper. Before fifteen minutes had elapsed, the operations officer phoned to tell him that there was a problem finding a replacement part in sufficient time to make the flight viable with his aircraft, so they were switching to a 727 instead, and that Nikos could stand down from duty.

Nikos thanked him and put the phone down. He was not unhappy to have been relieved of the flight. By the time they would have taken off again, it would have made it a long day. He stretched and yawned and made the decision to go home and relax. Getting into the car, he put on a cassette and took a leisurely drive home, contemplating how he would make his move on Jenny. He had already fixed the roster so Greg would be away for ninety percent of the month. That would give him ample opportunity to ingratiate himself with Jenny. As he arrived at his villa, he looked at his watch, it was four thirty. Pulling in the drive, he was surprised to see Hussein's car parked there. His senses suddenly alerted, so he decided to drive around the back and make an inconspicuous entrance. There should not be any legitimate reason for Hussein being here in his absence. He had seen him before his flight and there had been nothing out of the ordinary going on. Something told him that whatever was happening in the house was not above board.

He braked gently at the rear of the house, leaving his car door open to avoid alerting anyone to his presence. All was silence around the villa. He quietly unlocked the back door and went into the maid's kitchen. He was surprised that none of the servants were around. They were usually to be found gossiping together in the kitchen at this time of day. Staying in the back of the villa, he silently ascended the stairs until he came to the landing where the bedrooms were located. Tiptoeing along, he listened at each door, straining to hear voices. When he reached the guest bedroom, he was not disappointed. He could clearly hear the voices of Monique and Hussein in animated conversation. He heard Monique laughing; it had been years since he had heard her laugh like that. He was suddenly gripped with overwhelming jealousy and anger at the thought of another man making her laugh so happily. He had always thought that Monique was happy playing the part of the martyred wife. He thought that her upbringing, with its emphasis on "noblesse oblige," would prevent her from ever being unfaithful to him. He believed that she would stand by him for better or for worse. Now here she was, undoubtedly in the arms of Hussein, laughing and joking, perhaps it was even directed at him.

Unreason threatened to overwhelm him. He wanted to storm into the room and confront them both. However, reason prevailed and his manipulative logic clicked in, and he decided to wait and see what else transpired. In minutes, he heard all the confirmation he needed that his wife and Hussein were having an affair. The unmistakable sounds of lovemaking echoed through the door. Not trusting his emotions, he turned on his heels and returned to the maid's kitchen downstairs. There he waited until dark. It was nine thirty before he heard them coming down the stairs. He rushed outside and round to the front of the villa, hiding behind a large shrub in the garden. From there, he watched Monique and Hussein embrace at the door. Seeing them both in front of him looking so happy only served to fuel his anger which was now threatening to overtake him. The moment Hussein drove away, he stormed into the house, kicking each door open until he found Monique. Alarmed by the sudden noises, Monique ran downstairs from the guest bedroom that she was planning to tidy. Nikos confronted her as she stood on the stairs. "Whore! You are no better than the rest of them," he screamed, while leaping up the stairs two at a time to reach her. "You filthy whore," he said, grabbing her hair that was hanging loosely round her shoulders. "Call yourself an aristocrat, you are nothing but a disgusting whore," he said, slapping her fiercely across the face. "What do you have to say for yourself, whore?" he demanded savagely.

Filled with fear, Monique was unable to respond. Her silence only enraged him the more. "Speak, whore, and tell me all about it. Did you enjoy fucking him?" Still unable and unwilling to speak to him, she tried to pull away from his vice-like grip. Nikos was in a blind rage by this time, feeling her pull away, he tightened his grip on her and started to shake her. "Speak, you filthy whore!" he said, slapping her again on her face. Using all her strength, she twisted out of his grip, trying to escape him. He grabbed for her again, knocking her off her balance and down to the bottom of the stairs. Seeing her lying on the floor awakened the beast within him. He jumped down the stairs and began kicking her in the side. Every time she struggled to her feet, he slammed her down to the floor again, kicking her repeatedly. Eventually she collapsed, unable to move anymore. Nikos spat on her and left the house.

Hussein left Monique feeling uplifted. He did not feel like returning to his villa nor did he wish to run the risk of an encounter with Sherrifa. Instead, he decided to drive back to the airport and finish up some work that he had left pending. Arriving at the airport, he stopped in at operations to see what was happening with the flights.

"There was a small snag on KA 202 this afternoon. They returned to base thirty minutes after takeoff. We had to switch the flight to the 727, but everything's running on time now, sir," reported the operations officer. Hussein was overcome with a feeling of foreboding, knowing that it was Nikos' flight that had returned to base. That meant he had been in town since at least four o'clock this afternoon. He went quickly to his office with an overwhelming sense that all was not well with Monique. He dialed her number, hoping to speak to her. If he got Nikos he would say he was phoning to ask about the technical issue this afternoon. The phone rang and rang but there was no reply. His feeling of unease was intensifying. He decided to return to Monique's villa, and if Nikos was around, he would use the same excuse about the afternoon's technical snag. As he drove back down the highway, he allowed himself to think of the worst. Had Nikos returned back to the villa and seen them both together? If he had, then he dreaded to think what state Monique might be in. He knew that Nikos had a savage streak in him. He hoped to God that his suspicions were unfounded.

When he reached Monique's villa and saw the front door wide open, he feared the worst. He went swiftly inside and called her name. Hearing a muted groan, he turned and saw her lying like a broken doll, battered and bruised at the bottom of the stairs. Fear overwhelmed him as he rushed to her side. *Oh please, God, don't let her be dead*, he prayed. Touching her face, he was relieved to find that she was warm and breathing. "Monique, Monique," he whispered, putting his hand underneath her head. As he did so, he felt a sticky wetness, and he pulled his hand out to find it covered with blood. Fear stirred within him again at sight of the bloody gash on her head. "Oh God, Monique, what have I brought upon you?" he sobbed.

Slowly he felt her move. "Monique, Monique, wake up my darling," he pleaded. Her eyes flickered open and registered confusion at first. As the memory of what had happened returned to her, she screwed up her face in pain. "Darling, don't try and move too much, I'm afraid that you might have some broken bones," he said gently.

Ignoring his advice, she shuffled up onto her elbows and tried to stand. Hussein grabbed her arm to steady her. Cringing in pain, she made it to her feet. "I don't think I am too badly hurt. It is just my left side that feels strange," she said breathlessly.

"Let's get you into the den where you can lie down."

When he had got her settled in the den, he suggested that they call the company doctor.

"No, I don't want to make a fuss. I'm sure I'm all right," she said.

"Look, darling, I am equally sure that you are not all right. You need medical attention. Who did this to you, Monique?" he asked, already certain of the answer.

"Nikos," she answered simply.

"Did he see us together?" he asked.

She nodded, the pain showing in her eyes.

"Oh God, I'm so sorry, my love. I wish I'd been here to protect you," he said with anguish. "You should not have borne this alone. Somehow I will make it up to you."

Monique just put her finger up to his lips to silence him. The effort to speak to him was too great.

"Darling, we must get some medical help for you," he insisted.

"What am I going to say happened to me?" she asked.

"We will say that you fell down the stairs. Now let me call the doctor," he insisted.

"No, I prefer to keep this quiet if possible. I'm sure that nothing serious is the matter with me," she implored.

Hussein thought for a minute and then made a suggestion to Monique. "Listen, darling, let me call Jenny. She doesn't live very far away, and she has enough medical expertise to know if you need attention or not. I'll tell her that you have had an accident and that you don't know whether you should call the doctor. I feel sure that Jenny will be discreet about it. What do you think?"

She considered his words for a moment and decided it was probably a good idea. "Very well, give her a call."

Hussein phoned operations to find out Greg's number. It was Greg who answered the call.

"Greg, this is Hussein. I'm sorry to disturb you at this time of night, but Monique has had an accident. She has fallen down the stairs and looks in a bit of a bad way, but refuses to see the doctor. I was wondering if Jenny could come and have a look at her. She doesn't want to make a fuss, but I would feel happier if someone with medical knowledge saw her."

"Of course, Hussein, I'm sure Jenny would be only too happy to help. Let me call her for you." He quickly shouted to Jenny and explained the situation.

"Look, we will be there in about ten minutes. Jenny says to keep Monique still until we get there."

Hussein closed the phone, happy to have someone else to help him. Greg and Jenny arrived promptly. Hussein let them in, explaining that he had dropped in on his way from the airport to have a word with Nikos about the flight this afternoon. He was not in, but Hussein had found Monique at the bottom of the stairs. Jenny went quickly into the den and began to examine Monique. From the paleness of her skin, she could see that Monique was in shock. As she assessed Monique's injuries, she quickly came to the conclusion that she needed to be taken to the hospital for X-rays.

"Monique, I know that you don't want to, but I must insist that we take you to the hospital. You have, most certainly, some broken ribs, and I think that you may have dislocated your collarbone. But more importantly, the injury to your head may have concussed you and needs to be monitored. I can arrange for you to be taken care of at the University Hospital where I work. The staff will look after you well there, and I will stay with you until we know what's happening," said Jenny persuasively.

Monique gave in to Jenny's persuasions. Her injuries were beginning to give her a lot of pain now; she knew that to refuse further medical investigation would be foolhardy.

"Thank you, Jenny, I will be glad to go to the hospital with you. I'm sorry to be such a trouble to everyone," she said apologetically.

"Stop worrying about other people. You should be concentrating on yourself right now," reprimanded Jenny. "Besides, we are all friends, and what are friends for but to help one another when they are in need?"

Monique smiled her gratitude.

"I will follow behind the three of you in my car, if you don't mind driving Monique and Jenny to the hospital," suggested Greg.

"I am more than happy to do that, Greg," said Hussein gratefully as he wanted to ensure that Monique arrived safely at the hospital, where she could be looked after.

The two men helped Monique gently to her feet and guided her to Hussein's car. As she settled into the back seat with Jenny beside her, they heard the sound of a car pulling into the drive. Hussein got out of the car and saw Nikos walking towards them.

"What's going on here?" asked Nikos, feigning ignorance of the situation. Burning with rage, Hussein fought down his emotions and informed him of what he already knew.

"In your absence, Monique has had an accident. It seems that she has fallen down the stairs, and Jenny and Greg have been good enough to come out and help her."

For a moment, the two men faced each other with hatred burning in their eyes, both aware of the other's deeds. But knowing nothing would be gained by a showdown so they both backed off, knowing that it was necessary to save face. The game must be played well, no matter how provoking the circumstances.

Nikos quickly assessed the situation and responded in the appropriate manner. He had not seen Jenny at first in the darkness, and her presence made it imperative that he play the role of concerned husband. "My God, where is my wife? Is she badly hurt?" he enquired convincingly.

"She is in the back of Hussein's car with Jenny. We were just about to set off for the University Hospital," interjected Greg, who had walked over from his car.

Nikos walked hurriedly to Hussein's car and fussed over Monique. "My darling, what has happened? Are you in a lot of pain?" he asked her.

Fighting back her desire to spit in his face, she answered civilly for the sake of propriety. "I am in as much pain as you would expect, given the injuries I have."

"We must waste no time in getting you to the hospital. Can I get you into our car?" asked Nikos.

"No, I don't think that is good idea," interrupted Jenny authoritatively. "She has already been moved more often than is good for her, and to move her again would only give her more pain and could cause more damage."

"Okay then, I will ride along with you in that case," he replied.

"Fine, jump in," said Hussein unenthusiastically, resenting Nikos' intrusion.

Arriving at the hospital, Jenny ran ahead and informed the necessary staff members of the situation and returned with two orderlies who brought a trolley bed to collect Monique.

Nikos played his trump card at this point. "Thank you, Hussein, for all your help. I think I can take over from here," he told him smugly, knowing how much it would hurt him to have to relinquish Monique to his care.

"Right, okay, don't hesitate to ask if I can be of any further help," he answered, pain tearing at his insides at the thoughts of leaving Monique.

"Don't worry, I won't," Nikos replied with barely disguised malice.

Inside the hospital, Jenny efficiently coordinated matters, and Monique was quickly seen by the doctor and taken for X-rays. She was initially kept overnight because of her concussion and the shock she was suffering. Nikos insisted that he should stay at the hospital with her. But Jenny gently dissuaded him, seeing how much it disturbed Monique.

"Don't worry, Nikos, we will take good care of her, and I am going to stay here as long as she needs me," said Jenny.

"I will drive you back, if you like," volunteered Greg who was beginning to feel rather redundant. "You can phone me if you want me to pick you up later, Jen."

"Okay, love, but I think I will ask them to bring a bed in here for me for the night, and I will stay with Monique," answered Jenny.

"Jenny, that is so kind of you. I don't know how we are going to repay you," said Nikos ingratiatingly.

"I don't need any repayment, just seeing Monique back on her feet again will be sufficient," said Jenny with a smile.

After everyone had left, Monique began to settle a little more, although she was still shaking intermittently with the remnants of shock.

"You will start feeling better in a little while," consoled Jenny. "Unfortunately, we can't give you anything to calm you down because of the concussion you suffered. We need to keep an eye on you for the next twenty-four hours. Are you warm enough?"

"I am beginning to feel warmer on the outside now, but I still feel a bit icy on the inside, if you know what I mean," she responded.

"Don't worry, that is normal after what you have gone through. Would you like to have a warm drink?"

"Yes, I think that I could manage that. Oh, and Jenny, I forgot to tell Nikos that Roger is staying with his friend tonight. Will you please ask him to pick him up from school and explain what has happened? And ask the maid to take care of him until I am out of the hospital," she said worriedly.

"Of course I will, and if you would prefer, I am quite happy to have Roger stay with me until you are feeling better," said Jenny willingly.

"That is so kind of you, but I think he will be fine at home. My maid is very fond of him and has babysat for him since he was a baby. She is more like an aunt to him."

"Oh, that's fine then," answered Jenny, slightly disappointed that she would not have the opportunity to look after him herself. Leaving Monique briefly, Jenny went off to the staff room and made Monique a weak cup of tea and brought it back to her. She drank it down gratefully. The warm liquid began to restore her to normality. They chatted quietly for another twenty minutes until Jenny sensed that Monique was beginning to tire.

"Listen, I think we should try and settle down for the night now. The hospital routine begins at an unearthly hour, and then the sound of rattling trolleys and banging doors will be sure to wake you up. I am going to get myself a hospital gown to sleep in, and then we will put the lights off. There will also be someone coming in every couple of hours to check on you as well, so we better grab some sleep while we can."

Monique acquiesced gratefully. Fatigue had overtaken her, and she was happy to settle down.

It was, as Jenny predicted, a disturbed night, but happily Monique did not show any more signs of concussion. It was two more days before she was discharged from the hospital. She had made a good recovery but was still feeling very sore from the injuries to her ribs and collarbone. She was strapped up quite tightly but still able to move around with care. Nonetheless, she was truly happy to be back home again, away from the noisy hospital. Monique loved her independence and needed to get back in the swing of things again. Unfortunately, there was little that she could actually manage to do but walk around her precious garden and read books. Hussein had contacted her as soon as was possible after her discharge, eager to have firsthand knowledge from her. Nikos had kept information on her condition to a minimum, knowing that it would irk Hussein. That was all the retribution Nikos was likely to have since Sherrifa had been unsympathetic to him when he confronted her with the news of Hussein and Monique's unfaithfulness.

Nikos had gone to Sherrifa full of fury, hoping she would deliver some form of retribution, but all he was met with was indifference. "What on earth do you expect? She is still a young, attractive woman, and you are not taking care of her. It is not as if you have any kind of relationship with her," she said unsympathetically.

"Don't you even care that Hussein is sleeping with her?" he asked, hoping to provoke some emotion in her.

"Frankly, no, I don't. Besides, we have other fish to fry right now. Jenny is who you should be concentrating on now," she said sharply.

"But …" interjected Nikos. Sherrifa snapped,

"Get over it," cutting off his sentence.

"Okay, Sherrifa, whatever you want," he conceded, knowing it would do him no good to continue.

He left her villa shaking with anger, determined that somehow he would wreak vengeance upon his wife and Hussein. *At least I can do one thing: I can prevent them from having the opportunity to meet for at least a month. I have only local flights this month, and I will be watching both of them.* That thought brought him some small comfort. His thoughts turned to Jenny. *If Sherrifa wants her out of Greg's way, I am more than willing to comply. Jenny is going to be such a sweet victory.* He couldn't wait to feel her lithe, young body under him. With Greg away for the majority of the month, she would be his for the taking. *Soon*, he thought, *very soon*.

CHAPTER THIRTEEN

A step too far, Nikos makes his move

Greg came home waving about the new roster. "Jen, I've got the fullest roster ever this month. I am hardly home at all. The airline has, fortunately, been chartered to bring pilgrims from the Far East to attend the Hajj, and we are really pushed for crew. I'm truly sorry about this, darling. If you'd like, I could arrange for you to come on one of the trips with me. I am doing a New York trip at the end of the month. Would you like to come on that with me?" he asked consolingly.

"That sounds nice, but you have such a short stay there that it isn't really worth the jet lag, darling. I'll be all right, I have my work to keep me busy. If I change my mind, I will let you know. Now, come and eat this dinner I have slaved over," she joked, unwrapping the take-away meal that she had picked up on her way from work.

"Mmm, it looks delicious," he responded in kind.

"Jenny, you don't have to be a hermit while I'm away. There are some parties that we are invited to, and you can always go along with Monique and Nikos. They'll be only too happy to take you after what you did for them," volunteered Greg, trying to ensure that his wife was entertained in his absence.

"I will see," said Jenny doubtfully.

"Promise me that you won't just sit at home feeling lonely," insisted Greg.

"Oh, all right, if it will shut you up," she agreed reluctantly.

Jenny waved Greg off the following day, knowing she would be seeing very little of him for the next month. She was determined that she would fare better than she had during his absence when he was on the training course. Her day passed quickly in the usual hustle and bustle of the emergency room. By the time she left for home, she was pleasantly tired, although a little despondent at the thought of having lonely nights for the next month. As she pulled in at home, Hilda intercepted her at the entrance to her apartment.

"Marhaba, Jenny, how are you," she enquired in her friendly accented English.

"I am fine, though Greg is away at the moment. He has a very busy schedule this month," she replied.

"Yes, yes, he told me, and zat is why you are coming to have dinner with us zis evening. We are having some friends over, and you will enjoy zere company. Go and change and we will see you in an hour," she told Jenny fussily.

"Oh, thank you, that will be nice," said Jenny, brightening. She and Greg had been on other occasions to Hilda and Fouad's dinner parties, and they were noisy, gossipy occasions where everyone felt at home. It was a world away from the stiff formality and protocol of the airline parties. The evening turned out to be a lively affair that was enjoyed by all. After the first course of delectable food, Jenny found herself in the company of a young woman whom she had met at a previous party. She was a young, sparkly Arab woman named Hannah, who was in her early thirties and seemed to know what everyone in town was doing. She spent quite some time talking with Jenny. She wanted to know all about her work at the hospital, and if it was true about Dr. Khalil and the divorced Canadian girl getting married. Jenny smiled and told her what she knew.

"Zat is interesting. You know zat eet ees very unusual for Arab men to marry divorced foreign women. She must be very beautiful," said Hannah, pushing for more information.

"Candy is my good friend, and I can tell you that she is not only very beautiful but also a very warm and sensitive person. I'm sure they will make an ideal couple. He is very much in love with her," Jenny informed her.

"But, doesn't she have three children?" enquired Hannah, her eyes getting bigger and rounder.

"She does, indeed, but it does not make a lot of difference to Dr. Khalil. He would take her if she had a dozen children. Besides, the children are looked after mainly by her in-laws, although she sees them regularly."

Hannah was practically falling off her seat at this latest disclosure. "But didn't her ex-husband object to her remarrying? You know zat is is very unusual in za Arab world," she said incredulously.

"Well, Candy's ex-husband is an airline pilot who is more liberal than most Arab men, so perhaps that has something to do with it," volunteered Jenny. "Yes, yes, zat must be it. Za pilots have a different life to za rest of us. You know, zey are very spoiled, and zey are allowed to get away weez so much."

"Yes, that's what they tell me," said Jenny with a smile, hoping Hannah would change the subject.

"Of course, you are married to a pilot as well," remembered Hannah.

"Yes, I am. He is away at the moment, in the Far East."

"You must get very lonely," she told Jenny sympathetically.

"Yes, it can get lonely when he is away for a long time," she replied philosophically, thinking of the lonely night she would be spending later on. *The first night is always the worst*, she thought to herself.

"Do you travel very much weez your 'usband?"

"Not as much as people would imagine. Often their trips are so short that there is little point in going with them. You just get tired and bad tempered from the travelling. I would rather be rested and fresh for him when he comes home."

Hannah nodded her approval. She obviously thought Jenny was the right kind of foreign girl to be married to an Arab man. She seemed to have her priorities right. She proceeded to tell Jenny about a forthcoming trip to the States. "My 'usband has got a fantastic deal from 'is travel agent, and eet ees much cheaper zan just buying za ticket from za airline."

"Oh, yes," said Jenny, trying to look enthusiastic, "which travel agent did he use?"

"Ah, eet was Phoenicia Travel. Zey are very very good," said an enthused Hannah.

"I seem to have heard of them before," said Jenny, trying to remember where she had heard that name before. In a second, it came back to her. It had been Talal, who said his family ran a travel agency here in Kharja and that he was responsible for taking groups of tourists to the Holy Land for tours. The thought of Talal sent a jolt through her. She had believed that she had shut him away in a dark and distant part of her mind. But the thoughts of him churned up her neat and orderly mind, leaving her feeling suddenly vulnerable and insecure. "I remember, I met the brother of the travel agent on a flight once, and he told me about his work," she said.

"Zere are four brothers," said Hannah conspiratorially, "and zey are all so good looking. Zey have zose lovely green eyes. We theenk zat green eyes are very special here in za Middle East." Hannah leaned forward and whispered in Jenny's ear, "Eet is said zat one of za brothers works for za resistance in Koudara." Hannah seemed particularly proud of this piece of information and waited to see Jenny's response.

"Oh, that sounds very dangerous," she replied, trying to fight down the feeling that it might be Talal who was the one.

"Yes eet ees, but zey say he ees very clever and avoids being caught," she said, assuming the air of someone who had inside information.

"And do they know which brother it is?" ventured Jenny, unable to conceal her interest.

"No, no one knows which brother eet ees, but I theenk zat eet ees Talal, because he ees za only one zat ees not married. He ees different from za others too. He ees like za pilots, very liberal."

Jenny's heart had leapt involuntarily at the sound of Talal's name. She would have liked to have pressed for more information, but Hilda was hustling everyone to the table that was filled with delicious desserts that she had prepared. No one needed encouragement, as Hilda's desserts were famous. Everyone filled their plates full with exquisite Arabic pastries, stuffed with all manner of delicious fillings. Hannah moved on from Jenny during dessert, eager to impart the news of Dr. Khalil and the divorced Canadian girl to the willing ears of the other female guests. Jenny chatted with others until the end of the evening, trying to rid herself of the thoughts of Talal that kept creeping into her mind. By the time she left, she was wide awake and troubled with the ever-present thoughts of Talal. Sleep was difficult for her that night; she tossed and turned trying to get Talal out of her thoughts. In the end, she resolved that she would speak to Dr. Khalil the next day and ask him if he had any knowledge of Talal or his brothers being involved in the Resistance. With this plan of action made, she managed to fall into a light, unsatisfying sleep. She was glad when it was morning and was able to set off for work. At least there, her duties precluded the possibility of dwelling on unbidden thoughts.

She threw herself into her work with great energy and began to feel more in control of herself and her thoughts. By lunchtime, she felt significantly brighter. As usual, Candy came to join her and they ate lunch together. However, on returning to the emergency room after lunch, she saw Dr. Khalil's door open. Pausing at the door, he looked up and smiled, "Can I do anything for you?" he asked in a friendly manner.

"As a matter of fact, perhaps you can. Last night I was at a dinner party and one of the guests was mentioning your cousins. She said that not only did they have an excellent travel agency, but one of the brothers might be involved with the resistance in Koudara. I just wondered if there is any truth to it?" she asked in as neutral a manner as she could muster.

Khalil looked intently at Jenny, making her feel uncomfortable. He had been unprepared for such a query. Putting his pen down, he answered her. "Come in and sit down, Jenny. I imagine that you are asking this because you have met Talal and fear that it might be him."

Jenny reddened and nodded, unable to hide the truth from Khalil's searching look.

"Well first, let me put your mind at rest. There is always talk about unconventional people being part of the Resistance. But that is all it is, talk. You should not take dinner party gossip too seriously. Secondly, as I have already indicated, Talal is an unconventional man. It is quite clear that he is more than a little interested in you. What you do about that is entirely your business, but be warned, he is not a man to be taken lightly. If you involve yourself with him, you might be getting into something that you wish you had never started. He is my cousin, and I care for him deeply. He has many admirable qualities, but he is no ordinary man. That's all I can really tell you," he concluded, affording her one of his deeply compassionate smiles.

"Thank you, Khalil, I appreciate the information," she said with a somber face and left the room silently. Returning to her work, she once more resolved to banish Talal from her thoughts.

Nikos' fingers toyed with the telephone on his desk at work. *Was now the right time to begin his seduction of Jenny?* Greg had been away for a week, and he knew Jenny was invited to the Lambert's party this evening. Greg had conveniently asked Nikos to keep his eye on Jenny, and to make sure that she went out to functions with Monique and him. *Yes*, he decided, *now was the time*. Picking up the phone, he dialed her number. It was six o'clock in the evening, and she should be home from the hospital.

"Hello," said Jenny, glad to have the phone ring and break the silence of the apartment that she had just entered.

"Hi, Jenny, this is Nikos. How are you doing without that husband of yours?" he said cheerfully.

"Oh, not bad under the circumstances, I'm keeping busy with my work at the hospital during the day, and I am reading a good novel in the evenings," she replied cheerily.

"Well, I was phoning to see if you are going to the Lambert's this evening. Monique was saying that she would like to see you again," proposed Nikos.

"Oh, I wasn't really planning on going. I don't like going to these do's on my own," responded Jenny, wishing that she could have some company but not wanting to put Nikos and Monique to any trouble on her part.

"Well, I don't think that is good enough, Madam Youssef. You cannot hide yourself away just because your husband is out of town," he told her with mock sternness. "You must come along with Monique and me tonight. Besides, Greg made me promise not to let you sit at home every evening, so I am not going to take no for an answer."

"Well, I suppose I cannot refuse, in that case," she replied, happy to escape her lonely evening routine.

"We will pick you up at eight then. See you later."

The relationship between Nikos and Monique had not deteriorated since his attack on her, only because there was nothing left to deteriorate, and their cold, formal indifference prevailed. He refrained from alluding to her indiscretion with Hussein, because to do so only served to inflame him, and there was nothing right now that he could do about the situation except prevent Hussein from having the opportunity of seeing her alone. Nikos arrived home at seven o'clock. "Are you ready, we are taking Jenny to the Lamberts," he barked through Monique's closed bedroom door.

"I will be ready in half an hour," she informed him. He quickly showered and dressed and selected his most expensive cologne for the evening. He wanted to be as attractive to Jenny as possible. As he descended the stairs, he saw that Monique was already waiting for him in the hallway, and he could not bite back a sarcastic comment. "We are looking stunning for the lover boy this evening," he said, noting her elegant cocktail dress and shiny, upswept hair.

"Yes, he's worth it," she shot back at him.

"Let's go," he rattled at her, in the tone he reserved for cabin staff that were not showing sufficient respect for his authority.

Obediently, she followed and sat silently for most of the drive to Jenny's apartment. Before he went to collect Jenny, she looked Nikos straight in the eye and said, "If you have a shred of decency in you, you will leave Jenny alone."

"That's rich coming from a whore like you," he spat at her. Predictably, Nikos attitude was completely changed when he came back with Jenny. He was charming to both women.

The Lambert's party was attended by the usual crowd, plus a couple of ambassadors, who lived close by. Jenny was happy to see Betty there and started to make a beeline for her. Seeing this, Nikos swiftly intercepted her and told her with mock sternness that she must not hide herself away talking to Betty all evening, and that he would be coming to claim a dance from her when the music started. Jenny assured him that she would look forward to their dance later on, but she must spend some time with Betty as she had not seen her for some time.

Betty greeted her warmly, but was, as usual, blunt but accurate in her observations. "He's after ya'," she said, jerking her head in Nikos' direction.

"Oh, Betty, do you still believe that?" she said, laughing off the suggestion.

"Listen to me, Jen, I've been here for many years and most'a that time all I've had to do was to watch what was goin' on at these parties. It happens too many times for me to surely know it when I see it," she stated emphatically.

"Well, let me tell you, Betty, when I needed to get to England quickly a few months ago, Nikos went out of his way to help me, and he has been nothing short of a gentleman with me ever since."

"Well, whaddaya' expect? Do ya' think he would be unpleasant to ya'll? He wants to make a good impression on ya'," insisted Betty.

"It's not like that Betty. He doesn't come across that way at all. He's friendly without overstepping the mark. No, I think that this time your unerring instincts are wrong," she said, closing the subject.

"We'll just wait an' see, shall we," said Betty, determined to have the last word on the subject.

At this juncture, Sherrifa and Hussein arrived. She looked resplendent in a new Yves Saint Laurent gown. Her eyes darted across the room as she mentally noted who was present. A smile of satisfaction touched her lips as her eyes alighted upon Jenny. She gave a quick nod of approval to Nikos; she had hoped that Nikos would persuade her to come out and play.

Hussein looked around the room and noted where Monique was, and as soon as was respectable, he would go and join her. It had seemed like an eternity since he had seen her last, although it had only been a matter of weeks. The last time he had seen her, she was broken and bleeding. He was relieved to see her looking so well and radiant, with no visible signs of her former injuries. He looked over to where Nikos was standing, and for a moment, their eyes met in hostility. But Nikos looked away, knowing Hussein had the upper hand. There was nothing he could do to keep his wife away from Hussein tonight. Sensing this, Hussein moved quickly amongst the guests, spending only a short time discussing shop with other pilots. Monique was chatting with Peggy Gallagher when Hussein came over. "Hello ladies, how are you both this evening?" he enquired, his eyes resting upon Monique.

"Fine, fine," said Peggy, excusing herself from their presence with a little wave. She knew the look that Hussein had given Monique. She herself had been the recipient of such looks a long time ago when Nikos was pursuing her. She left, feeling the guilt of the way she had behaved in those days. She had believed Monique to be a cold, uncaring woman. Now she could see things clearly as they were. Nikos was the deceitful, selfish person who sought only to fulfill his own base desires. Thank God she had walked away from that hell. She was happier now than she had ever been, and she was grateful for her kind and gentle husband. They now had a good relationship based on mutual understanding and a newfound respect, and it was working. She left them, wishing them all the best. If two people ever deserved a little happiness, it was them.

"Monique, darling, it is so good to see you looking so well again. You have no idea how badly I've felt, not being able to see you in person after taking you to the hospital. Talking on the phone just doesn't satisfy," he said tenderly, giving her hand a discreet caress.

"I feel much better now, and the thoughts of seeing you again helped raise my spirits and get me back on my feet again," she told him truthfully.

"How is that bastard treating you? I hope he is not making life unbearable for you." he said.

"Life with him has been unbearable for a long time. He insults me at every opportunity about you and me, but other than that, it is not too bad. I have gotten used to his evil tongue over the years."

"God, I wish I could get you away from him somehow. I swear that, sooner or later, we are going to have a life together with our children."

Nikos had been watching Monique and Hussein talking together. He resented his wife's obvious happiness at being with Hussein. Feeling the jealousy and anger well up inside him, he left the group of pilots he was talking to and interrupted their intimate conversation.

"Well, well, well, this is intimate isn't it?" he mocked them.

Monique gave him no time to finish his apparent cutting sarcasm. She smiled at Hussein and remarked, "You must excuse me, Hussein. I haven't seen Sherrifa for such a long time, so I am going to have a chat with her." Hussein smiled his understanding and stood to one side to let her pass.

"It's a real nice piece of ass, isn't it?" said Nikos. indicating Monique's seductively moving form.

"Shut up, you piece of excrement. It's quite evident that you have no respect for your wife. Don't include me in that. She is a wonderful woman, who has the respect of most of the airline for putting up with a low life like you for all these years." he growled with more than a hint of a challenge in his voice.

Sensing the rage within Hussein, Nikos backed off, fearing a showdown. The last thing he wanted to do was to upset Sherrifa or Jenny at this point.

Claire Lambert declared the buffet to be ready, and invited everyone into the dining room to fill their plates. Nikos seized the opportunity to ingratiate himself with Jenny. Seeing her with a very sparsely filled plate, he cajoled her, "Come along now, Jenny, you must fill your plate up with this lovely food. We can't have you wasting away while Greg is flying. Here, let me help you," he said, picking up an Arabic delicacy. "Try these, they are stuffed vine leaves, I can highly recommend them." He picked one up and popped it in her mouth. "Just try it. You will love it, I am sure."

Jenny obligingly ate the proffered delicacy. "Mmm, it's really delicious," she said enthusiastically. It had a wonderfully piquant taste. "Yes, Nikos, I will have some more of those please."

Nikos helped her to choose the most tempting dishes on the table. Over the many years that he had spent in the Middle East, he had become a connoisseur of the fine foods of the area. Much of it was similar to his national Greek food, but he had come to prefer the Middle Eastern versions with their carefully blended spices and herbs.

As the meal ended and the music began, Nikos claimed his promised dance from Jenny. The music was soft and slow, giving him the opportunity to put his arms around her and hold her close. It was all he could do to keep a polite space between them, Jenny had been on his mind for so long, and thoughts of making love to her had occupied his thoughts regularly. He wanted her, he could feel her warming to him and *soon it would be time*. "Jenny, every time I see you, you look lovelier. Greg is such a lucky chap," he ventured.

"I'm sure that you say that to all of the ladies," she laughed, making light of his comments.

"You may have heard exaggerated stories about me, Jenny, but I assure you I do not give compliments readily. You are an outstandingly beautiful woman who deserves to be complimented," he said seriously.

Jenny was unsure of how to take the compliment, so she changed the subject. "I'm glad to see Monique looking so well again after her accident."

"Yes, she's feeling much better now. Both Monique and I are so grateful to you for the help you gave her that night. Needless to say, if there is ever anything that I can do for you or Greg in the future, don't hesitate to ask."

"That's kind of you, Nikos, thank you."

"How are spending your time while Greg is away? Are you keeping busy?" asked Nikos.

"Well, I am always busy at the hospital during the day, but I do get a bit fed up in the evenings. However, I've got a good novel on the go at the moment, which is keeping me entertained," she told him.

"Listen, don't sit on your own in the evenings. Come over and join Monique and me. We would love to see you more often," he urged.

"Are you sure?" she asked cautiously. She had been thinking to herself that it would be a good idea if she got out a little more in the evenings, but she really did not have anywhere to go now that Candy spent most of her evenings with Khalil. She knew she was always welcome, but she felt that she could not impose upon them too often. If she went to visit Monique and Nikos sometimes, that would help to break the monotony of the evenings, she thought.

"What do you mean, am I sure? Of course, I am sure. I would not have extended the invitation if I wasn't sure. Listen, all you have to do is pick up the phone and say that you would like to visit, and I will come and pick you up. In fact, I will make it easier than that. On Sunday, I will be coming in from a flight at around seven o'clock. I will stop by on my way from the airport and pick you up, and we can all have dinner together. What do you think about that?" he said persuasively.

"Well, that sounds wonderful. I would love to join you," she answered, happy to have something else planned while Greg was away. She would enjoy Monique's company. They had become closer after the accident, and Jenny found that she really liked her. After penetrating Monique's superficially aloof exterior, she had found a warm and caring woman underneath. Yes, she thought she would enjoy furthering their friendship.

Nikos was delighted at this latest turn of events. He had been planning to move in on Jenny tonight, but Sunday would be so much more appropriate. After she had shared a dinner with them, she would be in a more malleable position. Sunday was only two short days away, *and then dear little, Jenny, you will be all mine*, he thought smiling to himself.

The rest of evening progressed pleasantly, the only shadow being when Sherrifa tried to make polite conversation with Jenny. Although her intentions were to be charming and win Jenny over again temporarily, she was unable to control her acid tongue when she came face to face with her. "Allo, Jenny, 'ow lovely you look zis evening as always," remarked Sherrifa, almost choking on the words. "I am 'appy to see zat you are not sitting at 'ome while Greg is off flying." Unable to resist the opportunity of a slight, she added, "After all, I am sure zat he is not sitting miserably in his 'otel room, ne c'est pas?"

"On the contrary," returned Jenny sharply, "with the exceptionally busy roster he has this month, I imagine he will be trying catch up on as much sleep as possible. He will be quite happy to be in his hotel room rather than the cockpit for a while. Now, if you will excuse me, I really must ask Nikos and Monique if they are ready to leave as I have an early start in the morning."

Jenny walked away, leaving Sherrifa fuming. *Somehow, I can never get the better of that bitch*, she thought. *The trouble is, she is not afraid of me. One day, though, I will watch her crawl away from me.*

Jenny approached Nikos and asked what time he was planning to leave. He shot a quick look over to Sherrifa, checking to see whether she had any objections to his leaving. Seeing his familiar glance, she nodded her approval.

"Whenever you are ready to go, Jenny, I will just go and collect Monique," he effused. The drive to Jenny's home was cordial. Nikos made most of the conversation. Both Jenny and Monique were feeling tired, Monique from the lingering effects of her recent injuries and Jenny from her exhausting day at the hospital. As they pulled in Jenny's drive, Nikos insisted that he see Jenny right into her apartment.

"Really there is no need, I am fine," protested Jenny.

"No, I promised Greg that I would keep an eye on you, and while you are in my care, I must insist in seeing you safely into your house," he said charmingly.

"I will not be long, Monique darling, keep the car doors shut," he added with false concern.

Monique did not grace him with an answer, but told Jenny that she would look forward to seeing her for dinner on Sunday evening. She knew Nikos was manipulating events so he would be able to spend the maximum amount of time with

Jenny while her husband was away. She also knew that she was powerless to stop him. *At least,* she thought, *if Jenny is actually in my presence on Sunday, it cuts down on the time he can be alone with her.*

Nikos escorted Jenny to her door and waited while she opened it and put on the light. "It has been a lovely evening, Jenny. I have enjoyed it so much, escorting two beautiful women out for the evening is more than I could ask for," crooned Nikos charmingly.

"Thank you, too, it has been so nice going out tonight. Much better than sitting in with a novel," she said smiling.

"Don't forget Sunday. I will come and collect you after work," he reminded her.

"You know, it will be no problem for me to drive over. It would save you an extra journey," said Jenny helpfully.

"Absolutely no, I have already told you, when you are with me, I take care of you from start to finish. I want to be sure that you arrive and get home safely. You know how bad the traffic situation is, even late at night here." He wanted to ensure that she was best placed for his seduction.

"Yes, that is true. I never feel that confident driving at night. If you're sure, I will be happy to concede," she said gratefully.

"That's the spirit," he said, reading more into her last innocent statement than was intended.

Concede, he thought, *what music to my ears. She does play the game after all.* In his elation, he bowed and took her hand with mock gallantness. He kissed it, and then with a huge grin, he left.

Jenny joined in his laughter, unaware of the reason for his sudden lightness of mood. She waved him goodbye and thought how nice it was to see a lighter side to Nikos. Oblivious to his future plans for her, Jenny happily showered and retired for the night, recalling only the pleasant events of the evening and bidding the absent Greg a goodnight wherever he was. She fell into a deep, trouble-free sleep.

The following two days went by quite slowly for Jenny. There were, happily, fewer admissions in the E.R. and Jenny found herself with time on her hands. She spent some of this unaccustomed leisure time chatting in reception with Candy, who was also kept less busy as there were fewer relatives wanting immediate news of their loved ones. Much of their conversation concerned Candy's forthcoming wedding. Although sanction had been granted from Farris and his family for the wedding to go ahead, there was much squabbling in their family over protocol as to who should be invited to the wedding and who shouldn't. "I tell you, Jenny, I am sick to death of hearing from my former in-laws. They keep telling me that I have to invite this cousin and that cousin or it will cause a family rift forever more. I'm glad they are all being supportive, but they are just about taking over," said Candy despondently.

"What about Khalil's family, aren't they helping you?" enquired Jenny. "Well, yes, they are, but they have elected to take a back seat in all of this. They are very quiet people and don't like a lot of fuss. Thankfully, they don't impose their wishes on me. Khalil is also keeping a low profile regarding the ceremony. He just says, make all the arrangements, send me the bills and I will turn up on the day," she sighed.

"It does sound like a bit of a fiasco. I wonder why the two of you don't just elope and save all the shenanigans."

"You know, that's the most sensible thing I have heard in a while. Perhaps that might be a way out," she said brightening.

"You could always take a flight to Greece and have a private ceremony there. I heard one of our ground engineers and his fiancée did that. Only in their case, his parents disapproved of his choice of wife and they eloped. But nonetheless, they are married and his parents finally came around to accepting the girl. They gave a big party afterwards for all the family and friends, and everyone was placated."

"Jenny, you are a darling. I am going to ask Khalil what he thinks about that idea. It certainly sounds good to me," she said, grinning from ear to ear.

Taking her leave of Candy, Jenny checked her watch and saw it was getting close to home time. She looked around the E.R. to see if any patients had made their way there. Finding that there was nothing and no one that needed her ministrations, she decided to take her leave. Dr. Khalil gave her a cheery wave as she left, remarking that it would be nice if they were this quiet again tomorrow. Jenny nodded her agreement and went on her way. As she drove home, she felt happy that it was Sunday and that she would be amongst company and would not be alone. She was looking forward to having dinner with Monique and Nikos.

On her way home, she began reflecting on her life. She was feeling Greg's absence keenly; the evenings especially seemed to drag by. Not having him there to look forward to at the end of the day, to share supper with, was making her feel quite depressed and lonely. She was hiding this fact well, not wanting any of her friends to know how she was feeling, understanding it was a situation she would have to come to terms with as an airline pilot's wife. *If only I had a child*, she thought, *it would take the entire sting out of the loneliness. Perhaps it won't be long before Greg starts the infertility treatment. At least if we know it's impossible for us to have children, then we can go ahead with an adoption.* She knew from her experience on the children's wards in England that she was quite capable of loving someone else's child. There had been a couple of times whilst she was still a trainee nurse, before she had learned to stay impartial, when she had become very attached to children in her care, and it had been an awful wrench for her when they were discharged. She knew intuitively that the great emptiness inside her could be filled only by having a child of her own to care for. It was easier when Greg was home with her, but his long absences brought all her stifled feelings to the surface.

Arriving home, she showered and changed for the evening. Nikos arrived promptly at seven and whisked her off to his car. "You look lovely as always, Jenny," said Nikos, giving her an admiring glance.

"Thank you, you are as charming as ever," she replied lightheartedly. She was in the mood for joviality and hoped she would see more of Nikos' lighter side again.

Monique greeted them both at the door and ushered Jenny into the lounge. Nikos excused himself to shower and change. "How was your day, Jenny?" enquired Monique pleasantly.

"Well, it was rather quiet today. I'm glad there are fewer patients, but at the same time, I prefer when it's busy, especially when Greg's away. If I'm exhausted by the time I get home in the evening, then the chances are I will have a good night's sleep. But when I have had little to do, I often find it hard to sleep in the empty apartment. It always seems so much bigger and scarier when Greg is away," said Jenny, surprised at herself for being so honest.

"Oh, you don't have to tell me about that. I remember when I was first married to Nikos and he brought me out here. I was unbelievably lonely when he was away on trips. Back then, the country wasn't as developed and the airline was still small. Nikos wanted to get as many flying hours notched up as he could, and I was stuck at home on my own for days on end. Sometimes, I thought I would die of boredom and loneliness. Until that is, little Roger was born, and my life changed completely to the good," she concluded laughing at herself in retrospect.

"I imagine it must have been quite hard for you. At least I have my job, which is fulfilling, and through that, I have met many nice people too. I really don't know why I am complaining," she said, feeling slightly ashamed.

"You are complaining quite legitimately," insisted Monique. "You are young, and your husband has been away for some long periods this year. Things will get better, especially when you start a family. Then the shoe will be on the other foot. You will not have the time to be lonely, and your husband will be missing having your undivided attention," she said sagely.

"Oh, I do hope so," sighed Jenny.

Appearing in the doorway, Nikos remarked, "Well, this sounds like doom and gloom in here, and we can't be having that tonight. Monique, darling, what has the chef prepared for us this evening?"

"Well actually, I have cooked something for us. I have made some beef and mushroom stroganoff, followed by chocolate mousse. I hope you will both enjoy it."

"Mmm, I know that I will," said Jenny, touched that Monique had gone out of her way to prepare something herself.

"Sounds good to me. Shall we go through? I am starved as I haven't eaten anything since morning," Nikos informed them.

Monique shouted through to Roger, who was in the den. "Roger, vien ici, pour le diner."

"Oui, Maman," he replied instantly.

As he walked into the room, Jenny felt a pang of jealousy at the way the mother and son exchanged loving looks.

"Roger, I would like you to meet Jenny. She is married to Captain Greg. She is the nurse that helped me so much when I had my accident."

"I am very pleased to meet you," he replied, in perfect English. "I am so glad you were there to help Maman. I am very grateful to you."

"As are we all," interjected Nikos, not wanting to be outdone by his son.

"It was a real pleasure. You have a very special mother," Jenny told Roger.

"Yes, I know," he replied seriously.

The dinner was beautifully cooked and presented. It was clear that Monique was an excellent cook. Jenny found herself coming back for second helpings, and was deeply impressed with the chocolate mousse. "Monique, you must give me the recipe for this chocolate mousse. It is sheer heaven. I have never tasted anything so good," she said enthusiastically.

"The recipe is a French one given to me by my mother," she said, a slight cloud passing over her face at the mention of her mother. To speak of her family that had cut her off for marrying Nikos was still painful. The worse thing of all was them being right about Nikos. So many times she had regretted her actions in marrying him. She fervently wished that she had listened to her family, who had told her that he was unsuitable for her. Their reasons for finding him unsuitable might have been the wrong ones, but the advice had still been right.

"Well, I must have the recipe. I will copy it down before I go, if that's all right," said Jenny, noting Monique's temporary distraction.

"Of course, it is all right, but you mustn't be thinking about going home now. It is still early. Do you like playing cards? I thought we might have a game together. Roger has just recently learned to play poker, and he insists that I play poker with him at every free moment. It will be a real treat for him to have a game with us," she said laughing.

"Well, I think I can just about remember how to play poker. Perhaps you can help me if I get stuck, Roger," said Jenny with a smile.

"It will be my pleasure," he responded, his English as perfect as his French.

The evening sped by, with much laughter at the enormous stakes of play-money that Roger was betting. He, of course, ended up the winner, and had to be threatened with everything but the kitchen sink to get him to go to bed. "No, Roger, you must go and sleep now, as you have school in the morning. You are already so excited that it will take you till dawn to calm down, I imagine. No more argument, bed," insisted Monique.

With a look of mock heartbreak, he reluctantly left the room and went to bed.

"What a lovely son you have," said Jenny to Monique and Nikos. "He is not only extremely handsome, but he is adorable as well. He will soon have many admirers."

"Thank you, it is truly hard not to spoil him," said Monique. Nikos turned away, disassociating himself from the conversation. Roger was his son, but he had showed little interest in him as a baby, and now at a time when he might be of some interest, Roger no longer bothered trying to win his father's affections. He had seen him humiliate his mother too often to have a shred of affection left for him.

Sensing Jenny's intention to leave, Monique insisted that they all have a bedtime cognac. "That way, you will be sure to sleep tonight, Jenny," said Monique with a wink, eager to keep Jenny from Nikos' clutches for as long as possible.

"Well, if you insist, but I must make a move soon. I feel bad that Nikos still has to drive me back home," said Jenny, hoping that she was not imposing.

"Don't worry about me," interjected Nikos. "You know us pilots are used to irregular hours, and besides, we have thoroughly enjoyed your company."

Monique smiled and went to arrange the drinks. She returned with the cognac and a box of luxurious chocolate mints, which she proffered to Jenny. "Do have one just to finish the evening off," she insisted.

"I don't know about finishing the evening off, it will be finishing my waistline off," she groaned.

"There is absolutely nothing wrong with your waistline, and a few little calories are not going to spoil it. Besides, you can always work it off at the hospital tomorrow," insisted Monique.

"I shall definitely have to. There will be no lunch tomorrow for me after all I have eaten today. It was all so delicious, though," added Jenny.

"You are welcome at any time to come and join us, Jenny. In fact, if you have some time off during the week, why don't you come over and spend the day with me?" said Monique hopefully.

"I will certainly do that when the hospital can spare me for a few days," she replied, thinking how nice it would be to spend some time with Monique. However, knowing how much she needed her job to prevent her from being lonely, she knew there would be few occasions for them to spend time together. Smiling brightly, she thanked then once again for the pleasant evening and insisted that she had to go. Monique watched Nikos and Jenny leave, feeling as if she had just sent Jenny like a lamb to slaughter. She only hoped that some modicum of decency would stop Nikos from moving in on her.

Nikos was animated on the drive to Jenny's. The thoughts of finally getting close to her had lifted his spirits. It had been many a year since he had last felt this way. Reaching her apartment, he walked her to the door. Jenny began to thank him and bid him goodnight.

"Jenny, I would feel much happier if I saw you right into the apartment, then I can rest assured that you are completely safe," he insisted.

"Oh, you fuss too much," she said, "but if it makes you feel better, come on in and see that I am safe and sound." She opened the door and went into the sitting room. "See, everything is in order, and I am quite safe. Please don't worry about me anymore. You need to get your sleep," she told him positively.

"Don't worry about me, I'm used to going without sleep after so many years in the flying business. In fact, I am not in the least sleepy. Perhaps we can have just one more nightcap before I have to go?" he asked persuasively.

Jenny did not really want to have another nightcap, but for the sake of goodwill, she acquiesced. "All right, what can I get you?" she asked.

"Whatever is your pleasure," he told her.

"To tell you the truth, I feel that I have had quite enough to drink this evening. I was planning to have a cup of herbal tea."

"Hmm," he replied, "in that case, make mine a brandy."

As she left to prepare the drinks, he settled himself on the sofa in preparation for his later moves.

"Here we are," she said, returning with the drinks. She put his brandy in front of him and started to settle in a nearby armchair with her tea.

"Don't sit over there. It will be much friendlier if you sit next to me here. That way, I won't have to shout," he said, enjoying the way she was prolonging the chase.

Unhappy about Nikos's suggestive manner, she reluctantly complied with his wishes.

She settled next to him and tried to keep the atmosphere light and cordial. "So, what shall we talk about?"

"We will talk about how beautiful you are Jenny and how long I have been waiting to be alone with you," he whispered, reaching his arm out behind her shoulders.

Jenny froze. She began to see how stupid she had been for letting herself get into this situation.

"Listen, Nikos, I think you have the wrong idea. I'm sorry if you got the impression that I want to start something with you. I don't, I have just come to enjoy Monique's and your company. I thought that we are friends," she said panicking inwardly.

"Jenny, you can drop the act now. It's me you are talking to, and I can see through that innocent guise of yours. Come here," he said, pulling her roughly towards him. He grasped her tightly round the waist and head, forcing her to receive his fevered kiss. "Oh, Jenny, Jenny, this will be so good."

She tried to pull away from him, but the harder she tried, the more he tightened his grip. Jenny was terrified; he was ignoring her pleas to stop. She struggled hard to pull away from him, afraid of the brute strength that he was using on her. With a supreme effort, she pushed him away and managed to struggle free of him.

"Get out, get away from me!" she shouted, running for the door and planning to run outside if necessary.

"Shut up, you little whore, you know that you want it too," he snarled, reaching her side in seconds.

He grabbed her and dragged her to the sofa again. He threw her down and began to tear the clothes off her. Jenny began to scream, hoping that Fouad or Hilda would come to her aid.

"Shut up, bitch, no one is going to hear you," he said, covering her mouth with his hand.

Jenny's heart was pounding; her body was trembling with fear. Never in her life had she been this afraid. As she continued to struggle, he continued to tear off the rest of her clothes with his free hand.

"This is going to be the best fuck you ever had, you little prick-teaser. You will be begging for more," he snarled at her.

Oh God, help me, cried Jenny silently, as he unzipped his trousers and began to force himself into her. Jerking her head away for a second, she let out a shrill scream of sheer panic. *God, let someone hear me*, she prayed. *Please, let someone hear me.* The curtains were still opened, and she hoped someone might come past and see what was happening to her. As he tried again to force himself into her unyielding body, she let out another piercing shriek.

For this, he struck her savagely across the face and yanked her from under him, throwing her face down over the arm of a chair. From there, he pushed her face in a cushion and began to penetrate her from the back. "You are going to get it one way or another tonight, so you may as well cooperate," he grunted vilely in her ear.

Jenny's strength was ebbing, and she felt as though she was suffocating from a lack of oxygen. The fight was leaving her, her body became limp as she succumbed to this indignity. Hope of rescue had left her, and she felt alone and abandoned.

"That's right, just relax and you will enjoy this," he told her, unaware of her fear. *Some women liked it rough*, he reasoned. *She was just one of them. She was just dragging out the chase as long as possible.* It did not once occur to him that she did not want him.

Jenny had become limp and lifeless, awaiting the final indignity to be forced upon her, when she heard the sound of the front door being kicked open. She heard footsteps striding quickly towards them, but with her face buried in the pillow, she could not see who it was. She prayed fervently that it was someone who would come to her aid. In a second, she felt Nikos being dragged off her back and the sound of a scuffle. As she raised her head, she was amazed and relieved to see Talal. He had Nikos by the throat and was pushing him against the wall. There, he hit him across the face. Nikos tried to fight back, but

Talal's superior strength prevailed. He half-pushed and half-kicked him out of the apartment. "Get out of here, you cowardly dog, and don't you ever lay a finger on her again or else it will be the last thing you ever do!" he shouted at him.

Closing and locking the door, Talal turned to the trembling and shaking Jenny. He quickly went to the bedroom and took a blanket off the bed and wrapped it around her. He led her to the sofa and sat her down gently. Gratefully, she leaned on his broad shoulder, feeling the warmth of his body against the deathly cold of hers. Talal wanted to take her in his arms and console her, but he was careful not to impose himself on her. He could see that she was deeply in shock, and he did not want her to feel that she was in any danger from him.

Despite her ordeal, she sensed no threat from Talal. On the contrary, she wanted to bury herself in his arms and forget what had taken place. They sat for some time like that, until finally the tears came. Then Talal felt confident enough to put his arms gently round her and console her. As she sobbed, the shaking began to subside and normality reinstated itself. "Talal," she said shakily, "how is it that you are here?"

"I have been in town for a few days, and I have tried my best to stay away from you. But knowing that your husband is out of the country, I decided that I could not give you up without at least one more try. The truth is, I have driven by your house many, many times this week. Tonight, I came to the door but found you were out. I decided I would wait for you and talk to you when you returned. When you came back with him, I was devastated. I thought he was your lover. I stayed around for a little while, but when I saw you sit down next to him on the sofa, I decided I had seen enough. I began to leave, but with my feeling in chaos, I stood for a while on the hill and looked at the ocean. It was then that I heard your scream. I ran back here as fast as I could, and well, you know the rest."

"I am so grateful you are here," she whispered.

"So am I," he told her tenderly. Talal made Jenny some tea and insisted she drink it, then led her to the bedroom, still wrapped up in the blanket he had put around her. "Come on now, you are going to get some sleep. That is the best medicine for you."

"I, I, c'can't," she stuttered, trying to tell him how afraid she was.

"You are going to go to sleep, and I am going to stay in the room with you. I will sleep on the floor, just like a guard dog," he told her.

"No, please, just lie next to me so I can feel you there," she whispered.

"Whatever you want, I will do for you. I just want you to feel safe." Talal took his shoes off and got onto the bed beside her. Putting his arms around her gently, he rocked her until her exhausted body finally gave way to sleep.

CHAPTER FOURTEEN

Recovery

Jenny spent a reasonably comfortable night with Talal. She did not enter deep sleep, only that superficial, aware kind of sleep where the mind refuses to let the body take over its autonomic functions. She awoke several times on the verge of panic, but finding Talal next to her, settled back into her half-sleep. As the dawn light crept into the room, she roused and became fully awake. Responding to her change of breathing patterns, Talal awoke and smiled at her. "How are you feeling now?" he enquired softly.

"I feel a bit of a wreck, but at least I'm calmer now, thanks to you. I don't know how I would have coped if I had been left on my own last night," she said gratefully.

"It's better not to think of what might have happened, just concentrate on what did happen and the fact that you are now going to be all right again in a few days," he urged.

"Oh, I have to go to the hospital," she said, suddenly remembering her daily responsibilities.

"Jenny, you are not in any fit state to go and work today. Have a look at your face." Walking over to the dressing table mirror, she took a sharp intake of breath as she looked at her face. It was bruised and swollen all down the left side where Nikos had hit her. Talal came up behind her and put a reassuring arm around her. "Don't worry, it will look better in a few days, but I think until you have got things together, you should call in sick at work. I'm going to stay with you until you are feeling able to be on your own again."

"Oh, Talal, that's so good of you," she told him, grateful of his presence, "but haven't you got work, a group to take to Koudara or something?"

"Don't worry I will take care of that. I have some vacation time coming, and I will take it now. When does your husband get back?"

"Not for another ten days," she said, feeling slight guilt over Talal's presence. But there was no one else she wanted to be with, not even Candy. Talal had rescued her, and he could protect her from anything that might endanger her. She felt safe with him.

After taking a long, hot shower, Jenny called Candy at home and told her she had a flu bug and would not be coming in to work for a few days. When Candy volunteered to come over and keep her company, she told her she did not want to pass the bug on to her and that Hilda was taking good care of her. As the day progressed, Jenny grew more confident. Seeing this, Talal suggested they go out together to the hotel where he was staying, so he could pick up some of his clothing.

"I would go on my own, but I don't want to leave you on your own just yet," he told her gently.

"Yes, that's fine. I don't want to be alone just yet. I will come with you," she agreed readily.

They drove in his car to one of the quality hotels in the town. "I won't be very long. Will you be all right in the car until I come back down? I don't want you to be seen coming into the hotel with me in case people get the wrong idea," he said thoughtfully.

"I'm sure I can manage," she replied, surprised at herself for feeling vulnerable at the prospect of such a short time alone.

As he left the car, she watched his tall, athletic body stride purposefully towards the hotel entrance. *What a handsome man*, she thought, *and how considerate he has been to me.* As he disappeared through the hotel entrance, the thoughts of the previous evening began to close in on her. She was finding it hard to comprehend what had taken place. She closed her eyes, and the memory of the terror that she had experienced began to well up inside her. This time, her medical training took over. Aware that she was still in shock, she took some deep breaths and concentrated on what was happening around her. With great difficulty, she managed to push the traumatic thoughts to the back of her mind. By the time Talal returned, she was fairly composed but very grateful to see him again.

"I have sorted everything out. I have talked to my family, and they know that I'm taking some time off. I hope that you don't mind, but I told them they could contact me at your number, but only if it was an emergency."

"No, I don't mind. There will be only you and me to take the call. I can't see that it will cause any problem," she reasoned.

"Let's pick up some food and go back", suggested Talal.

"Yes, that sounds like a good idea," she agreed, feeling, for the first time since the incident, the stirring of an appetite.

At Sherrifa's villa, Nikos was relating his version of the previous night's events to her.

"What the hell happened, you fool?" demanded Sherrifa, looking at Nikos's bruised face. "How are you going to explain the state you are in to everyone?"

"I told Monique that I surprised some thieves trying to get into Jenny's apartment, and they put up a fight," he said sheepishly.

"And she believed you?" she said sarcastically.

"No, I don't think so," he replied. Indeed, she had not believed him but was discreet enough not to embarrass Jenny with a call. She only hoped Nikos had got his just desserts and that Jenny was unharmed. She would wait until the dust had settled and cover stories had been concocted before she approached Jenny.

"Well, in any case, it doesn't really matter whether she believes you or not. It is essential that others do, and that we get the English bitch to corroborate the story. I will take care of that," she hissed. "What did you do to her that another man had to drag her away from you?" she demanded.

"You know how it is. She had been leading me on for the last few weeks, and when I moved in on her, she started playing rough. I thought that was the way she liked it, so that's the way I gave it to her," he said boldly.

"You stupid fool, you read the whole thing wrong, and now you have messed it all up," she said accusingly.

"Well, I don't think so. I did some thinking last night, and I believe that she did not respond to me because she already has a lover boy. Isn't it just a bit too convenient that he was there to rescue her? He's a good-looking man, and he certainly seemed to be possessive of her. He threatened to kill me if I went near her again," he said confidently.

"Aha, at last, we have her Achilles' heel," declared Sherrifa, her quick mind making all the relevant connections. "I think that you are right. We might yet be able to show Greg that his sweet little thing is just as prone to weaknesses as we all are," she said, smiling for the first time.

"It does explain quite a lot, doesn't it?" said Nikos, unable to comprehend that Jenny would reject him without cause. He reasoned that she had rejected him only because she was involved with another man. That, he was able to accept.

"I will have to contact some of my friends and find out who the mystery man is," proclaimed Sherrifa, with more than a little triumph in her voice. She would talk to some of her father's friends in the Secret Service who would willingly find out any information for her. There was very little crime in Kharja, and they would relish the opportunity of following and identifying a potential criminal and being of service to one of the top families in the country. She would, of course, ask them to be discreet, for her sake.

"Nikos, I want you to keep out of Jenny's way. Just leave the rest up to me now," she ordered, her mind already occupied with her next moves.

"It will be my pleasure. If I never see the little bitch's face again, it will be too soon," he said venomously.

The days spent with Talal were beginning to speed by. Jenny had nearly overcome her ordeal, thanks to Talal's constant care. She had fended off potential visitors when they phoned, saying that her bug was quite virulent and that she was being well looked after. When Sherrifa phoned, she simply told her that she was ill, and when Sherrifa spoke of the thieves that Nikos had tackled outside her apartment, she told her, with tacit cooperation, that they had not been back. Jenny was aware of the need for discretion. The fact that this story had been constructed for her was quite convenient, and it was something she could tell to Greg.

By day seven, her bruises were nearly gone and were undetectable with camouflaging makeup over them. Her spirits had returned, and she was able to laugh and joke and was free of fear. Talal had not tried to impinge on her space. After the first evening, he insisted on sleeping in the spare room, telling her that if she needed him, he would be there. His reassuring presence was all she had needed. After the third night, she was able to sleep normally again. Now the undeniable current of feelings that she had experienced in Talal's presence began to return. That evening, after they had eaten dinner together, Jenny put a cassette of Julio Iglesias on and invited Talal to dance with her. He needed no encouragement; he had been waiting for her to make the first move. They swayed together to the soft, romantic Spanish songs until Jenny reached up and put her arms around his neck and pulled his face towards hers. They gently kissed, both experiencing a rush of desire. Their kisses grew in intensity, until Talal gently pulled away from her.

"Why?" she asked, puzzled at his action.

"Because if I don't stop now, I won't be able to," he said tenderly.

"But I don't want you to stop," she said coaxingly.

"I want to make love to you more than anything else in the world, but I am not going to do it now. I don't want you to associate me with what you went through with that other bastard. I want to come back to you afresh, and then we can make love without any negative thoughts that could turn you away from me. And when we make love, it won't be here. This is another man's house, and I will treat it with as much respect as I can under the circumstances," he explained.

Jenny appreciated the wisdom of his words. "I understand, and I have made a decision that I do want to see you. I cannot argue with the feelings that I have for you, and these past few days have shown me the kind of man that you are. Yes, I will wait for you and look forward to the time when we can make love. I will have to reconcile myself to the fact that I am being unfaithful to my husband, and be responsible for the consequences," she said honestly.

"We will share the responsibility. Whatever happens, I will stand by you to the best of my ability. I am so happy that you have come to a decision about us. Let's just see where life is going to take us." He pulled her close and gave her a warm, gentle kiss that was disturbed by the shrill sound of the telephone ringing.

"Hello," said Jenny.

A deep, rather rough-sounding voice spoke to her in broken English. "Madam, excuse please, I have to speak with Talal."

Turning to Talal, she told him the call was for him. Taking the phone, she watched his face become serious. He spoke authoritatively to the man on the phone, though she was unable to decipher any of what he was saying as he spoke so quickly and in a different dialect to the one she had grown accustomed to. He put the phone down firmly and looked at her regretfully. "My sweet love, I have to leave tonight. I am so sorry, but it is an emergency. I would not leave unless I had to, and you can rest assured of that. I know that you will be fine now. Go back to work tomorrow so that you are kept busy."

"How long will you be gone?" she asked, wondering what kind of emergency could take him away at this time of the evening.

"I can't say exactly, but it will be within a month. Think of me every day. You will be in my thoughts daily." And with an afterthought, he added, "And pray for me." Jenny stood and watched as he quickly gathered his belongings from the spare room. Sadness surged through her at the thought of his leaving, but she fought it off knowing that it would not help Talal to see her breaking down as he left. He took her gently into his arms and gave her a tender kiss and left without looking back. To see the pain of their parting reflected in her eyes would be more than he could bear. He walked away with his heart aching for Jenny, with the uncertainty of their future gnawing at him. He steeled himself to face his commitments to others who relied upon his leadership.

Jenny watched him walk away, knowing that he felt the same wrench at parting. She closed the door and stood behind it for a long time, unable to move. Her thoughts were in chaos and the pain of parting was tearing at her like a knife. Finally, she took a deep breath and moved back into the lounge. The trauma of Nikos' attack had abated only to be replaced by a burning passion for a man she still knew relatively little about. *How am I going to deal with this?* she asked herself. *How can I face Greg when he returns?* The questions kept flooding her mind until she remembered the words that suddenly made sense to her now: **"Play the game well."** *Yes, it does make sense,* she thought. There is no doubt that I am morally and emotionally committed to two men, and right now, I simply have no answers. I would only hurt Greg if I told him of my feelings towards Talal. *All I can do is play the game well,* she reasoned, *and that means I must maintain my composure and learn to deal with the feelings I have for both men. The acceptance of feelings for one does not automatically cancel feelings for the other. I will continue as before with Greg, only telling him the constructed story of Nikos' encounter with the thieves. Talal's intervention need not be mentioned.* As the evening wore on, Jenny found herself relaxing, able to deal with her emotions more clearly. She sipped a large brandy and soon fatigue set in, and she slept as well as could be expected under the circumstances.

Waking the next morning feeling fit, though somewhat confused, she peered at her face to see if any signs of Nikos' assault were still visible. She decided there was nothing that couldn't be hidden by heavy makeup. Fortunately, Leila had given her a free sample of pan-stick makeup to try. She had given her it after the bombing, when the strain of work had begun to show on her. After she'd applied it as Leila had instructed, she was pleased to see that it covered all the greenish-yellow traces of the bruises that still remained on her face. Satisfied with her appearance, she dressed and went to the kitchen to prepare some breakfast. As she filled the kettle, she became acutely aware of Talal's absence. A feeling akin to nausea shot through her as the closeness of the past days spent with him filled her mind. *Oh God, I miss him already in a way I have never experienced before.* She closed her eyes and allowed thoughts of him to fill her mind. She remembered their parting the night before, and how he had asked her to think of him every day. She thought of him with both love and gratitude for what he had done for her. *Talal,* she spoke aloud quietly, *know that I love you and that I am waiting for you.* Remembering his last words to her, she said an unaccustomed plea to God to watch over him and keep him safe. Returning to the toast she had prepared for herself, she found herself devoid of any appetite. She just drank her coffee and left for the hospital.

At the hospital, she was greeted warmly by friends and colleagues and quickly immersed herself in patients' ailments in order to forget about her own heartache.

She met Candy for lunch, and she was bursting to tell her of her latest news. "Jenny, you know what we were talking about the other week concerning that couple who eloped to Greece to get married?"

"Mmm," answered Jenny, not really concentrating.

"Well, look," said Candy, pulling out a large, gold wedding ring from a chain round her neck. "You are the only one that knows. Khalil said it was all right for me to tell you. We are going to break the news to everyone else this Friday," she said, grinning from ear to ear.

"Oh, Candy, I'm so happy for you. Don't worry, I will not tell a soul. In a way, it is perhaps the best thing that you could have both done. It will be a shock to those closest to you, but I am sure they will understand in the long run," said Jenny positively.

"Yes, that's what we thought. We are planning a large party for next month. Make a note in your diary. I will need all the support I can get on that evening."

"I wouldn't miss it for the world," she replied enthusiastically.

"Now, what about you?" said Candy. "I see that the flu has taken its toll on you. You must have lost a couple of kilos, at least, and I see that you are wearing heavy makeup, which is most unusual for you. I guess that you need a little more time to recuperate."

"Oh, do I look that bad?" asked Jenny, putting her hands up to her cheeks, aware that the last few days had taken their physical and emotional toll on her.

"No, no, don't be silly. Let's just say that if you were a catwalk model, you would have achieved your look. It's just because I know you so well that I can see when you have had to resort to artificial aids to make you look healthy, which is something that you usually never need. And, what's more, I'm going to get us a nice fattening dessert. They have got chocolate pudding on the menu. You look better with extra kilos," she told Jenny in a motherly tone.

Jenny smiled her agreement. Being at the hospital, she found her appetite returning and felt the need to build herself up. Talal had ensured that she ate meals and got enough rest, but now she needed to take control of her life again.

By the time Greg returned, she was in much better shape emotionally. Her feelings towards Talal remained strong, but it had not diminished the feelings she had for Greg. When he returned, he was full of concern for her. "Darling, Nikos told me about the incident the other week when he surprised thieves trying to break in here. It must have been awful for you. Thank God that Nikos was there to look after you."

Jenny was unable to give any response, other than a weak smile and a nod. The thought of Nikos churned up feelings of fear and revulsion in her, and it sickened her that he was turning the situation into one where he emerged as some kind of hero.

"I can see that it really shook you up, love. Look, don't worry, I'm around a lot more this coming month, and I will make sure you are safe," he told her with a reassuring smile.

"Dinner is just about ready," said Jenny, changing the subject.

"That's nice of you, darling. You didn't have to bother. We could have gone out or had a take-away. I know you have been at the hospital all day and must be tired too."

"Don't worry, it's nice to have a home-cooked meal sometimes," she said, aware that she was trying to assuage some of the guilt over her actions with Talal.

She had found herself unprepared for the guilt she had been experiencing all day at work as she anticipated Greg's return. Time had hung heavy since Talal's departure. She thought of him faithfully every day and whispered a little prayer for his safety. For her own sanity, she only allowed herself to think of him for a short time every day, still feeling the intense pain of their parting but still aware that she needed to function normally in front of Greg and at work. The absence of any word from Talal made things even more torturous for her. She longed to hear just a reassuring word from him, telling her how much he meant to her. It was hard to hold on to the memories and the belief that he would return to her, but she was prepared to do so for him.

It was three weeks before she heard any word from him. He contacted her at the hospital through Dr. Khalil. "Jenny, could you come in here please? I have a call for you," said Khalil in fairly serious tones.

Jenny responded quickly, slightly alarmed at Khalil's tone, and for a second she wondered if something had happened to

Greg. Her heart beating slightly faster than usual, she took the phone from Khalil, who left the room closing the door quietly behind him. "Yes," she said cautiously.

"Don't sound so alarmed; it's only me my love," said Talal.

"Oh, where are you?" she asked relieved and delighted to hear his voice again.

"I'm not in the country at the moment, but I will be arriving next week. I can't wait to see you. I have made arrangements to stay in a friend's villa during that week as he is away on business. I will contact you again when I return. I love you, angel, please wait for me?"

"I will, I will," she said tenderly.

"I have to go now, but keep me in your thoughts as you are in mine. Farewell, angel," he told her, his voice choking with emotion. He loved Jenny with a passion hitherto unknown to him.

"Goodbye, love, be safe." She kept the phone in her hand for a few seconds, trying to assimilate what Talal had told her. He had seemed to convey so much while at the same time telling her very little. She had hardly any opportunity to speak; he had done all the talking. He had not told her where he was or what he was doing, only that he would be coming sometime next week. She replaced the receiver slowly, having digested the information he had given her. She now began to wonder what Talal had told his cousin Khalil, in relation to her. Surely it looked suspicious, him wanting to have a private conversation with her at the hospital. She debated whether she ought to think up some legitimate excuse for him having to talk to her.

At that moment, Khalil walked in. "Can you arrange to take a blood sample for the new admission in cubicle three, please? Try and get hematology to rush the results through quickly. I'm worried about hepatitis. There has been talk of an outbreak in the refugee camps," he told her seriously.

"Right away, doctor," she told him, glad that she did not have to concoct a story for him. His facial expression suggested that it was not necessary, yet she believed that she could still sense a faint air of disapproval from him.

The days following Talal's call saw Jenny in a bright and animated mood. Her eyes shone and her complexion took on a peachy bloom. Fortunately for her, Greg would be away for three days during the latter half of the week when Talal was due to arrive. She decided that she would spend the night with him on the second night of Greg's absence, feeling that to meet him on the first night would somehow be more callous in regard to Greg. She constantly wrestled with the guilt of her proposed actions, but she was aware that no amount of guilt would be sufficient to prevent her from sleeping with Talal. The feelings that she had for him were too overwhelming to be ignored. She almost felt compelled to be with him.

Sherrifa sat tapping a pencil impatiently on the pad next to the telephone while she was kept on hold as Lieutenant Mubada, her contact at the secret police was being located. She had not identified herself initially when she spoke to his assistant, but when he came on the line again to say that they were still trying to locate him, she barked fiercely in Arabic at him, "This is Madam Al Fayez speaking. How much longer must I wait?"

"Sorry, sorry, madam. Please just wait a moment. I will have him on the line for you immediately," he told her, almost cringing. *I hope that she will not ask who I am and have me fired,* he thought. In seconds, he had located Lieutenant Mubada and informed him that Madam Al Fayez was on the line for him. He strode into his office quickly and picked up the phone. "Madam

Al Fayez, I am honoured to have you call me. How can I be of service to you?" he asked in his most ingratiating tone.

"You remember I asked you some time ago to find out who a certain foreign woman was meeting? Why have you not reported back to me about it?" she asked him in a slightly impatient voice.

"Madam Al Fayez, please forgive the delay, but I have nothing to report to you, and I understood that you wished me to be discreet. That is why I did not contact you. I have had my men watch this woman night and day, and there is no one coming to her house other than her husband and their friends," he answered apologetically.

"Yes, yes, but are you quite sure?" she persisted.

"I am quite sure, madam, but we will continue the surveillance for you."

"Yes, do that, and I will contact you again in a few days," she shot back impatiently at him, slamming the phone down.

"It is my pleasure to be of service to you, madam, goodbye," he said into a dead telephone line. Sherrifa had already closed the line, having no wish to listen to the ingratiating, mock humility that people in lesser positions afforded her. *How long do I have to wait to nail that bitch*, she thought to herself. *She seems adept at keeping herself looking squeaky clean, but my instinct tells me that she is not as innocent as she appears. Just one false move and I am going to have her and her delicious husband.*

Jenny started work early, the day of Talal's return. She wondered whether he would call her again at work. She hoped he would, but the day passed without word from him. It was just as she was leaving work and walking to her car in the hospital car park when a tall, shadowy figure emerged from a nearby building.

"Jenny, come over her," a familiar voice called softly to her. In a second, she knew it was Talal, and she was at his side in an instant. He put his arm around her and led her to a small empty room. He closed the door and took her in his arms and kissed her with a passion that surprised her. She felt the familiar spark of electricity ignite between them. They had to force themselves apart as their need to be together was so strong.

Breathless, Jenny said, "It is so good to see you again. I have missed you so much."

"I have missed you too, beloved. You don't know how much. Will it be possible to see me this week?"

"Yes, I am alone from Wednesday till Saturday. I thought that it might be more proper to wait till Thursday to meet."

"I can understand what you mean, but I must urge you to use every moment that we can be together. The passage of a day is not going to make our time together any more ethical, my love. We don't have all the time in the world," he pleaded gently with her.

"Yes, you are right. We will meet on Wednesday," she quickly conceded.

"Listen, my love, I will take the opportunity from now until Wednesday to travel over the border to Koudara. I have some paperwork that needs attention. I will phone you at home early on Wednesday evening and tell you how best to meet me."

"That sounds fine to me," said Jenny, smiling at him. In truth, she was pleased that she would not have to deal with both Greg and Talal being in the country at the same time.

Tuesday and Wednesday passed interminably slowly for Jenny. Thoughts of Talal constantly invaded her mind, and she longed to see him and be with him again. By the time Wednesday evening came, she was so wired she could not relax. When she returned home, she headed for the shower but decided that a bath would be better in case Talal phoned, fearing that if the shower was on, she would not be able to hear his call. She was just finishing her bath when the phone rang.

"Darling, listen carefully to me. In one hour, drive to the Plaza Hotel and you will see me in my car in the car park, and then just follow me. Do you understand?"

"Yes, love, I will see you in an hour, bye." Jenny dressed and put on some light perfume and had a quick sandwich before she left. Talal was waiting as promised at the Plaza, where they rendezvoused. He then drove ahead of her for about fifteen minutes until they arrived at a palatial villa. Talal signaled for her to follow him into the drive. There was an empty double garage, and Talal indicated that they park their cars inside. He led her into the villa through the garage and upstairs into a spacious reception room that was furnished with tasteful luxury.

"Wow, who owns this place? It's fabulous," remarked Jenny.

"A friend," said Talal, taking her into his arms. In seconds, Jenny was consumed with passion for him. She felt her skin burning hot and her whole body aching for him. They discarded their clothes in moments. It was impossible to say when they began their lovemaking. From the time they drew together on the bed, their bodies melded together as one. Jenny gasped with pleasure as he touched every sensory nerve in her body. She could feel the virile strength of his hard body inside her. They moved together in blissful union. She felt close to oblivion as she neared orgasm. Nothing was real other than this moment of ecstatic passion.

Talal whispered to her, "Can I spill my seed inside you?"

"Yes, yes," she responded. Not caring that they had used no protection, she wanted to feel him ejaculate inside her. She needed fulfillment from him. Her words triggered his climax. Every muscle in her body seemed to contract as she came. Talal groaned in ecstasy as he felt her orgasm. They rocked to and fro until their passion finally subsided.

"Sweet, sweet, Jenny, you are so beautiful. I have never made love so completely to anyone ever before. I felt as though our souls were entwined, as if we were together in some magical place, far removed from the restrictions of this world," he said in breathless tones, gently caressing and kissing her face.

Jenny could not answer him. Emotion was choking her throat, and she simply looked at him. The look was sufficient for Talal; her eyes adequately expressed her feelings of love for him. They lay together in a state of complete oneness. Jenny felt fulfilled in a way that she had never done before. Her whole body was attuned to his, and as she lay with him, she listened to the beat of his heart and imagined that it was beating for both of them. One heartbeat, one breath, one love, for them both. Jenny had planned to return home to sleep that night, but she could not bear to leave his side any more than he could bear to let her leave.

The next morning, they rose early and shared a breakfast of coffee and cereal together before leaving. "Darling, can you find your way back to your place from here?" enquired Talal. "I will drive in front of you and lead the way if you can't."

"Don't worry, I have worked out where we are. If I drive around to the other side of the villa, I should come out on the coast road, and I can just follow that home," she said with a hint of smugness.

"Clever girl, I can't fool you. I can see that," he said playfully.

"You would not ever try to fool me would you, Talal?" she asked, allowing a deeply hidden doubt to surface.

"Never, Jenny," he said, taking hold of her shoulders and turning her to look him square in the face, "don't ever doubt me. I cannot say right now what our future may be, but never, never doubt me. I love you deeply, and I have feelings for you that I have never experienced before. Until the day I die, you will be my love. I have never before thought the convention of marriage to have any virtue. Since I have met you, I have changed. I have wanted to possess you, to own you, just to ensure that you will always be at my side. I know how selfish that sounds, but yet I have wanted it. Of course, I would never trap you that way. I want you to be with me of your own free will, for us to stay together as long as our love is strong."

"Oh, Talal, that makes me feel so much better. I already feel as though I belong to you in some way, perhaps that we have always belonged together. I can see that marriage is in many ways a hypocrisy. Neither Greg nor I have kept our marriage vows, and believe me, there was no one *less* likely to break them than me, and yet I have done it. I do feel guilt at what I have done, but I honestly feel that what we have is somehow just as sanctified as the institution of marriage, perhaps more so. Oh God, I am so confused."

Talal embraced her firmly. "Do not trouble your mind with justifications. Allow yourself to feel all the good of what we have together. We share an uncommon love, and we should cherish it. Let the future take care of itself. We will meet every challenge as it comes. I may not always be there in the flesh to help you, darling, but I will be with you every second in spirit."

Jenny absorbed his words and felt the stronger for them. "Now, darling," she interjected lightly, "I have to get back home and do something about the way I look. I can't go into the hospital looking like this."

"You look wonderful to me, but I think that sexy dress might send out the wrong signals," he said appreciatively. "However, I'll have no complaints if you want to wear it for me again tonight. You can come tonight can't you?"

"Wild horses couldn't keep me away. Shall I just drive over here at around the same time?"

"Yes, my love, that will be wonderful. I will be waiting for you," he promised.

Jenny returned home, showered and changed into her uniform. She looked at her reflection in the mirror and saw that her face was shining with happiness. She felt marvelous, she looked marvelous and she was madly in love with someone who seemed to adore her. When she had first fallen in love with Greg, in many ways, it was she who had adored Greg and he who had allowed her to. What she had with Talal was different; she had never felt before the intenseness of reciprocated love. Even relationships that she'd had before meeting Greg had never come close to this. She felt uplifted, exhilarated, ecstatic. The morning at work passed by fairly routinely. Dr Khalil afforded Jenny a penetrating look, noticing her dewy bloom.

She met Candy for lunch, and she also noticed the new air of exhilaration that Jenny exuded. "What have you been doing to yourself? You look like a million dollars. A new beauty treatment or what?" she demanded.

"Oh, I'm just in a good mood," she replied, trying not to give anything away, but at the same time, wanting to tell Candy about her new love.

"Well, I wish that I could look that pretty just from being in a good mood. It must be more than that. Come on out with it? You can't keep secrets from your best friend, you know?" she said, more joking than serious.

That was all Jenny needed. She looked around her cautiously to see if anyone was within earshot before disclosing her news. "Candy, this is going to come as a shock to you, and I'm certain that you are going to disapprove, but I have just got to tell someone."

"What, what?" asked Candy, her curiosity aroused.

"Candy, I am having an affair, but by calling it an affair makes what we have sound cheap and tawdry. I have fallen in love with someone who loves me too. We share something that is hard to describe to others. The bottom line is that I have never in my life experienced the emotions that I do for him. Please don't judge me too harshly. I know that I should not be doing this, but I don't seem to be able to stop myself," she said half-elated, half-remorseful.

"Oh, Jenny, I don't know what to say. Let me guess, is it that cousin of Khalil's, Talal?"

"Yes, how did you know?"

"I didn't know; it was just a guess. I saw the way he looked at you that time in the cafeteria, and Khalil said at the time that he hoped that Talal hadn't got designs on you."

"Why did he say that?" asked Jenny, suddenly worried that he might have a reputation as a philanderer or some such thing.

"When I asked Khalil, he was a bit evasive. He only said that Talal was a man not to be taken lightly and that he tended to live his life to extremes. Jenny, I am truly happy to see you this elated, but you must be very careful. It is one thing when a man has the occasional fling in this country and quite another when it is a woman. Be very, very discreet, won't you?" cautioned Candy.

"Of course, I will, but please understand that what I am feeling for Talal is something far removed from an '*occasional fling*.' Believe me, I would not have entered into something this serious if that was all it was," Jenny exhorted with great emphasis, wanting to demonstrate the justification for her actions.

"I know, I know, and it must be very hard for you now trying to deal with your feelings for Greg. Do you still care for him?" Candy asked, trying to smooth Jenny's slightly ruffled feathers.

"I do still care for him. Strangely, I still have the same feelings for him that I always have, but they have become downgraded since I have been with Talal." She was tempted to tell Candy about the Nikos incident but thought better of it. "Greg is very special to me. He has tried to be so thoughtful and good to me since his indiscretion with Sherrifa. But compared to how I feel about Talal, there is no comparison. That's all I know. I cannot excuse it. It simply is what it is," Jenny offered.

"Take care, Jenny, and enjoy the happiness that you are having now. But always be on your guard, and if you need help, you know that I will always do what I can to help you," Candy concluded, smiling understandingly at Jenny. She wanted her friend to enjoy life better than she had been doing in the past, but warning bells were sounding off in her head. She resolved to talk to Khalil about it later.

Jenny longed for the day to end so she could be back in Talal's arms again, where she felt safe and secure and the whole world could be shut away. They met again at the villa and spent another night of passion together, reaffirming their love for one another and drawing closer in every way.

"Darling, tomorrow will be the last night we can be together for a while," said Jenny, sadness tingeing her words.

"I know that all too well, my love, but it is too painful to contemplate at this moment. We will face it when it comes," he replied, all the while his mind trying to solve unsolvable problems of reconciling his love for Jenny with his commitments to others.

Candy poured a drink for Khalil and herself and settled down on the sofa of her apartment, where they were both living temporarily until the formalities of telling everyone that they were now married had been completed. They had already chosen a large family villa near the coast where they would move in with Khalil's children very soon. The villa would be big enough for Candy's children to come and stay for extended periods, a compromise that had been reached between Farris' family and herself. "Darling, I want to ask you about something, but I want you to be very discreet about it."

"Of course, sweetheart, go right ahead. I'm listening," Khalil encouraged.

"It's about Jenny. She told me something that concerns me. She's having an affair with your cousin Talal," stated Candy directly.

"I had suspected as much," he said in a resigned voice. "What's the state of play?"

"She says they are seriously involved. The only thing I worry about is her safety, and I don't want her to get hurt."

"I understand completely. She's had a tough time of it, and I want her to be happy too. I doubt that Greg is the kind of man who would act hastily if he discovered what she was doing, and he is hardly in a position to say much to her in light of what he has done. And you know that the airline people have a moral code all of their own, or should I say immoral code."

"You're telling me," interjected Candy, alluding to her years married to Farris.

"I had hoped they would settle down to a happy married life together and start a family one way or another. I did not imagine Jenny to be likely to get involved with anyone," reflected Khalil. "I believe it must be something special for her to take the risks she is doing with her marriage. But for it to be Talal is bad news."

"What do you mean?" she asked concerned.

"Listen, darling, Talal is a good man, and I have no doubt that his intentions with Jenny are the best. The problem lies with the nature of his work. He is involved with some politically sensitive issues which leave him vulnerable," he told her hesitatingly.

"What do you mean? I thought he was some kind of tour guide, taking foreigners to visit historical places. I imagined him to be a historian or something in that line," posited Candy.

"Ostensibly, his job is as a tour guide for the family travel agency, but as I understand it, he works undercover for the government giving information about potential terrorist attacks. What I am telling you must not be repeated, Candy, not even to Jenny. If Talal feels she should know, he will tell her. The only reason that I have any knowledge of this is because of some of the people I met after Shadia was killed. I was so angry, that for a time, I thought to join the resistance movement and vent my anger in that way. However, after long deliberation, I found that my calling to be a doctor outweighed my own personal need for revenge. You cannot be committed to saving lives when you are involved with the taking of lives," he explained.

"And is Talal aware that you know about him?" enquired Candy.

"Yes, yes, he is. I spent some time with him after Shadia's death where my suspicions were aroused. I told him what I suspected, and he did not deny it. However, he did not tell me anything more either. But he did help me to get myself together. He is a deeply philosophical man who sees the world differently to most of us."

"Wow, what a lot to take in," Candy observed. "That makes me even more concerned about Jenny. Could she be in any physical danger?"

"No, I don't think that is likely, but what worries me is that Talal cannot offer the kind of stability that I imagine Jenny needs. Plus the fact his work must, inevitably, put him in danger."

"You know," said Candy, looking thoughtful, "I wonder whether we have pegged Jenny wrongly. I know she appears to be a very conventional individual who likes routine and stability but consider this: She meets an exciting, foreign airline pilot while she is nursing in England, and within six months she has already married him and moved to a totally foreign environment. Furthermore, if she needed stability so much, would she have married an airline pilot? When she had the trouble with Greg, she had a lot of time to sort her life out in England, and what did she do? She elected to come back here, with all that it entails. I think Jenny might be a bit of a dark horse, even if she does not know it herself yet."

"Putting it like that, I think you might well have a point. I wish the whole affair had never started, but since it has, there is little we can do but stand by Jenny if she needs our help," agreed Khalil.

"I hoped you'd feel that way, darling. I too wish that it had never happened, but since it has, there is no point in being judgmental about it. We can only do our best for her since she has no one else here to turn to if things go wrong," she told him smiling, happy that the man she had married was such a supportive husband, who was able to see things in an unbiased manner. She pulled him close to her and playfully bit his ear. "Come here doctor, I think I need a checkup and an immediate examination. Where would you like to start?" she said, offering him an enticing bare shoulder.

"Oh, I think I should start at the top and work my way down," he replied playfully, entering into the spirit of the game.

The day of parting for Jenny and Talal came all too soon and overshadowed their lovemaking. "How can I leave you, my precious angel?" said Talal. "These few days have been a heaven on earth for me. I adore you, I want you to be with me always, and yet I know that I have to leave tomorrow, with all the uncertainty of not knowing when we will be able to meet again."

"I know," agreed Jenny, "my heart is already aching and we haven't even parted yet. Life can sometimes be so unkind. Have you no idea when you will be back in the country?"

"My angel, I wish that I could say for sure, but in truth, I cannot," he answered regretfully.

"Surely the work that you do for the travel agency cannot be so uncertain. I imagine you must have groups booked up well in advance," she countered.

Talal sighed and lay back on the rumpled, white sheets of the bed, squinting at the ceiling. "Jenny, you are no fool, and to allow you to become suspicious of my movements can only serve to destroy our relationship, and God knows, that is the last thing I want to do. Listen to me, darling, what I am about to tell you might affect our relationship, but I am guessing that you would rather be faced with the truth and have the opportunity to make some decisions here and now than to stay in ignorance."

Jenny felt the blood in her veins turn to ice. She could not imagine what Talal was about to tell her, only that it sounded threatening. She could not bear to be torn away from this man whom she had come to love so passionately in the past few weeks. "Tell me, Talal, whatever it is, just tell me," she told him, swallowing hard.

"I am not at liberty to give you any details of what I am about to tell you. Please try and be understanding and know that I love you more than life itself," he said, cradling her in his arms. "You know that this part of the world is very unstable politically and there is much that goes on globally at higher levels that is blatantly unfair and corrupt. To these ends, I work for the government in an undercover capacity in order to, somewhat, redress the balance. The travel agency work makes a perfect foil for my movements around the world. Jenny, my love, I have told you this because I love you and you have a right to know. Needless to say, keep what I have told you in the strictest confidence, to speak of it could put both of us in danger. Now, please darling, tell me you understand and that, at least for now, we can continue our relationship together."

326

Jenny let her head fall on his shoulder in relief. She had not known what she had feared he would say, but although it was stunning news, she felt able to deal with it. "Talal," she said seriously after a small silence, "I don't quite know how to respond to what you have told me. I need to ask you some questions."

"Go ahead, I will answer you the best that I can."

"There are two questions. The first, how dangerous is the work that you do?"

"I will not lie to you, it is very dangerous."

"Okay, second, will you always do this work?"

"Jenny, until I met you, my work was my life. I have always held strong views about political and social injustice and have only ever felt fulfilled when trying to redress the balance in some way. It began in university when I was studying for my degree in politics, economics and philosophy. The very nature of the courses gave me an unusual perspective on life. I was heavily influenced by the philosophical aspect of the courses and developed a strong sense of justice. I feel strongly for the underclasses of the world who do not have the wealth or political importance to have the ear of the world leaders. I understand their struggle, and the work I do allows me some influence on events, and I hope that I do it wisely. Since I have met you, my Jenny Wren, everything has changed. Before, I was willing to give my life for a cause that I believed in, but now I am becoming protective of myself. I look for safety first rather than justice. I long to be with you, and I want you to leave Greg and be with me forever. But right now, I don't know if that is a possibility. God, Jenny, I don't know whether I will ever be able to get out of this life that I lead. Believe me, I will do everything I can to be with you. Jenny darling, if I can sort my life out, will you leave Greg and be with me?"

Jenny's head was spinning. Events were moving faster than she could assimilate them. However, she knew beyond a doubt that she loved Talal and would go with him to the ends of the earth if he asked her. For the first time, she was glad that she had no children with Greg to consider. "Talal, I will gladly go with you wherever you want. Just get out of this dangerous life you are living now. I will leave Greg. What I feel for him cannot compare with what we have together," she told him tenderly.

"Oh, Jenny, you don't know what this means to me. I love you so much I ache. Let me see what I can do when I go back this time. Somehow I will find a way for us to be together. Trust me, I will move heaven and earth for you, for us."

"Yes, please make everything all right, Talal. I couldn't bear to lose you. You are everything to me now."

They clung to each other tightly as if trying to hold the moment of parting back. They made love one more time. Their passion spent, tears ran down Jenny's cheeks.

"I know, darling," he told her, wiping the tears away, "I will be back before you know it. Don't tell Greg anything until you hear from me. I know you will be safe with him until I come back. We will face things together when I am with you." Jenny just nodded, incapable of speaking, emotions constricting her throat. Talal got up from the bed and brought an ice-cold cloth and wiped Jenny's face. "This will make you feel better," he said tenderly. She was grateful for the cold cloth on her face, and she took it from him and pressed it to her throat and took a long, deep breath.

"Thank you, love, I feel better now," she said, finding her voice and affording him a weak smile. Drinking a final cup of dark, strong coffee, they reluctantly went their separate ways.

As Jenny returned to her apartment, the dawn was breaking and the brilliance of the sunrise made her feel deeply fatigued. The night had sped by with all of their talking and lovemaking, and they had not slept at all. She looked at her watch and, noting that it was five o'clock, resolved to try and have a couple of hours of sleep before she left to work. She managed to close her eyes and drift off until the alarm rang at seven forty-five. She dressed for work without showering. She wanted to keep the faint smell of Talal, which lingered on her skin, to comfort her for as long as possible. She steeled herself to be professional at work and immersed herself in the welfare of the patients. By the end of the day, she was exhausted, and she returned home to take a long, hot shower in preparation for Greg's arrival later that evening.

She was preparing a light supper for them when the telephone rang, and it was operations.

"Hello, Madam Youssef, thees ees oberations, Affif sbeaking. I have a message from Captain Youssef to inform you that he is delayed in ze Gulf for twelve hours. He weel see you, lunchtime tomorrow," he told her politely in good but accented English.

"Thank you very much Affif for passing the message. If you speak to Captain Youssef again, please tell him I will see him at lunchtime tomorrow."

"Yes, madam, you are welgome," he told her and closed the line.

Jenny exhaled loudly and thanked God that she did not have to see Greg this evening. She was exhausted, and she ached for Talal. She could almost feel him around her. She put the food in the fridge and headed straight for bed, where she slept soundly till morning when the alarm awoke her. She decided not to go in to work, not even for half a day. She was still very tired, and her body was demanding more rest. After phoning in to work, she closed her eyes and slept solidly for another three hours. Surprised at her lengthy sleep, she got up and dressed in preparation for Greg's arrival.

Greg arrived home full of smiles and apologies for the delay the night before. "Sorry about last night, love. We developed a technical just before takeoff. I hope it didn't put you out too much?"

"No, I didn't mind too much. It gave me an excuse not to go to the hospital today. I was feeling a bit tired and had a long lie in," she told him smiling.

He peered at her. "Mmm you do look a bit pale, love. You mustn't go overdoing it. Are you all right?"

"Oh, yes, yes, of course I am," she replied guiltily. "How are you? How was your trip?" she countered, turning the focus away from herself, remembering the unspoken dictum of "playing the game."

"It was an interesting trip I have got some news. I don't know whether you will like it very much, but after the initial part, it is all good," he said excitedly.

"Do tell me," she said, feeling his excitement.

"Well, there have been some high-level meetings going on lately, and the bottom line is that Hussein called me into his office this morning and told me that the airline is going to buy some more wide-bodied jets. This time, it will be the Tri-star. The deal has been made, and the first crews have to go to the States in ten days' time for the course. Jenny, Hussein said if I chose to go on the course, he would make me fleet captain on the Tri-star. What do you think of that?" he asked her, beaming from ear to ear.

Thinking quickly, Jenny smiled at him and answered, "In this instance, I don't think it matters what I think, but it is quite clear what you think. That something so important to you simply cannot be ignored."

"Oh, Jenny, are you sure you don't mind? It will mean being on your own again for about six weeks. Is that all right?"

"I survived before, I will survive again!" she told him with mixed emotions. She really needed the time on her own. Having to be with Greg now was becoming a constant strain on her especially as she now felt so committed to Talal. The guilt and deception nagged at her relentlessly. She wanted to tell Greg but did not want to hurt him. Without a doubt, she still cared for him, but her heart was telling her that Talal was the one that she truly belonged to.

"You can always go to England, darling, if you want and visit your folks while I am gone," Greg said halfheartedly, not really wanting her to. He preferred her to be in his country where he could have some control and influence over her.

"No, I won't go to England. I've plenty to do at work. I've have quite a good routine, and I don't want to break it," she told him, conscious that she wanted to be accessible to Talal at short notice. "Don't worry, I will be fine here."

"Are you sure, love?"

"Yes, perfectly."

"In that case, I had better call Hussein back and tell him that I accept the post of Fleet Captain. They need to know as soon as possible so that the roster can be adjusted," he concluded with a broad grin, pleased that he had encountered no problems from Jenny about his prospective lengthy absence.

CHAPTER FIFTEEN

Trials and tears

Sherrifa impatiently tapped the pencil on the notepad next to the telephone as she waited for the switchboard at the Muhabarat to answer. When she finally got put through to Lieutenant Mubada, she snarled at him, "My God, man, if there was a real emergency, half of the town would be dead before anyone got through to the switchboard here!"

"Madam Al Fayez, I am *so* sorry you had to wait, but we get so many calls. It takes time, you know. And rest assured, if there were an emergency in the town, we would know of it before anyone had the chance to phone and tell us about it," he said, trying to placate her.

"Hmmm," she growled, "well, do you have anything to report to me?"

"Madam Al Fayez, this is very difficult. You see, in fact you are quite right about the foreign woman. She is seeing someone. My man followed her the other day, and she met someone and stayed with him for most of the night."

"Aha," Sherrifa interjected, "I knew I was right. Now tell me who he is, and I will not trouble you any further. In fact, I will commend you to my father."

Mubada considered the benefits of being commended to Sherrifa's father. It could mean promotion or at least a debt of gratitude that he could call in some time in the future. However, the implications of what was involved in this matter were too serious to be overridden. "Madam Al Fayez, you must understand that there are some things over which I have no authority. In fact, I doubt that there is anyone with enough authority in this department to tamper with the affairs of the man that this foreign woman is seeing."

"What do you mean?" she barked, outraged at the fact that information was being withheld from her.

"Madam, please do not distress yourself. I am *so* sorry that I cannot be of more help to you, but if I disclose the name of this man to you, it would be a serious matter. He has security clearance of the highest level. If there were any way that I could help you, believe me, I would. It would be more than my life is worth to tamper with this man. Do you understand?"

Yes I understand all right, thought Sherrifa. *The bitch has beaten me again. At least I know that she is whoring around, though, and it is only a matter of time before she slips up.* She understood from Mubada's tone that he was truly unable to disclose the man's name, and there would be no point in pushing the matter. In fact, she probably had enough information for her own devious needs. "I understand your position. You have done what you can, thank you."

"You are most welcome, Madam Al Fayez. We will continue to keep an eye on matters for you, and if anything more develops that I can help you with, I will let you know."

"Shukran, ma salami," she told him, ending their conversation.

Mubada was thankful for the courteous ending to their verbal exchange and her wish for him to "go in peace." He had been unsure of how she would take the information that he had for her. Women like her did not expect to have information withheld from them. In the event, she was fairly reasonable.

Feeling reassured, he called his secretary to bring him a Turkish coffee as he lit up an American cigarette and dragged on it deeply.

"Nikos," Sherrifa barked in the telephone at him.

"Yes, chère, Chichi, how can I help you?" he fawned ingratiatingly. Since his incident with Jenny, he was aware that he had lost some of Sherrifa's goodwill, and he was eager to reinstate himself in her good graces.

"Get over here when you have finished at work. I want to talk to you."

"Immediately, chèrie, I have little left to do this morning that I cannot delegate. I'll be there in half an hour."

Nikos arrived promptly, bearing a large bunch of flowers. Sherrifa grunted at them and handed them to her maid to take care of.

"Listen, Nikos, you were right about the man who tackled you that night. He is her lover, I have it on good authority. The only problem is, he has some kind of top-level security status and I cannot find out his name. Even if I did, there would be little that I could do about it. People like him are protected and those he associates with. However, it does not alter the fact that she is having an affair, and sooner or later, Greg is going to get wise to the fact. Little Miss Purity will not have the guts or moral fortitude to keep both men. She will feel obliged to tell Greg that she has someone else. Then, Nikos, I will have dear Greg all to myself."

"That sounds great. So you are just going to play a waiting game then?"

"Well, I might just have to let it slip to Jenny that she has been seen with another man, just to move things along a little faster," she said with a laugh.

"Well, I salute you, Chichi, as usual. You have played your hand well. Poor little Jenny will have been beaten, but then she had no chance against you really," he toadied.

"Well, she will probably get away with more than I wanted her to. But that is only due to the status of her lover."

"Sherrifa, I don't like to say this, but what if this lover of hers wants to marry her or something? She will still be in the country and possibly in a position of influence," he cautioned.

"Nikos, sometimes I think you have learned nothing in all your years here. If she divorced Greg because of her infidelity, it would be an outrageous scandal. There would be no way that they could live in this country. They would be virtual outcasts, they would be forced to live abroad. But then you are assuming that this man would actually want to marry her," she sneered in incredulity at the thought of a man of high position wanting to marry a little English slut.

"Well, he did seem very involved with her," he said, touching his face in remembrance of the heavy blows that had been rained upon him.

"Ha, he is likely to be amusing himself with her. It is my guess that he is some kind of agent for the government and men like that do not make permanent liaisons. He will use her for his pleasure and then move on, leaving her without a protector. Then she will have to slink off back to where she came from."

"Yes, yes, you are right, of course," he told her, but he still had the feeling that she might be underestimating Jenny and the whole situation. However, Sherrifa was happy now, and he was in her good graces. He was content to let things lay.

Hussein put his pen down on his oversized ink blotter and stared hard out of the window. He hadn't had the opportunity

335

to be with Monique since the fateful night of the accident, for which he was still carrying an enormous burden of guilt. He knew he would likely carry the guilt for the rest of his life, to have been instrumental in hurting the very thing that he loved was unthinkable to him. No matter how removed he was from the action of violence, he knew that his association with her had been the instigation for Nikos' violent assault on her.

Despite the fact that he was talking to Monique regularly on the phone, he ached to be with her. His life was becoming more and more meaningless without her. His next move was to talk to his parents and tell them of the situation between himself and Monique. He had already spoken to his brother, who lived in Canada and who had begun making arrangements for him to apply for a residency permit that would allow him to work there. He had also contacted colleagues in the airline industry there, and they had assured him a job flying with an airline if he got the relevant papers. *It will not be a prestigious job. It is only a little airline, flying prop-jobs, but I will be happier doing that than living this farce,* he thought. *At least what I achieve there will be due to my own merit, and not just because I happen to be the husband of Sherrifa Al Fayez. When I know that I have definitely got the residency permit, I will approach Monique and see if she will come with me there.*

He picked up the phone and dialed Monique's number, the sound of her voice was always the best part of his day. He could feel the depth of her love for him despite their enforced separation. They talked together for around half an hour, both reluctant to end the conversation. "It is not always going to be like this, I promise you, darling. Things will change, and we will be together," he told her sincerely.

"I hope so, darling. It is my dream. Until then, I just wait for your calls every day. They make my life worth living," she assented, her gently accented English making her sound like a vulnerable little child.

"I love you," he told her, kissing her through the phone, willing her to have faith and wait for him.

"And I love you too," she reciprocated before they closed the line.

Jenny had welcomed her solitude since Greg's departure. Lately, she had been feeling unusually tired, and the strain of having to pretend in front of him was becoming unbearable. She settled down into a routine of work at the hospital and returning home to rest and read, or listen to music. She refused all invitations to go out in the evenings. Somehow, she did not feel the loneliness that she had experienced during Greg's previous protracted absences. She constantly thought of Talal and wanted to be instantly available in case he should call. Two weeks had already passed since Greg's departure, and she had heard nothing from Talal. She had taken to listening to the news in Arabic every evening at eight o'clock and acquainting herself with the local political situation, knowing Talal would be, in some way, involved. Her lessons in classical Arabic had finally paid off as the news broadcasts were only given in the classical tongue. She was not able to understand every word, but she was able to piece together enough to give her an overall picture of events. Lately there had been much tension in the streets of Koudara, with many angry demonstrations by the local people who had taken to the streets to protest about unfair taxes and oppression. Certainly, the situation was heading towards another crisis. Jenny hoped fervently that Talal would be safe and not get caught up in this latest violence.

"Ish malak y'aki?" "What troubles you my brother?" enquired a scruffily dressed paramilitary soldier, noticing Talal's uneasy silence.

"Oh, nothing," replied Talal, unwilling to discuss his personal torment with anyone.

"Your face and silence tell me otherwise," continued the soldier, unwilling to give up. He loved him like a brother; Talal was a man that he and his men aspired to emulate. He had showed unfailing courage in the face of danger and inspired the men to fight on in times when they felt downtrodden and despondent of the future.

"It's personal, Sadiq. It is something that I have to work out on my own."

"Talal, how can you tell me that it is personal? We have stood side by side in the face of danger many times, and we are like family. Whatever troubles you, troubles me. Speak, tell me of your problem."

Talal looked squarely in the eyes of Sadiq, knowing that he was right. Nothing could, or should, be hidden from this man who had shared so much with him. "Sadiq, when you kiss your wife goodbye before a mission, how do you feel?"

"Aha, I see the direction of your problem. My wife is my inspiration. It is because she and our children are so oppressed that I come to fight. I would gladly die to secure their liberty. We are poor people who have no political voice when we are treated badly. The best that I can do is to pray to God to help me, and stand and fight for our rights, with others like me. It tears me apart to leave her and my children, knowing that I may not see them again, but it would be a worse pain to stay and do nothing. I am resigned to my fate. But your fate, my brother, is different than mine. You are not poor, you are not without influence, and as yet, you have no wife." Pausing for a second, he looked at Talal deeply and continued. "What woman has wrought this change in you?" he asked kindly.

Talal looked down at the floor, not wanting Sadiq to see his Achilles' heel. "I have met a woman who has changed my whole life. From the moment I set eyes on her until now, she never leaves my thoughts. I want to be with her always. Now I am calculating the odds the whole time, looking for my safety before justice. I feel like a traitor and a coward towards you all, but I cannot help my feelings. I love her. She is like a breath of spring in all this turmoil. I see my future in her eyes, and it beckons to me with an irresistible force. But I am trapped. How can I get out of this? I will never be able to escape, and they will never let me alone," he said despondently, fighting back tears of futility.

"My brother you have stood many times and fought with us when you could have walked away. You have never ceased to help us in any way that you could. We owe you a debt of gratitude that is impossible for us to repay. There is no shame in your words or feelings. You have a right to a future and a life of peace and happiness. Together, we will find a way for you to get out of all of this. It will not be easy, but I think I know a way."

Talal looked doubtfully at Sadiq and listened to his words, but as he spoke, he began to see that his plan could work, namely because Sadiq was the only man powerful enough to carry it off with any success. "But," cautioned Sadiq, "you must not breathe a word of it to anyone, not even your beloved. She must know nothing. All this will require exact timing and expediency.

"You would do all this for me?" asked Talal disbelievingly.

"You are my brother. I cannot do less," said Sadiq with a smile. Talal's spirits instantly began to rise. He straightened his stooped shoulders and took on an air of purpose. Happy to see Talal so restored, he slapped him hard on the shoulder and started to laugh. "There is nothing that is impossible, remember that, and also that your brothers would do anything to help you!"

Hussein was firmly resolved to leave Sherrifa and the airline. He had spoken to his family and told them of his intentions. They were sympathetic to him, understanding some of what he had endured over the years. Ever since his brother's move to Canada, his parents had been considering emigrating there too, and spending their retirement there. Hussein's news simply served as the catalyst for their decision. Most of his extended family was far enough out of Sherrifa's reach for him to be able leave her without any repercussions on them. He planned to ask his son Samer to join them too. He hoped he would choose to be with him and Monique rather than Sherrifa. Fortunately, the prevailing law of the country afforded the father custody of children when they reached seven years of age. However, he would never insist that Samer come with him, so it would have to be his choice. It would be good to see Roger and Samer together. They were of a similar age and they always got along well together. *God*, he thought, *I hope that I can pull this off. It will be the fight of my life, but this time, I have no intention of losing. I will face Sherrifa this very night*, he decided. *There is no point in delaying.*

Sherrifa was in a good mood when he returned that evening. She had spent the afternoon at the beauty salon and intended to go and play bridge with some of her friends that evening.

"Good evening, Sherrifa," said Hussein, trying to attract her attention.

"Can't you see that I am leaving now?" she spat at him, giving a dismissive wave over her shoulder as she walked by.

"Sherrifa," he said firmly, the commanding tone in his voice stopping her in her tracks.

"Yes, what is your problem?" she asked, annoyed to be diverted from her planned evening's entertainment.

"Sherrifa, I need to talk to you on a very important matter. Can we go into the salon and talk?"

"You had better make it quick. I have plans for the evening, and I am already late."

"The conversation will be as long or as short as you want to make it," he told her.

"Then I imagine it will be very brief," she snapped. They walked into the salon and faced each other squarely, neither one of them wanting to sit down and give the other a height advantage.

"Sherrifa, you know that our marriage is a sham. I have continued with the pretence for the sake of my family, and I cannot deny also for the sake of all the prestige of rank and power you and your family have conferred upon me. But I can no longer continue this way. I am desperately unhappy. I have found someone whom I love and want to marry. I want my freedom from you, Sherrifa," he told her frankly.

"Ha," she mocked, "you leave me? You haven't got the guts. Besides, I will ruin you and your family. I will make sure that everyone in the town socially isolates them. They will be cut dead by all of the top people in the town. I will make you look like a skirt-chasing free-loader."

"Sherrifa, you can no longer do that. My parents have travelled abroad to join my brother and his wife, where they have

341

emigration papers waiting for them. They do not plan to return. As for my extended family, they are well out of your reach. They are not working here. They are working in the Emirates where they need no protection from your family," he said with some satisfaction.

Sherrifa fumed at being outmanoeuvred, but she quickly recovered, remembering that she could still threaten him with loss of position in the airline. "It will not be much of a life with this new woman of yours being demoted to a line captain and being ignored by everyone," she snarled.

"Sherrifa, you can stop your threatening. It is not going to work. I too plan to leave the country. I am quite prepared to lose the status I have gained in exchange for a life where I have someone who loves me and a chance of a happy family life."

"You stupid fool," she spat at him, "you would give all this away for a roll in the hay with an ageing, has-been, French aristocrat. She is not worth it." Sherrifa was beginning to get anxious. She knew that Hussein was basically an altruistic man whose honour would always come before money. She had been sloppy lately, not keeping tabs on the movements of her in-laws, and she had underestimated Hussein's feelings for Monique.

"Please, do not speak of Monique in that manner. She is a decent, not to mention beautiful, woman who has suffered at the hands of your lapdog Nikos for more years than I can remember. I will happily leave all this." He gestured around him with a look of disgust on his face. "For she is everything I want. I would happily live in a shack with her," he said, leaping to defend Monique.

Sherrifa fumed with anger at this. Hearing Hussein speak of Monique's beauty and dignity was more than she could endure. Her own insecurity about her looks was beginning to tell. Jealousy overcame her, and she stormed from the room shouting,

"This isn't over yet, you filthy son of a bitch. I will bring you and your French hag to your knees."

"Not this time, Sherrifa," he shouted after her. Sherrifa stormed up to the privacy of her bedroom, where the force of her anger finally turned to tears. She felt vulnerable. If she did not have the protective umbrella of her marriage to Hussein to lend respectability to her position, she would lose much of her power. Her position as wife of a top airline executive gave her freedom and license to carry on much as she pleased. If he divorced her, she would have to return to the protection of her father. He made a fine protector, but there was no way she could continue her lifestyle with the latitude she enjoyed as Hussein's wife. Instinctively, she picked up the phone and dialled Nikos' number. It was Roger who answered, and she did not waste any time on pleasantries. "Get me your father quickly," she spat in French at him.

"Who may I say is calling?" he asked politely.

"Madam al Fayez," she barked.

"Just wait one moment please." Roger called his father, who snatched the phone uncivilly from his son.

"Sherrifa, chèrie, what a pleasant surprise, how are you?" his attitude changing to one of pleasant subservience.

"Get over here now," she commanded him.

"Yes, chèrie, right away." He knew by her tone of voice that something serious had happened, and left immediately for her house.

On arriving, he found Sherrifa unusually distraught. "Chèrie, what has happened? Why are you so upset?" he said, leading her to the sofa in the salon and keeping his arm firmly around her.

"Hussein wants to divorce me and marry your whore of a wife," she snarled.

"What? I thought that was a passing fling," he said incredulously.

"No, it seems they are both so disgustingly noble that they have to forfeit everything for their love," she said with biting sarcasm.

"Are you telling me Hussein is prepared to lose everything he has here for Monique?" he asked incredulously.

"In a word, yes."

"He must be a fool, that is all I can say. As for her, I don't give a damn, but I understand what it will mean to you, chèrie. We must find a way to stop them."

"Yes, but Hussein has made sure that I have very little leverage. His immediate family have all emigrated so I have no influence there, and he no longer wants his position in the airline," she said helplessly.

Nikos understood the situation all too well, and he too stood to lose much if she was no longer married to Hussein. "Don't you worry, we will sort this all out," he said, a plan already formulating in his devious brain. "Listen, chèrie, there is a way out of this. The area that you are not thinking in is Monique. I can see two ways we can use her to our advantage. Firstly, you have friends in the Muhabarat haven't you?" She nodded.

"Well, you could arrange for her to spend a little time in jail on some trumped-up charge. Of course, I will be out of the country on a long-haul flight at the time and know nothing of it. Secondly, if that does not make them cool off, then I can claim custody of Roger while we are in this country. She will not leave her precious son, even for the love of her life," he said, pleased with his devious suggestions.

"Nikos, darling, you are wonderful. What would I do without you?" she said thankfully. "What a brilliant strategy, I can ensure that she spends quite a long time in jail, and not even Hussein will be able to secure her release. She will soon crumble under all that pressure." Sherrifa felt in control of her destiny again, knowing that the minute Hussein made a move from the house she would give the word for the police to move in on Monique and have her arrested. The trump cards would be all in her hands again.

The following day, Hussein phoned Monique to tell her that he had spoken with Sherrifa and told her everything.

"Hussein, darling, does this mean that we can be together finally?" she asked in disbelief.

"There is little she can do now. For once, I think that I have outmanoeuvred her. There is nothing to stop you from walking away from Nikos now. Will you do it?" he asked anxiously.

"Do it? Of course I will do it. Just tell me when we can leave so I do not have to stay a moment longer than I have to, after I tell Nikos about what we are doing," she said with joy and relief.

"I have been thinking about that. In light of his past violent performance, I think it would be better for you to talk to Roger and then just pack up and leave. You can leave Nikos a note, telling him you are leaving him. Once we get out of the country, we can both start divorce proceedings against our respective spouses."

"Yes," said Monique, "I agree, I think it would be better all around to do it that way. When shall we leave?"

"There is a flight to the States the day after tomorrow; that will give us a chance to get our things together. We will stay a few weeks in the States, which might fool people into thinking that we are going to settle there. I want as few people as possible to know exactly where we are going. We will take our time before we finally move to our new home. Nikos will be away on a flight when we are due to leave, so there should be nothing to get in your way. Do you think Roger will give you any problems about leaving?" he asked, this one last worry needing to be allayed.

"Roger will not mind at all. He often asks me to leave here. He has no love for his father, and to be with you will be a bonus for him. You know he adores you," she told him reassuringly.

"Thank God," he exhaled, "then it is arranged. I will call you tomorrow after Nikos leaves. We will go through the final details of our departure, then I will come and collect you in a taxi a couple of hours before the flight the next day."

"Darling, I cannot wait, and I am sure I won't be able to sleep until we leave. At last we can be together, no more sneaking around. You have no idea how much I love you, Hussein," she told him breathlessly.

"Yes I do, my love, and I cannot wait either. Forty-eight hours is not long after all we have endured, but still it seems an eternity to me too. I must go now, beloved. I have so much to arrange here and elsewhere, putting my affairs in order and transferring things abroad. Bring only the minimum of clothes for you and Roger, and only the very minimum of personal souvenirs. I will buy you and Roger new things when we get to our new home. I want few reminders of our old life."

"There is little that I want to bring with me, I too want to forget. Take care, my love, I will wait for your call tomorrow." She closed the line with a gentle kiss into the receiver. She was elated, and she began to sort the clothes that she and Roger would likely need into easily packable piles in drawers, so she could just transfer them to the suitcases the following day. She waited anxiously for Roger to return from school that day. She had not mentioned anything about her affair with Hussein to him, but she guessed Roger did have some inkling of it, and seemed to give his tacit approval.

"Ah, Maman," he greeted his mother with his usual roguish smile.

"Hello, Roger dear," she replied in English.

"Aha, I see it is an English-speaking afternoon today, Mother?" he stated in jest. "I assure you that my English grades are excellent, and I do not need any subtle coaching."

"No, Roger, it is not that, but I do have to have a very serious talk with you."

"What is it?" he asked slightly worried.

"Don't worry, I will do nothing if you are not in complete agreement with what has been planned."

"Tell me, Mother," he asked anxiously.

"You know that your father and I have not had a proper marriage for many years and that I have been quite unhappy for a long time."

"Yes, yes, I know that," he interjected, hoping that at last she would leave the monster who called himself her husband and his father.

"Well, I will come straight to the point: I have been seeing Hussein romantically, and we have fallen in love. He wants you and me to go to Canada with him and start a new life together. He hopes you will choose to come too and that we can all be a family together."

"Well, why are we standing here then?" he told her, grinning from ear to ear and feeling both relief and elation. "Shouldn't we be packing or something?"

Monique embraced her son, tears pouring down her cheeks. At last, she could offer him something better than the life he had been living with Nikos. They spent the rest of the afternoon talking and planning the future. Roger had never seen his mother look so radiant and animated, and he too was happier than he could remember.

The following day, Hussein had put all his affairs in order. He had prepared a letter to be given to the chairman of the airline the day after his departure to the States, giving his resignation.

He had told everyone that he had a business meeting there, and he did not want the inevitable huge scandal to unfold until he and Monique and Roger were out of the country. Hussein had contacted his son by phone and told him of his plans to leave and asked if he wanted to come with him. Hussein was delighted when Samer begged to be allowed to come out of boarding school right away. Hussein made all the necessary arrangements for him to come out of school and arranged for him to fly to the States to join them. Samer was overjoyed, at last he could look forward to something more than his cold mother and the equally cold boarding school that had been his unhappy life for so long.

In the afternoon, Hussein returned home to start packing his things. There was precious little to take anything other than the necessary clothing. By evening, everything was in order and completed. He had spoken to Monique and told her he would pick her and Roger up at eight o'clock in the morning. As he settled down for the night, he thought of what he was leaving behind. Apart from his work at the airport, there was absolutely nothing that he would miss. Everything that he held dear would be with him in his new life. He closed his eyes and drifted into a dreamless sleep.

The next morning, Sherrifa was around when he began to leave. She was under the impression that he was going to the States on a business trip. She had checked with her sources at the airport, and they had confirmed this. He had only his usual Samsonite suitcase with him, and there was nothing at all to arouse her suspicions. She went about her business, not wishing to speak to him if it could be avoided. She had come to the conclusion that he had, after all, chickened out of his planned move. At seven twenty, a cab came to pick up Hussein. Sherrifa caught sight of it as it left. Usually he had the driver take him to the airport when he was going on a business trip, immediately arousing her suspicions. *That conniving bastard*, she thought, *he is trying to pull a fast one on me. He really is going to leave me, and without a word.* She was filled with anger, spurred on by her own self-serving need to protect her comfortable and prestigious way of life. The phone was in her hand in a second. "This is Madam Al Fayez, get me Lieutenant Mubada now," she rapped out in Arabic to the switchboard operator.

"Right away, Madam Al Fayez, I am ringing through right now for you," swiftly answered the cringing telephonist, making the necessary connections and fearing any repercussions should she be kept waiting.

"Madam Al Fayez, how may I be of service to you?" answered Mubada cautiously, wondering why she was calling him openly. He calculated that it was not connected with the other matter that he had been helping her with.

"Listen, it has come to my attention that a foreign woman may be trying to smuggle her thirteen-year-old son out of the country without her husband's consent. It is even possible that she has convinced my husband to help her. She is, in fact, a great liar who will say anything to get her own way. Her husband will be devastated when he learns of his son's departure. He even stands by his wife in spite of all her infidelities and lies. The poor man worships her." She paused for a moment to create the right effect. With a stifled sob, she continued, "I, I believe," she faltered, "that she is having an affair with my husband. She is leaving the country so that he may visit her more easily, and without me finding out." At this point, she feigned some more choking sobs for Mubada's benefit.

"Madam Al Fayez, this is a terrible thing to happen. I am ready to do whatever I can to assist you," he answered swiftly. He was intensely suspicious of her story, knowing her reputation for infidelity. But when the chips were down, he had more to fear from Sherrifa and her family than from Hussein, even though he was a national hero. *Besides*, he reasoned to himself, *if this woman was kidnapping her son without her husband's knowledge and Hussein was involved with her, they deserved to be stopped. No doubt Sherrifa's father will be grateful to me if the whole thing is handled discreetly, and that could mean an immediate promotion for me.*

"Oh, I am so grateful to you," she sobbed.

"What was it exactly that you had in mind, dear Madam Al Fayez, if I may ask?" he posited with sympathy, understanding the need for discretion and caution.

"Well, I think if you asked your men at the airport to stop Madam Monique Stianou from leaving the country and detained her in jail until her husband returns, it would be the most satisfactory way forward. Undoubtedly, my husband will try to intervene, but I hope I can rely on you to keep him discreetly to one side until she is removed from the airport," she told him decisively.

"Madam Al Fayez, I will leave for the airport immediately and handle the matter personally. You can rest assured, all will be done with the utmost discretion. I understand that we do not wish to have your husband's image tarnished through being involved in such a tacky affair?" he offered.

"You understand perfectly, Lieutenant, and if all this goes well, you will be amply rewarded for you loyalty."

"Oh, no, no," he countered, in the expected manner, "I want only to help you. It is entirely unnecessary for you to reward me for simply doing my job, but I must ask you, do you know which flight this evil woman will be taking?"

"I cannot be sure, but I imagine that it will be the morning flight to the States, but it could actually be any flight. And there is just a possibility that I may be wrong about them leaving, but I do not think so."

"Don't worry, leave it all in my hands. Whatever the situation, I will handle it for you."

"Thank you, please keep me informed at all times," she said, a smile of intense satisfaction forming on her lips, feeling the heady surge of victory rising within her.

Lieutenant Mubada immediately put a call through to his men at the airport and told them to detain Monique at all costs until he arrived there.

Sherrifa felt elated. She was now in control of the game. If Hussein and Monique were trying to leave today, then she would be the one who stopped them. With Monique in jail, Hussein would have to come to her for help when he found out who was pulling all the strings as he did not have sufficient influence with the Muhabarat to free Monique on his own. Next, she put in a call to Nikos in Karachi, he was sunning himself at the hotel pool when her call came.

"Nikos, listen, I think that Hussein and Monique are trying to leave on the flight to the States today. I have informed my friend at the Muhabarat who will ensure that Monique is stopped from leaving the country on suspicion of kidnapping. I have told him to be discreet and keep Hussein well away from any possible scandal."

"That is wonderful, chèrie I admire your beautiful mind. What do you want me to do?"

"When you come home this evening, I want you to be the world's best father, who is devastated by the thought of his wife taking his beloved son away from him."

"I can do that, chèrie. Is there anything else?"

"Yes, Monique is going to be in jail. Does it bother you that she might be in there for a while?"

"No, I hope the bitch suffers. I don't give a damn about her."

"Good, then leave things to me."

351

"Whatever you want, chèrie, au revoir."

Sherrifa called for her maid. "Bring me breakfast," she ordered. There was nothing to do now but wait until Mubada called. She lit a long cigarillo and inhaled deeply, feeling pleased with her morning's work.

Monique and Roger were packed and ready when Hussein drew up in the taxi. They had only the minimum of luggage, so they were on their way in minutes. The drive to the airport was quick and pleasant, the elation that all three of them felt at their prospective journey made the atmosphere electric, with even the cab driver joining in their excitement. At the airport, Hussein took charge of all the travel documents. As soon as the check-in staff saw Hussein, they sent someone out to take his tickets and passports and check in their luggage.

"Good morning, Captain Hussein," greeted the clerk, "let me take care of your things."

"Thank you, Atif," replied Hussein, noting the badge on the clerk's jacket, as he always made a point of addressing employees by name where possible. "Can you also take care of Madam Stianou's documents and her son's as well, please?"

"Of course, sir, it will be my pleasure." He returned within five minutes with all the necessary work done.

"Thank you, Atif, I appreciate your assistance."

"You are more than welcome, sir," said Atif, who admired Hussein for his fair and unbiased treatment of staff and even more so for his heroic actions in the hijacking.

"That's about all from down here, darling," he whispered to Monique. "We may as well go through security and into the first-class lounge, where we can have a coffee and bite to eat."

"That would be nice, neither Roger or I could manage much breakfast this morning, and I must admit to being a bit hungry," responded Monique enthusiastically.

"Mmm, yes please," echoed Roger.

The three of them walked upstairs to security and began the tedious process of body and bag searches. When they arrived at the body search area, Hussein and Roger had to go through the men's section whilst Monique went through the women's.

"See you in a couple of minutes," said Hussein waving to Monique.

"Okay, see you," she waved back.

Roger and Hussein went inside to be searched, but before they had finished, an official at the airport came to the cubicle to ask for Hussein. "Excuse me, Captain Hussein, there is a problem in operations. Can you please go over there? I have a car ready for you, sir."

"Look, can't you see that I am about to leave on a flight soon? Can't someone else take care of whatever it is?"

"No, sir, my orders were to bring you right away. There seems to be an emergency."

Reluctantly, Hussein agreed to go. Turning to Roger, he said, "Listen, son, meet your mother outside and tell her that I will be a little late but not to worry. I will see you either in the departure lounge or on the aircraft."

"Yes, sir, I will," replied Roger, still unsure about how to address Hussein, but he had enjoyed the way that he had referred to him as *son*.

Hussein was whisked off in the airline car, and Roger made his way to meet his mother. He expected her to be waiting for him. He looked all around but could not see any sign of her. Finally, he went up to the woman security officer to ask about his mother.

"What is your mother's name?" barked the woman.

"Monique Stianou," replied Roger.

"Come with me," she told him gruffly, pushing him towards an office at the side of the building.

Inside the office, Lieutenant Mubada was waiting, "Sit down, please," he told him.

Roger obeyed, beginning to feel increasingly alarmed.

"What is the purpose of this trip you are taking?"

"Where is my mother?" demanded Roger.

"Never mind that now, just answer the question."

Roger thought hard. His mother had told him not to say anything about their plans to anyone. She had told him to say they were taking a holiday in the States, where they would be staying with friends. "We are taking a holiday, sir. Now please, tell me where my mother is," replied Roger politely.

"It has come to our attention that your mother is attempting to take you out of the country permanently without your father's consent, and in this country, that can be considered kidnapping."

Roger was panicking now. He wanted to see his mother desperately, and he did not know how to handle this situation. He wished fervently that Hussein was around to help him.

"Look, sir, I have told you that we are going on holiday and that is the truth. My mother is not trying to kidnap me at all. My father is a pilot for the airline here, and my mother and I often travel places together. I do not know why you are trying to say this about us now."

Mubada felt a little sympathy for the boy, for without the intervention of Sherrifa, they would have all left on their flight without problem. He found both the mother and the boy to be decent types, not at all what Sherrifa had suggested.

"Listen," began Roger again, "if you will, contact Captain Hussein Al Fayez. He has been called to Operations, and he is travelling on the same flight as us and has been helping us. He will tell you that we are just going on holiday," he said pleadingly.

"I am sorry, but you will have to wait here until this affair gets clarified."

"But where is my mother? Please tell me."

Lieutenant Mubada had been putting off telling the boy for as long as he could in order to get as much information out of him as possible. "Your mother has been taken to jail until this affair can be clarified," he said dispassionately.

Roger gasped unbelievingly, "What do you mean, taken to jail? That is impossible. My mother has done nothing wrong."

"Well then, this affair will soon be cleared up, won't it? And you will all soon be on your way."

"But the flight leaves in an hour," argued Roger.

"You can forget about going anywhere today, young man. It will take at least two days before things are sorted."

Roger's world seemed to be crashing round him; he didn't know what to do or where to go. In his panic, his mind seemed to be working at light speed, and suddenly, he had an idea. "Look, my mother is a French national, and I demand that the Embassy be contacted. If you do not, I will contact them myself."

Mubada did not really want the Embassy involved with this because it would only complicate things. Even though he was legally within his rights to arrest Monique, it was not really good policy. He needed to know how badly Sherrifa wanted this woman in jail.

"Okay, wait here and I will see what can be done," conceded Mubada. He went into an adjoining office and phoned Sherrifa.

"Madam Al Fayez, all is as we expected, and the suspect has been transported to jail."

"Wonderful, well done, Lieutenant, where is my husband?" responded Sherrifa, feeling great satisfaction that her plan had succeeded.

"He was called away to operations on a phony emergency, and I expect he will be breathing hard down our necks soon."

"Ha," laughed Sherrifa, "make him sweat it out."

"Madam Al Fayez, I am anxious to do everything that you want, but I have a small problem at this end."

"What is it?" she barked.

"Well, Madam Stianou's son is necessarily distraught about his mother's arrest, and he is demanding that the French Embassy be called. Of course he is within his rights, but it will complicate the affair if they are involved. It will not stay, well, discreet."

Sherrifa had not given much thought to the boy's reaction. In fact, she had not thought the whole thing through thoroughly at all because of the time constraints that had been upon her. Her devious mind quickly came up with a solution.

"Listen, tell the boy that you will contact the Embassy, and in the meantime, I will deal with the situation. You will say that I am on the way to the airport now to come and take care of the boy and help his mother to get released."

"Yes, Madam Al Fayez, that is an admirable solution. I will talk to the boy now." Mubada related Sherrifa's message to Roger, who received it with mixed emotions. Of the times that he had met Sherrifa, he had been polite to her, and in return, she had made the expected clucking noises over him. Roger could always feel the insincerity in her voice and manner. Other than that, he knew her by reputation only. She was a prominent figure and so the subject of much speculation and gossip at school, and from what he had overheard of his father's conversations with her, he knew her to be less than a loving wife. Her coming to pick him up here made things difficult, especially as he and his mother were about to leave the country forever with her husband. He could only wonder whether she knew. He hoped fervently that she did not, and then she would be able to get his mother out of jail with one phone call.

Sherrifa arrived within forty minutes, escorted by her chauffer, wafting into the office on an air of importance and expensive French perfume.

"Roger, you poor child, you must be worried sick. Come with me now, and we will sort this silly mix-up out in no time," she cooed at him in French. She then turned to Mubada and seemed to be berating him for his actions, though Sherrifa's Arabic was too fast for Roger to make out.

"Come now, Roger, let us get you out of here. This is no place for a young man to be delayed in."

"Merci Tante Sherrifa, I am most grateful, but can you arrange for my mother to be released as soon as possible, please?" he begged her.

"Of course, of course, I am working on it already. Now let us get back home, where I can give you a good meal," she fawned.

Roger was relieved to go with her since she seemed totally unaware of what her husband and his mother and himself had been about to do. He believed that she would secure his mother's release as soon as possible.

In operations, Hussein tried to find out who had sent for him and for what emergency, but to no avail. No one seemed to know who had recalled him, and all were very apologetic. Hussein began to get suspicious and phoned through to the first-class lounge to see if Monique and Roger had arrived there yet.

"No, sir, they are not here yet, but there is still another forty minutes before boarding. Perhaps they are in duty free doing a little shopping," offered the pleasant sounding ground hostess.

Hussein knew they would not be doing any shopping and began to wonder if something had gone very wrong. He then phoned through to security to find out if they were still there for any reason. When he got through, someone told him to hold the line. Within a minute, Lieutenant Mubada came on the line.

"Can I be of assistance, captain?" he asked politely.

"Yes, can you tell me if Madam Stianou and her son have cleared security yet?"

"Ah, there has been a problem there, sir. I think it would be advisable if you came over here, and I will discuss it with you." Hussein's blood ran cold; he knew something was wrong. He took the car himself and raced to the departures area. He found Lieutenant Mubada waiting for him. Inside the office, Mubada proceeded to tell Hussein that Monique had been arrested on suspicion of kidnapping.

"That's absurd," he said infuriated. "She must be released immediately. She is the wife of one of the senior pilots and a good friend of the family."

"Ah, yes sir, but unfortunately she was reported by a very reliable source. There is nothing we can do at this moment until the charge has been investigated and the woman's husband returns to the country," he said, enjoying his little power play. Under normal circumstances, he would have been kow-towing to Hussein.

"And who is this 'reliable source'?" he asked, almost knowing the answer before he spoke.

"The source, sir, is Madam Al Fayez."

"Thank you, Lieutenant, where is Madam Stianou's son?" he asked without emotion.

"Madam Al Fayez came and took him to your home. She is looking after him."

"Thank you for your assistance," said Hussein, turning swiftly to leave before his face reflected the violent emotion that he was feeling. He would not give this obvious pawn of Sherrifa's the satisfaction of reporting any visible reaction from him to her.

Admiring Hussein's composure, Mubada offered, "For what it's worth, I did not enjoy taking this action, but I had little choice."

358

"That is entirely your affair, Lieutenant. Now if you will excuse me, I have urgent matters to deal with." Hussein turned smartly on his heel and walked out of the building and headed for his villa. He was now shaking with anger at Sherrifa's behaviour. He had no idea how he was going to free Monique from prison, but his first priority was to ensure Roger was being properly taken care of. As he drove, he wracked his brains to think of any contact that he might have who would have enough influence to get Monique freed. He felt wretched and powerless until he remembered the letter of resignation he had left with his secretary to be given to the chairman after his departure to the States. The last thing he needed now was to give up his position at the airport. At least there, he could still wield a little power if he were still in his job. He pulled over to a nearby telephone box, fervently hoping it was operational. Luck was with him, and he quickly got through to his secretary. "Hania, have you sent that letter to the chairman yet?"

"No, Captain Hussein, I was about to send it with a driver in about half an hour. Is there a problem with it?"

"Yes, yes, there is," he said, relief flooding through him. "Will you please take it to my desk and lock it away with your set of keys? There are important reasons why it should not be sent just now. And I have also cancelled my business trip to the States. It is possible that I will be in the office later on today. There has been a bit of a crisis on a personal level that I have to deal with."

"Don't worry, Captain, I will take care of it, and if I can be of help with anything else, please let me know." Hania, like so many of the people who worked for Hussein, would do anything for him. He was always a concerned and understanding boss who treated his employees in an egalitarian manner and with great respect.

"Thanks, Hania, I will keep you posted, goodbye now." He continued his drive to the villa, his mind racing, unable to come up with an immediate solution to anything. He decided to ensure that Roger was comfortable and then go visit Monique.

Hussein pushed the door of his villa open and strode forcefully inside, looking for the whereabouts of Sherrifa and Roger. Before he had taken more than a few steps, Sherrifa appeared out of the lounge, all smiles.

"Oh darling, there you are. I see that you have been able to postpone your business trip to the States. I am so glad, now we can sort out this awful mess with poor Monique."

Hussein looked daggers at Sherrifa. In that moment, he felt capable of wringing her expensively decorated neck. "Where is Roger?" he demanded.

"He's right here, the poor little soul. He is distraught with worry about his mother," she said, leading him into the lounge.

"Roger, are you all right, son?"

"Yes sir, I am all right, but as you can imagine, I am extremely worried about my mother. Can we do something right away?"

Sherrifa jumped in at this point, "Roger, Lieutenant Mubada is already doing all he can to expedite things. There is very little that we can do but sit and wait, my dear boy."

"Well, can you take me to see her, please?" asked Roger, looking directly at Hussein.

Hussein understood his need to see his mother, but really felt that it would distress him to see how his mother is being treated there. "Look, Roger, I don't want to disappoint you, but I really feel that you would be better off waiting here at the villa. Why don't you go to Samer's room. There are probably some things that would interest you there. I know he has an enormous collection of videos. Perhaps you can watch some of them till I get back. I am going right now to see your mother and see if anything more can be done. Come with me now, and I will show you where his room is."

"Okay, sir, if you think that is best." Roger eagerly followed Hussein. He was desperate for them to be alone for a few moments so he could speak freely, as too was Hussein.

They climbed the stairs that led to the bedrooms, and when they were out of Sherrifa's earshot, Hussein told Roger, "Son, I am so sorry about this. I'm afraid that we have been set up, and your poor mother is taking the brunt of it. Rest assured, I will do everything I can to get her released as soon as humanly possible."

"I don't doubt that for a minute, but I feel so helpless. I cannot bear to think of Mother in jail, and also I worry about what my father will do when he comes home this evening," he said desperately. With Hussein saying they were being set up, Roger was fairly sure Sherrifa was behind all this, and he felt most uncomfortable being in this position, having to pretend everything was perfectly normal when all knew that it wasn't. But his mother had always told him to be polite to everyone under any circumstances and never divulge personal information to anyone. With Hussein, he felt safe enough to speak openly. "Is it your wife that is behind this?"

Hussein looked at Roger's face and knew that lying would be futile. "Yes, son, I believe she is, and that is what is complicating the issue," replied Hussein in a disheartened manner.

"In that case, I imagine that the police lieutenant is involved in the plot too."

"Yes, you are quite right," he replied, admiring Roger's perception. "Well, when I mentioned to him that I wanted to contact the French Embassy and tell them of the situation, the lieutenant seemed to change his tone with me and become more cooperative. I believe that we should contact the Embassy and see if they can help, for I am sure that he did not."

Hussein felt heartened. Somehow, he never thought of Monique as being French. She had been in the country and part of the airline for so long, that she did not appear foreign to him in any way. He rebuked himself for not thinking of contacting the Embassy himself. He had met most of the ambassadors to the country at various functions so he would be able to appeal to them on a personal level as well as an official. He picked up the phone and dialed Hania's number.

"Hania, can you find out the name and direct telephone number of the French ambassador and then call me back at home immediately? And please, only speak to me. Do not give the information to anyone else."

Hania could feel his urgent need for discretion and assured him that she would do it at once. Within fifteen minutes, she had passed the relevant information on to Hussein, and he contacted the ambassador personally. "Good morning, your Excellency, I am Captain Hussein Al Fayez. You might remember that we have met several times."

"Of course, I remember," replied the ambassador. "How could I forget the famous captain who prevented the hijacking so adeptly. Your deeds are often discussed in ambassadorial circles. In fact, we all concluded that you ought to be in the diplomatic corps with your obvious skills of negotiation," he concluded light heartedly, obviously happy to talk to Hussein.

"Ambassador, I will come straight to the point. I would like to ask your help both officially and personally."

"Certainly, I will be delighted to help in whatever capacity I can. Please go ahead and tell me what the problem is," he answered in a more serious tone.

"A dear friend who is a French national has been mistakenly arrested for allegedly trying to smuggle her own son out of the country permanently without her husband's knowledge or consent."

"What is the lady's name?" The ambassador became serious.

"She is Monique Stianou, and she is married to a Greek national."

"Ah yes, I am acquainted with Monique. She has done a lot for our cultural centre, and I know her family in France well. Don't worry, I will do everything I can to put pressure on the authorities."

"Thank you so much, can I leave you a couple of numbers where you can contact me as soon as you hear something? Right now, I am going to visit Monique and see what I can do for her."

"Yes, that will be helpful." After closing the line, the ambassador called his secretary to bring him all papers pertaining to Monique and her son. He put his head in his hand and began to think of the best method of handling the situation. He hated to deal with anything where local police were involved with French nationals. It always needed extreme amounts of tact and diplomacy. He knew Monique well and could not bear the thought of her being locked away in jail. Besides, unbeknownst to Monique, he had been giving Monique's family in France regular updates on her welfare. He would hate to have to tell them about this. The papers arrived on the ambassador's desk promptly, and within minutes, he saw that he had problems. Roger was born in Kharja, thus conferring citizenship upon him. Although being a dual national, he was subject to local law whilst in the country. This would make the situation very difficult. The authorities would simply say that they had even more of a case, as they would look upon him as being Kharjan. Nevertheless, Monique is French, and he would do everything in his power to ameliorate her situation.

Hussein left Roger at the villa and was already halfway downtown to visit Monique in jail. His spirits were somewhat restored now. He felt he had made a positive step in contacting the ambassador. At least he could offer Monique a little hope when he saw her.

Monique looked around her spartan prison cell and sat down on the uncomfortable bed with its coarse grey blanket on it. She put her head in her hands as if to weep, but somehow tears were not forthcoming at this moment. Ever since she had been questioned and taken into custody, she felt a deep sense of futility overtake her. Instinctively, she knew that all her protestations of innocence would be ignored, and she felt the conniving influence of Sherrifa behind the whole affair. She knew it would be even beyond Hussein's power to get her released without Sherrifa's sanction, and she knew all too well what the price of her release would be. It would cost her the only man that she had ever truly loved. She had no idea how much further Sherrifa would dictate the terms of her life. Certainly Nikos would comply with anything that Sherrifa wanted, and as things stood now, she could not even affect the rights she had over Roger. It would take very little for Nikos to claim custody of him in Kharja, where she had few rights. Roger had the right of citizenship here and Nikos would, no doubt, ensure that he claimed it for him should it be required. That could mean that she would have to stay as a chattel of Nikos's, or leave the country without her son. The thought was unbearable, but nonetheless, she refused to give in to the situation. She wracked her brain to think of any possible means of getting out of her predicament. She knew she could not do it alone and waited impatiently for Hussein to arrive, as she knew he would.

Monique was pacing round her cell when the huge, sneering female warder shouted at her in crude English to follow her. As Monique came to the cell door, the warder pushed her roughly in the direction in which she was to go. She walked through a long corridor that led to a row of offices that ran at right angles to the corridor. The warder pushed her again towards the last office in the row. Monique stood outside the office until the warder opened the door for her, and inside she was relieved to see Hussein. He was ashen with the guilt and worry over the whole situation. He was relieved to see Monique bearing up under the intolerable circumstances she was in.

"Darling, darling, I am so, so sorry. I'm doing everything I can to get you out of here," he told her, clasping her hands in his. He desperately wanted to take her in his arms, but with the hawk-like eyes of the warder on him, he knew that restraint was the best option. He did not want to behave in any way that lent credence to the charges against her.

"I know how you must feel, but first tell me, where is Roger and is he all right?"

"Don't worry about him. Sherrifa has him with her at home. I know that it does not sound an ideal situation, but at least he will be with me. I don't think Nikos will want to take responsibility for him just now."

"I just want to know that he is being taken care of," she said, sounding more relieved.

"Listen, darling, try not to worry about Roger. I will do everything I can to keep him safe. Right now, the priority is to get you out of here. You may have already guessed who is behind this sorry mess."

"Sherrifa?" she interjected with some ferocity.

"Yes, unfortunately, that is right, which makes things difficult for us. However, Roger came up with the idea of contacting the French ambassador. He is very concerned about the case and promises that he will begin negotiations to get you released as soon as possible."

"That is a good idea, I admit, but I doubt that you know Roger was actually born here in Kharja, which means that I have few rights over him if Nikos claims custody," she said sadly.

"Damn, damn, damn," he said, covering his face with his hands, "I didn't know that, and it certainly complicates things. But no matter what, he did promise to help, and I am sure it will help your case if the ambassador gets personally involved."

"Yes, it certainly can't hurt. But you are not telling me what I really need to know. What is it that Sherrifa wants in exchange for my freedom?" She steeled herself for what she knew was to come.

"Darling, you know her, how self-serving she is. She needs me to lend respectability to her disgusting lifestyle. I will agree to her demands if nothing is done to release you by this evening."

"Don't be in such a rush to agree, Hussein," she said with courage. "I am not made out of cotton wool, and although this place is unpleasant, I am prepared to stick it out for a little longer if there is a chance that we can resolve the situation without you having to serve a life-sentence as Sherrifa's puppet." She was determined not to give in so easily to Sherrifa's demands. She was prepared to fight and suffer for Hussein if she had to.

"No, darling, I cannot bear the thought of you being in this horrible place all alone for a single night. I cannot allow you to do it."

"Listen to me, Hussein," she said seriously, "do you imagine that the life I have been living for so many years with Nikos has been better than being in a prison? He has used me and abused me. Being here is not that bad. Certainly if the French ambassador becomes involved, no one will violate my civil rights here. I will be in no danger. And more important, are you willing to give up on us so easily? I am not going to give up without a fight. I don't really know how we are going to tackle this, but I am not ready to give up yet. It's time we make a stand," she said with determination.

Hussein considered her words and admired her courage. He always underestimated Monique's strength. He remembered her courage during the hijack and understood that she was capable of enduring a considerable amount of discomfort. She certainly did have a point, and he truly wanted to start a new life with her. The thought of spending the rest of his days being manipulated by Sherrifa, and only sneaking time alone with Monique, was not a future that he could settle for.

"Darling, are you quite sure? It will be hell for me thinking about you here."

"It will probably be a worse hell for you than for me. I have already suffered the indignity of arrest. It is not going to get any worse than that for me. I trust you to take care of Roger; he will feel safe with you. Let Sherrifa and Nikos do their worst. I am not going to give in without a fight, and I will not make it easy for them."

"So be it, my love," he whispered, admiring her courage, "but I will not let it go on indefinitely."

"I know, go now and be with Roger. He will be in more need of someone than I am right now," she said and smiled at him.

"I will take good care of him, don't worry. I intend to go back to the airport. I will take him with me, and he can stay with me in my office."

CHAPTER SIXTEEN

Endings and beginnings

Jenny's routine had altered little in the last few weeks. She worked hard at the hospital by day and relaxed at home in the evening. She received invitations here and there in Greg's absence but rarely accepted. Occasionally, she went to have dinner with Candy and Khalil now that they were established in their new home, but apart from that, she felt little inclination to associate with the airline crew. She already felt divorced from them.

She began taking on new imperatives, as her loyalties were to Talal and to the world that he would soon be taking her to. Even though she had heard nothing from him in the last four weeks, she did not doubt his feeling for her. She could feel the bond between them strengthening, and neither time nor distance dulled her feeling for him. She knew he would come to her as soon as was humanly possible. Jenny looked at her reflection critically as she dressed in her uniform for work. She looked all wrong, her face was pallid and her features seemed to align themselves in manner over which she had no control. She had lost weight in spite of regular meals, and her usual stamina was beginning to let her down. Tiredness was becoming familiar. She thought perhaps that it was the constant heat. It was said that the health of Western women often began to fail because of the constant heat and exposure to uncommon viruses. Indeed, some wives of British crew members spent at least six months of the year out of the country because of the heat. *Oh God, I hope that will not happen to me*, she thought. *But still, if it does I probably won't have to stay here much longer. If Talal is able to leave, we will probably go somewhere where the climate is kinder.*

With this thought, she picked up her car keys and set off for the hospital. As she entered the emergency room, Dr. Khalil was waiting for her. "Jenny, there is someone in my office who wants to see you," he told her with the suspicion of a smile on his lips.

Jenny's heart leapt; she knew instinctively that it was Talal. "Can you spare me for a few moments?" she asked pleadingly.

"Of course, take as much time as you want," he told her indulgently. Although he had not exactly come to terms with Jenny's infidelity, he had resolved not to condemn her for it. She asked so little for herself, and gave so much to the patients, that he was happy to assist in anything that gave her pleasure. Besides, Talal was his cousin, and he did not want to rob him from his happiness.

Jenny rushed to Khalil's office. Talal was standing behind the door, and the minute she entered, he closed it and took her in his arms and kissed her passionately. "Hello, my Jenny Wren, it has been so long, and I have missed you so much."

"Talal, I can't believe that it's you. Let me look at you."

She surveyed his tall, lean frame and handsome face. As always, she was transfixed by his beautiful green eyes. She was overwhelmed with feeling for him. "I love you so much, Talal Khoury, you have no idea," she said playfully.

"Oh yes I do, angel, and to prove it, I have just made the final arrangements to change my life to be with you for always," he told her, smiling in triumph.

"Oh, I can't believe it. Is it true?"

"Yes, my love, but we must wait a little yet. I expect that I will be free to come to you before the month is finished."

"How did you manage it, darling?"

"That I can't tell you now, love. You will just have to believe in me." He stopped and looked at her seriously. "Jenny, I want you to promise me one thing."

"Yes, anything," she agreed, slightly alarmed by the seriousness of his tone.

"Promise me that no matter what you think has happened or what you hear, you will not give up on me."

"Of course, I won't. How could I?"

"I wish I could tell you more but I cannot. All I can say is that things are going to get worse before they get better."

"Don't worry, my love, no matter what happens, I will wait for you." He took her in his arms again and held her head to his chest and stroked her hair as if she were a child.

"Darling, I have to leave now. I am on my way to the airport. I am going to make preparations for our new life. God, how I wish you were coming with me right now and that everything was over."

"Me too, darling," she echoed passionately.

"The next time I come here, I will be free of the life I have been living. I will come to you here at the hospital. It is relatively safe for me here. I know Khalil will help us when the time comes. We will face Greg together, and then I think it would be best if you are ready to leave right away.

"Yes, darling, I will have everything ready. I have thought so many times about how I can tell Greg about us. There is no kind way, and the only thing that makes it a little easier is knowing that he has committed his own infidelity."

"The truth will hurt him for a while, but he is young enough to get over it quickly."

"I hope so," said Jenny with a note of sadness in her voice.

"It will all work out. Don't worry, angel. In a year's time, we will look back and see how everything will have worked for the best, even for Greg, I am sure. I must go now, my angel, or I will miss the flight," he said reluctantly.

"I know that you must go, but I long to begin our new life together. I hope it will be somewhere cooler than here," she said, lightening the mood.

A fleeting smile swept over Talal's face. "Don't worry, I promise you that it will be much cooler than here, angel."

He embraced her for the final time. As he slipped out of the door, he whispered once again, "Wait for me no matter what, Jenny Wren."

"I will, I will," she promised him.

After he left, Jenny felt both elated at the prospect of them sharing a future together and despondent at the shortness of his visit. She walked out into the E.R. looking for work to take her mind off things. It was unusually quiet, and Dr. Khalil walked over to her. "Jenny, are you all right?" he asked, concerned at her appearance.

"Yes, why?"

"I have noticed that you have been looking very pale lately, not yourself, and you have lost weight. Are you taking care of yourself properly?"

"Yes, actually I am. In fact, I have been very lazy lately. I do nothing in the evening but eat and lie about, reading and listening to music. I do seem to be less energetic, though. I think it might be the constant heat that's getting to me."

Khalil looked doubtful. Jenny was too young and vital for the effects of the heat to be telling on her so soon. "Well, I am not convinced. Unless you start looking a lot healthier soon, I am going to insist that we take some blood samples from you. It is quite possible that you could have picked up any number of diseases here," he told her firmly.

"Okay, you're the doctor," she agreed, not unwillingly. Her appearance had been worrying her, so she decided she would give herself another week, and if things did not improve, she would take the tests. Jenny returned to her duties, trying to blot the pain of Talal's departure from her mind. She loved him so much she could hardly believe it herself. Although she knew he was going ahead to arrange their future, she could not shake the feeling of intense loss that had fixed on her. *Work*, she thought, *and more work will be the antidote to my misery.* The E.R. was quiet that morning, so she told Khalil that she would help out on the medical wards if he needed her.

"Okay, Jenny, but take it easy, please. Work isn't always the answer to all your woes, you know," he said, understanding her desire to work.

"I know, but it does help with the pain," she replied frankly.

"Go on then," he conceded.

Jenny was always welcome on the medical wards, as she did not hesitate to do all and any of the required jobs, no matter how menial.

"Jenny, you should take a break now. Eet ees past the time of your lunch break, and you look very tired," said Amina, the ward sister. Jenny looked up from making a bed for a new admission.

"Alright, Amina, I will go after I have made up this bed," she replied.

As she finished the bed, a wave of nausea engulfed Jenny and blackness overcame her. When she awoke, she was lying on the bed that she had just been making with Amina rubbing her hand. "Are you all right, Jenny? I have called Dr. Khalil. He will be here in a moment," she said, alarmed at Jenny's loss of consciousness.

"Yes, I think so, what happened to me?" asked Jenny, feeling dazed and confused.

"You were bending over making thees bed, and when you stood up, you just collapsed onto the floor," she told her calmly.

Khalil arrived looking worried at hearing that Jenny had collapsed. "Now, I think we are going to have to take those tests a little sooner than we anticipated, Jenny," he told her, concealing his worry with a charming, crinkly smile.

"Well yes, I suppose you must," she said, knowing that argument was futile.

"What we will do is keep you in overnight for observation. We will transfer you now to a room of your own and do an array of tests on you, and try to discover what is the matter with you. Candy was taking a day off today, but I will ring her and ask her to come and keep you company," he told her firmly.

Jenny started to protest. "Don't disturb Candy on her day off. I'm sure she has so many things to do in the new house."

"What rubbish, can you imagine what trouble I will be in if I go home tonight and tell Candy that you collapsed at work and were being kept in the hospital? No, Candy will want to know what is happening with you, and there is nothing in the new house that is more important than the welfare of her best friend," he insisted.

"Okay, I give in," she said weakly, but very glad that her friend would be there to give support and keep her company.

Candy arrived within the hour, and she was shocked to see how pale Jenny looked. "What on earth have you been doing to yourself?" asked Candy.

"I don't really know, but something seems to be wrong. They are going to take tests," said Jenny with an air of misery.

'Oh, cheer up, it can't be anything too bad. You just don't look after yourself properly. When they do the blood tests, all they will find is pizza and falafel coursing through your veins. I have told you before that you cannot subsist on a diet of take-away foods," she said jokingly.

Jenny knew that there might be some truth in what she was saying. When she was on her own, eighty percent of her food comprised of take-aways. Lately, she had been too tired after work to make a proper meal for herself.

"Hmm, well I hope it isn't anything more than that. The last thing I want is to be laid up with anything more serious just now," she said reflectively.

"Why so serious?" asked Candy.

"Talal came to see me this morning, and I know that I love him more than anything in the world. I have decided that I'm going to leave Greg and be with Talal on whatever terms are possible," she said anxiously. "I can't be ill now. There is just too much to face."

"Look, you must slow down a bit. I swear if Talal knew you were in this kind of shape, the last thing he would want is for you to be fretting over the future. The most important thing is for you to concentrate on relaxation and recovery."

Candy looked at Jenny, and she did not seem very convinced by her words. "Look, you must relax, Jenny, or you are not going to be going anywhere with anyone," she said firmly.

"You don't understand. There is much more to it than you think." Jenny's words were cut short at that point by one of the junior doctors arriving to begin some tests on her.

"I have come to do some tests on Jenny. If she does not mind you being here, I do not," he said smilingly, and acknowledging Candy's new status as the wife of Dr. Khalil.

"Please, please, stay Candy. I can do with some moral support right now."

"Don't worry, wild horses would not drag me away," she reassured her. Candy stayed till late in the evening, when Jenny finally began to relax and unwind. By ten o'clock, Jenny was soundly asleep and Candy crept out of the room silently.

The next day, Jenny felt and looked much better. She was proclaimed well enough to go home, but was ordered to rest. Dr. Khalil looked at her seriously. "I don't want to see you here at the hospital to work for another week, and to ensure that you do rest properly, Candy will be coming round every day to visit, for long periods of time. Have I made myself clear?"

"Yes, doctor," she said with mock subservience, "I promise to take things easy. And thank God that Candy will be coming to visit or else I would go stir crazy stuck in the apartment with no one to keep me company."

"Go now, Candy is waiting downstairs in reception. She will take you home, and I will pick her up after I finish work tonight," he told her with a smile. "Oh, and I expect that I will have the results of all the tests by the time the week is finished. I will ring you at home when they are all complete."

Jenny met Candy downstairs. "Well, you look much better today, and as you have been put in my care for the week, I have made up a program of things to entertain and amuse. We are going to have some fun, but nothing too strenuous," she said with an air of authority that clearly showed that she would brook no argument from Jenny. She happily succumbed to Candy's ministrations, knowing that it was the best and fastest possible means of recovery. From her own experience as a nurse, she knew that good company and laughter were often the means to a speedy recovery.

Hussein was running himself ragged in his attempts to free Monique from jail. He had called in every debt he was ever owed but no one had the power to overrule Sherrifa. The situation at the villa was a stalemate. Sherrifa had declined to be moved by any pleas from Hussein to have Monique released. She had equally declined to be moved by Lieutenant Mubada's pleas to release her because of the pressure that he was getting from diplomatic quarters. The French Embassy was pulling out all the diplomatic stops it could in an attempt to get her released from jail.

Sherrifa had contacted Nikos and told him to go sick on his out-station, thereby delaying the situation. Once he arrived in Kharja, she knew Monique would be in a much stronger position as the situation would have to be resolved. Right now, delaying tactics suited her and were her best weapon.

Roger was bearing up bravely through the whole ordeal. Hussein spent as much time as he possibly could with him, convincing him that his mother was in good health and was as comfortable as could be expected. Roger knew, with certainty, that Hussein was doing everything that could be done for her, although it did not help the dreadful ache in his heart that he felt because of her incarceration. He hated Sherrifa with a passion and avoided contact with her whenever possible. He could see right through her feigned concern and attention. *Dear God*, he prayed, *please get my mother out of jail and out of reach of my father and his evil friends. It would be so wonderful if Hussein could be my father and Samer my brother. Then we could all be happy together.* Tears were stinging his eyes, but he refused to give way to them, as he had to stay strong for his mother's sake. There was a gentle knock on the door.

"Come in," said Roger.

"Hi there, son, are you all right?" Hussein asked, looking at his troubled countenance.

"Yes sir, I am fine," he said bravely. "I just wish that this was all over and we could all go away together."

"I know, I know, there is nothing I want more. And believe me, I won't stop until we are all together."

"Have you heard from my father?" asked Roger stiffly.

"I'm afraid that he is still reporting sick, and any attempts to get hold of him on the phone seem to be fruitless. I don't know where he is hiding himself," said Hussein, trying to make the situation sound more respectable than it actually was. His efforts were wasted on Roger.

"I hate that bastard. If I could get my hands on him, I would kill him for what he has done, and what he is still doing to us," he exploded angrily.

"Roger, I understand how you feel," Hussein said to placate him. "Don't you think I feel the same? I know that I have not suffered the way that you and your mother have over the years from his abuse, and there is nothing I would like better than to physically punish him for what he has done. But that is not the way forward. We are going to win this ordeal without stooping to violence. Just hold on tight and believe that we will win through, and we will, I promise." Hussein walked over to Roger and took him in his arms. "Don't worry, it will all be over soon."

Roger welcomed Hussein's comforting arms around him, and the tears that he had been choking back for so long began to spill over. "It will be all right, won't it?" he asked pleadingly.

"Yes, I swear it will."

Hussein felt almost as wretched as Roger. He did not know how this affair would be resolved, but he would move heaven and earth to make things right for them.

That evening, Sherrifa had arranged a small dinner party for some personal friends that occupied positions of importance and requested that Hussein be there.

"Why are you doing this Sherrifa? What do you think you are going to gain in the long run?" asked Hussein scathingly.

"I will gain you back, my darling. You legitimize my position, and being married to you suits my lifestyle. That's it in a nutshell. Now, I will expect to see you at dinner," she said smugly.

"And if I refuse?"

"I imagine that Nikos will have to be even more ill than he currently is, and Monique's sojourn in prison will be so much the longer," she said maliciously.

"You whore," he spat at her.

"I take it you will be there then?" she said smugly. He did not bother to answer her. She knew that she was holding all the cards, and he could not afford to upset her. He would be there, but only for Monique's sake.

The guests arrived for dinner by eight o'clock, and Hussein was present. He endured the evening even though his thoughts were with Monique. He even wondered wildly whether he could bring up her plight to them and perhaps solicit their help. *Nothing else had worked,* he thought, *but it might be worth a try.* He waited for the right moment after they had finished dinner. He had been cultivating one of the guests who was an official in the Ministry of the Interior. "You know, I have quite a problem on my hands at the moment," he said as impartially as he could.

"Well, is it something that I can help you with?" asked the official. He liked Hussein and thought of him as a hero ever since the hijack, and he genuinely wanted to do something for him.

"Well, one of my crew's wife has been mistakenly arrested for kidnapping, would you believe, her own son? They were leaving the country for a short holiday. Unfortunately, her husband is out of the country and not contactable, and it is making it difficult to clear up the whole issue. The poor wife is a foreigner and has no one much to help her. I have done what I can, but it seems that she cannot be released until her husband returns," he said with great restraint.

"This is ridiculous," said the official. "Give me the phone, I will speak to someone immediately and get her released."

Hussein's heart leapt. "I will take you to the hall. You can use the phone there," he said, trying to hide his elation.

"Oh, darling," interjected Sherrifa, "are you talking about that dreadful Stianou woman? You know that I have been doing everything in my power to help her, but I have found out from the most reliable sources that she is nothing better than a whore. She has been running around with men for years behind her husband's back. Now, I have heard, she actually was going to leave the country without his knowledge, taking his much-loved son with her. We are keeping the poor child here ourselves, you know, as he is quite distraught. I honestly don't think that we can risk getting this woman released until her husband returns. If she managed to slip through our fingers, then we would be to blame. And how could we face her poor husband then? I know it sounds a little harsh, but I have ensured that she is being well looked after in jail." She turned to Hussein, looking most concerned. "I wanted to discuss this with you, darling, but you were working so late this evening that I haven't had the opportunity."

Blood rushed into Hussein's face, and he had to conceal the fact that he was shaking with anger. He could not trust himself to speak, so he just nodded to her.

The official was immediately aware of the tenseness of the situation. He wanted to help Hussein, but he dare not go against Sherrifa's wishes. He suspected there was more to the affair than he was aware of. Deciding to err on the side of safety, he recanted. "Oh, of course, I should have known that you would be doing everything possible to help her, Sherrifa, and in the light of what you have just told me, I think it would be a wise precaution to wait until her husband returns."

Sherrifa smiled over at Hussein, her eyes shining with triumph. Her face clearly told him, *you can challenge me anytime, but you won't win.* Hussein felt the sting of defeat about him;

he felt humiliated and small. He hated her. It took him all his strength of character not to walk out of the room in disgust. He did not know where to turn to next. He was exhausted from nights without sleep, and no longer felt in control of his life. He politely excused himself from the gathering and walked out of the room with as much dignity as could be mustered. Everyone there could sense his humiliation, and felt a good degree of sympathy for him. They all knew Sherrifa of old and how ruthless she could be, but none of them were in a position to challenge her. Knowing so well the special relationship that she enjoyed with her father, none of them would risk upsetting her and incurring his wrath.

The doorbell rang with some urgency shortly after Sherrifa's little speech to the official from the Ministry of the Interior. The maid rushed to answer it, and Hussein was surprised to see Ezert, Sherrifa's brother enter the house. Despite their former friendship, he had not visited them for years. "Where's Sherrifa?" he demanded.

"She's inside in the salon. Is there something wrong?" asked Hussein, his anger temporarily forgotten because of the serious look on Ezert's face.

"It might be wrong or it might be right, depending on whom you are. Come with me. You need to hear this."

Obligingly, Hussein followed him, at a complete loss as to what Ezert was saying. Sherrifa looked up in surprise to see her brother standing there. She never willingly sought out his company nor him hers. Other than obligatory family gatherings, they never saw or spoke to each other. "Darling, how unexpected, do come in," she effused, going to kiss him in the traditional greeting.

"Save it, Sherrifa," he told her brusquely. "I have bad news for you." He looked round the room and wondered briefly whether he should speak to her privately, but immediately decided against it. All who were gathered there were counted as her close friends who never hesitated to do her bidding. It would be interesting to see how they responded to the news. "Sherrifa, I am sorry to tell you that our father suffered a massive heart attack two hours ago, and despite every possible attempt at resuscitation, he died an hour ago."

Silence descended on the room, as no one knew quite how to react to this sudden, unexpected news. Sherrifa's face became ashen. She tried to speak, but words failed her. Knowing that because of the law of primogeniture, Ezert was now the sole heir to his father's massive fortune, and those gathered around felt distinctly uneasy. Ezert was known as a fair and decent man, who distanced himself from his sister and those who toadied to her.

Now the power base had changed. Without the indulgence and protection of her father, Sherrifa was going to be stripped of her power. She felt her insides turn icy cold, and fear and nausea were choking in her throat. Ezert was now going to be a powerful man in the country, and by his actions tonight, he made it clear that his sister would not be offered his indulgence or protection. Together, the guests stood up and paid their condolences to the silent and stunned Sherrifa, and again, even more effusively to Ezert. They filed out of the room and left silently, all of them slightly worried about their positions of prestige now that their benefactor had died.

Hussein was equally stunned by the news; nothing was more unexpected. He looked at Sherrifa's shocked countenance, and for a fleeting instant, he felt pity for her. Seeing that she was in shock, he ordered the chauffeur to bring the family doctor for her immediately and asked her maid to take her to her bedroom. After she had been taken from the room, Ezert and Hussein faced each other. Ezert was the first one to speak, "It is poor circumstances to greet you again, old friend, but truthfully, I have been too ashamed to continue our friendship ever since Sherrifa began to treat you so badly. There was little I could do, to intervene, so for the sake of my own embarrassment, I stayed away. Can you forgive me?"

"There is nothing to forgive," said Hussein generously, and the two men shook hands.

"You no longer have to live in her shadow, Hussein. If you want to divorce her, you will get no resistance from me, or anyone else. I will personally see to that. Your position is secure at the airport for as long as you want it, and you can count on my help whenever you need it," he told him sincerely.

Tears of relief stung at Hussein's eyes, and he swallowed hard. "Thank you, Ezert, you have no idea what this means to me. I have an immediate request to ask you. A dear friend has been put in jail, at Sherrifa's behest, and I would like her immediate release. Her son is staying here with me, and they are very dear to me. If you can arrange it, I will go and collect her immediately." Ezert went to the phone and asked to speak to the person in charge and was put through to the duty officer and explained the situation. The duty officer wanted to be helpful, but he knew Lieutenant Mubada was handling the case personally. "Sorry, ya Sidi, but I think that you should speak to Lieutenant Mubada personally. I will give you a number where he can be reached."

Ezert quickly contacted the lieutenant and explained the situation. Initially he was reluctant to cooperate, but hearing the news of Ezert and Sherrifa's father's death, his tone changed immediately. "Oh please, accept my most sincere condolences. Of course this changes everything. I will come to the Muhabarat personally right away and ensure Madam

Stianou's release. I would like you to know that I had great misgivings about keeping her locked up," he said with cringing subservience.

"Obviously not great enough," said Ezert sarcastically. "I will be coming with Captain Al Fayez to collect her within the hour. I hope everything will be in order by then."

"Yes, yes, of course, Sidi, I will take care of everything, I will see you there."

When the two men arrived at the Muhabarat, Monique was waiting in an office with all her belongings. Hussein was overjoyed to see her. She looked a little pale and thinner but not too much the worse for her ordeal. He picked up her things and led her towards the door.

"Monique, this is Sherrifa's brother Ezert. We are friends. There is a lot to tell you, but I'll wait until we get home. But to put your mind at rest, everything is going to be all right."

Relief flooded through Monique at Hussein's words. She was too overcome to speak so she just smiled at him. Recovering quickly, she asked about Roger. "He is at home. I did not tell him I was coming to get you for fear of something going wrong. He's going to be so happy when he sees you."

Arriving back at the villa, Hussein was told that the doctor had been and Sherrifa had been sedated. She was expected to sleep through the night. Hussein led Monique to the room where Roger was staying and knocked on the door. Roger's sad, subdued voice answered, "Enter." Roger could not believe his eyes when he saw his mother standing there. "Maman, you are here. Merci, mon Dieu." He ran into her open arms and embraced her, hugging her so tightly that her breathing became difficult. Hussein left them together for a while before he stuck his head back in and asked Monique to come and join him when she was ready.

Hussein explained everything to an incredulous Monique and Roger. "Does this mean that you can be free of Sherrifa now, that you can actually divorce her?"

"Yes, my love, and we don't have to leave the country either. If you are agreeable, we can stay here. I don't imagine that Nikos is going to be coming here for more than a passing visit as he will have no job anymore, so I thought until we both have our divorces, and for the sake of propriety, you and Roger can live in your villa. I will sell this place and rent a small apartment until we are free to marry and get a place of our own. What do you think?"

"Oh God, this is all so sudden, my head is spinning. Yes, yes, that sounds like the right thing to do. I don't mind staying here at all. I am quite accustomed to it, and I believe I would miss the people and the life here," she said smiling.

"I want to call Samer tonight in London and tell him what has happened. He can catch the first flight out here tomorrow morning."

"Isn't it a little late, darling?" observed Monique.

Hussein had lost all track of time. It was already well after midnight. "Yes, it is a bit, but hang on, with the time difference, it won't be too late in England," he calculated.

He made the call and arranged for his son to arrive on the flight the following day. That done, he felt more relaxed. "Darling, you must stay here tonight. There are plenty of spare bedrooms, and I don't want you and Roger to be alone at your villa."

Monique was happy to stay there, even though she was under the same roof as Sherrifa. She could not face a night being alone after her ordeal. Hussein took her to a spare room, "The first thing I want is a long, hot shower," she proclaimed.

He gave her plenty of time to shower and change into her night clothes before he knocked again at her door. "I thought that I might keep you company, if that is all right?" he ventured.

"Please do," she answered enthusiastically.

That night, they lay together in each other's arms, neither wanting to make love, only to hold and reassure each other. The exhaustion of what they had endured was finally beginning to tell. They both eventually fell into a deep, dreamless sleep, to wake the next morning feeling heavy-headed but nonetheless happy. After dressing, they ventured downstairs, hoping they would not have to have an unpleasant encounter with Sherrifa. However, Hussein found an envelope addressed to him on the coffee table. It was from Sherrifa, informing him that she had now returned to her family home to support her mother through this time of great loss. Should he need to contact her, she would be there until further notice.

"Well, I credit her with knowing when to make a dignified exit," remarked Monique.

"Yes, I am just thankful that she has gone."

Roger came downstairs and joined them. "Good morning, son, what do you say we all have a good breakfast together? I believe that is what we were going to do before our plans were so rudely interrupted," quipped Hussein.

"That would be wonderful. I am really hungry," announced Roger, looking happy for the first time in days.

The cook was dispatched to make a mountain of pancakes and anything else she could offer for breakfast. Within twenty minutes, the table was laden with pancakes, fruit, eggs, pastries and freshly baked, herby breakfast pizzas.

After their meal, they sat replete with food and started to plan their day. "Aren't you going in to the airport today darling?" enquired Monique.

"No, I have phoned Chuck, and he is taking care of things for a few days. He will only contact me if it is an emergency. I want some time to get to know my new family. I will just be gone for a little while this afternoon when I go to meet Samer's flight. Then we can all be together," he said with some satisfaction.

"Look," said Roger, "there is a large car with a diplomatic number plate on it coming up the drive."

"I expect that it might be the French ambassador," said Monique. "He has been visiting me every day while I was locked up in that awful place. He has been very good to me."

Hussein went to the door before any of the servants could answer it. It was indeed the French ambassador with another man, who looked rather like a diplomat.

"Hello, welcome, I imagine you have heard the good news," said Hussein.

"Indeed I have, and if my sources are correct, Monique is here, is she not?"

"Yes, both she and her son are here with me," he replied.

Turning to the other man, the ambassador said, "Please let me introduce you to my very good friend of many years, the Marquis d'Aberville, or less formally as Monique's father," he said smiling. "I know that this is rather a surprise for you and perhaps something of a shock to Monique, but I have been discreetly keeping Monique's family informed of her welfare for many years now, and of course when this unfortunate affair happened, her father wanted to help her however he was able to. He arrived this morning on the flight from Paris."

Recovering quickly, Hussein invited them to come in. "Please, please, come in, I'm very pleased to meet you, and I am sure that Monique will be happy to see you too," he said, hoping that Monique would indeed be happy to see him. He knew that there had been opposition to her marrying Nikos and that had been the basis for the rift between them. He hoped that now she was divorcing him, their relationship would be restored. He led the two men to the salon where Monique and Roger were sharing a joke together. As Monique's eyes alighted on her father, she stopped in midsentence, shocked by his presence. She stood up but was uncertain of what to say or do next. In an instant, her father stretched out his arms towards her, inviting her into his embrace. She ran into his arms and sobbed, "Papa, you are really here?"

"Oui, ma petite fille, it has been too long."

Neither seemed to want to let go of each other's embrace. Finally, Monique called Roger over to join the embrace. "Roger, this is your grandfather, come and give him a kiss."

The three were happily reunited. Hussein and the ambassador left them to talk together. The ambassador turned to Hussein, telling him, "I believe everything will work out well for them now. And, if I am not mistaken, I believe that the Marquis will welcome someone of your standing into his family. I will certainly recommend you," he said with a twinkle.

"How do you know?" asked Hussein, surprised at his knowledge of his relationship with Monique.

"You would be surprised. I have my sources, but you know, the way you look at her gives it all away," he said with a merry grin. "Anyway, I must go now, duty calls."

"Thank you for everything you have done," said Hussein.

"No, thank you," he said sincerely as he disappeared into his waiting car.

Sherrifa wasted no time in contacting Nikos after reaching her mother's home. She was as close to her breaking point as she had ever been in her life. It took her all her effort to keep her voice steady. "Nikos, we are finished here. My father is dead, and my brother is running the show now, and he hates me. I am at my mother's house, and Monique is out of jail and is with Hussein and Roger at my villa. There is nothing left for us here. You will certainly be out of a job, and I cannot move now that Hussein is going to divorce me," she lamented.

"Oh God," he said, as the full enormity of her words dawned on him. "What the hell are we going to do?"

"Listen, I have a plan, get back here and sell everything that you can, and then get a visa for Canada, if you do not already have one. I have heard that it is relatively easy to get a resident's permit there in certain areas. I have some money that my father put away in Switzerland for me. With what we can raise together, we can start a business or something there. I can't live here anymore after the freedom I have enjoyed. The West is my only choice. What do you say?"

"Darling, Chichi, what can I say? You are always the one with the brilliant ideas. Of course I say yes to what you want. You know that your happiness is everything to me," he fawned, knowing that being with Sherrifa was his best bet. He had no friends in Kharja, and his wife and child would never take him back. Sherrifa was his only way forward.

"Good, then call me here when you arrive, and we can complete everything."

Jenny's week of recovery would be finished the following day. Both she and Candy had enjoyed a week of good food and enjoyable pursuits, to which Jenny had responded positively. Her former good health had returned to her, and she was more in control. Greg was due back the next day, and also as it was the end of the month, she expected to be hearing from Talal. She had not confided any more of her plans to Candy, feeling that it might compromise Talal's position in some way. She would tell her everything when she was safely away from Kharja. "Candy, has Khalil got the results of my blood tests back yet?" asked Jenny.

"I think he is expecting them all to be ready tomorrow. Don't worry, I am sure that everything is all right. You look wonderful now," she said comfortingly.

"It's just that I am anxious to get back to work, and Khalil won't have me back until he is satisfied that the tests are clear," she said worriedly, wanting to be available at the hospital so Talal could contact her with ease. She also needed to take some of her essential clothing there so she could leave quickly with Talal.

"Listen, I will tell him to hassle everyone to ensure that your tests are all ready in the morning. In fact, I will go in and get them personally from the laboratory, and if they are not ready, I will stand there until they produce them. Is that good enough?" she said jovially.

"Thank you, Candy, you know what they are like in the lab if you don't push them."

"Yes, and Khalil did not push them because he wanted to ensure that you had enough time off to recover properly," confided Candy. "I'm certain you will be back at the hospital tomorrow."

"You are both so kind to me. You are the best friends I have ever had," she said emotionally, suddenly aware of how much she would miss them both.

"Why so emotional kid? You know we are always here for you," said Candy, sensing her mood.

"Isn't that Khalil's car pulling up now?" said Jenny, glancing out of the window. "You had better not keep him waiting. He has seen precious little of you this week."

"Oh, don't worry, he hasn't suffered," said Candy with a conspiratorial smile as she left.

Jenny looked at the time, and it was getting on for eight o'clock. She would just have time to eat a quick snack before settling down to hear the evening news. She had stopped trying to eat her supper in front of the television when the news was on. Invariably, the reportage contained horribly grotesque images of atrocities that had been committed around the world, and she was unable to keep her food down. Her meal finished, she switched on the television and put her mind in gear to translate the classical Arabic. It was getting much easier now, she thought, congratulating herself. The news from Koudara was bad that evening. There had been uprisings on the streets, and there had been fatalities. As the camera focused on a man who had been an eyewitness, Jenny listened with interest.

"How many fatalities were there in the disturbances?" asked the reporter.

"There were many injured people and one man was shot dead," said the witness, sounding distressed.

"And have we any idea who the dead man is?"

"Yes, he is a prominent figure in the area", he said, tears filling his eyes. "He will be missed greatly. His name is Talal Khoury."

"Well thank you, sir, let's hope that his death won't lead to further uprisings. Now back to the studio," concluded the reporter.

Jenny's blood ran cold in her veins. She felt nausea rising to her throat, and she ran to the bathroom and vomited. She began to shake uncontrollably. Oh God, no, no, please don't let this be happening, not now. She must have stayed in shock for about an hour, not knowing what to do. Finally, she recovered enough to think to call Dr. Khalil. "Hello, Khalil, this is Jenny. Have you heard the evening news?"

"No, we were just having dinner. Is there something wrong?" he asked, concerned by her tone.

"Yes," she said, her voice beginning to fail her, "they said on the news that there has been trouble in Koudara and that Talal is dead," she sobbed.

"Oh God, no, I was afraid of something like this. Look, Candy and I will be round right away. Just sit down and try to relax until we get there."

They arrived at Jenny's apartment within the hour, both of them insisting that she should come and spend the night at their apartment.

Her feeble protestations were overruled by Khalil's insistence. "No, Jenny, you are coming with us. Put a few things in a bag, and we are leaving now."

"Come on, Jen, I will help you," said Candy.

After they reached the house, they tuned in to the local radio station that had regular news bulletins so Khalil could confirm what Jenny already knew. "I am afraid what you heard seems to be right, Jenny. There is not much we can do tonight. I will make some calls tomorrow morning and find out whatever I can. Let's all try and get some sleep."

Jenny lay in bed for hours until sleep finally came, she succumbed to the enveloping blackness, hoping that she would never awake from it if Talal was no longer in her life. She would rather be with him in death than to live without him.

It was about four o'clock in the morning when she awoke with a start, gasping for breath and sweating all over. She was consumed with the kind of irrational fear that is only experienced by those waking from a nightmare. The fear seemed to envelope her, it was only when she heard the plaintive chant of the Muezzin calling the faithful to prayer did the fear begin to dissipate. She began to feel reality descend upon her again, but with it came the awful knowledge of what had happened. Tears began to roll down her cheeks, but she could not allow herself to succumb to her inner misery. To do that would be to acknowledge that Talal was dead, and right now, she could not do that. She stayed in her room until she heard the sounds of people up and about. She decided that she wanted to go home. She desperately needed to be alone. She made a good show of being composed in front of Khalil and convinced him to take her home on his way to the hospital. As he dropped her off, he told her that he would do everything in his power to find out what had happened and let her know as soon as possible.

"Thanks, Khalil, I appreciate what you have done," she told him. Khalil was astute enough to know that Jenny was still in shock but did not want to force a showdown with her to stay with them. He would let her go home for a while but ensure that she was checked up on regularly.

Jenny went around her apartment mechanically. Her maid was already there, polishing and scrubbing, unaware of Jenny's misery. She tried to find things to occupy her until her maid left. Then she began to try and put her life in some perspective, the tears that she had been stifling back choked their way out in great heaving sobs.

The phone rang shrilly, bringing her back to reality.

"Jenny, I'm afraid that I cannot find out anything more about what happened to Talal other than what we already know. But I do have something else that I have to tell you right away. Can I come over personally and give you the news? It is about your tests."

"No, Khalil, whatever it is you can tell me over the phone. Greg is back in a little while, and I need to talk to him. I have decided to go back to England," said Jenny firmly.

"Jenny, I don't know how you will take this news, but I hope you will take it positively. Your tests have shown that you are pregnant and are slightly anemic," he said, hoping the news would cheer her.

"Oh, oh!" she said, her hand dropping to her belly, "pregnant, are you sure?" she gasped.

"Quite sure, Jenny, I'm surprised that you had not suspected something yourself," he said, encouraged by her livelier tone.

"No, I didn't, I often have irregular periods, and I have had so much going on. It was not something that I was watching for. Look, thank you for this, now I must go. I can hear Greg at the door," she said hurriedly.

"Okay, Jenny, but I want you to come in to the hospital for a prenatal check."

Greg walked through the door smiling. The minute he saw Jenny, he knew something was wrong. "God, Jenny, you look awful. What's wrong?" he said worriedly.

"Please, Greg, sit down and just listen. So much has happened to me," she said with as much composure as she could.

"Okay, Jen, fire away," he said, lightheartedly trying to hide the fear that was beginning to creep over him.

Jenny told him everything that had happened to her, including Nikos' attempted rape. She told him of Talal's reported death and finally about the news that she was now pregnant.

"Oh, Jenny, what a mess." He struggled for the right words. He still loved her, but he did not know what to say to her.

Greg sat silently for some time before he spoke again, this time his voice was measured and controlled. "Jenny, I know that you are probably numb at the moment, but listen to me. I still love you no matter what you have done, and I don't want you to leave me. I don't expect anything from you, except to just be here. No one will know that the baby isn't mine. In fact, there is just a chance that it might be, so please stay here, and we will be a family. You will gain nothing by going back to England. I will take good care of you. I saw Hussein at the airport and things have changed. He is divorcing Sherrifa, and he says

393

that my future prospects are very good in the airline," he said persuasively.

Tears filled Jenny's eyes, and she did not know what to say.

Greg passed her a tissue and said, "Don't say anything now, just promise me that you will think about it, and not go anywhere for now."

Jenny just nodded, knowing that she was in no fit state to go anywhere, and now her baby needed her strength to be well and cared for. As the morning wore on, Jenny began to adjust to her new condition, the new life inside her gave her hope. She knew that, he or she, was all she had left of Talal.

Seeing Jenny more settled, Greg went over to see Fouad, to see if he could fill him in on what had been going on in his absence. Jenny made herself a cup of cocoa and decided to have a lie down on the sofa. As she put her head back on the cushions, the phone rang shrilly, making her jump. She felt so tired she wanted to ignore it.

"Hello," she said wearily.

"Hello, Jenny Wren, I am waiting for you."

Review Requested:

If you loved this book, would you please provide a review at Amazon.com?

Lightning Source UK Ltd.
Milton Keynes UK
UKHW041101290320
361021UK00001B/16